Kitchen Addiction!

Lizz Lund

ISBN-10: 1466397659
ISBN-13: 978-1466397651

LizzLund.Author@gmail.com

For my wonderful husband, Chef Andrew Mark –
my knight in shining Armetale.

ACKNOWLEDGMENTS

This is my debut novel, so very special thanks and mentions must be made to friends and family who provided boat loads of moral support and hand-holding: my extraordinarily patient husband, Andrew Mark; my best pal, my sister Kate; and my jolly troupe of GF's: Polly, Robin, Carla, Barb and Jill. I would also like to thank my old college roommate, Susan Green for her enthusiasm, support, and providing very useful information.

Special thanks also to the Humane League of Lancaster, for allowing me a 'photo op' with a resident of its Kitty Colony.

Additionally, I am very grateful to my wonderful and kind editor from across-the-pond, Nicholas J. Ambrose of Regarding the Hive.

And, as always – much love and thanks to Mom, Dad and Pat.

DISCLAIMER

This is a silly story about silly people with silly problems for readers who want an easy laugh fast. There are no metaphors, symbolism, morals or literary goals contained. English majors: keep out.

The story you are about to read is completely fictitious. All of the characters, groups and events were concocted from my own imagination and too much raw cookie dough. Any similarities to actual people are completely coincidental and/or delusional.

Some of the geographic locations referenced are actual places. Others are completely make-believe. There is a Lancaster Polo Club, and the riders and their patrons are a nice bunch of people. To the best of my knowledge, their Chukker Tent has not been set on fire, but there's always next season. There is also a Lancaster Police Department. I imagine they're a nice bunch of folks, too – although I've never met any of them or visited any of their precincts and sincerely don't plan on it. Same goes for the U.S. Marshal's Department. For the purposes of this story, all persons and groups herein are made up from pixie dust.

Some of the recipes in this book were made and tested. Most were not. If you make any of these recipes, you're on your own. You might want to have a frozen pizza handy as backup.

So grab a beverage, your favorite forbidden food and scrunch down in your comfy chair. Put your feet up, crack open the book and enjoy.

CHAPTER 1
(Friday)

I leaned my face against the screen door until my forehead waffled. I smelled onions, peppers and kielbasa cooking in my kitchen. Again.

I come home for lunch every day to feed my cat and my cockatiel and sometimes myself. With the exception of my pets, I live alone. And with the other exception of my neighbor Vito, who's usually here. Like now. Vito's retired, a good guy, and considers himself a bit too much like family. Which means he's in my kitchen more than I am.

I bought the townhouse from Vito over a year ago and still can't summon up the chutzpah to make him relinquish his spare key. Or to change the locks, in case of hurt feelings. But that's mostly for sentimental reasons. Or as Ma puts it, seventy mental reasons.

My half of our adjoined homes belonged to Vito's late wife Marie, who went on her final shopping trip to the HomeWares in the sky long before she could feather the 'Her' part of the 'His and Her' nests they'd bought as retirement presents for each other.

But that's me. Sentiment matters and anything resembling a hard cold fact hangs out in the lunch meat drawer until the fuzzy stuff complains. This outlook sometimes frustrates my executive-style Ma, who's from the no-nonsense style Bronx. Ma scraped her way up, with and without Dad, to pearl-earringed Ridgewood,

New Jersey. She lost her Bronx accent long ago and hates it when environmental factors sometimes kick my 'Joisey' into gear. When my sister and I were kids, the only thing that gave Ma away were the occasional screams accompanying a wooden spoon upside our heads. Other than that, she seems perfectly L. L. Bean.

I'm Mina Kitchen – Mina being short for Wilhelmina. I'm named after a great-grandmother I never met and plan to thank in the hereafter by prodding a heavenly fork in her virtual side. Not because of inheriting her weird name, or even weirder nickname. It's mostly for inheriting her oddball catering disorder.

Family legend still regales Fat Friday of '55. Great-Grandma Mina – Dad's grandma – invited neighbors for a dinner that included a 25-pound turkey with all the trimmings. Which would have been fine, except the turkey dinner was prefaced by a ham, hot dogs, lasagna, meat loaf, barbeque ribs, roast beef and Yorkshire puddings, stuffed cabbage, stuffed shells, stuffed grape leaves, moussaka, and a pork and sauerkraut casserole. And three different kinds of bread. And rolls. And salads. And don't forget the carrot Jell-O mold. And never mind the appetizers served with the cocktails and hand-made bar trimmings before that. But I wax foodie; I love this story. It always ends happily ever after with, "And no one was able to roll away from the table until eleven o'clock that night." Although that might have been because Grandma Mina served one pie per guest, just to balance out the trays of blintzes and ice cream and all.

For the record, the legendary guests to Fat Friday included: Mr. and Mrs. DeMicco; Yorgios and Hale Papadopoulos, with their toddler and Gramma Papadopoulos; Bob Dietrich and his secretary Cheryl; and Sid and Sally Klingenbaum with their newly barmitzvahed triplets. Whether Great-Grandma cooked all that food to impress, or because she was diversity sensitive, we'll never know. All we know is that this was the first and last time Bumpa – my great-grandpa – let her cook for large and/or diverse crowds. They still had some humdinger dinner parties post-Fat Friday, Ma says. But Bumpa put the spatula down about Mina's cooking for more than four guests. From then on, only bonafide caterers covered neighborhood parties. Bumpa's heartburn couldn't handle the menus, plural.

I gritted my teeth, accepted my household and entered. The smoke alarm went off, the cockatiel shrieked and Vito jumped up and down at the smoke detector with a potholder in one hand and a giant Modess pad in the other. I walked to the back of the kitchen and opened the screen door, and turned on the exhaust fan. The air was confettied with cockatiel fluff. I was also pretty sure it was sizzling in the pan alongside the kielbasa. Just another normal lunch in my abnormal household.

"Sorry, sorry, sorry, Toots," Vito apologized in his usual triplicate. "I just gotta ask you to do this favor for me, so I thought I'd pay up front and make yous a nice, hot lunch."

Of course that was precisely what I wanted, it being August and feeling like 1,000 degrees. Vito's heart was in the right place. But I sometimes wondered what occupied the space his brains were supposed to rent.

"Anyways, I got an extra load of dry cleaning I was hoping you'd take over for me," Vito explained, waving the giant Modess pad at the smoke detector. I looked closer. It was a Swiffer pad. "I was gonna do a quick Swiffer after lunch." He blushed. I'd finally broken down and bought a Swiffer Wet Jet last April and it was still Vito's favorite toy. My rugs and furniture might be full of bird fluff and kitty fur but you can eat off my kitchen floor most any day, thanks to Vito.

Sadly, Vito is also a dry cleaning junkie. I don't know why he owns this many dry clean only clothes. But unquestioning schnook that I am, I make a few runs a week to the dry cleaner for him. I drive past it on the way to work anyway, so it's no biggie. And what the heck, it accrues bonus Swiffer points for me, too.

"Sure," I said. "I'll pick up Monday's drop-off, too."

"Well sure, you wouldn't want to pick something up without dropping something off. It confuses people."

"Right..." I said and grabbed a bunch of carrots out of the fridge, then went to the sink to wash and slice them. I had to. It was the only available produce.

Vito shook his head. "Tough week?" he asked. I sighed and nodded.

I'm the office manager for Executive Enterprises for Job Intuitive Technologies, otherwise known as EEJIT. This morning was the usual – I'd spent the better part of it listening to a litany of complaints from my boss Howard, in counterpoint to Roger Stumpf's emailed inventory of grievances. Roger is EEJIT's area rep for our largest client, Buy-A-Lots. Roger spends most of his time in Buy-A-Lots' regional office, which is located near some farmlands outside of York, toward Baltimore. Consequently, Roger emails a lot of requests, and complaints. Roger helps Buy-A-Lots exec folk use EEJIT's sales and marketing software, Predict-O, which is supposed to make lots of little Buy-A-Lots pop up all across the country. Sometimes they even wind up across the street from each other, like a nice tight knit Old World family.

So, at the end of most weeks, I mostly want to forget about my boss and his star employee and sauté something. It's making me become an increasingly reluctant office manager, which could be a problem. The pay is okay; my boss is not. This set up also fuels the maternal fires back in Jersey. Ma just can't understand why I work where I'm "so obviously unappreciated." I keep reminding her there's this little thing called a mortgage, complicated by monthly supplies of Cockatiel Clusters and Kitty Cookies, not to mention the occasional happy hour. And there's also my own inertia.

What this all boils down to is when all is well at EEJIT, I'm invisible and I like it that way. But when anything goes wrong, I'm the goat. As a result, my catering disorder usually peaks by Fridays. Luckily, on some weekends, my friends ask me to cater their parties. So far, it's gone like clockwork. Mostly.

While Great-Grandma Mina's catering crazies tried to please a broad spectrum of people, mine are about soothing a broad spectrum of stress. The more stressed I get, the louder I up the food volume. My familial claim to catering disorders was when my college roommate asked me to give a dinner party for her and her fiancé to celebrate their engagement and new digs. Her mother, father, sister and aunt arrived. His father and mother arrived. I served up 8 trays of canapés, 9 different cheeses, 4 vegetable crudités trays and 3 sushi platters followed by a buffet of beef stroganoff, chicken curry, vegetable risotto, Caesar salad and a jar of homemade pickled beets per person. To this day, I have not lived it down. Especially the pickled beets.

The basement door banged loudly. I glanced across. Two large, furry white paws held the bottom of the door and shook it for all it was worth. "I think Vinnie's hungry," Vito said, stepping back, armed with his spatula and his trusty Swiffer pad.

Last summer my best friend, Trixie, deposited Vinnie at my front doorstep. Trixie's an ER nurse who works the graveyard shift and every other shift in-between. Vinnie is a cat who used to belong to the old lady who lived in the apartment upstairs from Trixie. Her neighbor moved onward and upward to what we hoped was a heavenly condo in the sky. Her last wish, which she told Trixie during her final trip to the ER, was for Trixie to find a home for her Vincent if she left the planet before he did.

So now Vincent is my very large orange tabby. To put him in perspective, he looks like a small mountain lion. To keep his ego in perspective, I call him Vinnie. He has white tuxedo markings, white mittens and socks and impossibly large blue eyes. Unfortunately his right eye is slightly crossed, which we figure is the reason for some depth perception issues. Like when he leaps from table to floor and a lamp or toaster gets in the way.

I grabbed some Smackerel Mackerels – Vinnie's favorite treat – and slid my leg across the door to keep him in the basement for the moment. "Here," I said, putting some of the treats on the top step in front of a pair of large, glowing eyes.

"Fhwankyoo," he said, and began crunching.

I closed the door to the basement and poured myself some ginger ale. I figured that would wash down the bird fluffed kielbasa and eggs pretty good. And besides, it was the only cold beverage I had in the fridge except for a few stray beers and a swig of cranberry juice.

The phone rang. Marie screamed, held onto her perch and flapped her wings in a demented attempt to lift off, cage and all. Vito looked frantically for a pan cover, and waved the Swiffer pad at Marie and the cloud of nuclear fluff hovering over the stove.

I coughed and answered the phone.

"Oh, I got you at home!" It was Ma. I'd been coming home for lunch everyday since I bought the place last year and she still acted surprised when I answered the phone. "I just wanted you to know I'm sending some swatches in the mail," she began.

I gazed at my Technicolor walls reprovingly. Traitors. Ma's visit last Easter left her horrified when she realized my walls matched my psychedelic Easter eggs. Ever since then, the walls have been on Ma's side and continue to fink me out.

My walls are lacquered in various nail polish colors – tangerine, lilac, electric blue and some kind of silverish geometric wallpaper – by various flavors of tenants; Vietnamese, Lithuanian, and apparently some kind of Middle Eastern judging by the Arabic lettering on the fuse box in the garage. I also have multiple cable hook-ups in each and every room – including the bathroom and downstairs powder room. Why the powder room is anyone's guess: who watches TV in the potty?

I also wonder if my house might be under some kind of Homeland Security surveillance, because sometimes I hear clicking sounds when I'm on a long distance phone call.

Anyway, from what Vito's told me, it wasn't his sainted Marie's fault that she didn't get around to redecorating after they bought both houses. According to Vito, her last stroll in my backyard ended with a fatal stroke before she could switch her swatch. So I was pretty sure she was forwarding heavenly paint ideas at Ma. You know what they say: those we lose are always with us. I just didn't think they were supposed to be only a paint swatch away.

Ma's been mailing me paint swatches since I've moved in. No notes, no messages. Just swatches. I finally stopped opening them and stashed the envelopes in the bread drawer.

"Thanks, I'll look out for them," I lied. "I gotta go, though, I'll be late back from lunch. Bye." I rang off.

"I can get the clean stuff from you before the Brethren Breakfast tomorrow," Vito continued, setting a dinner plate full of the fluffed egg mess in front of me.

I looked at him blankly.

"You forgot, didn't you?" Vito asked.

He was right. I'd completely forgotten about the Brethren Breakfast. Tomorrow was the third Saturday of the month, which meant it was St. Bart's turn.

St. Bart's Episcopal Church is my godmother's church. Aunt Muriel is a card-carrying Episcopalian. (Really – they honest-to-God give you a card. I guess it's in case you're proofed.)

Aunt Muriel was and is Ma's best friend since they both crawled out of the swamp somewhere around the dawn of time.

They'd even evolved from the Bronx together soon after high school graduation. Long before I was born, Muriel and Louise slipped into power suits and accent-free white collar voices like second skins. A couple of divorces and a few broken glass ceilings later, they are success stories. Ma belies her years and generation as a freakishly astute techno nerd. There isn't a piece of digital wizardry she hasn't test driven or owned. This explains her fast-tracked VP position at SUZ, a top tier IT company. It also explains her sometimes being slightly embarrassed about me. I'm not quite a Luddite; I just refuse to own a cell phone and still play vinyl.

Aunt Muriel, on the other hand, invested in diamonds: specifically engagement rings. Aunt Muriel married well and divorced better, more than once. This last time she has remained single, much to Uncle Max's chagrin, considering their prenuptial agreement.

What this all means is that I'm the guarded offspring while Ma lives in Jersey and Aunt Muriel paves my way in the land of the Amish, where she moved with poor old Uncle Max. Here's to lucky seven.

Anyway, I'm glad to help with the Brethren Breakfasts, especially since this also keeps my catering disorder at bay. Although I don't usually attend church services, unless Aunt Mu makes me. I usually attend Sunday brunches, with a preference toward New York Times denominations.

Unfortunately, last Easter combined both church and brunch. Since it was my first new homeowner holiday with Ma visiting, I got excited about making brunch for Ma and Mu after Easter services. So I got a little nervous – which was probably why I made enough Chicken Divan crepes to feed a small army, accompanied by mandarin orange and bamboo shoot salad. And Waldorf salad. And a fruit tart. And chocolate mousse in phyllo flowers. And a seven-layer Peach Melba torte. With some Easter egg truffles, Jordan almonds and gourmet jellybeans on the side. By the time Ma and Mu got to the jellybeans, they formed a newly united front designed to make my walls tasteful and dial down my catering disorder. They signed me up for the monthly Brethren Breakfasts: my menu mania would be used for the common good. I also got enrolled in an alternating swatch-of-the-week club.

"I did forget," I admitted to Vito, looking at the little pieces of fluff and seed hulls in my eggs, "but I'll be there."

"7:00, you know." He stared at me.

"I know, I know." Happy hour tonight wouldn't be very happy knowing I'd have to get up at the crack of dawn tomorrow morning. But culinary curiosity always gets the better of me, and I go.

There's a fierce competition between First Meth and St. Bart's. First Methodist sponsors the first Saturday of the month for the breakfast, St. Bartholomew does the third. The breakfasts are held at the neutral zone of the downtown Unitarian Church.

The Brethren Breakfast (or Breakfast Wars, as I call them) began innocently enough with some friendly competition about protein-packed breakfasts for the needy. Since then it's escalated into a full blown rivalry that comes loaded with lots of pork and dairy by-products. If it escalates any further, the winning church will be the one responsible for creating the most new Heavenly memberships caused by arterial blockages.

Those who volunteer for either camp quickly learn you are not simply called upon to serve: you are enlisted in an all-out cholestoric war. I let myself get assigned as principal egg slinger, in the hope that the volume of eggs I cook for others will eventually displace what I cook alone. I read somewhere that people who are on serious diets allow themselves a favorite dessert once in awhile as a reward. So, once a month I scramble eggs for 225 people or so. I also limit my grocery trips to last just 18 minutes. I figure I can't cook what I don't have.

I told Vito I'd be there, and offered to drive him. "Thanks anyway, Cookie," he said. "But I gotta do some errands before I do the breakfast." Errands? What kind of errands does anyone besides Farmer Brown run before 7:00 a.m. on Saturday morning?

I gave Marie some of my seed-encrusted eggs, poked around the burnt kielbasa and onions and swigged some ginger ale. Then the doorbell rang. Marie shrieked and threw her seed cup upside down. Vinnie stuck both paws out from under the basement door and rattled the door — BANG-BANG-BANG. Marie sent up more hysterical fluff. I walked down the hall shaking my head, opened the front door and gasped to see Evelyn DeSantos.

Evelyn DeSantos heads the Breakfast Wars. Evelyn whips up the troops to maintain the frenzied rivalry between both denominations. Some call her Evil-yn, but only if they're sure she's visiting her grandkids out of state.

"Come on in," I said carefully.

She stepped in with all the due caution one should muster toward my Disney-puked walls. "Just for a minute," she said, with an askance glance at my electric blue hallway with silver and pink wallpaper borders. Then again, it might not have been the walls: most of her glances usually seem kind of askance because she draws her eyebrows on herself. On good days, she looks like a demented French child ran amuck with a marker. But at least they match her black helmet hair. Today Evelyn's eyebrows sported a cynically bemused look: her right eyebrow arched up, and her left eyebrow sloped down.

Both Evelyn and her eyebrows took in the hallway and smiled at me. I smiled back and wished I had a pot of something to stir.

"Hey, Evie," Vito said, sauntering into the foyer, holding a spatula in one hand and his beloved Swiffer pad in the other. "How's tricks, kid?" Vito sparkled his senior vintage savoir-ick. I shuddered. But Evelyn was made of stronger stuff.

"I came by for my package, Vito, but I didn't find you at home," Evelyn said. "I recalled Wilhelmina was your neighbor. When I saw her door open I thought I'd ask her to remind you. I do need it before the breakfast tomorrow." She smiled and raised her eyebrows, but they waved in opposite directions and scared even Vito. I cringed. Vito was clearly out of his depth.

"Sure, Evie, sure; I was plannin' on gettin' it to yous tomorrow morning. I was just tellin' Mina here I had some errands to run before the breakfast tomorrow, and yous is one of them." Vito smiled enthusiastically, showing off spaces where his molars ought to be.

"I will be seeing you both for the Brethren Breakfast in the morning," Evelyn commanded.

Vito and I exchanged glances and gulped. I was really glad Vito had reminded me. I'd have been a goner otherwise.

"No worries, Evie," Vito said. I smiled and nodded. Evelyn nodded and left. I didn't hear a car start up or drive away, so I figured she re-mounted her broom and left. Vito and I exhaled.

"Ya know, I never mind helping a body out," Vito said. "But this breakfast thing Evelyn has with First Meth is going a little over the top."

"Ditto. Even for me."

"She's already got me buying her six hams. And now it ends up I also gotta cook three of them, because there's not enough room in the church ovens, with the sausages and bacon and casseroles and all." Vito looked at me nervously. "Ya don't think Evie's got somethin' special up her sleeve for this week, do yous?"

"Fastnacht French toast?" I ventured.

Vito looked at me. "Fastnacht?"

"You know," I said, "the fatty donuts they sell right before Lent."

"Oh," Vito said thoughtfully.

I pondered, then mused aloud, "Actually, if Evelyn wants to be super authentic, she'll make sure they're homemade Fastnachts, made from potato dough with lard, fat and butter and cut into squares." I paused, then added: "And, of course, dusted with confectioner's sugar."

"Huh," Vito replied. "We better be on our toes next Spring," he said.

Just then the basement door rattled with the force of what I guessed was Vinnie's head or a lion-sized battering ram. Marie shrieked. "Guess Vinnie wants out of the basement," Vito said. "Ya can't blame the fella. It's all sunny and bright outside and he's stuck down there."

Normally, Vinnie hangs out in the basement until I put Marie upstairs at lunchtime. Then he trots upstairs and hangs out, until eventually he falls asleep on his side of my bed. Some nights I end up sleeping too, when he's not snoring or talking in his sleep.

Vito was right. Even though the lights were on for Vinnie, I'd felt guilty about this for a while. I checked the time and was my usual late. "C'mon, Marie," I said, lugging her cage upstairs.

I got Marie tucked in 'her' bedroom, and the phone rang. Again.

"I can get it for you," Vito yelled.

"Thanks," I yelled back, closing the door to Marie's room and heading downstairs.

"Well of course, Muriel, I remember yous too," Vito said. He smiled with his bridge-free grin into the kitchen phone, receiver to his ear, Swiffer hand resting on his hundred pound hip. He was the vision of domesticity. "Yes, ma'am, Mina's right here." He handed the phone to me.

"Mina? It's Aunt Muriel," the godmother said.

Aunt Muriel usually calls on Fridays, to help steer my weekend social life. As a result, I've rubbed shoulders with many of Lancaster's elite – mostly retired. "I wanted to remind you about the breakfast tomorrow morning."

Were they really this short-handed? "Yes, I know; Vito and Evelyn reminded me," I said.

"Oh, good." Aunt Muriel sounded pleased. "And I have some new paint swatches for you, dear, so I'll bring them with me. Remember, Sunday we're having brunch after church. And then we're off to polo," Aunt Muriel sang off.

I hung up and sighed. Apparently I would be attending at least one church service before Christmas. Well, my weekend plans were made.

I looked up at the clock and counted. If I drove at 45 mph through the 25 mph streets back to work, and got all green lights, I'd at least make it into the parking garage sort-of-maybe on time.

I opened the door to the basement and Vinnie sprang out and stretched his 48-inch long torso. I put his bowl and a box of Kitty Cookies on the counter while he stood up on his back legs, placed his front paws on top of the counter, and peered into his empty bowl. "Maw-wuphf!" he said.

"I know you want more. It's coming, it's coming," I muttered. Yeeshkabiddle.

"Man, he sure is a big cat," Vito said. He always says this when he sees Vinnie. Which is a lot. "Ya sure he's not some kind of special cat, like Maine Coon or somethin'?"

"Mainly mountain lion," I replied. I emptied a handful of treats on top of Vinnie's Kitty Cookies and presented his normal lunch to him. Vinnie replied with his usual, "Oh-kahyyye!" I put the bowl down on the floor, hollered my farewells and hurried out.

I was just getting into the van when Vito came running down the driveway after me. "Hey, you almost forgot!" he said, holding his gym bag full of dirty dry-cleaning. He was right. I had forgot. No wonder people were always calling to remind me about stuff.

He tossed the bag on the front seat next to me. "Sorry, Vito," I said. He gave me a 'fugheddaboudit' wave and I started to take off. I hoped that old ladies, strollers and excitable squirrels stayed off the streets until I got back to my desk.

I drive a dull brown Dodge Caravan, a vehicular hand-me-down from my sister Ethel and her husband Ike. Before the van, which I dubbed The Doo-doo, my '90 Ford Escort gasped its last fumes as it entered the slow lane, just past the entrance ramp near Nutley Street on Route 66, during a visit to Ethel and Ike in Northern Virginia. That night I had my 15 seconds of fame on the 10 o'clock news. Apparently I had single-handedly backed traffic up into downtown DC as well as Route 29 until 8 o'clock that night. At the time, I was more than happy to accept the offer of a used, reliable vehicle. The price – free – was right and the timing was perfect. Even if it was a poop brown van.

My driveway has the approximate pitch and slope of Mt. Everest, so it's a matter of habit while undoing the emergency brake to double-check my rearview for neighbors' cars and smartass kids. But what to my wandering eyes should appear but a galumphing Great Dane and Mr. Perfect, in his baseball cap reading, 'John Deere'?

Okay, he was wearing more than a cap. But not much more. Tanned torso, cut-off jean shorts and the dopey John Deere baseball cap. A minus 4 for the baseball cap but a definite plus-plus-plus for the abs and the rest. I'd seen him before, of course, in one of my more memorable feminine moments hauling my new second-hand club chair out of the back of the Doo-doo. The chair is not a heavy piece of furniture, but it probably made me look like Amazon Woman picking it up all by myself. And of course at the time I was sporting a sweat-drenched T-shirt, soggy pony-tail and no makeup. I also bonked my noggin getting out of the van. (Luckily, I didn't pass out or get concussed.)

By the way, I'm a forty-something and sometimes pass for a less-than-forty-something on my happy days or in dark piano bars. I have shoulder-length mousy brown hair that is thick and straight and without any noticeable amount of grey. I'm also considered to be exceedingly tall by vertically challenged boyfriends: I'm 5'10" in my stocking feet. In the spirit of boyfriends past, please do not insert basketball player jokes here. I'm also slightly accident prone which, combined with my kitchen addiction, is generally not a good mix.

Mr. Perfect saw me staring at him in the rearview mirror. I wiggled a 'hello' with my fingers, and he and Marmaduke loped off. Why, oh why, does any female stumble across her Mr. Perfect at the wrong time? Like when we're not perfect? I sighed. And then I burped. Vito's lunch hadn't done much for me except sabotage my insides. The botched opportunity to chat up Mr. Perfect was also not very settling. Urrrp.

Now I was seriously late. So, as Fate would have it, every traffic light turned red on me from Millersville Pike up through Manor Street. The one green light I raced toward at Mulberry I forfeited to a pack of fire engines. When at last I pulled into the Prince Street garage, I came up behind someone entering a parking garage for her very first time. A wizened, woolly, permed head peered out the driver's side window and stared blankly at the huge lettering of the machine's instruction: 'PRESS HERE FOR TICKET'. I sighed. I undid my seat belt, got out and walked up to the 100-year-old would-be parker. I pressed the button and handed her the ticket. She looked up at me confusedly through Coke-bottle lenses. Then she watched the gate go up. A moment later, I saw the light go on over her head. She smiled, waved thank you and floored her Camry for all it was worth, leaving me behind in the fumes.

I coughed, got back into my car and ignored the silent parade behind me that was backed up Prince Street, probably well past Clipper Stadium. I have to admit it: people in Lancaster are super polite. If this kind of thing had happened in New Jersey, horns would be leaned on and various dialects of hand signals would be displayed, not so subtly. As an official Jersey transplant, I've found the hardest thing to get used to about Lancaster – besides the bucolic scenery and fresh air – is how nice everyone is to each other. It's scary.

I found a parking spot then hightailed it into the parking garage elevator. I raced out of the elevator, through the courtyard, and into the lobby to wait for a few thousand years until an elevator showed up. There are only seven floors in the old Armstrong building on Chestnut and Queen and it almost never fails that you have to wait a lifetime for an elevator's arrival — and even longer when you're running late. I drummed my fingers impatiently on the receptionist counter. Then I heard three simultaneous chimes as a trio of empty elevators opened at once. I got into what looked like was the least threatening elevator and pressed 7 for the 'Penthouse'. Ha, ha.

I began walking to my desk, when someone grabbed my arm and pulled me inside the IT lab. "Leave your purse here," Bauser whispered.

"You're mugging me?" I asked.

"Seriously, How-weird's on a roll." Bauser shook his head. "So leave the bag here and make like you were in the bathroom or something so he doesn't know you just came back from lunch."

"Bauser, girls take their handbags into the ladies room all the time," I said. "But thanks for the heads up," I said, with a virtual pat on his head.

I opened up the IT lab door, stepped back into the hall and found myself breast-to-face with my boss, Howard (or, as we not so affectionately call him, How-weird.)

"MINA!" Howard screamed into my cleavage. "WHERE HAVE YOU BEEN?!"

"Lunch?" I said.

The little vein running up the center of Howard's bald head throbbed. I gulped.

"Everyone's out to lunch! You're out to lunch! Roger's out to lunch! And Buy-A-Lots' execs are out to lunch! Now those crazies are griping Predict-O is being used by arsonists!"

Bauser was right. How-weird was on a roll. I tried to muster all the intellectual wit I could from my energy-absent lunch. I took a deep breath, opened my mouth to explain, and let out a very loud burp.

Howard threw his stubby little arms up in the air and stomped off. Bauser fell backward into the lab convulsing. I blushed.

"Man, oh man, that was like totally the best response ever," Bauser hooted.

I sighed. Three years I've been with EEJIT now and each year I get depressingly decreased raises accompanied by increased hints of termination. Belching in my boss' face clearly wasn't helpful.

Bauser – known only to his mother as Ralph Bausman – took off his glasses to wipe the tears out of his eyes. Well, I thought, at least my dyspepsia provided comic relief.

"So what's going on?" I asked.

"Okay, seriously, babe, you are not gonna believe this," Bauser grinned. "You know How-weird's pet Buy-A-Lots project?"

I knew all too well. "Yip. Help Buy-A-Lots put a store on every corner of every town all across the country."

Buy-A-Lots pays EEJIT a boatload of money for the Predict-O reports, because Predict-O is supposed to find them the best possible new store locations. When Buy-A-Lots ran the program, and Predict-O forecasted Lancaster as the best place to open up their next new store, they went nuts. There are six Buy-A-Lots here already, and all of them are bleeding money. Both EEJIT and Buy-A-Lots couldn't understand the results from the data – but here in the Lancaster office, we sniggered. If you stay here for more than 48 hours, you realize that Lancastrians are frugal people. Very, very nice, and very, very frugal (in other words, cheap). So it was no surprise, then, that Buy-A-Lots execs couldn't believe our data was telling them to open up a seventh loss leader.

"Babe, remember how at contract renewal Roger talked Howard into letting Buy-A-Lots pay only half for Predict-O so we could keep the contract? The other half's bet on the new store opening up in Lancaster on time and being a lean, mean cash machine."

"Right. So what's the catch?"

"The new store on Fruitville Pike. It's burned down. Again."

Oh. So that's where the pack of fire trucks was going.

This was the second time a fire 'happened' to the same new store. The first time was an accident, the paper reported: a workman's torch was left on when it was supposed to be off. Although the gossip with the senior crowd during that Brethren Breakfast was that none of them were too unhappy about it. Especially since no one got hurt. (You see how nice Lancaster folks are?)

So that explained How-weird's meltdown. It was common knowledge that if the new store didn't go up on time and wasn't super profitable, How-weird would get the boot. I sighed. This could make my position even worse. Who knew who would replace Howard? Someone even more awful? Or maybe he'd fire me on his way out: his last hurrah, that kind of thing. I started to read the writing on the wall: scapegoat for hire.

"Welcome back, Mina," Lee said smugly as she sashayed past me.

When she was past, Bauser said, "Man, she is such a witch."

I shrugged. Ever since I'd been hired, Lee's jealousy for my office manager position flared at every opportunity. I figured it was mostly because she's a dyed-in-the-wool busy-body. Part of my 'other duties as required' includes being the closest thing we have to an HR department. Consequently, I help people deal with a lot of health benefit issues, which means I end up knowing a lot more about their personal lives than I'd like to. Someone like Lee would definitely use this information for no good. But luckily, Lee is a QA technician who reports to Achmed. And it seems that Achmed likes to keep her pretty busy so he can check out his stock investments and eBay.

I shrugged bye-bye to Bauser and trudged back to my cube. I looked over at Norman's cube across from mine, and saw him lying on his towel. Norman stretches himself out on the floor of his cube every day at exactly 2:00 p.m. Clearly it was half-past nap time, since he was already settled in. It was also a clear sign that I was even later than I thought. Crap. I plopped myself down in my chair and stared at the corporate logo screensaver. I logged in and waited for my email inbox to open. Since lunch, another 185 new emails had rolled in. I clicked on the 'Message from' column and confirmed what I already knew: 90 percent of these were from How-weird, whose office was less than twelve feet from my cube. I sighed, then reordered them by date and time to trawl through the missives in order.

I started to open the first email from How-weird when my phone rang. "Mina Kitchen, EEJIT," I said automatically, while trying to decipher the content of How-weird's first bold-face, red 14-point email.

"Girlfriend, you are not going to believe this!" Belinda hissed into the phone at me from across the miles.

While I had to endure How-weird and the occasional stray Amish buggy, poor Belinda endured various levels of dysfunction in EEJIT's corporate offices in Atlanta.

"Ken is on a rampage," Belinda whispered in a voice so low only a bat could hear it. But I got every word. We'd perfected the office phone whisper until we could hear each other's pulse.

"He's joined the club, huh?" I said, still perusing How-weird's emails, which had grown from 14-point bold red to 20-point purple, highlighted in yellow, and pulsing against a black border. I wondered how he did that. It was pretty eye catching. I'd have to look into it.

"Ken is actually sweating," Belinda said.

This was significant. Ken is about 7 feet tall and weighs 90 pounds. When he visits Lancaster and stands next to Howard, he looks like a giant fork standing next to a 4x4 meatball. The effect is pretty humorous. Especially since Ken's gestures are pretty effeminate, and Howard is a confirmed homophobe. This means that after one of Ken's visits, there is usually a mass exodus to the restrooms so we don't all pee in our collective pants.

"What's the deal?" I asked.

"Didn't you hear? You're out there, for Pete's Sake!" Belinda was a Baptist. Saying 'Pete's Sake' for her was significant cussing.

"Okay, I'll bite. All I heard is that Buy-A-Lots' new store on Fruitville Pike got torched again."

Belinda sighed. "And did you know the same thing happened out this way AND in Buy-A-Lots' corporate hometown?"

"Really?"

"And they think all three store sites were selected by using guess-whose Predict-O system?"

"Hey!" I smiled. Sometimes Fridays weren't so bad after all.

"And you know that fingers are pointing every which way, and Ken ain't gonna take the heat for nothin', neither," Belinda said. She was right. When it came to passing the buck, Ken made How-weird look like a rank amateur.

"Anybody hurt?" I asked. I had to. It was the nice thing to do, and I was still trying to fit into Lancaster.

I heard Belinda smile. "Nope."

Cool. But also weird. It meant there had to be some actual arsons going on. Since all three stores were already under construction, they weren't exactly the world's best kept secrets. Especially with all the PR Buy-A-Lots made sure was in play.

New stores and store openings were announced in every major newspaper.

"And get this," Belinda squeaked into the phone. "All three fires were set off by flaming –"

Her sentence was cut short as she fell into one of her coughing jags. Poor Belinda has asthma that's probably irritated by the same source that heats up my catering crazies at EEJIT.

"Are you okay? You wanna call me later? Or email?" I offered. There was, after all, no reason why EEJIT should ruin her weekend by landing her in the ER.

I listened for a response, and heard nothing. "Belinda!" I said, then jerked in my seat. I'd scared myself by speaking out loud into the phone like a normal person.

I heard some crackling and a snort. "Heeeeee-heeeee-heeee."

"Belinda, are you gasping?" I went into Commando mode. "Hang up the phone!"

"No-oooo..." she whispered back at me. "I'm t-t-t-trying not to – p-p-pee myself! Heeee-heee-heee!"

Oh. She was laughing. I'd never heard her laugh before. In fact, I'd never heard anyone laugh at EEJIT. Ever. Although I'd heard lots of sighing.

I got curious. "So what's the big 'heeee' about?" I asked, sensing Belinda wiping the tears from her eyes.

"Phew!" she gasped. Then, matter-of-factly, she said, "Every fire was caused by flaming bags of feces."

"Huh?"

"Bags of doggie doo – on fire! Hee-heee-heeee..."

I clapped my hand to my mouth so I wouldn't LOL. Wow. TGIF! I started to snicker – and that made Belinda snicker more. Then she ended up having a real coughing jag. "Gotta go," she gasped and hung up. This damn company.

I finally stopped and blew my nose hard. I started to pull myself together when I looked over and saw that I'd woken Norman. "Sorry, Norman," I said. I really was. Norman is the only person who helps me when things get so bad I bang my head against the desk. Usually by folding up his towel and placing it in front of my forehead.

"That's okay," he said. He looked at me incredulously. "Did something good actually happen?" he wondered aloud to me.

I scurried across the aisle bent kneed, so How-weird or Lee wouldn't see me above cube height, and plopped down next to him on his towel. I told Norman about the Flaming Fecal Flingers. Then we both kept trying from laughing so hard we turned red and tears streamed down our faces. In the end my bladder couldn't take it anymore. I squeaked, "Bye," and crawled back to my cube.

I bent my head over my keyboard and tried to think of something to stop convulsing. The image that ended up coming to mind was Howard sitting across from me at a table in a restaurant, eating. With people nearby. That worked. I grabbed a tissue and blew and walked quickly toward the Ladies' Room.

I was just in front of the Ladies' Room door when How-weird bellowed, "Mina, get in here now!"

I apologized to my bladder and moped back up the hallway to How-weird's office.

"We are in a lot of trouble here," he began. Oh good, I thought. The 'we' was code that I was going to get HA'd – hollered at.

"Buy-A-Lots' being sabotaged by arson!" Howard hissed conspiratorially, leaning over his desk, nose to navel with me. His breath reeked: it smelled like day-old liver. I had to step back to keep my eyelashes from melting.

I exhaled his fumes and took in the data. Buy-A-Lots. Sabotage. Arson. He didn't mention the doggie poop, but I couldn't help but think of it anyway and the corners of my mouth twitched. I looked down at the floor, trying to pretend I was at a funeral. Heck, actually being at a funeral would be better than being here. At least the dearly departed would have let me go to the bathroom. My bladder burbled.

"The police might be on their way here! To question us!" Howard squealed.

"Huh?"

"The cops picked up on the connection with the fires near Corporate and here," Howard sweated. "Now it looks like the Feds may go in on it." Howard stared up at me, pretending he had achieved a normal adult's height. "Buy-A-Lots is not happy," he ended, squinting at me, mostly because the sun was blinding him.

"Okay," I said, hoping for closure and an excuse to relieve my bursting bladder.

"Okay!? Okay!? It is not okay!" How-weird yelled at me in his bold, red, 14 pt. font voice.

I sighed. Howard threw himself back into his executive-like pleather chair. His eyes rested just above his desktop. He waved his eyebrows at me. "Buy-A-Lots is EEJIT's biggest client," Howard said from between gritted teeth. "If the police or Feds can prove there's a connection between the arsons and the Predict-O software, we've had it! No client will feel safe using our product if they think for a moment that Predict-O could be used by terrorists!"

Arson. Terrorists. Right. Uh huh. Gotcha, How-weird. Maybe he ought to cut back on that caffeine...

Howard rubbed his balding head with his fat hairy fingers. I winced. Luckily for me, Howard thought I was wincing in agreement with his terrorist theory. Actually, I bet a lot of people wanted to burn a Buy-A-Lots. It's just that very few people would actually go to the trouble to do it.

Howard's phone rang and he immediately leapt to answer it, as usual. Howard's completely paranoid about not answering his phone at all times, in case it's corporate. No matter how many people are in his office for a meeting, we all know that if the phone rings, we wait. Manners, schmanners. I hand signaled bye-bye to Howard and closed his door before he could motion me to sit and watch him talk.

Once I'd finished my visit to the Ladies', my bladder wasn't so anxious and I felt lots better. I also felt lots more curious. Why did Howard immediately conclude it was terrorism through software?

I looked at the clock. Happy hour was less than 20 minutes away. I figured a cocktail or few would help smooth my edges. I thought about putting on some makeup, but decided against it. I was only going to meet K., for heaven's sakes. I straightened my shirt, and saw I was covered in orange Vinnie hair. Then I shook my head, and seed hulls sputtered out onto the floor. I sighed. With my luck I'd meet the man of my dreams. I hoped he liked pets.

I headed back to my cube, swimming upstream against co-workers taking advantage of Howard's door being closed at 4:45 p.m. on a Friday. The phenomenon was virtually unheard of.

Howard's door is always open so he can corner some unsuspecting programmer and force him to work the weekend. Even Lee waddled quickly past me. At least by shutting How-weird's door I'd done something helpful.

I shut down my computer and slunk out behind Norman – and then Howard's door opened. Norman turned and stared deer-in-headlights back at me. I shook my head and motioned for him to escape. As Howard came out, I stepped around to block his view, offering Norman his route to freedom. I'm a bit protective about Norman. He got married for the first time recently; he's in his mid-50s, and the gal he married has three teenage daughters and four horses. This means Norman spends a lot of his at home time in the barn or the basement. Except this weekend the girls were visiting their dad. I'd hate it if Howard ruined Norman's weekend by asking him to work through it. Again.

"Everything okay now, Howard?" I asked innocently, swaying from side to side to block his view of Norman's exit. Howard jumped up and down, trying to look past me, but probably only got a good view of my tummy.

"Oh, sure," he sneered.

"Well, so long as everything's okay..." I replied, and drifted toward the door.

"Everything's just hunky-dory!" he said, throwing his paws up in the air and stomping on his little feet back toward his office.

"Okey-dokey," I said out loud to no one and made a quick exit, stage left.

I left the garage and drove happily along toward the House of Happy, hoping for a parking spot within walking distance.

The House of Happy's 'Snappy Hour' involves a jazz combo and a lot of gay men, making it my friend K.'s favorite Friday night spot. K. is my very dear friend, and yes, K. is really his name. He actually changed his name legally – for unknown reasons and an unknown sum – to the letter K. With a period. Sadly, 'K.' in conversation is usually mistaken with 'Kay', which is a weird name for a guy, even a gay one.

Most Friday evenings, K. and I flip a coin about where to meet, since meeting a lot of gay men doesn't exactly improve my love life. Although it should have improved my walls. But, maybe this

Friday night would be different. Maybe I'll meet an enthusiastic house painter. I smiled. Things might be looking up.

I quickly parked the Doo-doo, then strolled cheerily to the House of Happy on Queen Street (K. once proclaimed, in all seriousness during a very unsober moment, that this would be the street where he would meet the man of his dreams). As I began to climb the steps of the brownstone where the bar was, I stopped and palmed myself in the forehead. I'd forgotten all about Vito's dry cleaning.

I reached the top step and met Miss Marianne at the hostess podium. Miss Marianne is about 90 years old and has worked at the House of Happy since the first horse and buggy pulled up. She knows my friends, and more importantly, she likes me. I asked her to let them know I'd be back.

"Sure, hon." She winked at me from beneath teased magenta hair and large pink and black leopard patterned eyeglasses.

I squealed off the corner lot, cursing myself for not remembering about the stupid dry cleaning before I left work. Then I could have simply walked across the street. Now I had to drive all the way back. I re-parked in the garage, and hurtled across the road with Vito's gym bag of dirty duds to Lickety-Split Laundry.

I plopped Vito's gym bag onto the counter, and Mrs. Phang, who couldn't have been more aptly named, took the bag and unloaded it beneath the counter muttering something in Vietnamese that did not sound complimentary.

She frowned at me. "You have ticket?"

I sighed and began to dig through the dumpster known as my purse, piling stuff on the counter. I wouldn't have been surprised if I had found one of Mrs. Phang's relatives living amongst the rubble. Finally, I found my wallet without piercing my finger on the lost pin I discovered. I smiled, and Mrs. Phang snarled back. I quickly opened the wallet and several hundred receipts plopped out along the mess. Mrs. Phang smiled, and with surgical precision picked out the receipt bearing her logo so I could ransom the laundry I'd dropped off for Vito last Monday.

Mrs. Phang brought Vito's box of shirts out, and placed them on the counter, keeping a hand on top of the box. "You know, shirts weddy Weeeensday," she scolded me.

"I know, Mrs. Phang, but I really couldn't pick them up until today," I sighed.

"Shirt weedy Weeensday, you pick up! No wait 'til Friday!" she instructed. Yikes. I might actually have to break down and get a BlackBerry after all, just to keep up with Vito's dry cleaning schedule.

I went through our usual ritual of trying to pay for Vito's shirts, and Mrs. Phang continued her ritual of putting me in my place. "No – Vito regular customer! We get check! You take!" Like I said: Vito is a dry cleaning junkie. And he'd definitely found his source.

I scooped up my mess and shoved it back into my handbag as I pretended to ignore Mrs. Phang's laser beam glare at my forehead. Then I grabbed the shirt box and left. As I stood on the corner and waited for the light, I considered wimping out and going home and sautéing some onions and garlic and mushrooms in olive oil with rosemary as the base for some kind of recipe. I could always call Miss Marianne and she'd explain for me, maybe. Then I reconsidered. K. would never forgive me. And he'd probably confiscate my grocery bonus card, too.

So I trundled the clean-shirt box and myself back into the van and chugged back to the House of Happy. I walked up the steps into the martini bar and 'Snappy Hour', and what I hoped was the beginning of a halfway decent weekend.

But no one was there. Not even a mouse. Or a K. I sighed.

An oh-so-brightly-expecting-a-large-tip bartender came up to me. "Hell-ooo! Aren't we in a festive mood!" he sang at me.

"Actually, not so much," I replied honestly.

"I know a fan-TAB-ulous Cosmo that will change your spirits!" he gushed. He really was determined to get that tip. I sighed. He was right – at least about the drink. Mostly because any beverage at House of Happy comes in a seriously fan-TAB-ulous glass that I swear makes your drink taste better.

A few minutes later, I gratefully accepted my Cosmo, fan-TAB-ulous glass and all, and it was pretty good. I started to feel my spine untwist itself out of its weekly spiral. Then K. walked in.

"It's been that kind of week? Again?" he teased, pointing accusingly at my Cosmo glass – which stood empty. Huh. I guess I was a lot thirstier than I'd thought.

"Again! Times two!" K. laughed. We got our Cosmos, and 'tinged' our fan-TAB-ulous glasses to TGIF.

Armand sauntered in, and my spirits lifted higher. Armand is also a good friend, and definitely not gay. In fact, he doesn't even look remotely happy. And tonight he looked especially sullen. But that was because it was a Friday. Fridays are supposed to be the Mondays of Armand's work week. Armand makes his living – and a very good one at that – as a very silent headwaiter at one of Lancaster's very uppery eateries.

But for Armand, waiting tables is about much more than monetary compensation. Waiting is Armand's passion. He disdains those who do not have a true interest in the Waiting Profession, and abuse the privilege of serving the dining public by participating in this endeavor for a mere paycheck.

As it turned out, last week Armand encountered a scheduling 'mix-up' at work. In other words, his manager was annoyed with him, and so he rescheduled Armand from profit bearing weekends to tip-barren weeknights. Apparently, the new schedule was still in negotiation.

I smiled widely at Armand. Armand glowered back. "Wodka!" he commanded the bartender. Three smallish frozen vials of expensive vodka appeared on the granite bar, before the bartender skittered to the far corner to escape Armand's glare.

We 'tinged' to working weekends for Armand, non-working weekends for me and my cronies at EEJIT, and to the health of K.'s very solvent interior design clients.

The bartender continued to placate us with more frozen vodkas, sliding them before us and darting back to his corner. Other patrons arrived and crowded the bar. Smoke, gossip, jazz and a jovial crowd hemmed us safely inside Snappy Hour. I chatted, got jostled and generously shared my drinks with the shoes and elbows of those around me. Life was good.

There was a lull in the music when the penny dropped.

"Supper Clubs! Oh yes! We must!" K. said effusively.

"Huh?" I asked, drifting back from my happy planet Wodka.

"I heard about this from my friend Gillian," he said. "What you must have, my dear, is an entree-VOUS... Understand?"

"Nope," I answered.

"Well," K. began, "it's like a speakeasy, but for fine cuisine! Apparently enough haute cuisine chefs and gourmands are done with the highbrow, linen-tablecloth, silver service thing. So now these people invite you to their private residences for fabulous food at great prices. It's like a big party, with everyone sitting at the same table. It's a true gourmet experience!"

Armand fixed himself into the conversation scornfully by asking, "Who are zee vaiters?"

"There are none!" K. said, throwing his hands up and sailing the remnants of his frozen vodka over our heads and into a hanging plant.

"How do you know about this?" I asked. "And how do you know they're not some kind of scam to rob you? Or sell your organs while you're lying naked in a bathtub?"

"Oh no-ooo! That's just the point. It's a very exclusive friend-of-a-friend-of-a-friend thing..."

K. bobbed from Armand to me. Armand and I responded by trying to sip the remnants of our drinks in unison. Instead, we succeeded by bumping elbows and hurling our drinks backwards over our shoulders. Oh well. I decided it was Lancastrian for good luck.

K. checked to make sure there were no hostile reactions to our vodka missiles.

"They are invitation only, like dining in someone's home," he said.

"But you are served!?" Armand asked.

"Oui!" K beamed, tickled to pull out another of the few foreign phrases he knew. K. hadn't done very well with foreign languages in high school and was just a teensy bit jealous of Armand's accent. He was always endearingly proud when he could throw in a foreign phrase.

"...and you PAY for being invited?" I ventured for the necessary cash information.

"Mina, dear, you pay for the experience; it's not just a meal!" K. had an annoying way of making hunger tantamount to treason. As if anyone would consider eating because they were hungry.

"Right then," I said, and looked into my very empty glass, imagining I was swirling something fuller. "And the board of health licenses?"

"And zee drink license. These are allowed to sell?"

"Oh, you are both just too much! I'll ring up Gillian! Gillian will know! We should all go and try this! It'll be fun!"

I muttered an oath. Armand placed a curse. Someone baptized our shoes with a gin and tonic, and we took that as a cosmic hint to pay the tab and leave.

The clock in the Doo-doo informed me that it was 9:00 p.m. as I clambered in. Then an APB flashed across my brain. I'd completely forgotten about Vinnie and Marie — and more importantly, their dinners.

I was in a hurry, so I caught every red light back, of course. When I finally arrived home, I walked into the front hall and was relieved to see light from the basement. In my panic I forgot I always left the basement lights on for Vinnie so he can find his litter box easily and not explore alternative venues. Like the rest of the house.

I turned on the hall lights. Out came Vinnie, chastising me with, "Brrrllll! Gete!" for partying first and mommying second. He was right.

I got out two cans of Finicky Fare and went into our supper time routine. "Okay, which do you want?" I asked, holding the cans out to him. "'Sardines with Aspic Yick' or 'Gizzards in Goop'?" I asked. Vinnie pushed his face against the Sardines with Aspic Yick. "Aspic it is, sir," I said. "Aspica to you, you spica to me. Har, har." I know it's weird but Vinnie thinks it's punny.

I emptied the can into Vinnie's dish, fending him off while he stood up and pounded his front paws on the counter at me. If I come home some night to find him banging a fork and knife in each paw on the counter, it really won't surprise me. I put the dish down in front of him and turned on the rest of the downstairs lights before I went upstairs to check on Marie.

Marie greeted me by screaming, "Beee-yoooo!"

"Hello to you too," I said, patting her on the head and scratching behind her ears. After that I gave her fresh seeds and water. "I'll come up for you in a bit and then you can watch TV downstairs." I know it sounds simple but all Marie wants is to sit on my lap and watch a little TV– her one vice. She could have it. After I got Vinnie safely stashed behind closed doors, that is.

I came back downstairs and turned on the TV and poured myself what was left of the cranberry juice. I contemplated the contents of my fridge and found a surprise dinner and note from Vito. I set the Tupperware dinner next to the microwave. Vinnie finished his dinner and did his after dinner fetish-washing as I microwaved my ungourmet feast of pirogues and ham. The microwave binged and I took my meal, such as it was, into the living room, turned on the local news and chewed.

"Yet another fire has engulfed the new Buy-A-Lots store at Fruitville Pike," the burly anchorman announced. "Police are not ruling out arson."

A commercial came on, and I thought about Howard and Myron and work and Monday. I couldn't take more bad news, so I turned the TV off. I looked at my dinner. I couldn't take any more bad tastes, either. I wandered into the kitchen, dumped the dinner and pawed through my cupboards. I found a bag of mini-marshmallows, graham crackers and chocolate chips. I opened up a trusty recipe for s'more pie and improvised. While that was baking, I defrosted some frozen chicken breasts in the microwave, chopped an onion and set up a pot to make some Thai-like curry. My timer binged; I took out the s'more pie and set it on a baking rack on the counter to cool. Meanwhile, all the ingredients for the curry were in the stockpot and starting to simmer, so I opened the cupboard door to inspect my spices.

That was when Vinnie decided to hop up on the counter and loop his tail around the glass bottle of hot sauce in the cupboard. It smashed with a clatter on the counter, splashing hot sauce across my face – and directly in both eyes. "Shit! Shit! Shit!" I yelled. Blinded, I staggered toward the kitchen sink, tripping over Vinnie and stubbing my toe hard against the fridge. He hissed back at me, and I heard a loud plop. There was no point in looking: I couldn't. I held my head under the kitchen faucet and rinsed my eyes and my face, as well as most of the counter and a lot of the floor.

When I was able to open my eyes, I wished I hadn't. My s'more pie lay upside down on the kitchen floor next to Vinnie, who was attempting to lick off the melted marshmallow goop on the back of his tail.

I moved the stockpot off the heat and cleaned up what I could of the splattered hot sauce. Then I pulled some marshmallow gunk off of Vinnie.

A couple of hours later, my kitchen was still dirty, Vinnie remained sticky, and I felt guilty. I was a closet late-night binge cooker. “You won't tell anyone, will you, Vinnie?” I asked him. Vinnie thwacked his tail and sauntered off with a pot holder stuck to him, and I went upstairs to bed, resolving never again to cook alone.

CHAPTER 2
(Saturday)

Well before my alarm went off, I woke with a throbbing foot and head, and the realization that I couldn't see. "Don't panic," I told myself. "It's probably left-over hot sauce."

I made it to the bathroom sink without tripping over Vinnie, and splashed water on my face. Then, carefully, I pried my eyelids apart. Eeech! My eyes were so bloodshot the whites of my eyes weren't white anymore. They were completely red. And the hot sauce had also apparently made an equal impression on my face, too. My entire face looked like a giant sunburned blotch.

Vinnie darted under the bed with a concerned, "Grrlll?" and watched me from his hiding spot. Apparently he didn't recognize me, either.

"C'mon," I said, with a scratch of my fingers on the sheets. He emerged and hopped onto the bed for his snuggle. I petted him and discovered a wad of tissues glued to his tail. Well, at least he'd gotten rid of the potholder. Vinnie purred, stood up and put both his paws on top of my shoulders: his own special kitty hug. He started to clean my face with his sandpapery tongue, which would have been very sweet if it hadn't felt a lot like being exfoliated by a Brillo pad.

"Thanks, Vin. I love you too."

He stopped sanding my face and I headed to the shower. As I limped into the bathroom, I glanced in the mirror. Vinnie's kisses had removed a layer of the blotch, and part of my face along with it. I looked like a sunburned baby's bottom.

When I finished, I got out and reached over Vinnie to grab a towel while he sat vigil on the bath mat. Vinnie doesn't approve of showers – particularly the water I drip on him when I get out – and he muttered something that bordered on rude as I stepped out.

I dragged a brush through my hair and tried to ignore my lobster face in the mirror. I put my hair up in a wet pony tail, threw on my favorite Barnstormers T-shirt and oldest jean shorts, and felt a lot more ready for the day and hash slinging. And some seriously high octane coffee. And jelly doughnuts. I sighed. I knew there were no jelly doughnuts in my Jackson Pollack a la Vinnie stained kitchen.

I headed downstairs and deliberately averted my eyes from the myriad hot sauce splatters. Instead I headed straight to my new BFF, Mr. Coffee. I threw in some water and high-test coffee grounds and waited. Upstairs, Marie shrieked. I sighed. I trudged back upstairs, and gave her fresh seeds and water. I stroked her little pinhead and pulled out some of the 'done' casings from her new feathers coming in.

"Sorry about missing your programs last night. There wasn't much on, anyway," I said.

"Bee-you!" she replied cheerily. It doesn't take much to make Marie happy.

I trotted back downstairs to set out Vinnie's bowl of Kitty Cookies. Then it was my turn: extra-strength coffee and Extra Strength Tylenol. It was 6:00 a.m. I slugged myself into the living room and watched the end of an old movie and started to feel better. I dozed. I know I dozed because the knocking at my front door woke me up.

"Sorry to come by so early, Toots," Vito apologized. "But I figured you were up because of the lights on and on account of the breakfast and all."

"Mrgmph," I mumbled.

"Anyways, would ya mind if I got my clean shirt box from yous now? I gotta couple of errands to make before breakfast," he said. Pre-dawn dry cleaning? I was too tired to ask, but I'd remember to file it away for later.

"Ummm… sure," I said.

"Thanks, Cookie," he whispered.

"Why are you whispering?" I whispered back.

"I figured Vinnie and Marie was asleep."

Oh. "No, they're up and fed."

"Geez, you get up early on a weekend," Vito said. "Umm... where's the box, Mina?"

"Backseat of the Doo-doo. Garage..." I mumbled, and lay back down on the sofa.

I heard Vito trudge through the garage and collect his precious dry-cleaning shirt box. He came back into the foyer and I felt him watching me prone on the sofa.

"Hey, smells like you got coffee brewing already?" he asked.

"Yup. High-octane. Help yourself." I gazed over at TV and closed my eyes again.

"Thanks!" Vito smiled and waddled into the kitchen. Then he screamed, "HOLY GEEZ, WHO GOT WHACKED?"

Oh. I guess I hadn't really noticed the full effect of the attack of hot sauce a la Manson Family Mountain Lion. I felt Vito walk through the living room from behind closed eyes and heard him stop in the dining room. "And Holy Pirogues, what happened to the carpet?" he asked.

"Hot sauce."

"Geez. You weren't cooking alone, were you?"

I shrugged. "Vinnie was here," I said.

Vito sighed. "You know, if you put salt on it right away, sometimes it takes the stain out. But now it's dried. I could mix up some salt water and we could try spraying it on," he said. He came into the living room and hovered over the sofa. "You want I should try?"

I opened my eyes and stared at Vito staring at me.

"Did you have a make-up malfunction or something, Toots?" he asked. I explained about the hot sauce eye wash. "Wow, are your blue eyes red. But they're very patriotic looking and all. Hey, if you want, I can make your apologies to Evelyn?"

Gosh. "Naw, it's okay, I'll manage," I said. Besides, I figured if I didn't cook for a couple hundred people soon, there was no telling what would happen if I cooked at home alone again.

Vito puffed up. "Well if that's the case, yous can't drive like this. I'll make some calls and do my runs after the Breakfast Wars." He smiled at me conspiratorially. "Anything you want, kid? We got about a half hour. I can make a run?" he asked. I shook my head. "How about some jelly donuts?"

That made me perk up. "Well, if you happen to have a spare jelly doughnut at home, I wouldn't mind it," I said.

Vito grinned from ear to ear. "I don't," he said, "but I made a run for Abe Cooper just yesterday night. I'll ask him."

"Vito – it's not even six-thirty!!"

"Hey, it's okay. He has early golf games; he's definitely up by now. Besides, I have a key," Vito said. Vito had a key to Abe's place too?

"I'll be right back!" he said, and huffed himself out the front door. And locked it for me, since he had his key and all. I sighed. My home life was confusing at best. Even if I did change the locks I bet that Vito would still find a spare somehow. Sometimes that made me worry about Vinnie, in case Vito let him out by accident. And our arrangement also had me wondering about my future sex life. That is, if I ever got one.

Vinnie stuck his head out from under the sofa and nuzzled my hand. "Brllll???"

"Yeah, he's alright. He means well, anyway," I said.

The local TV woman began to broadcast the end of the world again, so I pushed up from the sofa and headed back into the kitchen. I was halfway done with my coffee when Vito let himself back in.

"Ta da!" he sang. He pulled an enormous grin, and this time I noticed the spaces where his teeth ought to have been actually had, umm... teeth.

"Huh?"

"Jelly doughnuts! Raspberry, even!"

I smiled. "Thanks, Vito." He kept smiling so I kept looking closer. Besides, I'm nosey. "Gee, Vito, your smile seems a lot brighter today," I lied.

"Naw, it's just there's more of it," he beamed. "I thought I lost my bridge, but I found it cleaning out the car yesterday." He smiled a Game Show Host grin at me.

"Oh, that's great," I said. "Thanks for the donut. I'm just gonna gulp this quick and then finish getting myself together."

"Sure, sure, sure, Toots!" He nodded and left, leaving me wishing I didn't have an image in my mind of him – or anyone else

– coming across a mouthful of dentures alongside Buddy Burger wrappers, tissues or other standard-issue car trash. Yechhhh.

I bit into the jelly donut then washed it down with the super leaded coffee. "Grrlll???" Vinnie purred at me, rubbing his arched back just above my knee. He stuck to my shorts.

It was a little before 7:00 a.m., so I figured I better go get Vito. As I headed toward the door, Vinnie chattered amiably from behind me.

When I came out, Vito was waiting in a folding mesh porch chair, wearing mirrored sunglasses. "I figured you wanted your privacy," he said. I shrugged, and we plodded down our attached lawns and got into his Lincoln Town car. The car smelled great – like Easter. I turned around and saw three large pans covered tightly with foil and remembered about the hams. "By the way, it was nice of you to leave me dinner last night," I fibbed, determined to act Lancastrian.

"Sure thing, Toots."

We drove off toward the Breakfast Wars.

When we were on Duke Street, Vito banged his forehead on the steering wheel. "Stupido!" he muttered.

"What's the matter?" I asked politely. I didn't really want to know, but I figured it was probably the Lancaster way to feign interest if someone bangs themselves upside the head on their steering wheel.

"Nothin', nothin', nothin', Toots," Vito said automatically.

We pulled into an alley off of Duke Street that leads to the parking lot where lawyers pay a premium Monday through Friday, but parishioners and soldiers of the Breakfast Wars park for free on weekends. We got out of the car and I followed Vito, who was lugging his box o' dry cleaning, to the kitchen entrance. Inside, I strained to see in the dark, following down the steps behind him. Compared to the 90-degree muggy air in the parking lot, the stairway down to the kitchen felt cool. But it was still pretty early. The afternoon promised temperatures of over 100 degrees and a humidity index over 90. The kitchen promised worse.

Luckily when I entered, the kitchen – with only the oven going – was a balmy 102 degrees. And once I got the egg pans going, Hell would feel like a tropical paradise.

Evelyn greeted us at the bottom of the stairs bearing her standard issue meat cleaver. Aunt Muriel stood behind her, furrowing her brow. "You're a little late, dears," Evelyn said. I mumbled an apology without looking at her. Then she turned her deathly gaze toward Vito. "I expected you a bit earlier."

"Hey, Evie, it's not our fault," Vito said. "Just look at Mina's face and her eyes. And she stubbed her toe. She shouldn't really even be here."

I stood flamingo-style and stared at them. Evelyn and Aunt Muriel peered at my pink face and red eyes. "Oh dear!" they both commented.

"Well, put on some sunglasses!" Evelyn said, and Aunt Muriel handed me her pair of bling-studded shades. Vito and I looked at each other and shrugged. Typical Evelyn. She'd got the volunteer by the throat and she wasn't letting go.

I put on Aunt Muriel's shades. Vito patted me on the shoulder, and I limped over to work with Ernie while Vito went to his usual station of utensil bundling. It was funny to think that a guy with such big pudgy hands could be so nimble fingered. But Vito made tucking plastic forks, knives and spoons in a napkin a form of Episcopalian Origami.

"Here you go, kid," Ernie said, holding out a spatula to me.

Ernie's about 73 years old and always calls dibs on the egg whipping. He cracks a couple dozen eggs or so, whips them up, then passes them to me. I throw the mess in a couple of pans to scramble. Once my batches are done, someone else schleps them over to the serving counter and throws them in chafing dishes. When the doors open at 9:00 a.m., people line up. The honest truth is for some people this will be their only decent meal – maybe their only meal – of the day. It makes my culinary crazies feel almost worthwhile.

Ernie started cracking eggs while I melted butter and oil in the frying pans. I reached into my back pocket and dug out an orange bandana, folded it and tied it around my forehead. I'd figured out long ago that sweat dripping from my forehead into frying pans wasn't too hygienic.

"Sunburn?" Ernie asked me.

"Hot sauce," I replied, lowering Aunt Muriel's shades.

"Really?" Ernie arched his eyebrows. But something was wrong. I stared at Ernie and his rumpled forehead trying to figure out what was missing. He saw my stare, and started chuckling. "Oh yeah, heh. Got a little too close to the grill yesterday and WHOOMPF! My eyebrows fell out cinders."

"Gee, that's too bad. But they'll grow back in," I said.

"Yeah, sure. Hey, maybe they'll grow back in red, like they were when I was 20. You think?" Ernie winked at me. "Hey, better yet," he whispered, "maybe I could color them in with a marker like Evelyn, huh?" Ernie nudged me in the ribs and we both grinned. "See, when you smile you look almost human!" he beamed.

I got the first batch of eggs scrambled but I didn't know who was ferrying them to the warmer. Ernie's lined up bowls were there, but he had been going back and forth with Vito carrying in the hams. I looked around and couldn't see him. I shut the heat off the pans and looked around for some transportation help. Then I heard Vito come back down the stairs with the last ham, getting cornered by Evelyn. Eeek. Since I had to save the eggs, I figured I might as well save Vito, too.

"Hey, Vito," I interrupted Evelyn's interrogation. Vito's face flipped the volume on the hopeful factor.

"Yeah, Cookie? Yous need a hand?" he asked.

"Or two," I said. Vito grinned back. Evelyn scowled. At least it looked like she was scowling. But it was kind of hard to tell if it was really a scowl or not. She might have been happy, but her eyebrows looked mad.

Vito lumbered across the kitchen and through the maze of food, supplies, volunteers and serving paraphernalia. Once he got within hearing range he whispered, "I owe you, Toots."

"What's with her this morning?" I asked.

"Aw, she's a little sore with me on account of I couldn't do my errand early this morning like I planned, and she was my first stop," Vito explained. "Anyways, so I gotta do a little favor now for Evelyn and stop over her house in a little bit."

Vito ferried the scrambled eggs over to the warmers, which were immediately confiscated by Aunt Muriel, Norma and Ray. Norma and Ray are a couple in their late 60s. The three of them are usually assigned to serve up the breakfast items. Which is a good thing since they're the most presentable looking among us. Norma and Ray always looked clean and pressed. I think they sleep standing up, like horses.

Once I got done with scrambling all the eggs, I felt like I'd sweated off ten pounds. And Ed, who held the line next to me at the stove, still pumping out pancakes, was just as sweaty but a little scarier looking – mostly because both his eyes unfortunately face in opposite directions. It makes conversations and wise cracks a little tricky; you aren't really sure whether he's talking to you or the persons on either side of you.

"I gotta go now, Toots, but I'll be back," Vito said, holding his beloved dry cleaning box next to him.

"Thank you, Vito," Evelyn waggled at him. "I'm sure Ernie can help Mina," she said.

"Oh sure, Evelyn; no problems here," poor Ernie said, snapping a salute at his peeled egg forehead. I had a funny feeling it was gonna take a long, long time for Ernie's eyebrows to grow back. Fingers crossed he wouldn't be tempted to borrow Evelyn's marker.

Off Vito went with his box o' shirts while Ernie and I kept scrambling.

A feeling suddenly struck me, and I peered about the kitchen. All at once I was sure we were missing more than Ernie's eyebrows.

"Hey, Ernie," I wondered out loud, "Where's Henry?"

Ernie's face kind of blanched. "Umm... I think he had some kind of an accident yesterday so he couldn't be here," he fluffed. Hmmm, I thought. Weird.

My toe started to throb peacefully, so I tried not to think about missing volunteers. Instead I began to really miss my Extra Strength Tylenol. Youch. Now it felt like a cozy one thousand degrees in the kitchen. Everyone was passing around pitchers of ice water, which was good since I was probably the only person under 50 there. The thought of limping from person to person performing CPR was not particularly attractive. Not that I was at this point, either.

We finally got the breakfast buffet ready and assembled cafeteria-style on the counter: scrambled eggs, pancakes, scrapple, sausages, sliced ham, bacon, French toast, hash browns, grits, fruit, milk, juice, biscuits, and pans of macaroni and cheese casserole. And there was more in the dining room for people to help themselves to: iced cinnamon rolls, turnovers, pies, layer cake, muffins, donuts, hot and cold cereals, coffee, tea and hot chocolate.

Each Breakfast War I would mentally cross myself and pray that there would be no suicidal diabetics or arterial bypass patients partaking of the complimentary repast. It was an easy task, fortunately: we all held hands and said a prayer before serving. Jorge, the verger, was always at each breakfast and always led us. Today's prayer ended with, "...and we're extremely thankful for our continued blessings from Groceries Galore and especially thankful for the donation of the many hams from Friends of Vito." Huh. I didn't know Vito an organization of friends. Other than his Breakfast Wars buddies. At least, none that I had ever met.

After the blessing, Norma, Ray and Aunt Muriel lined up in their latex hospital gloves to serve the masses. Although Aunt Muriel replaced her diamond cluster rings over her gloves. Is she a class act, or what?

I spied the dirty pots and pans and sighed. Usually I stay and help with the cleanup, but I'd kind of had enough for one hot sauce/mangled foot morning. But Vito was MIA with the Evelyn errand. Then Vito's head popped into the kitchen. "Pssssst, Toots," he hissed. I looked at him and hope returned. "C'mon," he waved and ducked back up the stairs. I hopped out and hoped I'd slide under the radar. I hopped right into Evelyn.

"Hi-iiiii!" I beamed from under my sweat soaked orange bandana. Evelyn looked a little earnest, even though her eyebrows were scowling.

"Thank you, dear," she said. "I know how uncomfortable you must be. Please make sure you have yourself looked at. Oh, and by the way, Mina, Vito mentioned the, ummm... splatter on your floors from the accident. Be sure to use salt; it's marvelous for removing stains." Evelyn patted me on the arm and walked by me, cleaver and all. Wow. Lancaster folks sure have this nice stuff down to a tee. And they're also very up to date on stain removal, too. Useful, yes?

I limped back up toward the street and was relieved to feel the temperature drop instantly. Vito had the Towncar running and the AC blasting. Hurray for Vito! I got in the car and looked at the thermometer. Now, at about half past ten, it was only 102 degrees with 92 percent humidity. I didn't even want to think how hot the kitchen must have been to make this weather feel cool.

"Boy am I glad you got back when you did," I said. "My dogs are barking. And so are their puppies." I slid my toes up onto the dashboard.

Vito shook his head. "You're gonna get that looked at, right?" he asked.

I looked at my toe. Then I saw the big gash on the top of my foot. "I'll see how it goes Monday," I said. Vito shook his head again.

We drove home in amicable silence, sailing through green lights all the way through town. Typical. Maybe I had some kind of red light magnet attached to my van.

Once we were home, Vito pulled into his driveway. We both got out of the car and I was just about to shut the door when I saw Mr. Perfect jogging around our cul-de-sac with Marmaduke. I stood there with my hand on the door handle, frozen.

Mr. Perfect rounded the circle with his hound and stared right at me and grinned. "Hey," he greeted with a wave and jogged on by.

Hey, he said. That's friendly, right? So maybe I didn't look so bad! I grinned at that thought – and then caught my reflection in Vito's side view mirror. My face was slick, shiny and red, topped by the drenched orange bandana and lots of sweaty strands of hair poking up over top. I looked like a Muppet on acid.

"Hey, he seems like kind of a nice guy," Vito said. "Dunno about the dog, though," he added thoughtfully, and ambled toward his front door. I stood in the driveway and hung my head.

"Hey, Mina, you alright? Could I get ya something?"

I shook my head. "No thanks."

I shuffled up to my front door and re-entered the Fright Night II set that was my home. Ugh. I did not feel like housecleaning, much less deep boiling hot sauce stains – or possible blood stains, judging by the gash in my foot – out of rugs. But since I was a mess already, I shook it off, munched some Tylenol, and went to work.

I scrubbed the floors and Swiffered them. I felt guilty Swiffering behind Vito's back, but I figured he'd have more turns later in the week. Once I was done, I treated myself to a hotdog, a couple more Extra Strength Tylenol and a beer.

Of course, fridge-rustling sounds are a dinner gong for Vinnie. He sauntered up from the basement, stretching and yawning. Smart cat. He'd stayed completely out of the way while there was anything resembling work being done. I patted him on his head and gave him his leftover Aspic Yick from the night before. Then I took a piece of bread up to Marie. Finally it was my turn to get out of my sweat soaked clothes and into the shower.

I gulped some beer and set the bottle down on the bathroom sink. I was about to get out of my clothes when I caught myself in the mirror. Yikes! Much, much worse than Muppets on Acid. More like Meth Muppets. Maybe I was having an allergic reaction to the hot sauce? The thought made me feel squeamish. I thought about the 1980s remake of 'The Fly' with Jeff Goldblum. Was I really becoming Brundle-Rash?

I tossed the thought aside, and my sweaty gear along with it, and climbed into the shower. When I was done, I slipped on a soft T-shirt and some old lightweight jammie bottoms.

About then I decided it was half-past naptime. I hopped into bed and dozed and dreamt about buffets and kitchens and cats (oh my). When I woke up, Vinnie was curled up against me and the clock read almost four. I considered it, got up and sidled downstairs. I poured a glass of water and raised my glass to Vinnie. "Well, here's looking up your address," I said.

After toasting the cat, I went upstairs to feed Marie and apologize for not bringing her down for TV later. It was tough enough going up and down the stairs with my mangled foot, much less carrying the triceps-shaping cockatiel cage.

Back downstairs, I went through the usual dinner routine with Vinnie and held out his menu. "Okay, do you want 'Chicken Lips' or 'Edible Entrails'?" I asked. Vinnie purred his face up to the tin of slivered lips: we had a winner. I plopped the contents down into a clean bowl for him and shivered. Yeesh. And I thought Scrapple was what they squeegeed off the killing room floor.

By now it had cooled down outside to a tolerable 80-something degrees. I put on an old Tom Waits record, scratches and all. I opened the screen door from the dining room, so the music could stretch out to me on the deck, and Vinnie could check out the nature channel safely from inside. Then I opened up a new box of red wine, poured some into a coffee mug, and sat outside in my lounger and sipped.

There's a saying about the bluebird of happiness, and may it fly over you, yada yada. In my family we use this as a curse. Because we all know what birds do. They do doo-doo. Which one did, right into my mug o'Merlot after I drunk my first swig. Shit.

It was also the harbinger of more dirty stuff falling out of the blue.

"Psst, Mina," Vito hissed through the bushes that separated his yard from mine. I sighed. For a second I considered pretending I was asleep, but Vito toddled over through the shrubs. I fantasized about planting roses, barberries or anything else with thorns that would discourage future neighborly visits.

Tom Waits tucked into 'Jersey Girl' so I motioned shhh at Vito. He held both paws up to me in complete understanding and plopped down with his diet Coke in the other chair. As the song started to end, so did my peaceful evening.

"Mina, I hate to ask ya this," Vito said. "But I really got to get some stuff back from Lickety-Split Laundry, lickety-split, like."

"Huh?"

"I'm missing something I really need, and I gotta get it before they close tonight at six."

"Okay."

"Great! So you'll help me!"

"Huh?" I asked.

Vito gulped and took a breath and I swear I heard the gears in his head shift to Big Fat Lie mode. "You see, the thing is," Vito began, "Mrs. Phang kinda likes yous, and she really hates me. She always gives me a hard time."

"Are you kidding me?" I shrieked politely. He looked at me.

"Well the thing is, I really need to get a particular shirt tonight on account of because I'm going out somewhere... yeah, yeah, that's it! I'm goin' out somewheres and I need this particular shirt what Mrs. Phang's got ready for me."

Vito smiled at his massively fabricated whopper. But being my usual schnooky self, plus having had a Merlot and Extra Strength Tylenol cocktail, I let my guard down. "So what you're asking me to do is to go downtown and pick up dry cleaning for you – again,"

I emphasized, to make sure the guilt thing hit home. After all, guilt can be highly profitable.

"Well, when ya put it like that ..." Vito said.

"Yeah, I am."

"Oh."

We stared at each other Mexican Stand-Off Style. I had to hand it to him. He might have retired to Lancaster from Philly like he said, but he had all the tenacity of a Jersey guy. Huh. Go figure.

At last, I grimaced. "Okay, Vito, here's the deal."

"Yeah!" he said, patting my shoulder in thanks.

"Okay, I'm not really in a position to drive right now, what with my foot hurting and drinking wine and Tylenol," I said, emptying my glass into the planter next to me.

Vito's brow furrowed. "Okay." Clearly he was worried about the sobriety of my zinnias.

"So I'll pick up your laundry, but I can't drive there. You'd have to drive me there. And by the way, since you'd already be there, wouldn't it make more sense for you to just be polite to Mrs. Phang and pick up your own dry cleaning?" Ha.

"No! No! No! Mrs. Phang hates me! She'll put scorch marks in my best shirts!" Vito whined. I could totally empathize with his fear of Mrs. Phang. And ironing. I hadn't ironed a piece of clothing since 1982.

"Okay, look, I'll do it but you gotta get me there. And back," I added.

"Sure, sure, sure, Toots," he said.

I limped inside while Vito retreated. I turned off Tom Waits, put my raincoat on over my jammies and gimped out of the house and into Vito's Towncar. On the ride into town I readied myself to be dropped off in front of Lickety-Split Laundry. But Vito drove right past it, and parked in the lot near Central Market.

"Vito, don't you want to drop me off in front of the cleaners, and not a block away?" I asked.

"Ummm. No. I can't. On account of Mrs. Phang knows what my car looks like and I'm afraid she'll close up early once she sees it. She's done it before," Vito mumbled.

I wasn't buying it. "Vito, let me get this straight. You're so afraid of Mrs. Phang that it's okay for me to limp around the block with a sore foot and your dry cleaning because you're afraid she'll hurt your laundry?"

Vito gulped. "Yep."

"Here's a little clue: MAYBE IT'S TIME TO USE A DIFFERENT DRY CLEANER!" I glared at him.

Vito gulped and looked down and started the car. "Uh, maybe you're right, Toots... sorry... didn't realize your foot hurt you so bad," he mumbled apologetically.

Hrumph, I thought. Vito pulled up in front of the cleaners, gave me the cleaning ticket and I gimped inside. Mrs. Phang was waiting for me, adorned with one of her best sneers. "Why he park here? What he want?" she snapped.

I was in no mood. "This!" I answered, equally as snappy, slapping the cleaning ticket on the counter. Mrs. Phang jumped back a bit.

"No need shout," Mrs. Phang sulked, and she disappeared into the back room. I heard her rummaging for Vito's shirt amidst a lot of Vietnamese expletives. Then she returned with the usual shirt box and handed it to me. I took it and stared at her. "I know, I know, he regular customer, he pay by check." Yeeshkabiddle.

Mrs. Phang nodded brusquely, folded her arms and stared at me. "You go home, you put on cream! Get rid of rash!" she advised with a shout.

I stepped out of the building and walked over to the curb where Vito's car had been idling. Except neither Vito nor the Towncar were anywhere in sight. I rolled my eyes and wanted to do a Mexican hat dance on his shirt box. But I figured that would hurt my sore foot more, so I calmly slammed the box against a nearby lamppost. Something rattled from inside it. Great. It sounded like I'd knocked all the buttons off his shirts. I stood on the corner in my raincoat and jammies, leaning on the lamppost, watching all the tourists pass by.

Just then Vito pulled up to the corner and waved at me to hurry into the car.

"Where'd you go?" I asked, sliding into the car as Vito sped away from the curb. "What are you in such a hurry for?"

"Sorry, Toots. I was afraid I got spotted by a traffic cop and didn't want to risk a ticket. I just drove around the block," Vito said. I held on to the box and closed my eyes. When I opened them again we were parked in Vito's driveway. "Thanks again, Mina," Vito said.

"No problem," I lied, handing him the box and getting out of the car.

Vito put the car back into gear and waved goodbye to me. Boy, he must be in a hurry. He didn't even bother to change into the shirt he made me pick up for him. Huh.

I opened the door and Vinnie greeted me by rolling on his back and demanding a belly rub. I threw my raincoat over the railing and picked off a mousie toy that was stuck to his belly in more marshmallow gunk. I padded into the kitchen and peered into the fridge to see what might be playing for dinner. It looked like I was fully stocked with condiments but no food to wear them. Thinking pizza delivery sounded pretty good, I scrounged around for the phone book. Phone book in hand, I called PizzaNow! and ordered a medium white skinny pizza with onions, green peppers, tomatoes, mushrooms and anchovies. Things were looking up.

The pizza arrived, and I settled down to a pizza orgy for one and watched Stand Up Comic-palooza with a fresh Mug O'Merlot, sans birdie doo-doo. At a commercial I went upstairs and gave Marie some pizza crust. Then I settled back downstairs on the sofa. The last thing I remember was Vinnie curled up next to me on the floor, snuggling my hand.

CHAPTER 3
(Sunday)

I woke up on the sofa to Vinnie snuffling inside the pizza box and a Family Cook-Along rerun. I scooped Vinnie's head out of the box and petted him. He felt lumpy. I looked closer. A piece of pizza crust was stuck to him. Vinnie scooted away and ran into the basement. I got up, washed the gunk from my fingers and made some coffee. I poured a cup, lifted it to my lips and glanced at the clock. And then I gasped and spat the coffee back out again. It was 9:50 a.m. I was supposed to meet Aunt Muriel at church at 10:30. And for brunch afterward. And the polomathingy after that. Ack. Ack. Ack.

I grabbed some paper towels and swiped at the mess on the floor. At least Vito would have something different to Swiffer today. I threw some Kitty Cookies in Vinnie's bowl, and started quickly upstairs when my foot complained. I told it to report to Customer Service. I climbed the rest of the steps, fed Marie and got in the shower. A few nanoseconds later I was out again, wet, purple and red. There was a dull throb in my foot. My face glowed a shiny bright pink. And my eyes were still bloodshot. I shrugged. I figured I'd wear Auntie's sunglasses again. I pulled on a light-blue sleeveless linen dress and cute spikey white sandals, throb or no throb. I pulled my wet hair up into a quickie French braid, patted on some foundation, and finished with some lip-gloss. With any luck I might pass for sun-poisoned.

I dashed downstairs, grabbed my purse and stepped into the oven otherwise known as my van. I started the engine, regretting the non-working AC. I remoted the garage door open and lead-footed it down the driveway. I looked in my rearview and realized I'd almost smooshed Mr. Perfect flat on the curb, along with his Dinasouris Muttis. There he was again, greeting me in another moment of my time-challenged hysteria. Sporting his usual tanned torso under a white t-shirt. His hair was freshly washed and he wore a new, somewhat pissed off look. I waved a little in the rearview mirror at him, to which he shook his head and loped off with his hound. I leaned my head on the steering wheel and sighed. When I looked up, I saw Vito ambling toward my car all gussied up in his Sunday best: a powder blue leisure suit and white patent leather Pat Boone shoes. Good grief. We not only matched; we looked like we were going to the prom together.

"Hiya, Toots, you leaving for St. Bart's? Can I hitch a ride?" he asked.

I'd never seen Vito at a church service. Then again, I'm not a regular.

"Sure," I shrugged. "Hop in."

"Boy, I sure hate walking into a service all by myself."

I glanced at him and noticed he'd lost his bridge again. But I was proven wrong: we hit a red light. While we waited for it to turn green, he reached into his blazer pocket, withdrew his bridge and slipped it into his mouth. Then the light turned green. I floored it. I was determined not to stop at any more red lights with Vito or his teeth.

I parked the van on Mulberry and we walked toward church. Or really Vito walked and I limped behind, my foot barking at my cute spikey sandals.

Mulberry Street was a picture perfect slice of Americana on a hazy Sunday morning. Just the quiet hum of cars passing, cicadas, and someone washing breakfast dishes.

"You wanna sit together?" Vito bellowed shyly.

"Sure," I said, "but we have to look out for Aunt Muriel. I'm supposed to meet her."

"Oh, hey, that's great!" Vito smiled enthusiastically. Somewhere in the dim recesses of my ancient love-life, I vaguely recalled this was what attraction smelt like. Vito was oozing something very much like this at the mention of Aunt Muriel's name. Huh.

We headed into church and scoped out Aunt Muriel. I walked down the aisle and tapped her on her shoulder. She slid over, while I offered Vito first dibs to sit next to Auntie. Aunt Muriel's eyebrows flew to the ceiling and she pursed her lips together into an asterisk. Vito responded by flashing his game-show-host-with-bridge-in grin at her. I sat at the end of the pew and pretended to memorize the hymnal. But maybe things were looking up. My foot hurt a bit less, and my eyes felt adjusted. I took Auntie's sunglasses off. Maybe I didn't look like I had eyeball aneurysms anymore. Vito tapped me on my arm. I looked over, and saw Auntie waving at me to put her sunglasses back on. I put them on.

We went through the service with some confusion, which is typical for Episcopalians and visitors alike. We quickly realized poor Vito was a visitor. I tried to explain the Prayer Book vs. Hymnal vs. Contemporary Hymnal vs. Weekly Insert, nudging him when to pick up his hymnal, put his knees down, put his right foot in, put his right foot out, that's what Salvation's all about. The Eucharist began, and eventually it was our turn to walk up to the altar. I stood up and let Vito and Auntie out of the pew. Vito got ahead of us, but I figured we'd catch up. I shrugged at Aunt Muriel and she smiled her thin-lip look back at me. We shuffled up the aisle and took our turn to kneel – Vito, me, and Aunt Muriel.

The first pass with the Host went okay, with Vito starting the lineup. Then the chalice with the Blood of Our Lord was offered to Vito. Instead of gently guiding it to his lips, Vito grabbed hold and gulped it all down. Aunt Muriel's jaw dropped. I stared in amazement. I'd never seen anyone like tawny port that much.

Once the chalice was wrested back from Vito's fervent grasp, there were a lot of blank looks. While we were one of the last pews up to bat, there was still a line of people waiting to partake of the Eucharistic feast, which meant sharing the One Cup. Except that Vito had chugged it.

Suddenly the organist whipped up a Toccata, and vamped for sacramental wine time. This allowed for some new wine to get blessed asap. Tawny port might be getting a new claim to fame in the Episcopalian church. "We bless no wine before its time." Yup. It was eleven-thirty.

We kneeled for a while and waited for the sacramental backup to appear. Vito was polite enough to hang around kneeling with those of us who remained dry. New wine appeared, got poured into the chalice and was offered to the start of the line, beginning with Vito. Which was probably why Aunt Muriel reached across me and snapped it out from underneath his nose, and took a big swig. Just to be polite and not have Auntie look a little alcoholic, I took a big gulp too. What the heck – the worst anyone could accuse us of was being thirsty.

We ambled back down and through the chapel. Vito pulled me aside. "What are these little candles for?" he asked. I explained. "Oh. Well, then I'm gonna light a candle here, for my sainted wife, Marie," he explained, a little misty-eyed. Poor guy. He really missed his wife. Either that or all that tawny port had mellowed him out.

"Okay," I said, "you just put your offering in here, then light a candle. And I'll hang around in case you get... lost." I wasn't sure what other liturgical faux pax Vito might commit, but I hoped he'd used up his quota for the morning.

"Right, thanks, kiddo," he said.

He pulled out a wad of cash from his pocket. I stood bug-eyed: the roll of dough was big enough to choke an elephant. Vito put a crisp, new one-hundred dollar bill into the donation box. Well, at least St. Bart's could replace the port he'd guzzled with that, and then some. He lit a candle and bowed his head while I hovered around him, just to be sure he didn't set anything on fire. I stood, smiling limply as people tried to weave their way around Vito's girth and return to the sanctuary.

Once Vito's mumblings to the Almighty were done, he turned around and winked at me. I led Vito back down the aisle toward Aunt Muriel, who was on her knees, muttering and shaking her head. I hedged in ahead of Vito to kneel next to Auntie this time, in case she forgot where we were and hit Vito in the pew.

The service over and our handshaking with the vicar complete, we stood uncomfortably between the church and the Fellowship Hall. "Beauteous day!" Vito beamed at Aunt Muriel.

"Yes," Aunt Muriel replied.

"Anyone want coffee? We can grab a cup in Fellowship Hall," I asked and then felt Aunt Muriel's stilettoed heel stomp my hurt foot. "OWWW!!!" I yelled.

"Really, Mina!" she gasped.

"You pierced my foot!" I said.

"Oh," she said. "Beg pardon."

"Hey, yeah, some coffee would be great," Vito said, and smiled. "And maybe some ice for your foot, huh, Toots?" he asked. I nodded and Auntie and Vito ambled into Fellowship Hall. I limped behind.

Inside there were some of the members of the Breakfast Wars, plus a few of the enlisted kids. Evelyn stood in the kitchen, supervising the coffee service with her kinetic eyebrows. Ernie loaded the dishwasher, minus his eyebrows. Norma and Ray put out some sweets, wearing their pressed best. I looked and realized the coffee hour snacks were mostly leftovers from yesterday's Breakfast Wars. Lancaster folk must believe in the 'waste not, want not' thing pretty intensely. It was going to take me a long time to even think of serving used food.

Ed looked around in both directions at once, holding out a fresh pot of coffee and waiting to pour. But most people knew enough to wait until he set the pot down and left. You have to be kind of careful with Ed so you don't get hot coffee poured right next to you. I spotted Henry holding a coffee mug with a gauze-bandaged hand. Huh. If I didn't know better I'd say Henry's hand was pretty badly burned. But maybe he had let Ed pour for him last week.

"Hey, Henry," I said. "Missed you yesterday. Everything okay?" I asked.

Henry's face kind of paled. "Oh sure, yes, thanks for asking," he said, and then smiled at someone across the hall and hurried away.

Someone pinched my arm hard and I spun around and hurled my coffee smack into Aunt Muriel's chest. "What the?" I asked too late, realizing Auntie had pinched me to rescue her from Vito's verbal clutches. "Sorry, Aunt Muriel," I said lamely.

"Jeez, Mina, you could have scalded your Aunt!" Vito puffed up in defense of his afflicted object of affection. To Aunt Muriel's mortification, he pawed at the coffee stain in the middle of her chest with his handkerchief.

"Really, really, I'm quite alright! Thank you all the same!" Aunt Muriel spluttered. I guess she wasn't very happy about having her boobs blotted in public.

Aunt Muriel grabbed Vito's handkerchief and tucked it into her blouse like a farmer's wife settling down for a big Sunday dinner. Except that Aunt Muriel was definitely no farmer's wife, and she looked pretty upset. Even her diamonds spluttered. "Mina, I simply must go home and change. I cannot go to brunch like this. And certainly not polo," she finished.

"Pick you up at your house?" I asked.

"Yes please, dear," she said, and whisked away, the edges of Vito's handkerchief fluttering past her like a veil. I looked at Vito. We shrugged and walked back to my van.

We began to sweat as soon as we were back in the Doo-doo. As I started the van, I re-wished I had working AC. At the light on Walnut Street, I glanced at Vito and saw orange sweat trickling down his neck, where it began to form a dark brown line along his collar. I looked closer. Vito's hair was melting. By the time we pulled up my driveway, Vito's liquid hair had started to dry, making shoe polish lines around his jowls and neck. I sighed inwardly. I just didn't have the heart to tell Vito about his hair malfunction. Or the time. I had to be on the other side of town at Aunt Muriel's and then hightail it with her back downtown for the brunch thingy. But my foot ordered me to change shoes.

"I guess you can't come in for a minute, huh?" Vito asked. I shook my head. "No problem, Toots. I just wanted a little female advice about decorating, that's all."

Vito smiled and got out of the van and waved bye-bye. I sat still in amazement. Vito was asking the owner of Disney Puked Walls a la Hot Sauce stains for decorating advice. I wondered if his walls in his half of the duplex actually looked worse than mine.

I got out quick, walked inside and slipped in a puddle of kitty puke, falling smack down on my keester. Vinnie came trotting up from the basement and licked my nose. I shook my head, patted him and found a couple more marshmallows stuck to him. Then I saw some wet marshmallows in the puddle he'd left. Apparently Vinnie's cleaning himself of marshmallow gunk wasn't a good thing.

I grabbed a few hundred paper towels and cleaned the floor. I washed quick and got rid of my dirty duds. I stood in the bedroom in my underwear while Vinnie rubbed against my shin and stuck. There was still marshmallow glue on him. "Okay, buddy, that does it," I said. We trotted into the bathroom together. Vinnie stretched out on the bathroom floor belly up, and looked up at me. Apparently he didn't want any more s'mores, either.

I found out pretty quickly that pulling marshmallow gook out of Vinnie's fur was going to hurt me a lot more than it hurt him. His claws are pretty sharp. So I got a pair of scissors and cut off anything that felt remotely sticky. After I was done, Vinnie looked like a large stuffed toy that had been attacked by moths. But, as he purred and rubbed against me, he didn't stick. Progress.

I washed my hands, pulled on a pair of Capri length chinos and a hot pink sleeveless shirt. I matched that with a pair of hot pink flat sandals. My stubbed toe and pierced foot still complained, and I told them to mind their own business. I did a quick double-check at my make-up. My face looked pink (not scarlet), and my eyes looked less vampiric (more Dean Martin-esque). I'd probably fit in. I tossed some spare Tylenol in my pocket for back up, and went downstairs with my moth-eaten mountain lion leading the way. Out of the house I went, Auntie's sunglasses back on my face, hopped into the Doo-doo and then floored it across town.

I weaved my way across Millersville Pike, Columbia Avenue, Marietta Pike and into Auntie's development. I got to her house and let myself in through the garage door. "Hi, I'm here!" I shouted. No answer.

I walked into the kitchen and sat down at the table. The message light on Auntie's phone blinked. I wondered if the message was from Ma, then wondered what Ma was doing. Sometimes I miss Ma being in New Jersey, especially when I'm god-mom sitting. But I figured I'd get a call from her at lunchtime tomorrow about new swatches.

"In here, dear," Aunt Muriel called out.

"Where?" I asked.

"Bedroom," she said.

I walked into Auntie's bedroom and saw her standing in the middle of the room in her underwear and knee highs wearing a plastic grocery bag over her head. "Everything okay, Auntie?" I asked.

She pulled a pale yellow silk top over her head, bag and all. She removed the bag and stared at me. "It keeps your hair in place," she explained. That was a relief: for a moment I wondered if she was performing a very slow form of suicide.

She put on white linen trousers and slid her feet into matching yellow sandals. Aunt Muriel looked very nice, cool and collected. In contrast to me, I thought as I glanced at myself in her dresser mirror. I looked hot, pink and harried.

We took Aunt Muriel's Lexus and headed across town and brunched at 'Camille's'. We both love it there. It's like dining in a 1930s movie set. Different kinds of Art Deco lamps decorate each table, the windows are Frank Lloyd Wright-like, and vintage jazz music plays in the background.

We each ordered a Bloody Mary, then studied our menus to the tune of several fire engines in the background. "Oh dear," Aunt Muriel commented idly. I sighed, wondering if the Fruitville Buy-A-Lots got flambéed again and worried about facing EEJIT tomorrow morning. Aunt Muriel looked at me. "How are your eyes, dear?" she asked. I lowered her sunglasses. She pushed them back up on my nose.

Just then the GQ-like waiter we'd been admiring came back with our Bloodies. I picked mine up and took a sip. "Are we ready, ladies?" he said, smiling. For what? I thought idly, staring at his handsome face and movie star smile. I really needed to get a boyfriend. And a life. Auntie's was nice, but it was a loaner.

Aunt Muriel woke me up politely. "Mina?"

"Sure," I said, and we ordered. To my credit, I at least don't live up to my namesake's restaurant habits. Great-Grandma Mina vacillated horribly between menu items and typically wound up ordering two to three entrees as a result (with several doggie bags on the side.) I ordered only one entree.

In the amicable quiet that followed, Aunt Muriel asked hopefully, "Have you chosen any paint colors, dear?"

"Oh, there are a few I'm thinking about," I lied.

Aunt Muriel sighed and gnawed her celery. We both turned and looked out the window at a fire engine racing past us. I took a healthy swig of my Bloody Mary and pretended Mondays happen to someone else.

I went to split the tab with Aunt Muriel but she insisted on treating me. "Of course, dear," Aunt Muriel said, leaving

Handsome Harry a large tip. I also thought I saw her write my phone number down for him.

Back out in the street, the heat pummeled up at us from the sidewalk. Aunt Muriel's gadgety car thingies confirmed the ridiculous temperature with their feminine-esque electronic voices. "It is one-hundred and one degrees Fahrenheit, with a humidity index of 92, which will make the air quality seem like one hundred and seventeen degrees." Yeesh. How about just saying it's hot?

Aunt Muriel set her car's air-conditioning to freezing. A few minutes later, we pulled into her driveway and scraped frost off the windows. "What time's the polo thingy?" I asked, getting out of her car. Auntie's borrowed sunglasses fogged up: I tripped and fell flat on the driveway.

"Two-thirty, dear," she said, picking me up and leading me by the elbow into her kitchen. I took off the fogged sunglasses and looked at her kitchen clock. It was two o'clock.

"Shouldn't we just go straight there?" I asked.

"Oh no, dear! Not without our tailgate!" Aunt Muriel said, shocked. Tailgate? I thought. We'd just finished a three course brunch. Where does she put it? Aunt Muriel weighs about 98-lbs. soaking wet and has never had to diet. My dieting sensibilities are pretty much subdued by my catering disorder. Let's just say it's a good thing I'm not height challenged.

Aunt Muriel opened a cooler waiting by the fridge and carefully placed containers of cheese, crackers, nuts and crab spread inside, along with assorted pretty plates and silver utensils. Then she pulled out a painted box with a latch on it, and inserted a bottle each of red and white wine into it. I wondered if catering disorders were normal for polo? Maybe I'd fit in.

Auntie handed me a small boutique bag holding a rolled up cloth. "Careful with this, dear," she instructed. "Our wine glasses are in here, wrapped inside the table cloth and napkins."

"Are you allowed to bring wine to polo thingies?" I asked. Aunt Muriel stopped dead in her tracks and stared at me. Well.

We stashed the party loot in her car and took off up Route 30. Happily for me, this avoided Fruitville Pike altogether, so I could honestly not think about burnt Buy-A-Lots or EEJIT.

We wound up in the middle of a small farmers' town. Just a small main street; a few residences and the odd shop. Some dogs barked. "Are you sure we're going the right way?" I asked.

"Yes, of course. I've held a season pass since I've moved here," Aunt Muriel smiled.

"Oh," I said. Since Auntie had lived here for over a decade, this must be a pretty established outing.

We turned onto the exit for Route 772. Before I knew it, we saw a smallish lawn sign low to the ground at the corner on Church Street, next to the 'Alla Famiglia Italian Ristorante'. The sign read: 'Polo – This Way!'

Aunt Muriel made a left onto Church Street, then turned right onto a gravel road. We drove up to a woman wearing gold jewelry and collecting cash. Aunt Muriel slowed down and swooshed her electric car window open. "How are you?" Aunt Muriel beamed at the blonde behind the Elton John pink sunglasses.

"Lovely day for this, isn't it?" she beamed back.

"Oh yes!" Aunt Muriel tinkled some laughter her way, and we continued on. I shot her a sideways glance. Clearly she was out of her mind. Aunt Muriel's usual idea of an outdoor event was peering at it from behind a large window, preferably in a stadium box. I shrugged. Maybe we were going to watch the polo thingy from inside her Lexus.

We drove along, and I saw a large party tent set up. Next to it was an announcer's booth. I peered around but for the life of me couldn't see one building, much less a building large enough to fit a swimming pool. "Well, we're here!" she sang out brightly. I looked beyond her and saw Porta-potties and furrowed.

Aunt Muriel led the way toward the pseudo-wedding tent while I limped behind like Quasimodo, dragging the tailgate supplies between my hands and teeth. Tables and chairs were set up, and a bunch of people sat around enjoying their snacks. They seemed pretty friendly. Or well lubricated. Or both. Aunt Muriel directed me to a table, and I put our stuff down while she flitted from table to table. She lit on her last party: a table complete with silver champagne bucket, roses, crystal stemware, numerous hors d'oeuvre trays and a large Martini pitcher. It was impressive. There, she accepted a hug from a tall guy who chose to conceal his receding hairline by shaving his head altogether. But sitting right next to him was – ohmygosh-ohmygosh-ohmygosh – Mr. Perfect!! I pushed Auntie's borrowed sunglasses way back up my nose.

Aunt Muriel returned to our table and smiled brightly at me. "Sorry, Mina. I didn't mean to be away for long," she said.

"Not a problem," I said, waiting to pump her for an introduction to Mr. Perfect and Crew.

Then, all of a sudden, coming directly up to the tent, was a gal riding a horse! And then a guy riding a horse! In helmets! Aunt Muriel waved to them, and they waved back. I looked at her, puzzled. "The polo players, dear," she clarified in an obvious sounding tone.

"Polo?" I asked.

"Yes, dear. Those are players from our team."

"But where's the pool?"

"What pool?"

"For polo. Water polo, right? Like Marco Polo?"

Aunt Muriel slapped her hand to her forehead. "White," she said.

"Right?"

"White!"

"Right?"

"POUR THE WHITE WINE PLEASE, DEAR," Aunt Muriel shouted affectionately. I opened the bottle of wine, while Aunt Muriel explained through clenched teeth. "This is a polo match, Mina. As in polo pony," she grimaced.

"Oh," I said. I still didn't get it.

Aunt Muriel hissed kindly at me. "Polo is a field sport, like soccer, with horses."

OH! I thought. I GET IT! "Horse hockey?" I asked. Aunt Muriel sighed.

"Here's a paper that will help explain... and I'm sure the announcer will give some sort of an overview," she said, patting me on my head.

She poured me a glass of wine, and we watched as the match began. Amidst my casting furtive glances toward Mr. Perfect. A sort of half-time came and the announcer invited us to 'stomp the divots'. We got up with the crowd, and commenced to go a-stomping.

There in the middle of the field was Mr. Perfect, stomping contentedly with his pals. I stood stomped in my tracks, wine glass in mid-air. Aunt Muriel hissed at me. "Who are you staring at?" she asked.

"Ummm... I think that guy over there might be my neighbor."

Aunt Muriel shielded her eyes with her hand, looking across the field. Unfortunately, it was with her wine glass hand, which she dumped right next to her left foot. "Hmmm," she said thoughtfully, ignoring the fact that she'd imbibed under-age field growth. "I might have seen him before. Maybe at a benefit. I'll ask Marshal tomorrow," she said finally. I furrowed. So much for a timely introduction.

We managed to avoid the 'steaming divots' as directed by the announcer. Instead we sat back down, poured more wine and settled in to watch the rest of the game. The referee threw the polo ball down the middle of the field and both teams thwacked their mallets.

And then everything went black.

I woke up flat on my back with a scrambled head. Or at least it felt like that. But, I realized by comparison, my foot didn't hurt so much. So maybe things were getting better after all. I opened my eyes and saw flashes of light.

"Hope you don't mind! We like to scrapbook everything!" the bleach blonde polo maven said while clicking some pictures of me.

I blinked. Above me stood a cigar-puffing patron. I looked around and saw Aunt Muriel looming up from behind him like Godzilla v. Mothra. She pinched his cigar with lightning speed and extinguished it in a pitcher of water, screaming politely at him about my needing air. Well, at least Auntie thought it was a pitcher of water. Unfortunately it was Marshal's very large pitcher of martinis.

After the fire was put out, I sat clasping a sandwich baggie full of ice chips to my forehead. Or at least what used to be my forehead. Now it felt like it was about to give birth, evidenced by the egg on it that was becoming the size of the polo ball what bonked me.

A guy with a helmet and a numbered Jersey ran over to me. "Are you okay? Do you want an ambulance? We've got a doctor here..." he trailed off, gazing around and signaling said doctor.

Oddly enough, said doctor was also sporting a helmet and numbered Jersey. "How many fingers am I holding up?" he asked kindly.

I smiled stupidly and said, "Yes." Geesh. Was this embarrassing, or what?

"You might want to get that looked at," he said, producing a business card while addressing Auntie, who giggled uncharacteristically and took his card all too enthusiastically. Gack. I might have been bonked by my next uncle.

"It's no biggie," I said, crawling around on the tent floor on all fours, struggling to get up. "I'll just have them check my head when they amputate my foot."

I staggered up onto somebody's arm and let myself get led to a seat. Everyone was being very, very nice to me. But then again, they were all from Lancaster. I felt around my pocket for a stray Tylenol and munched on one. I still felt the Somebody's hands on my shoulders, and hunched around to take a gander.

OH-MY-GOSH-IT-WAS-MR.-PERFECT!!! Wow. And all it took was a little brain damage for a proper introduction! I struggled to look up at him, attempting a demure gaze. What I think I pulled off resembled more of a facial tick. Which was probably why he stared at me. I gulped. Well, now or never I thought.

"Hi, I'm Mina. I think we're neighbors," I stammered. Great. Maybe I could attribute stammering to having my brains used for Shake 'N Bake.

"Of course! I thought I recognized you!" Mr. Perfect beamed. "I'm your neighbor! Bruce! I walk David by your house every day! I live at the other end of the lane, opposite your dead end. Reg, Marshal, come here, look – a neighbor! At polo!"

Several painful feelings registered all at once, besides the ones banging my head and my foot. One: I prefer to think of my house on Clovernook Lane as being in a cul-de-sac, not a 'dead end'. Two: I thought it a bit callous to begin introductions to strangers while my forehead was still pregnant. Three: Bruce? Reg? Marshal? Arghhhh. It was all perfectly queer to me now. No wonder he looked perfect. He probably has longer morning ablutions than Aunt Muriel or Ma. And certainly more than me.

Reg and Marshal came over dutifully and feigned attentiveness at me. Which at least didn't hurt. Reg refreshed my ice cube baggie so my forehead wouldn't hatch prematurely, and Marshal shucked up an Appeltini. Not my all-time favorite drink, but desperate times require desperate drinking. Especially since the remaining wine was warm. Which was mostly because all the ice cubes were on my forehead.

"So you're Bruce," I repeated stupidly.

"And his Goliath is David!" creened Marshal.

"You should have brought him, Bruce," chided Reg.

"Well," Bruce began, "I would have, but he's so afraid of air horns." Air horns? Oh. That's what the large blasts of noise were. "They use them here to mark the end of the chukker."

So Bruce and Reg and Marshal told me what they knew about polo, and how they all worked in different restaurants, which explained why I usually see Bruce walking his Goliath – sorry, David – at lunchtime. "We haven't come up here in ages," Marshal confided, "but it's Bruce's birthday, and this is what the birthday boy wanted!" he sang happily.

I sighed. Well, it was nice to make some new friends. Even if they couldn't scratch a dent in my love life. Well, at least K. would be thrilled when I tell him about his expanded social circle. I looked around for Aunt Muriel.

Aunt Muriel spotted me – or, more precisely, my Appeltini – and good ol' Reg drudged up one for her, too. I looked over at Auntie and saw she'd pushed her hair way up past her forehead. This was odd. I looked closer and realized her bangs were singed right off. All that was left was a charred fringe. Well, I guess putting out cigars in pitchers of martinis is a bad thing. Luckily she was unaware. So I figured this was a good time to leave. "Uh, Aunt Muriel, I think I've had enough party, okay?" I hinted.

"Of course! Our poor lamb!" she gushed, petting the top of my head and peering intently toward the polo playing physician on the field. Luckily, Reg, Marshal and Bruce were close by, and offered to pack up and carry Auntie's tailgate party. I gratefully accepted for her.

We left the field and entered the climate cooled calm of Aunt Muriel's Lexus. This of course was when acute nausea set in.

"Aunt Muriel, pull over," I spat calmly, prepping to toss my cookies.

"Nonsense, dear, there's nothing here but fields!" Aunt Muriel sang brightly.

"I'm going to puke!!"

"Here? But you can't! There are no rest rooms!" she said.

"IF YOU DON'T PULL OVER I'M PUKING ON YOUR LEATHER SEATS!"

Auntie pulled over onto the edge of a cow field in a cloud of dust and pebbles. If the combination of wine, Appeltini, konk on the noggin and EEJIT neurosis wasn't going to make me puke, the stench of Amish fertilizer would. I lost my offending contents at lightning speed hurl. A pack of tissues immediately appeared in front of my face. "Here," Aunt Muriel offered. "Wipe," she commanded. I pawed at my mouth. "Here," she said again, producing a baby-size bottle of spring water. "Rinse, spit," she instructed. I rinsed, spat, and felt a little better. So did the several cows who'd lumbered up to the fence to see what all the ruckus was about.

"Come along, Mina. We're being stared at," Auntie sniffed. Stared at? There wasn't a soul in sight. Who was staring at us? Amish pot roasts?

I kept my eyes closed until we climbed up my driveway. We pulled up to see Vito standing in the middle of his garden, happily deadheading his overgrown Shasta daisies. Vito smiled at us, bridge and all, waving. I shot back what I hoped was a smile but felt more like a grimace.

I started to unbuckle my seatbelt when Aunt Muriel put a hand on my shoulder. "Stay right here, Mina," she ordered. The way I felt, not a problem.

Auntie got out of the car and she actually went over and talked to Vito voluntarily. I saw Vito nod his head up and down and pull out a bunch of keys. He fingered one and handed it to Aunt Muriel. Aunt Muriel took it and started for my front door, nodding over to the car, and me.

Vito lumbered over to my side of Auntie's car as fast as his fat feet could carry him. "Heya, Toots. How about I give yous a hand?" He frowned at me. "Heard you got a good shot to your noggin," he said, escorting me up my own front walk. Aunt

Muriel waited for us, glancing over her shoulder to make sure Vito was performing the chores she'd assigned him. She had just put the key in the lock, when I realized Vinnie was out and about the house and I was afraid he'd scoot out the front door. But Vito was ahead of me. "Hey, Muriel, hold on to Tootsie here," he said, smiling. "Sometimes her Vinnie boy gets a little enthusiastic about open doors," he explained.

Vito went inside. Aunt Muriel helped me follow. Standing in my hallway I saw my back door standing firmly wide open. This was about when Marie shrieked from the curtain rod and dive-bombed into Aunt Muriel's hair.

Have I mentioned that Aunt Muriel has an inordinate fear of birds? Actually, she's mostly afraid of them nesting in her hair. This became pretty obvious as I dislodged Marie's feet from Aunt Muriel's well hair sprayed doo. "C'mere, Marie," I screamed affectionately to the crazed cockatiel. I managed to get her on my finger and hastily went upstairs to put her back inside her cage. I wondered how she'd got out – but my thinking was kinda slow at the time, which was understandable what with the Tylenol and Appletinis and konkings and such.

I came right back down, and Vito shushed me. "Hold on, Toots," he whispered. "Muriel, close the back door," he directed. Vito, directing? Go figure.

Vito moved silently and agilely downstairs to the basement. It was then I dimly grasped that maybe Marie hadn't let herself out of her cage. Maybe someone was in my house. And maybe that someone was still in my house.

After what seemed like forever, Vito came back upstairs. He looked a little pale. "No one's down there, Toots," he said.

"Well, that's a relief!" I breathed.

"No, Toots. No one's there. Including Vinnie."

I ran to the back door, opened it and screamed, "VINNIEEEEE!" a few hundred times.

Dusk set. So did my hopes of ever seeing my cat again. It was bad enough my house had been broken into. Stealing my pet was a whole other realm of horrible. I sat down on the deck steps to think. Which was why I cried. Vito lumbered over through the shrubs. "I looked alls over by my place, Toots. I don't see him nowhere," he apologized.

"Thanks," I sniffed.

Auntie came up behind me. "Mina, I've been in every closet and under the beds," she said. I sighed. If Vinnie hadn't been missing, a huge wave of housekeeping paranoia would have swept over me. "I couldn't find Vinnie inside anywhere, dear."

Vinnie was gone. Really gone. "Uh huh," I said, wiping another puddle of salt water from my cheek. I looked at Vito. "You think someone took him?"

"Chrissakes, no, Mina," he said. "There'd be a note," he added nicely. I shot a worried look at him. "Aw, Vinnie would've bit them on the nose," he said. This was true.

"Mina, dear, we do need to call the police," said Aunt Muriel.

"Police?" I asked dumbly.

"Mina, your home has been broken into. Anyone can see that," she said.

"Well, uh, Muriel, do you, uh, think that's a smart move? For Vinnie's sake, I mean?" asked Vito.

"Whatever do you mean?"

"Alls I'm saying is what with patrol guys and all, crawlin' all around, dontcha think that might scare the kitty off?"

"He's not here, Vito. Mina, we have to report this."

"Maybe Vito's got a point," I said.

"Mina!" Aunt Muriel warned.

"Girls, girls," Vito said, holding up his hands and waving settle-down motions at us. "Look," he said, "why don't Muriel and I go through the rest of the house, just to see if anything major is missing? You know, like jewelry? Or cash?"

I did the only sensible thing I knew, and cried. "Yes, there's something major missing," I snuffled. "Vinnie!" Vito and Aunt Muriel stared at each other and ducked into my house. Clearly nobody was safe, or dry, with me.

So I had a good sob, and beat myself up for not leaving Vinnie in the basement as usual (who steals anything from a basement?) Bad enough imagining him lost, or hurt. Worse yet – what if he'd managed to get out onto Millersville Pike? Christ – deer get flattened out on that drag and no one even bats an eye! And, of course, even worse case scenarios hummed in the back of my mind.

These, and a zillion other comforting thoughts kept me sniffling on my back steps.

The screen door opened behind me and I looked around hopefully. Vito stood there holding a roll of paper towels in one hand, and Vinnie's bowl of Kitty Cookies in the other. He put the Kitty Cookies on the step next to me, and handed me a paper towel. Then he took one for himself and blew loud. I looked up at him – his eyes actually looked red-rimmed. Wow. I guess he liked Vinnie more than he was scared of him, after all. Either that or Aunt Muriel'd scared him.

Aunt Muriel came back out. She grabbed a paper towel and dabbed at her eyes and blew her nose. Politely, of course.

"Well, at least whoever did this to you didn't expose your bird to the elements. Which would have been far worse. Hawks are very prevalent in Central Pennsylvania," she said. Vito and I stared at her, then each other. "Oh! Oh, my dear! Vinnie is much too big to be carried away by any hawk!" she added hastily. Vito and I looked at each other and sulked. Clearly Auntie hadn't seen some of the hawks out our way. Sometimes I was afraid for my neighbor's beagle.

So the three of us copped a squat on the back steps. An unlikely trio if ever there was one. Except for how we appeared in church. Waiting for Vinnie. Past dusk. Past a sliver of the moon. Past the first star.

Aunt Muriel's hand touched my shoulder. "Mina, I don't think anything of any genuine value was stolen," she said.

"Except Vinnie," I said glumly.

Ya know, Toots, if that's what yous thinks, maybe it's better to call the cops in. They might have an MO on these guys," Vito added hopefully. I nodded. At this point it couldn't hurt to post an ABP for a white and orange molting mini-mountain lion, with one crossed blue eye. You'd know him the moment he bumped into you.

The phone rang, and Aunt Muriel went inside and answered it for me. I heard a lot of 'uh huhs', so I got hopeful. Then she hung up and stuck her head back outside. Funny: while she held the door open to talk to me, I had to squelch an automatic response to tell her to close the door to not let Vinnie out. It was a moot point now.

"That was Beatrice," Aunt Muriel explained. I nodded. I knew that she meant Trixie. "I told her what's happened. She asked if it was alright to come over, and I said yes for you. I hope that was alright?"

I shrugged. "Sure." Though I wasn't really sure Trixie would understand. She thinks I'm overly-attached to Vinnie and Marie because I feed and water them daily. But it was still nice of her to offer. Especially as she and Aunt Muriel are pretty much chemically at odds with each other. They're a lot like black mollies and angel fish. Neither one matters a bit to the other. But put them in the same tank, and pretty soon you have dead angel fish. I read somewhere it's because mollies are chemically toxic to them.

I heard Aunt Muriel dive back inside the safety zone of public communications. She was dialing the phone and talking in some fairly officious tones. I guess she'd called the police. I was glad she was dealing with them for me, and for Vinnie.

A little while later I heard a car pull up. Trixie came out back, equipped with some Southern Comfort and a pack of Swank's. "You look like you just lost your best friend."

I hung my head and sniffled. "I did."

She shrugged, took out a small flask of Southern Comfort, and lit up a smoke. She hunkered down beside me and took a sip. "How long're you gonna sit out here for him?" she asked.

"As long as it takes," I sulked.

"Well, I like you, but I'm not sure that these steps aren't gonna hurt my butt before long."

I looked at Trixie. Even when she was blunt she was nice. But then again, she was from Lancaster.

She reached inside her pocketbook and pulled out a can from Finicky Fare's Gourmet Galore line: 'Bitsy Toeses 'n' Fuzzy Noses', Vinnie's favorite. Since the Gourmet Galore line also comes with a gourmet price – like a buck a can – he gets this at holidays only. The thought of bitsy toeses and fuzzy noses as food products generally makes me gag. Now I held back tears.

"Let's get this party going sooner than later," Trixie said matter-of-factly. "If I was scared of coming back home, especially if I'd been out when I knew I wasn't supposed to be out, it would take a lot more than Kitty Cookies to get me back inside."

I had to admit it: she had a point.

Trixie popped the lid and dumped the Gourmet Toeses and Noses on top of Vinnie's Kitty Cookies. “Now, come inside this house and figure out what’s been lost,” she commanded.

“But Vinnie!!” I cried.

“Aunt Muriel’s taking an inventory of your house,” she said warningly to me. I stared back blankly. “Sooner or later she’ll get to the bread drawer,” she clarified. Trixie knew about the paint swatches. “We’ll leave the door open. That way Vinnie can come right inside when he shows up. He’s probably just having a romp,” she added.

I took a swig from Trixie's bottle. “You realize this means fraternizing with Aunt Muriel,” I warned.

“Yup, and probably Officer Appletree.” She paused to take another swig of Southern Comfort, stubbed out her cigarette and pocketed the filter. “I came in as your Aunt was calling the police. He’s usually assigned to this side of town.”

“Too bad you used to date him,” I said.

“His wife thought so, too,” she added.

Poor Trixie. Always the cheater, and never the cheated. We’d both had our share of boyfriend troubles. Her ex live-in Chuck, pre-Appletree, lived a life of luxury thanks to his maxing out Trixie's credit card. He's been sending her payments ever since, so she won't press charges – which is how she got involved with Appletree. As for me, I moved to Lancaster after falling in love with the wrong boyfriend for the right reasons. Himself wanted a job in the country; I got a job. Himself spent; I paid. Himself left me with Marie, his cockatiel. I stayed and bought Marie and me the house. But, as Trixie says, I'm not the first girl to have had her ex flip her the bird.

“Okay,” I said.

I propped the screen door open and went inside the kitchen. A few seconds later a zillion flying bugs joined us.

Trixie and I paraded upstairs to make sure Aunt Muriel and Vito weren’t taking inventory of my underwear and socks. We ran into them in the upstairs hall, and I peered over Vito’s shoulder and into my bedroom. The floor was wall-to-wall clothes, papers, books, tissues – you name it. Aunt Muriel shot me a look. “Hey, I didn’t leave it like this!” I cried defensively.

I started to go in, but Vito extended an arm and stopped me. "We better not touch nothin' until the cops check this out," he said.

I looked inside the bathroom. The entire contents of my medicine cabinet and linen closet were strewn everywhere. My foot throbbed. I reached into my pocket and munched on another Tylenol.

The doorbell rang and Aunt Muriel slid past me to answer it. Vito and Trixie and I went downstairs behind her. Officer Appletree and Trixie glared at each other in the foyer affectionately. "Officer," Aunt Muriel began.

"Appletree, ma'am. Trixie," he greeted.

"Hi, Adam," she said, swiping a moth from her face.

Appletree looked down the hall and into the kitchen at the open back door. "You found the back door open like this? You don't have to leave it that way," he started, heading through the kitchen to close the door.

"No, we left it open. We figured whoever sacked Mina's place also let her cat out," Trixie explained.

"Oh, okay," he responded none too convincingly, schwooshing at bugs. "You have any idea what they took?" he asked, pulling out a pad for notes.

"Vinnie," I said glumly.

Vito and Aunt Muriel filled in Officer Appletree with the particulars. We clumped back upstairs behind Officer Appletree to re-survey the damage. "Any jewelry missing?" he asked hopefully. I opened my jewelry drawer and checked.

"Nope," I said.

"Your purse missing?"

"Nope,"

"You notice anything suspicious?" he asked Vito.

"No, no, sir," Vito stammered. "I was, uh... doing some, umm... errands around 3 o'clock, got back around 4:30 and was just taking care of the flowers out front."

"Thanks. That helps. Mr., uh...?"

"Spaghetti. Vito Spaghetti," Vito responded. "S-P-A-G-H-E-T-T-I. Just like the noodle." He smiled. Aunt Muriel and Trixie stared at me. I shrugged. At least Vito's last name was appealing.

Officer Appletree tiptoed over the piles of clothes covering the floor. I think he was afraid to step on a bra or something in front of Trixie. He looked over at the answering machine on my desk. There were two messages. "Have you played these yet?" he asked.

"No," I said. I crossed the room to play them, hoping one was about Vinnie.

"Mina, you're not gonna believe this." It was Bauser. "It's me, Bauser. The Buy-A-Lots on Fruitville Pike got torched again. And would you believe, our servers are down! Howard's gonna throw a fit. I'm gonna go in and try to take care of it now. Anyway, hope you're out someplace having fun. Gimme a call if you want. Otherwise I'll see ya at the salt mines tomorrow."

Second message. "MINA, WHERE THE HELL ARE YOU?" It was How-weird in full 20-pt. bold shouting mode. I winced. "Our servers are down! You realize, as office manager, you're supposed to accompany after hours staff, right?" He hung up.

"Your job description requires you to accompany after hours personnel?" Auntie asked.

I sighed. "It changes daily."

"That was a very hostile message," Appletree observed.

"Yeah, that's her boss," Trixie said.

"Oh, well," he said, and closed his pad. "If you want, we can give him a call, to vouch for what happened here," he said.

"Thanks," I agreed, and gave him Howard's contact information.

"But you might want to give the Animal Shelter a call," he offered. "Give them a heads up, and a description, in case your cat gets turned in." I nodded.

We trudged back downstairs and went room by room through the rest of the house. Which didn't take long. The main upset was in my bathroom. Every medicine and pill bottle I owned was thrown about the place. What kind of medicine were they looking for?

I thanked Appletree and said goodbye and watched Trixie exiting a little too closely behind him, which I ignored. Vito patted me on the shoulder and shuffled back over to his place. Aunt Muriel stood glued to the hallway floor. "I'm staying with you," she announced.

"What?" I asked, rubbing my forehead. I wished the lump would hatch soon.

"My dear, you can't take care of this mess by yourself. Especially with your head injury!"

I looked at her, about to argue, but realized once she left I was a hostage in my own home, since the Doo-doo was still at her place.

So she had a point there. Right at the top of my head.

I looked longingly out back at the deck. Still no sign of Vinnie.

When I turned back, Aunt Muriel was leafing through the phone book. "PizzaNow! Yes, we'd like a pizza delivered please," she began.

I shrugged. I guess having pizza for dinner, breakfast and then dinner again wasn't the worst thing that had happened to me so far. I looked up at the kitchen light and the swarm of bugs. I didn't think housing the insect kingdom would bring Vinnie back any sooner. I steeled myself to call the animal shelter first thing in the morning, as I shuffled to close the door.

Vinnie slid himself in-between my knees. I responded by tripping over him. "Vinnie!" I screamed, hugging all his girth.

"Well, at least that mystery is solved!" Aunt Muriel said. I hugged Vinnie and nodded. Aunt Muriel pulled the screen door all the way closed. "Your door doesn't close all the way," she noted. I nodded. I'd have to have it fixed. Was that how someone got into my house? Or did Vito visit and forget to lock up? I hadn't mentioned the spare key thing to Appletree. He might get the wrong neighborly ideas about me and Vito. Ick!

Auntie and I gave Vinnie the once over. Aside from some leaves and twigs plastered to the last remaining bits of marshmallow fluff, there was nothing wrong with him. I gave Vinnie his all-time favorite – above and beyond Chicken Toeses and Piggy Noses: genuine tuna fish. I started to open the can while Vinnie stood up on his hind legs and pummeled his front paws on the counter. Sometimes I wonder when he'll be able to use the can opener to help himself. "A-ch-aat! Mow! Mow! Mow!" he said in his kitty falsetto. I figure this translates loosely to, "Okay! Now! Now! Now!" I put the tuna in his bowl and watched contentedly as Vinnie guzzled.

The pizza arrived, and we let out a few swarms of bugs at the delivery guy. After Auntie and I ate, she went upstairs to rummage for a nightie. I lay on the sofa and channel surfed, with

Vinnie stretched out alongside me, and rested my eyes for a bit. I guess that was why Aunt Muriel shrieked, "Mina, get up!"

"Huh? What?!" I screamed back.

"Do NOT sleep!" Aunt Muriel commanded. But judging by my headache and my foot ache, I was gonna need all the beauty rest I could get. The other fly in the ointment was the fact I'd been munching on Extra Strength Tylenol all day. And some Southern Comfort.

I explained the dilemma to Auntie. "Well, alright," she mulled, "but I'm going to check on you hourly." Oh, goodie.

Aunt Muriel came back down, moved Vinnie and sat down next to me on the sofa, to keep me from lying down. "Oh, guess you found some jammies," I said. She was wearing my Hi!Hi! Kitty PJs. She looked cute in pink.

"Yes, thank you, dear," Aunt Muriel said, taking the remote from me and turning past the Menus for Many show I was watching and over to the local news. "I found you some jammies and left them on your pillow," she added.

Hint taken: I shuffled upstairs to change. Good old Aunt Muriel had cleaned the debris off the top of bed, and made neat little paths from the bathroom to the closet, edged with stacked, folded clothes. That was so sweet of her.

I washed up, fed Marie, and came back down. Plopping down beside Auntie on the sofa, we watched the end of the news together. That was when we saw the story about this afternoon's burning Buy-A-Lots on Fruitville Pike. We swatted at the moths. I looked at Vinnie to see if he could be useful at catching bugs, but he just lay prone on the floor with his left paw nuzzled over his nose, snoring peacefully. Aunt Muriel got up and went into the kitchen. Vinnie woke up and trotted behind her. This was weird. Vinnie doesn't usually follow her. So I followed Vinnie.

Aunt Muriel doled out a couple of mugs O'Merlot and we sipped. Vinnie stood up on his back legs and hugged Auntie's waist. Aunt Muriel pulled out a piece of pepperoni that was tucked into the jammie pocket and gave it to Vinnie. I stared at her accusingly. "The poor boy was famished from his ordeal!" she furrowed at me.

"Good," I said. "Maybe he'll develop a taste for bugs." I swatted at the cloud of gnats hovering over our heads.

"Oh, they'll all be gone by the morning." Aunt Muriel thwacked once or twice too. "Our boy certainly likes his pepperoni," she said.

Vinnie 'sat pretty' for her while she rewarded him with another piece of pepperoni, and then she went upstairs to bed. Vinnie trotted along after her. I hoped she wasn't sleeping with any more pepperoni in my pockets.

I turned out the lights. The sound of crickets chirping filled the living room. I lay down on the sofa, wondering how I would ever get used to sleeping with crickets. Then I heard Vinnie tossing his bowl of Kitty Cookies on the kitchen floor. I swore quietly and stumbled into the kitchen, determined to give him what for.

That was when I met Blossom the Possum. All twenty-seven pounds of her.

"Nice possum... nice possum... wanna go back outside to your nicem possum place-um?" I sang hopefully, opening the back door to let her out. Which only succeeded in letting in more insect life.

Blossom looked up at me, and continued to munch on Vinnie's Kitty Cookies with fierce looking, jagged jaws. Eech. Then she washed her face, burped, and waddled out. I closed the door after her just as a big fat fly landed on the counter. I thwacked him. I knew it'd make my karma suck, but I'd had enough of the Peaceable Kingdom for one night.

CHAPTER 4

(Monday)

I hate Mondays.

I woke up to gnawing sounds. Which was weird. What could Vinnie be crunching? Carefully peeling back my eyelids, I saw bright sunlight streaming into the living room. Which was also weird. The sun doesn't shine on the living room side of the house until almost noon. Then I watched as a small terrier chewed my rocking chair. I shoved him away and staggered into the kitchen. It was 10:45 a.m. It was Monday. I was supposed to have been at EEJIT a long, long time ago.

"Shit! Shit! Shit!" I cried, running up the stairs and headlong into Auntie brushing her teeth in the bathroom. "Why didn't you wake me up!?" I yelled.

She spat into the sink. "Your manager, Howard Blech, was notified by the police of your being robbed yesterday," she said. She rinsed and systematically spat again. "I contacted him personally this morning to let him know you have a doctor's appointment at 11:30. If you feel well, and if the doctor says you are fit, I will drive you into work."

Oh. Well. That explained everything. My life was now under maternal law. I leaned against the wall and rubbed my head. It felt sore but also like the swelling had shrunk. "Hey, I think the swelling's gone down!" I yelled happily.

"Ummm... I think you should keep this appointment, Mina. After all, you also need your foot examined." She winced at me and walked away.

I looked in the mirror. Yup, the swelling was down – no more pregnant forehead. In its place was a large, dark purple circle that was ringed in red and green like a bull's-eye. I gazed down at my stubbed toe, the cut on my foot and the spot where Auntie's stilletoed heel pierced me. Each was a wonderful shade of eggplant, delicately trimmed in pink.

Aunt Muriel and I turned as we heard gnawing sounds from downstairs. I figured it was the terrier eating my furniture again. "Whose dog?" I asked.

"Do you have a dog?" she asked, pulling a plastic grocery store bag over her head in preparation for getting dressed.

"You know I don't have a dog. I've got Vinnie," I said. "By the way, where is Vinnie?" I asked nervously. Aunt Muriel pointed her grocery bag encased head toward the bed. Vinnie lay sleeping on his side mumbling, with one paw covering his snout and the other clutching a half gnawed piece of pepperoni. "Oh good grief," I said. No wonder he hadn't encountered Fido in the living room. He had a pepperoni hangover.

I patted his belly and a lethal 'poof' pooted out his south end – the silent but deadly kind. Aunt Muriel still had her head in the bag. "You might want to stay in there," I warned, holding my nose. She nodded, and I headed back downstairs to settle the score with somebody else's dog.

I got Fido away from more rocker gnawing by bribing him with Apple At'ems cereal. He took the bait and trotted happily behind me into the kitchen. There I made a pot of coffee and heard the front door open. It was Vito.

"Hey, Toots, how's your head?" Vito smiled as he ambled toward the kitchen, carrying a white paper bag. "I got yous and Muriel some jelly donuts. I figured yous could use them..." He trailed off as I faced him, giving him full frontal forehead. He stared disbelievingly at my bruise and gulped. "Boy, that was some whack, huh?"

I shrugged, took the bag from him and set some plates and coffee mugs on the counter. We helped ourselves, and chewed quietly.

Vito looked down and finally registered the furniture crunching Terrier. This was because the dog was sitting pretty for Vito's jelly donut. "When'd you get him?" Vito asked.

"I have no idea."

"Gee, I always wanted a dog," Vito said wistfully. "Hey, if he doesn't belong to anyone, can I keep him?"

"Better check around first, Vito, just in case."

"You're right. Jeez, ya never know what walks through an unlocked door," Vito said.

I looked meaningfully at him. "Yep, one never knows," I agreed.

"By the way, Mina, if yous thinks you're going into work today, could you take this for me?" Vito asked, holding up his perpetual gym bag of dry cleaning.

I sighed. "Sure."

Aunt Muriel came down and shushed me upstairs to get ready to have my head examined. I got dressed, Vinnie still lay sprawled out on my bed, snoozing and pooting in bachelor bliss. I fed Marie, went back downstairs and left Kitty Cookies in Vinnie's bowl.

"Where's Vito? And the dog?" I asked.

"Vito took him for a walk to find his owner," Aunt Muriel replied. "Come along, Mina," she called after me. I trotted obediently behind.

We got to the doctors' and I signed in. Before long, a nurse called out, "Mina Kitchen?"

"That's me," I said.

She backed away. "Uh, just step over here so we can, uh, weigh you..." she trailed, keeping a good distance away from me. I sighed. Why is it when you feel like crap you have to get weighed? What good is that? You're there because you feel bad, right? So you have to feel guilty, too? I accepted her unacceptable weight reading and went inside an examination room where I perched on a bench and waited.

A few thousand years later, a guy I'd never seen before popped his head into the room. "Good afternoon, I am Dr. Singh," he sang.

"What happened to Dr. Dahler? Or Dr. Senz?" I asked.

"They are out of town at a very impressive conference, for which they will gain invaluable knowledge about the cosmetic medicines," he beamed. "I am their replacement for today's patients," he finished. Great. Leave it to me to get a temp. "So, what is the condition of which you would like to complain?" I looked at him questioningly. He'd got to be kidding. Where should I start? And how much time did he have? "Do you have a physical malady for which you wish to be cured?"

Oh. That stuff. "I suppose," I began, and explained about the konk on my noggin and mutilated foot.

"Oh, this is very, very bad," Dr. Singh said, shaking his head. "It is terrible to live with such pain. But it is this which will gain us the moral strength." He smiled at me. Oh good grief. I got a doctor of philosophy. "Here, please to let me examine your head," he continued, and invaded my personal space by stepping in-between my thighs. After that he proceeded to peer so closely into my eyes with his scope thingy that I felt his eyelashes flicker against my cheek. Oh well. At least he hadn't eaten pepperoni.

He stepped back and picked up my foot. I yelped politely at him. He looked at me and shook his head, tsking. He let my foot down and started to write in my file. Then he wrote something on a prescription pad. "Firstly, let me say this to you: you are very much in very much pain," he said. "Your foot has the contusion and has been lacerated with a wound, and also appears a bit pierced. And your head has suffered quite a blow by a round, heavy object." How observant of him. "I see from your file that you have not had a tet-a-nish shot in your recent personal history with this practice, yes?"

I gulped. "No..."

"Good!" And he beamed at me far too brightly. "Then we will have a registered nurse administer a tet-a-nish shot! As for your head, though, I am afraid there is not much we can do for it."

"That's pretty much the family consensus," I quipped. Dr. Singh stared back at me blankly. Clearly he thought more damage had been done than he'd assessed. He shook his head and ripped a sheet off his prescription pad.

"This is a small but helpful prescription for your pain," he said, handing the paper to me. I reached for it, and he withdrew it. "It is not to take during working or driving or eating or sleeping hours," he admonished.

"Oh, okay," I said. Must be just for playtime, then.

"And please to read all of the instructions accompanying this medicine, which will come forthrightly from your neighborhood pharmacist," he finished. He pressed a button on the wall and left the room. I shrugged and waited around for my tet-a-nish shot.

A short, round, snarling bleached blonde nurse shuffled into the room. I cringed. She opened my file. "Well, what do we have here?" she drawled at it. Obviously my input wasn't necessary. "Oh, you're the tetanus shot. Well!" She smiled at me. I cringed some more. "We'll just fix you up right here!" she said, and pulled a large syringe from her pocket. She wiped my arm with an alcohol swab and uncapped the syringe. This revealed something that looked like a large knitting needle with a propeller on the end. I winced. "Oh, this won't hurt a bit!" she jibbed, then jabbed my arm. "Now, this might feel hot later on. And it might cause a bump. And a little bruising. And you might have a headache. And some nausea. But nothing to be worried about," she concluded and handed me the charge sheet to take up front. I wondered why I needed the tet-a-nish shot, since I already had bumps, bruises, nausea and a headache? I sighed and wandered up front to ransom myself from the doctor's.

Ninety-five dollars later – inclusive of my discounted co-pay – we were back inside Auntie's Lexus and headed for the drug store, and then back to my place for Vito's forgotten laundry bag. I was going to have to start writing things down. I blackmailed Auntie into chauffeuring all this. If she didn't, I told her I'd bring Vito back to St. Bart's. She agreed. We got my prescriptions filled, picked up Vito's laundry bag, and finally she dropped me off at the Chestnut Street entrance to EEJIT. That was where I met all the other occupants of the Armstrong building milling and seething on the sidewalk. Of course Lee spotted me first.

"Nice of you to join us today, Mina," she sneered. "Too bad about your head. Guess it made some dent in your memory, huh?" she smirked.

Bauser came over and stepped between us. "I think Howard's looking for you, Lee," he said.

Her cheeks flushed red. "Really? Where?"

"Oh, I think over by the courtyard entrance," he said, and pointed. Lee swaggered away from us, then broke into a full jelly roll cantor as she wobbled around the corner. My head throbbed.

"Why's Howard looking for her?" I asked, afraid to find out I was being replaced as we spoke.

"He's not. I fibbed," Bauser said.

"Really! Good for you, Bauser!" I congratulated. Even though he was from Lancaster, I figured he had to be capable of the occasional white lie. After all, his dad was from Hoboken.

"You alright, Mina?" He looked at me warily.

"Yeah, I just look kinda bad right now." I explained about my weekend.

"Jeez, you'd have been better off staying here," he said. We looked at each other and winced. Clearly things were not exactly as they ought to be for my social life.

Bauser went on to fill me in about the power shortage and the aftermath. "Well, the thing is, I dealt with the power. No parts to replace, no shortages, no nothing. So I just hung around until the power came back on. About seven o'clock," he said.

"Okay," I said.

"Not exactly."

"Huh?"

"The fire started in our server room – seventh floor."

"What fire? I thought this was a drill?"

"No such luck," he responded.

He led me around to the corner opposite our building. From this angle, I could see the billows of smoke hurdling up into space from EEJIT's seventh floor offices. Oddly enough, it made me feel a little happier. I smiled contentedly and looked at Bauser. He looked puzzled. "All I can get from the firemen is that it's contained to the server room."

Crap. How-weird would have a field day pinning this on Bauser. And me. Especially since I wasn't with Bauser in the server room yesterday. My happy feelings went up in smoke.

"Don't worry," Bauser said. "I could do with a break. Collect some unemployment; have an extended vacation..." His eyes glazed over at the thought of endless nights on the Internet with endless mornings of sports shows.

I shook him. "Bauser, get real! If Howard pins this on you, it's not like getting laid off! It would be fired for cause!" I hissed. Bauser's glaze continued in its reverie. "You won't be able to collect unemployment!" I said.

That made him snap out of it. "Oh crap," he said quietly.

Just then we saw several fire marshal types gather groups of employees from various companies and shuffle them over to the courtyard. Bauser shrugged. "Now or never," he said, and I nodded.

We plodded our way back across the street, and gathered with the masses. I saw How-weird grouped with Lee and – yikes – also Myron Stumpf. And worse yet, what appeared to be a client. I hung my head.

The fire person held up a bullhorn and attempted to make some semblance of the carnage. "Ladies and gentlemen, I'm afraid that your offices will need to be shut down for the remainder of the day," he said. A few hundred employees from various businesses cheered and texted ferociously, while their supervisors cast accusatory glances and took mental notes. He went on, "I've met with the managers from each floor. With the exception of EEJIT," he added a bit tersely. Bauser and I exchanged cringes. We looked toward Howard, Lee and Myron, who were smoldering in a corner. I've said it before and I'll say it again: I hate Mondays.

I shrugged at Bauser, and headed off toward Howard. "Your funeral," Bauser called after me.

"Remember me kindly," I called back.

I stood in front of Howard.

"Geez, what is that thing? You got a hickey on your forehead?" Howard asked. Lee and Myron smirked.

"No, Howard. This is a wound I got after I nabbed the mook who broke into my house," I responded, projecting a mental tongue out at Myron and Lee. You can take the girl out of Jersey, but not the Jersey out of the girl. Can I lie, or what?

Howard paled and stepped back a few paces. "Well, then," he started, and pretended to chuckle, then continued, "hope you can help find out who the bad guys are here, Super Woman." He thwacked Myron across his waist; Myron bent over and coughed, while Lee coddled his back and sent accusatory looks my way. Howard and the Suit exchanged smirks.

"How'd this happen, Howard? Any thoughts?"

"Yes! Yes! I have thoughts!" Howard exploded. "You were supposed to be here with Bauser yesterday when the power went out! AND YOU WEREN'T!" he finished triumphantly.

"Yes, Howard, that's correct," I said. "I was unable to be here with Bauser during the power shortage because I was UNCONSCIOUS."

"Oh," Howard said. I looked at Lee and Myron. They stepped back a couple of feet. "Well, the fire marshal wants you to go through and show him all the office permits, safeguards and insurance and engineering records for the server room," he said.

"Howard – you established the office permits, safeguards and set up the insurance and engineering records for the server room, long before I started here."

"Yeah, well you know where they are," he answered. "Myron, Dick – looks like we can get that golf game in after all, gentlemen!" Howard smiled, slapping Dick the Suit's back. Dick coughed and spluttered a grin.

"I play too!" Lee exclaimed.

Howard smiled at her and replied, "Of course you do, Lee, of course you do." Then he, Myron and Dick the Suit chuckled off. Lee and I stood rooted amidst our mutual disdain for each other, but outflanked by our common contempt of corporate Dicks.

Lee huffed off. "Well I'm outta here. I got better things to do." And off she stomped.

Bauser sidled up. "That's what she meant by the memory dig. Dick Fellas, from Buy-A-Lots, was scheduled to visit. Lee was bragging about it in the Ladies' Room last Friday," he said. I squinted at him. "I heard her through the air ducts. Next to the Men's Room. It's pretty clear if you're standing on a urinal with your ear next to them, too." I shook my head. "So what's he want you to do now?"

"Escort the Fire Marshal through a few thousand pounds of paper."

Bauser sighed. "I'll help."

"You don't have to do that. You're not on the hook."

"Yeah, but you weren't even here when that paperwork was put in place."

"I should have been here with you yesterday."

"What? You and your cranial offspring?"

I shrugged. We found the Fire Marshal, and got ready to view the charred remains.

Archie Daley has the unenviable position of being investigating Fire Marshal for Lancaster. To that end, he is not cheerful, convivial or anything that might mislead anyone into thinking he particularly likes people or helping them. If you didn't know better, you'd think Archie cheered each time a Lancastrian's property was ignited.

"Can't turn the elevators back on until we know they're safe. Walk up," he ordered.

The thought of walking up seven flights did not thrill my throbbing foot. Or forehead. Or my newly stabbed arm. And the prospect of possibly having to resuscitate the sea lion hulk of Archie D. huffing and puffing up the stairs ahead of me didn't help, either. So I promised myself that if Archie passed out on the staircase, my foot would accidentally get lodged in his hind quarters and shove him down all seven flights of steps. It made sense to me; in case of emergency, break ass.

We reached the seventh floor huffing and puffing. Bauser and I gaped at the propped open glass doors. If How-weird knew about this security breach he'd bust a gasket. Smoke still hovered around the server room, thanks to the building's hermetically sealed windows. Some fans were set up to blow the smoke into the lobby. This made for a great Halloween effect but didn't seem to be exactly OSHA friendly.

"Over here, boss. Think I got it," a guy labeled 'Volunteer Fireman' called.

Daley sauntered past Bauser and me and met the guy outside the server room. Together the two inspected some smelly smoldering remains. "Oh, for crying out loud," Daley muttered.

Bauser and I joined them. "What?" I asked.

"This wasn't an electrical fire after all," said Daley.

"What do you mean?" Bauser asked.

Daley held up a charred bag of some supremely stinky stuff. "Found this in your server room," he gasped, waving his hand.

"Huh?"

"Someone set a bag of dog crap on fire in your server room. Guess someone doesn't like you." He and the volunteer fireman chuckled.

"Geez," the volunteer said, "just when you think you've seen it all."

"But that's impossible!" Bauser yelped. "I was the only one here! And the door was closed behind me!"

I cringed. Not only was this another proverbial nail in the Bauser coffin, courtesy of How-weird, it was definitely not good for me. I envisioned Howard's eyes lighting up at being the 'hero' for catching the 'hostile employees' responsible for further delays to Buy-A-Lots' new Lancaster store opening.

"Look, there has to be a logical explanation," I began, walking behind Bauser and into the server room that now doubled as a turkey smoker.

"Well, this here's your cause. We'll write it up for you, so you can take care of your insurance," the volunteer said with a grin. "Actually, arson's a lot easier to claim than electrical malfunction," he added. Well, at least that was good to know. And it was very nice of him. But he was obviously from Lancaster, too.

"Anyway, there's not too much more for either of you to do here now," Daley said. "The building's landlord's been contacted and he's sending extra security, so the offices can get aired out. I suggest you examine for any missing contents tomorrow, once we get the air cleared out here. It's not too safe health-wise as it is," he finished, looking at me – or, more precisely, my forehead – meaningfully.

I looked at Bauser, who was gently banging his head against the wall by the water cooler. I sighed and took out my pain killer prescription. "Want some?" I asked.

"Sure," he said.

I gulped a couple, and Bauser pocketed his for later. Probably for when he had a brewski at home.

"Need a ride home?" he asked.

"Yeah, but I have to hit the dry cleaner's first," I said.

"Vito?"

"Yup."

We said thanks and goodbyes to the volunteer fireman and Daley, who very kindly tried not to guffaw at our predicament. It's one thing to wish your office went up with the flaming bag of shit. It's another to have to tell your boss that that's what happened.

We went silently and sullenly back down the seven flights of stairs. We got to the street and schlepped away together from the police barricades and into the parking garage. There we took the elevator to the top level, where Bauser always parks his 1995 Aspire ("It aspires to be a car."). Some people like to park their expensive cars away from others to avoid scratches and dings. Bauser parks far away to avoid co-workers.

After Bauser removed a few dozen sci-fi paperbacks, old gaming CDs and leftover Buddy Burger wrappers and coffee cups, there was some room for me to sit down. I perched down on the front seat and nestled Vito's bag on my lap. Oddly, I felt better. Maybe it was the fresh air on the rooftop. Maybe it was escaping work early on a Monday afternoon. Or maybe the meds had kicked in. Even though I knew I'd have to re-lock and load the blame/burden thingy argument tomorrow with How-weird, for now I was free.

Bauser put on his mirrored shades, threw in a Ramones 'Best of' CD, and we started off. We trundled down the exit spindle of the parking garage and Bauser carded our way out. He hung a left and let me out on Prince Street in front of Lickety-Split Laundry. As usual, I wasn't looking forward to dealing with Mrs. Phang. But this time, since the meds were working, it didn't feel like such a big deal.

I walked into Lickety-Split Laundry with Vito's bag. No one was there. This was odd. After a few moments of waiting, I rang the bell on the counter. I figured this would piss Mrs. Phang off, but I knew better than to just dump Vito's dry cleaning and run. I looked out the window. Bauser was waiting in his Aspire, bobbing his head up and down to the Kinks. Or the Romantics. Whatever.

A nice, short, preppy looking redhead appeared. "Good afternoon, may I help you?" she asked me pleasantly.

Um. Okay. "Who are you?" my meds let me blurt out.

"I'm Annie," she said, beaming.

"Where's Mrs. Phang?"

"Oh, she had to step out for a while." Annie smiled, exposing endless miles of Kansas-stretched porcelain teeth.

Methinks I smelled a rural farmland rat. Mrs. Phang probably hadn't 'stepped out' since 1954. And I never noticed a 'Help Wanted' sign in the window, either.

"Can I help you today?" Annie smiled at me.

"Uh, yeah… sure…" I said, and handed over Vito's ticket for pick up.

"Just a minute!" Annie squealed, and ran the dry cleaning hook thingies through their paces. Which was weird, since Vito's shirts always came in a box. He never got back hanging goods. Annie stacked up an assortment of collar shirts, Hawaiian shirts and golf shirts on the hanging bar. She smiled and said, "That'll be $63.65."

Okay – this was definitely weird. Clearly Annie hadn't been broken in by Mrs. Phang to know that Vito's a regular, because she wanted payment from me and not Vito. I guess it was the meds, but I wasn't into any static. I gave Annie the $63.65, and took the clean shirts. "Do you have anything else you'd like to drop off?" Annie asked me.

"Oh, no, thanks… this is just my boxing gear," I lied, indicating the gym bag full of Vito's stuff that I still needed to drop off.

"Thanks! Come again! Have a happy day!" Annie called out after me.

I stood by the side of Bauser's Aspire, and banged on the window for him to help let our dry cleaning passengers in for a ride. I tossed Vito's gym bag alongside them. "Everything okay?" he asked.

"No… weird," I said honestly.

"Great," Bauser shrugged, and did an illegal u-turn back to Orange Street and drove to my house.

Bauser backed up into my mini-ski slope driveway. I guess he figured it was easier to maneuver a potential head-on collision than rear-end my neighbor across the street. He pulled up, grated all the gears on his emergency brake, and parked. I sat there for a moment, apprehensive, and leaning forward. I wondered idly who else might wander out from my house at me.

After listening to a final soulful chorus of the Ramones ("Hey, ho – let's go!") Bauser shut off the engine, and helped me lug Vito's dry cleaning into the house. I had a moment of panic, half anticipating Vito to accost me for his laundry on our conjoined front porches. Or worse yet, open my front door and let me into my own house, as usual. But luck was finally on my side: neither happened. I stepped into the front hall and sighed and itched my konked noggin with dry cleaning hanger. Bauser followed. I took Vito's 75-pounds of dry cleaning and stashed it inside the hall closet, along with his gym bag. Lucky for Vito I only have one coat.

Bauser's good with cats, and better with dogs. Especially his own dog, Jim, who is a three-legged Irish Setter. Bauser adopted Jim from the animal shelter a couple of years ago. Don't ask me how or why Jim's minus a leg. Some things you just don't want to know.

Vinnie ambled up to Bauser – always happy to meet another fella – and grll'd, "Hullo," to him, and rubbed against his legs. Upstairs, Marie shrieked. The usual.

"What happened to Vinnie?" Bauser asked, examining his oddly cut fur.

"Moths," I answered.

I opened my fridge for inspection. "I have one beer, some limeade and a Box O'Burgundy," I offered.

"Beer's cool."

"Okay," I said, and gave Bauser the last beer. I poured a mug of wine for myself.

Bauser scritched Vinnie and then offered to give him his dinner – Fishy Scales and Piggy Tails – while I zipped upstairs to give Marie her seeds and sips. I came back down, we turned on the tube, and plotzed. We probably looked like an old, disinterested married couple. Don't get me wrong. I like Bauser. And vintage punk rock is okay. But Bauser? Bauser's a great guy, but, hey – he's Bauser. Which is okay, because he feels the same way about me.

We settled on a pizza order – how many times now had I had pizza in the last few days? I'd lost count – and waited. I switched on the food network channel for distraction.

The doorbell rang, and Bauser and I got up to pay our halfsies for our pizza delivery. But on the stoop, instead of the pizza guy, we found Aunt Muriel and Vito. With Ma. There were several startling discoveries about this vision, not the least of which was answering my own doorbell. Usually, Vito does that. Also, I wasn't expecting Ma to visit. She stood silently on my porch texting her office BFF all about it.

Aunt Muriel's gaze quickly took in Bauser: single, male. "My gracious, Mina, I'm so sorry! We didn't realize you had company!" she cried giddily. A vision of various high school productions of 'Glass Menagerie' sprang into my head and I was singularly grateful Aunt Muriel hadn't declared, "My, a gentleman caller!" She was also costumed to play a part; she sported a wide orange headband. I suspected she was hiding her charred bangs.

"Hi, Ma," I said.

Ma hugged me, examined my forehead and checked the email on her Crackberry. Clearly she wasn't too happy about having a grand-noggin. I wasn't too happy that she wasn't the pizza guy. But we hugged and stood there.

"Hey, Toots, you gonna let us in or what?" Vito asked affably.

"Oh, sorry," I said, grateful for the consumed pain meds, tet-a-nish shot and mug o'Merlot. I shot Bauser a warning look. He replied happily by slurping his beer and returning to his pillow on the floor, and flipping the channel over to the sports network.

Vito ambled into the hallway with a large, foiled casserole pan. Ma wheeled in a small, metallic overnight bag. She reminded me about Ethel's and Ike's upcoming visit, and our planned familial Lancaster rendezvous – which, of course, I'd completely forgotten. She handed me a pack of swatches. Then she and Aunt Muriel frowned at my walls. Vinnie rubbed happily against Aunt Muriel, since she was now his official pepperoni connection.

"I have some things for you in the car," Ma said to me, looking up from her email. I sighed and started to go out the door. Vito 'tut-tutted' me and brought Ma's stuff in: several shopping bags, a box from the liquor store, several bottles of good red wine, and a cooler.

"Wow, your family's cool," Bauser smiled.

"Not cool; catered," I auto-replied. Genetics forbid anyone in my family to travel without a picnic.

Ma and Aunt Muriel unpacked the shopping bags and in minutes my countertops were covered with various kinds of gourmet cheeses, olives, deli meats, nuts, crackers, Absolut, Grey Goose, Chivas Regal and few bottles of a nice Syrah. There was also an assortment of new little bowls as well new sheets, a wine bottle opener and throw pillows, courtesy of Ma and her savvy shopping. What can I say? What Ma sometimes lacks in communication skills she makes up for in retail.

Vito'd plunked the huge casserole on top of the stove. While Ma and Aunt Muriel unpacked and admired the prizes Ma'd brought for me, I lifted up the foil on Vito's casserole to take a peek. There lurked a kaleidoscope of ground beef, onions, clumps of condensed soups, ziti noodles, shredded American cheese and beans. These were topped with an undiluted can of tomato soup, Velveeta slices and what looked like either kielbasa or a large Gardner snake nested in the middle. I gulped, thankful that Bauser and I had placed the pizza order.

Vito clapped me on the shoulder, as I let the foil back down to shroud the dead casserole. "Looks pretty good, huh?"

"Great," I lied.

"Hey, I know I'm only a lonely widower," Vito said, looking soulfully over at Aunt Muriel, who continued to ignore him, "but I know how to learn a thing or two. I got the recipe for this right off the Internet!"

"Hey, that's really great, Vito," I said. Since my curiosity often outranks my sense, I asked, "What is it?"

"Johnny Mazarotti's – a la Vito Spaghetti!"

Ma and Aunt Muriel froze in their tracks and stared at Vito. They looked like Bambi's Great-Gramma deer in headlights. "Johnny Mazarotti's'? I haven't heard that name since Karen Dervish, right, Mu?" Ma said, getting faintly puffed up and sentimental.

Mrs. Dervish was one of the gals who guided Ma along the pearl-stringed ropes of Ridgewood in the early 60s, when being snobby was intensely in vogue. Ma and Mrs. Dervish might not have been best-buddies, but they both belonged to the Mother's Mafia. I found out about this after I snuck my first cigarette and got slapped upside the head with Ma's wooden spoon.

"What's that for?!" I had wailed.

"For smoking!" Ma gritted back at me.

"How'd you know?" I cried.

Ma leaned in, and answered quietly, "Mothers know everything."

I believed that for a very long time. Until graduation prom when I found out that Mrs. Dervish's daughter, Alicia, had finked on me. Alicia willingly dressed in matching mother/daughter outfits with Mrs. Dervish until her freshman year of college. A couple years after college graduation, I heard that she'd moved out from her parents' home to do environmental work with unshaved legs in an even more unshaved section of Vermont, where I suspected she smoked other things besides tobacco.

"Oh, we haven't had Johnny Mazarotti's for a thousand years!" Aunt Muriel shrieked, clearly trying to not offend Vito but severely amused.

"Hey, these are Johnny Mazarotti's a la Vito Spaghetti!" Vito beamed.

All at once, Ma and Aunt Muriel fell suddenly silent. Since I had already witnessed the raw makings of the impending offal, I wondered how much Zantac I had. Especially with Ma sleeping over. But Aunt Muriel's a real trooper. She asked politely, "Oh, is this your own version, Vito?"

"Yup!" Vito smiled. "Ya sees, the ways I figured it, the secrets not just in the noodles, but in the secret ingredients!" We looked at him, smiling hopefully, and willing the secret ingredients not to be something too awful. Except I already had a pretty good idea. "Kielbasa, pork 'n' beans, potato chips, and my secret creamed garlic barbeque sauce! I made it myself!" Vito winked. I looked blank. "The sauce, I mean."

I gulped. Apparently the damage was far, far worse than I'd imagined.

The doorbell rang and Bauser sprang into action, clearly awakened, and sobered by the thought of creamed kielbasa barbeque casserole. "Pizza!" Bauser sang. "I got it, my treat!" Obviously Johnny Mazarotti had made an impression on him, too.

Vito looked down sheepishly. Aunt Muriel frowned at me. Ma sucked on an olive. "Sorry, Toots; I should have figured you'd have your own dinner plans," he said.

Oh, good grief. "Well, I did when it was only me and Bauser! Hey, this is great!" I smiled. "Now we can have olives and pizza as – ummm… – appetizers, and have the Johnny Spaghetti's as our main course!" I said.

"Well, hey, sure… great!" Vito beamed.

Dishtowel tucked neatly into his waistband, Vito turned on the oven. I don't know what I did in my past life, but clearly Vito sought to make sure I got served in this one. I looked over at Ma and Aunt Muriel for sympathy. They were too busy clawing inside their purses and clandestinely divvying up the various Rolaids, Beano and Mylanta they had between them. But I also got 'the nod'. I'd done the right thing by Vito.

So we also divvied up a lot of pizza, olives, gourmet cheeses and nuts for the first course, along with a generous amount of 'frothies' in the blender. Bauser stuck with his beer, tenderly fingering the pain pill I'd given him earlier like a talisman. I sighed and checked on Vito's casserole corpse in the oven.

I came back into the living room, and it looked like old home week. Ma and Aunt Muriel were cozily tucked up together on the sofa sipping frothies, while Vito was squashed happily inside the little side chair, with Bauser lying contentedly across the living room rug at his feet, looking a lot like his Irish Setter. Vinnie came in and perched happily in Aunt Muriel's lap, and noshed on a pepperoni slice she 'assured' me she wouldn't give him from her pizza.

After we chatted for a while and the smoke alarm went off, I took the Johnny Mazarotti's out of the oven and opened up the screen door. I set out some plates and forks and napkins for our buffet. I put the hot dead casserole on the stovetop, figuring a public viewing was safer. I'd have a private service with the remains afterward.

While we ate, Bauser and I filled everyone in about EEJIT, Buy-A-Lots and the flaming bags of feces. Typical supper talk. I finally started to feel like my house was homey. Even while Vito insisted on giving us his recipe:

Johnny Mazarotti ala Vito Spaghetti

- Large package dry extra wide egg noodles
- 2 pounds ground beef
- 2 large onions, chopped
- 10 garlic cloves, minced
- Vito's Secret Garlic BBQ sauce
- 2 pounds garlic Kielbasa
- 4 cans pork 'n' beans
- 1 can condensed tomato soup
- 2 cans condensed cream of chicken soup

- 1 hunk sliced Velveeta
- 1 package cream cheese

Directions:

1.Preheat oven to 350 degrees F. Grease the inside of a baking dish with Crisco or lard.
2.Bring a large pot of salted water to a boil. Add egg noodles and cook. When done, drain and set aside.
3.In a large saucepan over high heat, brown the ground beef, onion, garlic. Mix in the cans of pork ‘n' beans (don't drain), Cream of Chicken soup and cream cheese.
4.Smooth a layer of Vito's Secret Creamed Garlic BBQ sauce on the bottom of the baking dish. Place half of the cooked egg noodles on top. Layer with half of the bean and meat mixture and half of the Velveeta slices. Salt and pepper to taste, then repeat the layers with the remaining cheese as a top layer. Cover all with canned tomato sauce. Place 2 large kielbasa – whole – lengthwise on top of the casserole. Push into the center of the casserole, so partially ‘hiding’ but still exposed. Top with smashed potato chips, if desired. (Vito desired)
5.Bake in the preheated oven 30 minutes, or until the cheese is completely melted and the surface is hot and bubbly.
6.Take Bean-O. Then serve.

Finally, after some old-time MGM re-runs, Bauser went home. Vito followed behind. “Oh, I guess you got kind of busy to take care of my dry cleaning, what with the fire and all,” he said nervously.

“No actually, Vito; Bauser dropped me off and I picked it up,” I said, happy that I remembered and wasn’t going to disappoint him. I opened the front hall closet door, and displayed the plethora of hanging dry cleaning. “Ta da!” I sang.

Vito looked at me like feathers had sprouted from my ears. “What’s this?” he asked.

“Your dry cleaning. Which I paid for, by the way,” I offered with frothie induced enthusiasm.

“Whaddyamean you paid for it?”

Somewhere in the dim halls of my remembery was the idea that getting Vito's shirts on hangers – and paying for them – was weird. But what the heck – it's only dry cleaning, right?

"Look, Vito, there's a new girl there... she probably just didn't know you have an account... it's no big deal. After all, you're good for it, right?" I joshed.

"She didn't give you no box?" Vito asked.

"No..." I replied, feeling a twinge of righteous indignation. If Vito was going to be this much of a dry cleaning junkie he could meet, and pay, his own dealer. Hrmphh.

"What about the bag?"

"Well you know, I figured since she was new and all... it'd be better to deliver your bag to Mrs. Phang after she got back from her vacation," I said.

"Vacation?!"

"Well, yeah, I guess she has to take a day or two once every seventy years or so..."

"So yous didn't drop off the bag?"

"No – it's right here... I just forgot about giving it back to you, with everyone visiting and all..." I stammered.

"That's okay... that's okay, Toots... I'll just take this bag of dirty duds off your hands," he said.

"Don't you want your clean shirts?" I asked.

"I'll help myself tomorrows."

Vito left with his gym bag of dirty duds, while I stood in a dust of disappointment. I hung my head.

"Well goodnight, my dears. I must bid you adieu," Aunt Muriel called out at us, after checking to see Vito was well inside his house. I exchanged glances with Ma, and we shrugged. I figured Aunt Muriel was still a little paranoid about Vito, what with his church boob petting and all. She pointed at the prescription bottle of horse-size antibiotics. "Before I go, take these!" she warned. "For her infection. From the laceration," she explained to Ma, pointing at my foot.

"Oh, yeah, right," I said. I got some water, choked on a horse pill, and chased it with another pain med.

Ma and I got everything in the kitchen stashed away. The dishwasher hummed happily. Vinnie lay on his back in the middle of the living room a la cock-a-roach and pfffed more pepperoni fumes happily into the ozone. Ma held her nose and waved herself off to sleep in my room. I shrugged and trudged upstairs after her with a piece of pizza crust for Marie and got in my jammies. Then I headed back downstairs with a blanket, a pillow, and last month's self-help book purchase, 'The Cretin's Cavalcade for Kitchen Addictions'. I was glad the author obviously knew how to help with self-esteem, too. I made myself a little nest on the sofa and settled down to read behind closed eyes.

CHAPTER 5

(Tuesday morning)

Tuesday morning, I woke up around dawn to a Biblical scourge of smells. I looked around the living room and didn't see Vinnie. But clearly his pepperoni eating was a lot more toxic than I'd figured. I stumbled into the kitchen to open a window and found the terrier growling at Flower the Skunk over Vinnie's bowl of Kitty Cookies.

I scooted Vito's would-be-pooch away from Flower and into the basement. Flower responded by showering me and my kitchen with skunk spray. Then she waddled to the back door, looked over her shoulder at me with a dismissive glance, and pushed her snout at the gap in the door and let herself out.

Since I was now up and stinky, I decided it was time for Ma to be up and stinky, too.

"Ma-aaaa!!" I screamed congenially.

"Wha-aaattt!?"

Ma came downstairs and yawned. Then she choked. "Pew! What have you been doing down here?" she asked, holding her nose. I explained about the close encounters of the smelly kind. Ma leaned toward me and sniffed. "Phew! You stink!"

"Ya think?"

"Do you have any tomato juice?"

"You want a Bloody?"

"No, you fool! You're supposed to take a bath in tomato juice to get rid of skunk stuff."

"Oh. I have a six pack of individual cans. But I only have 4 left because K. and I had Bloodies a few weeks ago."

"What you need is a few gallons," Ma said.

I responded by crying.

"There, there, it's not your fault you're stinky," Ma said, patting my head from an arm's length away.

"Thanks," I sniffed. "But it's just everything… and on top of the burning dog poop job stuff, my head hickey and the shredded foot thing, I gotta smell bad now, too?" I blubbered.

"Maybe this is a good time to ask your neighbor for some help," Ma said sympathetically. I sighed. The last thing I wanted to do was invite Vito over for an additional visit. Especially while I, along with my kitchen, was stinky. Vito might never stop Swiffering. "After all, Vito does like that dog. And he'll probably be over here to Swiffer anyway," she finished.

She was right. "Okay," I sniffed.

Ma left me to walk across the front porch and negotiate with Vito for help. I trudged upstairs with 4 individual cans of tomato juice, wishing I could have brought the vodka, Tabasco, Worcestershire sauce, horseradish and a nice fresh lemon wedge along, too.

Let this be a word to the wise. The stinky wise, that is. Washing with tomato juice to get rid of skunk stuff does not work like the old wives' tale we've all heard about. It's more like being stuck with no running water for a week or two, and then settling to wash up with cans of Minestrone soup. It kind of masks your stinky smell, so you don't completely reek of BO. But you end up smelling like soup instead. Which got me thinking: it had been a long time since I'd made a nice vat of homemade soup. Since it was August, maybe I'd make a small stockpot of zucchini soup. I could serve it warm, with a dollop of sour cream on top. Or a bit of grated parmesan. It was comfort food, and lo-cal. How could I go wrong? And while I was on the Italian theme, with the zucchini soup and all, I could throw together a nice summer veggie lasagna, with squash and mushrooms and a light béchamel sauce.

I finished fantasizing about my summer menus once the hot water ran out. I got out cleaner, and about six recipes richer. I sniffed. I still smelt a bit like Flower. Should have used the tomato juice to make a Bloody after all. I'd still smell funny, but I wouldn't have minded so much. I pulled on a soft clean short-sleeve shirt and khakis, and trudged downstairs with my hair back in its usual wet pony tail.

"Oh-my-gawd!" Ma yelped and leapt away from me. This was not exactly the reaction I'd hoped for.

"What's the matter?" I asked.

Ma held her nose and tapped into the Borg. She put her Bluetooth in her ear. Seriously, her cell phones are pretty slick. I've only seen kids working Target or drug dealers use these. I hate to admit it, but Ma's techno savvy knowledge thingy is scarily impressive.

Ma got through to Aunt Muriel, and a lot of Mhming and "Yes, yes that's right… yes, you did hear me correctly," went on. I hunched on the landing. Vinnie came down from upstairs and looked around a little wide-eyed. Clearly the aroma was not conducive to his sensibilities either. He sniffed me, shook a paw and stalked back upstairs. I didn't blame him. I didn't want to sit near me either.

I didn't know what to do. So I cried. It didn't start out full-blown: just a few sniffs while Ma talked on her Borg Phone and paced around the front porch. Anyone not knowing she was talking on the phone would swear she was a raving lunatic talking to herself. And getting answers.

The whole situation reminded me of when in the sixth grade and I went to school all happy because I could show off my first pair of official bell bottoms. Ma had let me pick them out myself: Blind Your Eyes White, just like I remembered Marcia Brady wore on 'The Brady Bunch'. The day was great until recess when my best buddy Mona came up to me and tied her sweatshirt around my waist.

I'd gotten my first period. In fact, I was the only girl in the entire grade school to get her first period before matriculating to Junior High. Which was a shock. Because we all were convinced that Betsy Heffelstein was gonna be the one because she had to wear a bra. But there I was, in my brand new white bell bottoms, with a crimson splotch that looked like I'd sat on a stuck pig. So I had to go to the principal's office and call Ma – and then had to wait for her in Mrs. Heinz's office perched on a copy of the Bergen Record. I liked Mrs. Heinz. She had white hair that she rinsed each week to match her suits. That week was lilac – my favorite – so her hair was a misty shade of lavender to match the various styles of purple and grey suits.

Ma flew down to school and swooped me and a clean section of the newspaper back home. I told her I felt awful about the new slacks – they weren't even a full day old. But Ma went out that afternoon and bought me a replacement pair right away. And I didn't even have to beg. Go figure. Ever since then, Ma and I were on different terms.

Anyway, sitting on the landing bruised and stinky felt a lot like being in the principal's office. So I cried some more. Ma marched back into the hallway on a mission. Then she saw me. I palpably felt her put on verbal brakes when I saw her jaw clench to a screeching halt. Probably bit the end of her tongue in the process, I wagered. She took a deep breath, and in a strange tone I suspect she uses mostly for clients said, "Aunt Muriel suggests bacon. I saw Vito on the porch. He's bringing some over." She removed the Borg Phone from her ear and came toward me, and patted my shoulder – once again from a safe distance. "There, there, there. My poor lamb," she said. Although I noticed she wasn't about to get close to me. When you're stinky, you're stinky.

Vito came over with a pound of bacon. I took it and headed into the kitchen to find a frying pan. Ma slapped her hand to her forehead. "You're not supposed to cook it!" she yelled at me.

"Huh?" I replied.

Vito looked awkward. "Uh, I got some things I have to do," he said, and beat a hasty retreat.

Ma motioned to the hallway, then pointed to the stairs. "You're supposed to rub it on you. Where you got sprayed. It's supposed to get rid of skunk stuff," she instructed.

"Raw bacon gets rid of skunk stuff?" Ma nodded. "Doesn't sound very kosher," I said, taking the bacon upstairs. Vinnie trilled happily and trotted back upstairs underneath my feet.

I'm not so sure about the political correctness of rubbing bacon on yourself. But ever since Lady Gaga wore a brisket, it might not be such a big deal. Most of Flower's spray had gone on my knees and shins, so I rubbed the bacon there. Then I redressed and put makeup on. Vinnie licked my legs. I headed back downstairs a new fake woman. Ma looked sort of happy.

"See, I told you everything would be fine," she fibbed. "Now just stand there a moment." She sprayed me with cologne. I cringed. I hoped I wasn't going to smell like apple-smoked cologne.

I drove to EEJIT, and after helping another octogenarian negotiate the intricacies of the parking garage, decided to drive up to the rooftop and park next to Bauser. I knew his favorite spot by the piles of peanut shells littering it. Except that Bauser's car wasn't there. Which was weird, because he starts at o'dark hundred. I shrugged, took the garage elevator out and walked up the covered path to EEJIT.

The building's security guards were still in place. And the fans blowing out the smoke fumes were, too. I nodded to them – the security guards, that is – produced my ID badge and headed toward my desk. A lot of the cubes were empty, which didn't surprise me. I figured most of my co-workers didn't need much of an excuse to not work in smoked cubes. EEJIT, in its usual spirit of corporate decay, was open, forcing its employees to burn a vacation day if they didn't want to come in and work in the smoke. Unless of course they were looking forward to their families cashing in early on life insurance policies from inhaling a barrage of carcinogens. In which case it smelled like they had it made.

What got me in the door, in spite of the carcinogens, was curiosity. I had a few ideas I wanted to run past Bauser. Also, I needed Bauser's help dealing with the insurance stuff. I hoped he was coming to work. I couldn't imagine Bauser taking a day off since he had to literally be forced to neutralize his accumulated vacation days a couple years ago. That was because EEJIT used to let us carry over unused vacation time from year to year, mostly because a lot of the employees visit family in China, India, the Ukraine or other countries that are a good 14 hour plane ride away. Last year, another large corporation bought EEJIT and stood firm. Our new parent corporation, Effhue Ltd., refused to allow any more vacation carryovers, so everyone had to use up their accumulated time. As a result, a lot of my co-workers took month-long vacations last year. Consequently, we hired a lot of temps, who in turn made a lot of mistakes. So our projects took twice as long, because none of the project managers were allowed to factor in re-work time into development because of using temp contractors instead of the real developers.

Anyway, since Bauser accrued his benefit time since 1989, by the time the new corporate edict came around, he had almost 13 weeks of vacation time and 18 personal days. Once corporate realized Bauser is our IT department, a deal was made that forced him to take two weeks of vacation off in perpetuam, with the remaining time paid out clandestinely. Which made sense, considering his cash purchase of a 54" flat screen TV that he hung on his 108" long living room wall. So I guessed Bauser was taking off today, to keep up his end of the bargain.

I got to my desk, logged in, and waited for the one thousand and one diatribes from How-weird to appear, and sorted through for bonafide emails.

The phone rang. "Mina speaking, EEJIT," I said automatically.

"Girl, you are not going to believe this!" Belinda hissed at me.

"How you mean?" I whispered.

"Halloween?!"

I emailed her my question. Yeeshkabiddle. "Oh," she said after she'd read it. She knew that I knew better than to fool with her about Halloween. Baptists take Devil Worshipping Holidays pretty seriously. After all, she was going to go up in the Rapture while I was going to get blown to oblivion because of sporadic attendance to St. Bart's, Breakfast Wars or not.

"They put Bauser on the Plan," Belinda whispered.

"What!?"

"You better watch your back with Howard," she added, and hung up.

I stared at my screen. "Shit."

Norman looked up, came over with his towel and folded it up and placed it on the desk in front of me. "Don't let EEJIT give you permanent brain damage," he said kindly, preparing the space on my desk where I usually bang my head.

"It's pretty bad," I said, and told him about Bauser. Norman shook his head.

"This place gets lousier every day. I can't believe they opened the office for work with all this smoke," he said. Then he looked at me. "Hey, do you smell bacon?"

I got up and mumbled, "Thanks," then grabbed my purse and hightailed it to the Ladies' Room.

This was just too much. Especially for a Tuesday. So I started to cry. Then I tried not to cry – which only made me cry more. Which, in turn, made me look awful. Mascara tears streaked down my face. I blew my nose hard. Then I heard someone coming in.

Shit, shit, shit, I thought. I really didn't want to explain my Sad Clown face to any coworkers. So I ducked into the farthest stall, closed the door, blew my nose hard again and waited for the occupant to come and go.

The door opened, and I heard someone come in and run water. I was beginning to calm down. I began to think that maybe I could come out into the open with some kind of wisecrack and laugh my cosmetic disaster off. I was about to come out and face the gurgling music when I heard the door open again. And whispering.

"What happened?"

"What should have happened months ago. That goof-off Bauser's been put on the Plan," the other voice smirked. It was Lee. Big surprise.

"I didn't think Bauser goofed around. He hardly takes a day off," mouse voice stammered. Who the heck was this? I held my breath, pulled my feet up and eavesdropped.

"Let's just say he's finally been found out as being the world's largest paperweight," Lee smirked. "So he's taking his weenie day off to decide if he wants to take the Plan or quit."

"But he was working on his day off, taking care of the fire," Mousie began. And then stopped abruptly. Probably because Lee set her Shut Up Glare on stun.

"Yeah, he was here. And incompetent," Lee snorted. "The server room should have been locked down. He allowed the arsonist's entry."

I didn't think I could dislike Lee more than I already did. I was wrong.

"Well, anyway, who do you think will handle the server room?" Mousie asked. "We're having a lot of data problems called in about the website and Bauser always troubleshoots those between our servers and the host site."

Ohmygawd, Mousie was Maureen! Sometimes I had lunch with her! And we both kvetched about Lee together! I pinched my lips together and gnawed my tongue.

"Me, of course," Lee said. "After all, I took a course in web management," she added smugly.

"Oh, well, that's good to know," Maureen continued. "I've already got clients complaining. Thanks for filling me in about Bauser. I tried to find Mina to ask, but I couldn't find her."

Lee started to say something when Smyrna blew into the restroom. I pondered about slamming the stall door open Clint Eastwood style and letting them all have it ("You need office supplies? You need toiletries? Go ahead! Do you feel lucky, punk?") but my leg was falling asleep.

Smyrna announced, "Maureen, Howard is looking for you. He has the Buy-A-Lots executive in his office and they're screaming about the data downloads."

The three tsking workabees scuttled out of the Ladies' Room. I heard the door swing open. Then I heard Maureen's voice one last time as they departed: "Do you believe all this smoke? And, I swear, I think I actually smell bacon."

I unfolded myself, came out, rubbed my leg and washed my face. And reminded myself to keep my mouth shut and just chew if I ever had lunch with Maureen again.

I wandered into the kitchen in search of some high octane coffee and a sugar buzz. Since the server room's right next to the kitchen, most everything was either melted or smoked, with the combination of the fire, last night's power outage and it being a very hot summer. I started a new pot of old coffee, grabbed a semi-soft package of peanut M&M's and munched.

Norman shuffled into the kitchen. We stared at each other.

"Jeez, are you alright?" he asked. I explained about Flower and my scents. "Jeez, maybe you could go home sick?" he asked hopefully. I shook my head and explained about Ma and Vito and the Non-Peaceable Kingdom complete with swatches. "Oh, me too," he said. "The girls are all home. This is the week between music and equestrian camps." He sighed. "So it was come in to work or stay at home with my family."

I nodded sympathetically and we walked back to our cubes together, armed with our respective vices: my caffeine and chocolate-fix, and Norman with his carrots. I understand Norman's a vegetarian. But I still think breakfast carrots are weird. Couldn't he grab an apple or raisins or something?

We parted at our crate openings to strap ourselves in our chairs, hook back into the network and tap back into EEJIT's network. Or at least Norman did. I saw the note on my chair and sighed.

'SEE ME.'

It was from How-weird – obviously. In large, red 37-point ink. I was surprised he took the trouble to write it on a piece of paper, and not just my chair. I shook my head, grabbed a notepad and pen and trudged toward his office.

I got side-swiped by the Ladies' Room Regatta doing a fast shuffle off from How-weird's office. I peered in and saw How-weird behind his desk with smoke literally fuming in front of his face.

I knew I'd contemplated Howard disappearing in some kind of Rumpelstiltskin manner for a while now, but this was a bit over the top. Dick Fellas, the Buy-A-Lots exec, was sitting in the guest chair opposite Howard and choking. I looked at Howard and then at the pile of cinders under his desk, sending up the very, very smelly smoke.

"Hi, Howard," I waved. "Got your note... do you need me to order something?" I faked.

"WHERE WERE YOU?" How-weird shouted in 57-point, bold, shimmering italic purple at me.

"Umm, well I got a cup of coffee, went to the ladies' room; you know... normal morning stuff..."

"YEAH, WELL I GOT SOME NOT SO NORMAL MORNING 'STUFF' HURLED AT ME!"

"Huh?"

At this point, Dick Fellas recovered enough to explain. "Hello. It's Mina, isn't it?" He frowned. I nodded. He looked me up and down and clearly looked pained. "Well, MINE-ahhh," he drawled, "Howie here and I were discussing yesterday's concerns, when someone very rudely interrupted us during our discussion this morning by hurling, ummm... a bag of burning fecal matter... under Howie's desk here."

I glanced down. Right under the very center of Howard's desk was a smoldering, stinky paper bag, an indentation on it indicating where Howard's fat little foot had been: he'd clearly tried to stomp it out. That explained where the fumes were coming from. And the smoke. I was surprised the sprinkler in his ceiling hadn't gone off. I guessed he must have put it out in time. And then I saw that the contents of the smoldering bag was splattered all over How-weird's shoes, socks, pant legs, wall-to-wall carpet, computer desk, walls, and chair. Eww.

"My," I said. Howard gave a smoldering glare at me (no pun intended). I shrugged. "Wanna paper towel? Some Pinesol? Lysol? Clorox?" I asked.

"NO, I WANT YOU TO IDENTIFY THE LOCATION OF EVERY PERSON IN THIS OFFICE AT 8:58 THIS MORNING!" Howard blared through clenched teeth.

"I hardly think that's Mina's concern," Dick said pointedly to Howard. "After all, I've called People to take care of this."

Wow. He called People. I wondered what he thought I was.

"Actually, Howard, that might be kind of hard, with the exhaust fans going and all," I said.

"WHAT DO YOU MEAN?"

"I mean, unless someone has to use their card to get through the lobby's glass doors, there's really no way to tell who came in and when." Howard looked apoplectic. "Unless of course the building's security guards remember. Maybe they're taking some kind of notes?" I ended hopefully.

"CHECK WITH THEM!"

"Ummm... okay... Just a hunch here, but I'm guessing this takes priority over the insurance files?" I asked.

Howard gritted his teeth so loudly I swear he could have ground wheat. "INSURANCEFILESPLEASETAKEPRIORITY!" Ugh. I would have rather gone back and interrogated Chubaka the Guard.

Just then a couple of suits walked in. And stepped back out gasping. I looked at Dick, who looked at Howard, who looked back at me. I peered at the new suits. They both looked like they were from IBM, except they were wearing navy blue instead of corporate dinge. The guy, I didn't know. But I sure remembered the redhead.

"Good morning," the IBM-esque guy said, holding out a business card to Howard and Dick.

Howard stood up to take the card and shake hands, but ended up stepping further into the molten pile of poop. There was a disgusting 'sqwoosh' sound, and the bag puffed out yet more fecal fumes. The IBM dude dodged back out of Howard's office into the threshold. I wasn't far behind him. Dick look strangulated but there was no room for him to escape, what with the throng in the doorway. Howard smoldered.

"My associate and I were in the area, on a separate matter, but thought we should look in," he said through a pleasant smile. Howard looked at the guy's business card, turned green and fell back in his pleather chair.

"Gosh, you guys are really on it. I had no idea the dry cleaning business was that competitive," I said. Everyone looked at me. "I guess you're here because of the smoke smells in the carpet and such. And I'm sure Howard's pants need a really good dry cleaning now."

Red flushed.

"MINA, WHAT ARE YOU TALKING ABOUT? THESE ARE U.S. MARSHALS!" Howard shouted, waving the IBM guy's card at me.

"Really?" I said. I took the card from Howard and read it. I stared at Red. Had the fumes gotten to me? I could swear she was the new girl I met at Mrs. Phang's Lickety-Split Cleaners. Why else would I think she and this guy were peddling door to door dry cleaning services?

"Young, umm, lady," the old IBM-like guy began, "I think there has been some misunderstanding here. I'm a U.S. Marshal. And Ms. McMay is my associate." He smiled conclusively. "We were just leaving town but read about the Buy-A-Lots arsons, and EEJIT's recent troubles."

I stared blankly back at him. I really couldn't see the connection. Who didn't want to fling a flaming bag of poop at a Buy-A-Lots? Or How-weird, for that matter? "Coincidentally, Ms. McMay is from this area, so she convinced me to make a stop before we left," the guy – Mike Green – said pointedly, indicating Red. He finished, "We'll be on our way now."

"Sure, sure, no problem. Thanks lots for your help," How-weird replied, getting up from his chair and wiping his foot on the carpet. Real smooth, I thought. Ick.

Howard and Dick gave the U. S. Marshal and Red a custom tour back toward the elevators, with lots of backslapping on Howard's part. Poor Red.

I shuffled down the hall and into Bauser's cube. I opened the pen drawer where he kept his spare keys to his filing cabinet, and inserted a ruler. SNAP! went the mousetrap he routinely booby-trapped to break the fingers of snoops. I pulled out the dented ruler and adjoining mousetrap, opened the drawer and took out Bauser's spare keys.

I went through Bauser's files, which are really well organized, and took out all the pertinent insurance files. I also took out the hard-copy listing of everyone's hardware information, just in case there had been smoke damage and someone insisted they needed a replacement. Then I logged in through Bauser's system and used the company access codes to download more insurance stuff from the admin directory onto a flash drive. I closed out, gathered up the paper files and re-locked Bauser's cabinet. Although I thought the point was probably moot. I thought about replacing Bauser's finger-trap but figured I'd probably lose a finger setting it back up. So I pocketed the keys, and planned on handing them back to Bauser when I saw him. Which I hoped was soon.

I got back to my cube and sealed the files in an oversized plastic overnight pouch, since it was the only available unsmoked envelope in my cube. I figured this was safest since there were a bunch of odd/small sized notes in the files that probably shouldn't get lost.

Then the non-heavens rained down on me. And my cube. And my computer. And me. While the fire alarm sounded. Apparently the fire alarm sprinkler system did work.

Since Howard had also decided last month that part of my duties as Office Manager included being the resident Fire Safety person, I had to go cube by cube and get everyone out of the building. Which would be easy: I didn't think anyone was actually at EEJIT today besides me, Norman, the Ladies' Room Trio, and Howard and Dick. Mr. Green and Red had left the building before we started flinching in the showers. So I grabbed the overnight pouch, then began making my way up and down rows of empty cubicles and got soaked. I held my hand to my eyebrows Pocahontas-style so I could see across to Norman's cube. Norman was sitting at his computer with his towel draped over his head and his laptop. "HEY, NORMAN," I yelled, "YOU GOTTA LEAVE! THIS ISN'T A DRILL."

"I KNOW," he yelled back, "AND I'M WET, NOT DEAF."

Oh.

I clung to my pouch and purse and continued my rounds. Even through the men's room. Eeeeccchhhh. Once I was done in there and had stepped out again, I saw the IT lab door open. Inside was Bauser.

"WHAT ARE YOU DOING? THIS ISN'T A DRILL!" I shouted, tugging at his sleeve.

"I HAVE TO SET THIS INTO BACKUP," he screamed politely back at me. I shrugged, stepped into the hallway and wrung my hair into a puddle. "THERE," Bauser cried. "C'MON, LET'S GO."

"WE HAVE TO USE THE STAIRS."

"OKAY, LET'S GO," he replied, and started to lead me into the lobby foyer and to the stairway door.

"I HAVE TO MAKE SURE NORMAN'S LEFT."

We raced back to Norman's cube. Norman sat transfixed at his terminal. Bauser thumped the back of Norman's chair. "I'M COMPILING," Norman yelled.

"NO, YOU'RE NOT: I SET US INTO BACKUP MODE. YOU'RE COMPILING IN TEMP – IF IT'S NOT DROWNED," Bauser yelled.

"Shit," Norman said.

"IT'S OKAY; I GOT YOUR BACKUPS AT HOME."

Norman sat up, took the towel off his head and we left.

We made our way down the back stairwell, also deluged with showers, through the lobby and out the doors. Where a real thunderstorm was raining on our parade. I couldn't see a thing through the torrential mess, so Bauser and Norman led me by the elbows and under the awning of PizzaNow! across the street. I wiped my eyes and blinked. Once I was out of the pouring rain, I could see.

"Jeez, Mina," Bauser blew.

"What?" I asked.

"Talk about leading Helen Keller from the woods," he said. I squinted back. I looked over at Norman. He had somehow smuggled his laptop out with him. Wrapped in hermetically sealed plastic. Huh. I didn't know we had hermetically sealed plastic. Which was somewhat surprising since I was in charge of ordering that kind of stuff.

Bauser and I looked at him. "Are you logged out?" Bauser asked.

"No."

Their eyes locked. I was confused.

"Same session?" Bauser asked.

"Concurrent."

"Crap," I said.

"You mean there's more burning crap?" Norman asked.

"No; I forgot my stupid purse," I said.

"Are you kidding me?" Bauser asked.

"Well, I can't drive without my keys," I began. He shrugged. We heard the alarm go silent.

"We'll meet you at your house," Bauser said. I looked at him. Then I looked at Norman. Norman nodded.

"It's early in the day. I can't go home yet. The girls are still here," he replied simply. I shook my head. With my weird pets, odd neighbor and church lady crowd, who'd have thunk it that my house was any kind of sanctuary?

I gave Bauser the pouch with the insurance stuff and told him I'd meet him at my house. I wasn't worried about Bauser or Norman having to be let in, since Ma was camped there. Then I raced back into our building to the tune of sirens in the background. I limped back up seven flights of stairs to EEJIT, opened the door to the lobby and everything went black. Again.

I came to strapped to a gurney being hoisted down the stairs. Which was probably why I started screaming like a banshee, which scared the volunteer rescuers. They responded by dropping me. The gurney responded by racing down all seven flights and lurching bumper-car style out of the building, through the courtyard and into traffic. I shot out, clattering and screaming, smack dab in the middle of Queen Street.

Soon, a few confused volunteer Fire Police and ambulance workers surrounded me. Once they realized I was conscious and irate, they unstrapped me, picked up their gurney and went home. I rubbed my head and sat on the curb. A fella in a trench coat came up and looked at me, then stared at the building. "I'm sorry," I said, rubbing my head, "but I think all the offices are closed."

"I AIN'T NO DAMN OFFICE WORKER!" he raged. "I'M A BAG MAN!" Then he huffed away. This bagman was clearly not from Lancaster.

I tried to stand up but my knees saw double.

"HEY, MINA!" a voice called from what sounded like very far away. It was Trixie, and she was sitting on the curb right next to me. "Oh boy, you look like heck," she said. Heck? You see what I mean? That's about as edgy as it gets with Lancastrians. "C'mon, I'm taking you home," she said. I shook my head and saw stars.

"Ma," I bleated.

"I know," Trixie said.

"And Aunt Muriel. And Vito. And Bauser, and I think Norman… oh my."

"What is this, a convention? C'mon, you can't keep sitting here on the curb. Somebody's doggie will piddle on you." Made sense to me. "Although you might not smell too much worse. What in the world happened to you?"

I sighed and gave Trixie the punch list about Flower, tomato juice, a pound of bacon, and perfume. Trixie sniffed. "Well, you do smell mostly like bacon, at least," she admitted.

We got up – or that is, Trixie dragged me up, and I wobbled.

"Where's your purse?" she asked.

"Purse?" I parroted stupidly.

"THE THING YOU KEEP YOUR WALLET AND YOUR KEYS IN," she said loudly. Apparently Trixie was confusing being concussed with being deaf. I shrugged. Trixie shook her head, got me up, and marched me back toward EEJIT's offices. After accosting several policemen, EMTs and an off-duty nun (by mistake), Trixie gave up on my handbag.

"The officers said they'd keep an eye out for it," she said. Her eyes got slitty.

"You're not gonna use this as an excuse to get in touch with Appletree again, are you?" I winced. I couldn't take Trixie's on-again, off-again romance. It wasn't so much because of the other woman thingy. I just couldn't handle the lack of continuity. And her breakdowns always made me nervy. If Trixie could get broken down that easily over a romance, I didn't stand a water ice's chance in Central Market in summer. That is, if I ever weathered another romance.

Trixie replied, "I'm a taxpayer. Not using available police resources is wasteful." She looked off dreamily into the distance. I winced. Yeeshkabiddle.

Because I didn't have my handbag, I didn't have my car keys. So Trixie drove me home. We pulled into the driveway behind Ma's and Aunt Muriel's respective cars. Bauser's car was parked in Vito's driveway. A few other cars parked at the curb. The way my skull was thumping I really hoped all the other cars belonged to the neighbors. Or Jehovah's Witnesses. It didn't really matter, just as long as they were attached to persons who were not inside my home.

Trixie put her Jeep into park, pulled heavily on the emergency brake at the foot of Mt. Driveway, and shut the engine off. I saw the door to Vito's house open, and out popped Mike Green and Red.

"Hey, Trixie, lookit," I said, pointing my watermelon sized forehead toward Vito's. Trixie paused checking her lipstick and stared. "That's Mike Green, the U.S. Marshal who was in Howard's office," I said.

She considered, then said, "He's cute. For a Marshal. I guess. What was he doing in Howard's office?"

"Well, at first I thought it was because of Howard's dry cleaning, because the redhead who's with him was Mrs. Phang's substitute the day I was supposed to bring in Vito's dry cleaning and just picked up instead."

"Wait a minute, wait a minute," Trixie said, "you mean those two aren't a couple?"

"Nope."

Trixie applied more lipstick, fluffed her hair, adjusted her cleavage and hopped out of her Jeep quicker than you can say, "Date night." A guy in uniform – even a suit – is like the pull of the moon on the ocean to Trixie. She just can't help but make waves. I sighed and thought about banging my head but someone had just done that for me. I scrunched down inside the Jeep, closed my eyes and wished I was someone else.

“HEY, VEEE-TO!” Trixie sang out, waving her arms akimbo and galloping across my driveway to Vito's and up the front porch in two gazelle-like strides. Green and Red swung around and stared like raccoons caught in a dumpster while Vito poked his head outside the front door like a genuine culprit. Trixie stared at Mike Green and grinned. It made her look like Bloody Mary from ‘South Pacific’. Mostly because she forgot to check her lipstick and her two front teeth were smeared with ‘Blind Date Burgundy’.

Red stared at Trixie's teeth and Mike Green stared at Trixie's cleavage. Typical reactions from some not so typical visitors. Vito saw Trixie, exchanged stares with Red and Green, shrugged a ‘whaddaygonnado?’ with his shoulders and slunk out onto the front porch.

“Hey, Trix. How's tricks?”

“Oh, fine, Vito, just fine,” Trixie beamed. She was clearly triumphant that flouncing up the porch steps had yielded some good bosom bounces. I made a pact with myself not tell her about her teeth later. “Oh, so sorry, Vito! Didn't see you had company!” she lied. She might not have been from Jersey, but sometimes she could sling it with the best of us. No wonder we're buds.

“No problem, Trix, no problem,” Vito said. But he looked a little stressed, like there was a problem. “This here’s, uh...”

“Mike Green.”

“Oh, a pleasure I'm sure.” Trixie pumped his hands with both of hers, face beaming, as she held them momentarily captive between her breasts.

“And this here, is, uh,” Vito began.

“Annie McMay,” Red said.

Trixie turned all slitty-eyed again and glared from Annie to Mike, and then turned the Death Stun Stare on Vito. Vito knew better. “Annie's my, uh...”

“Niece,” Annie said, extending a hand toward Trixie. Trixie did all but snarl. She looked like a Doberman with lipstick.

Vito tried again. “And, uh, Mike… he's Annie's, uh...”

“Co-worker!” Mike Green exclaimed a la K., his wrist immediately going limp. Trixie winced. She shot a rocket glare at Vito.

"Nice to meet you," she lied to Mike and Annie. "Catch you on the flip side, Vito. Gotta get Mina inside." And with that she hastily flounced back to the Jeep.

I cringed for Trixie. Clearly she hadn't encountered the crush-on-the-gay-guy thing too often. She swung open her door, threw herself in the seat and rummaged around for a cigarette. "Stupid queers," she muttered, finding a half crushed butt in the ashtray, and shoved the lighter on.

"K.'s gay," I responded automatically.

"K. doesn't count. K. never tried to date me," Trixie said.

"You just met the guy! How does that qualify as trying to date you?"

"Well he might have. If he hadn't tried to fool me."

"How did he fool you?"

"He's wearing straight wear."

"Huh?"

"Two mismatched socks, tie has barbeque and/or chili stains on it, should have had a haircut a week and a half ago, and definitely does not have his nails done," Trixie snipped while puffing her cigarette stub and rearranging her boobs back into their June Cleaver position.

"Geez. You got all that from a handshake?"

"Sure. Appletree was good for something."

I gulped and made a vow not to become neurotic about the kind of information Trixie gleaned from me on a day to day basis. Yeeshkabiddle.

"C'mon. We really should get you inside," she said. "You don't look so good."

I stared ahead at Ma's and Auntie's cars, and turned and stuck my tongue out at Trixie.

"Back at you. But I'm going in with you anyway. Besides, I want to find out why maybe-not-so-gay Mike Green and Annie McMay are still gawking at you."

I looked up. She was right. But then again, what with my skull embolisms, skunk stinky smells and forehead hickeys, getting gawked at was hardly a surprise.

Trixie had me up and out of her Jeep almost as quick as she'd rearranged her boobs. She hauled me out the passenger side door, suspending me by my right arm. While she partially dislocated my armpit I thought Trixie might be taking her kick-boxing classes a tad too seriously. Which was probably why I held her nose and yelled, "OWWW!" at her, which got me dropped like a sack of potatoes. That was how I ended up sprawled on my keester in the middle of my driveway. I looked up and saw Mike Green, pseudo gay guy, transfixed by Trixie's boobs, while Red and Vito looked at me with long suffering looks usually worn by pictures of patron saints in museums.

"OH-MY-GOD-THERE-HER-IS! IS-HER-ALRIGHT??!" K. creened as he came bounding out my front door toward me, with ever a backward glance or three toward Mike Green. Clearly, K. hadn't missed any of Vito's introductions from my living room windows. I heard Trixie begin to snarl.

And so began my not-so-comfy public humiliation session, as a goodly portion of my tribe thundered out of my abode: Ma, Aunt Muriel, Bauser, Bauser's three-legged dog Jim, Norman, and – lo and behold – my sister Ethel, her husband Ike and their two Yorkies, Hansel and Gretel. While my sister's peers were into their kids, Ethel married into a canine version of the Von Trapp family. When she and Ike talked about having a big family, it was in reference to adopting canine brothers and sisters for Hansel and Gretel. Go figure.

While these thoughts oozed along, Bauser's dog Jim decided to nurse my face back to health while Hansel and Gretel fought over which of my sandals to gnaw. In the midst of all this, I lay writhing like a tortured bug in my driveway.

I shooed Jim away from my face and made it to a sitting position. I patted Jim on the head, said, "Good doggie" and then shouted, "Look, Jim, RATS!" and pointed at Hansel and Gretel. Jim gave out a, "WOOF!" and went after the Yorkies. Or the Ratties, as I call them. They took off in a pack down the front yard and circled back, onto my front porch then over to Vito's in a collective bounding leap. Well, at least Jim and Gretel did. Hansel got stuck in between the porch railings. Apparently he'd been consuming too many doggie Gingerbread Houses.

"OH, SWEETIEEE!! HOW ARE YOU??" K. screamed.

"I'M NOT DEAF YET," I screamed back.

"Oh, sorry," K. said. But he didn't look at me: his eyes focused on Green the whole time. Which, to my thinking, made Green look green. Maybe Trixie was right? But why?

Then Norman trudged over and held out his towel to me to help me up. What a bud. "Do you think you should go get an x-ray?" he asked.

Trixie shook her head. "I don't think she's concussed. She was strapped in, for Pete's sake."

"It's not like I was wearing a helmet, you know," I answered.

"Here, wait a minute." She raced to her Jeep and rummaged in the glove compartment. When she came back she was brandishing a pen-size flashlight. "Look up here." Then she shone a light into my left eye. "You're eyes aren't dilated. You're fine," she said, shutting off the pen light and clipping it into her cleavage. I sighed. I wondered how Trixie's ER patients fared. I made a mental note to avoid needing emergency medical services during one of Trixie's shifts.

I got hauled inside by the tribe, minus Vito, Red and Green. I hugged Ethel and Ike. "Sorry, I forgot all about your visit, and Ma's," I said.

Ethel shrugged. "We're just passing through for a few days. We thought it would be fun to catch up with you and Ma together, before we visit Ike's family in Connecticut," she said.

I looked out the door and saw Gretel pulling at Hansel's tail while he lay stuck between the spindles. "We better get your fatties inside," I said.

Ethel mumbled, "Only Hansel's fat. He's on a diet. He can't help it. He eats Gretel's cookies."

I got washed and realigned on my sofa in a clean T-shirt and shorts, complete with a shiny red and purple face. Meanwhile, Vinnie ate pepperoni slices from Aunt Muriel, along with Jim and Hansel and Gretel. Which made me pretty relieved that Bauser would eventually be taking Jim home. I wasn't sure where my sister and Ike were sleeping that night, but I was glad there was no room in my house for multiple pet pepperoni poots. Pew.

Ma came back from upstairs. "She must get lonesome being upstairs alone all day, so I installed a small TV and DVD player for her," she said. I reminded her that normally Marie's in the kitchen until lunchtime, while Vinnie lounges in the basement.

"The basement? Oh no; not for our dear boy," Ma and Aunt Muriel cooed in tandem. Vinnie looked up while Ma stroked his head. He grinned conspiratorially, bestowing a smile full of pearly white corn teeth, studded with pepperoni bits. I furrowed.

"Well, just so long as Marie doesn't have any more eggs," I said.

"You mean she's had eggs?" Aunt Muriel asked.

"Yup."

"But where are all the babies?" she asked.

We all kind of looked away. Especially Bauser. "She had eggs by herself, Aunt Muriel," I said. "There was no, umm... Mr. Marie."

"But if she already had the eggs..."

I shook my head. Apparently, biology – other than your own - wasn't exactly a school requisite back in the day.

Norman cleared his throat. "It's like, umm... ya know... chicken eggs. If there's no rooster to, um… ya know… then, um... they're just eggs. Like you buy in the store."

"Oh," said Aunt Muriel. "Can we eat them?"

We all cringed. Thankfully, Ma dove in. "Anyway, it doesn't matter. Marie's perfectly fine up there, and Vinnie's much happier not being locked in the basement," she said, snuggling her forehead up against Vinnie's. Vinnie responded by purring louder and schlurping Ma's nose. "Besides, she seems to really like musicals; especially Fred Astaire," she went on. We all looked at each other blankly and shrugged. Who knew?

After some altercations about going to the hospital vs. ordering pizza, we settled down with a cool drink and some hot debriefing. And a very, very cold ice pack on my head. I gave some not so Lancaster-polite snippets about How-weird, flaming feces, opportunistic muggers and incompetent fire police.

"But I don't understand about Red and Green," Trixie whined. "What were U.S. Marshals doing at EEJIT?"

"Something about Red being from around here, and seeing the flaming feces trouble with EEJIT and Buy-A-Lots, yada yada," I said. "Has anyone actually ordered a pizza? Or something for a cluster headache?"

"But why did you think Green was a dry cleaning salesman?" Bauser asked.

"I told you. Red was subbing for Mrs. Phang because she said Mrs. Phang was out on a vacation day," I began. "So when Green and Red showed up at EEJIT, right after the fire, I figured they were selling some kind of fire and smoke dry cleaning package."

"Wait a minute, wait a minute," Aunt Muriel chanted. "You mean to tell me that when you come back with Vito's dry cleaning, that Red was subbing for Mrs. Phang?"

"Uh, well, um, yeah. So what?"

Ma and Aunt Muriel clapped hands to their foreheads. "Oh boy," Aunt Muriel said, and headed for the kitchen and the Wodka.

We all took the hint and indulged in a makeshift happy hour. Then we chatted about my Girl Scout good deeds re: Vito and his dry cleaning fetish and the burning Buy-A-Lots.

"There's more," said Bauser. Norman nodded, and draped his towel around his shoulders. Then the doorbell rang; the pizza man cometh.

I knew that K. placed the pizza order when it came from Frederique's instead of PizzaNow!, and cost three times more. We all attempted to pay for the pizza, but Ma and Aunt Muriel won the stand-off while the delivery kid grew a beard. Aunt Muriel pulled out a credit card and handed it to the kid, trumping Ma's cash. "Not your credit card!" Ma shrieked.

"It's alright. It's Max's." Aunt Muriel smiled. "Part of our agreement. Emergency funds," she said. Ma shrugged. I nodded. It smelt like emergency pizza to me.

The delivery kid left with a big smile and a huge tip, thanks to Uncle Max. K. served up our pizza buffet amongst draped clean linens, bottles of red and white wine, individual bottles of sparkling water, candles, Mediterranean olives and a multitude of nice glasses I knew I didn't own.

Answering my quizzical expression, K. said, "Your mom called and said you were having a crowd."

I looked at Ma. She sucked on an olive.

"Well, I know how busy you'd be, ordinarily," K. offered. "And after all this – pew!" he said, waving his hand and lighting a match.

Pew was right. But this time at least it wasn't me. Jim lay sprawled in the middle of the dining room floor, gazing lovingly up at the largesse, and pooting pepperoni.

After opening up the screen doors, turning up the AC, and lecturing Aunt Muriel about the vices of pepperoni and pets, we figured we were defumagated enough to eat. We divvied ourselves up amongst the meal when the front door opened. It was Vito.

"Sorry, sorry, sorry, Toots," he said, apologetically holding palms toward us. "I don't mean to interrupt your plans here. I just wanted to see how yous was doing."

"I'm okay."

"Well just so longs as you're not knocked out no more."

Aunt Muriel leaped into the foyer. "Oh, Vito, we're so glad you're here!"

Vito flinched backward an inch at her brightness. "Huh? You are?"

"Why yes, aren't we, Louise?"

Ma brought up the flanks. "Yes, of course. Please come in, Vito," Ma said, and closed and locked the door behind him. And stood in front of it.

"Oh, well, if you ladies insist." Vito looked around, not sure what he'd stumbled into. He looked at me. I shrugged. Damned if I knew.

"Certainly, Vito," Aunt Muriel said. "Please, come in and do help yourself."

Vito stared at the gourmet pizza meal. "Hey, well now, don't mind if I dos." He smiled and waddled the rest of the way in.

We grazed the buffet, fed and coddled pets, and sipped. It was quite a spread: white pizza with ricotta and spinach; pink pizza with buffalo mozzarella, portabella mushrooms, sundried tomatoes and shrimp; summer pizza with artichokes, zucchini, tomatoes, green onions and fresh basil; a bow tie pasta salad with grape tomatoes, yellow tomatoes and tomatillos, au vinaigrette; an antipasto platter with prosciutto, salami, roast beef, smoked turkey, parmesan chunks and seafood salad; and a large tossed Mediterranean salad. And, for dessert, what appeared to be individual cheesecakes, along with some kind of raspberry brownie sandwiches. Only Trixie longed for pretzels. "What's a party without pretzels?" she whined. K. hung his head while I waved off Ma and Aunt Muriel. They would never understand the fetish thingy most of Lancaster – hell, most of PA – has for pretzels. Even I don't get it, and I live here. But I learned long ago not to refute it. The path of least resistance is best met by serving pretzels.

K. gave Trixie a breadstick and a salt shaker and told her it was an artisan pretzel. Trixie furrowed but dutifully dipped her breadstick in her beer and salted it. We finished the bountiful repast and sighed in blissful waist expanded stupors.

Norman cleared his throat. “Listen, I've got to get going. Janice is going to kill me. Unless she thinks I'm working,” he said. Bauser patted him on the back of his towel. “But listen, the thing is, I really need to get online to check my runs,” he said. “Actually, I need to check who's checking my runs.”

“No problem, dude. I've got packet sniffers out,” Bauser said.

Norman almost smiled. “Really? Wow, that's great!”

We stared at Norman and Bauser much the same way someone stares at their first plate of seaweed salad. “In that case, I guess I can have a beer after all,” Norman sighed. Then frowned. “Someone's got breath mints, right? It would be a long story for me if she smelt beer on me.”

“Who could tell with all this garlic?” Vito asked. K. shot Vito a look that screamed ‘Puh-lease’.

K. brought Norman a bottle of beer and a glass and set them down before him. Norman tried to unscrew the twist top – except he failed, because it wasn’t a twist top. Then Norman not only needed a bottle opener but some Band-Aids and a tourniquet. Ma got some Band-Aids and a supply of dish towels while Vito opened Norman's beer bottle with his teeth. We all winced.

Norman raised his bottle to Vito in thanks, and took a swig. He choked a little, but after another swig he seemed almost not unhappy. Then he began.

“Awhile ago, before all the news coverage, I was wondering about the coincidence of the Buy-A-Lots' fires. You see, not all the other fires made national press coverage like the coincidence of Buy-A-Lots' Lancaster location with EEJIT's Lancaster location, which any idiot could have seen. I mean, I recognized others before.”

“Huh?” I asked.

“There seems to be a pattern of burning Buy-A-Lots' with new store openings.”

“How'd you notice that?” I asked. Everyone leaned in.

"Well, because I had a discussion about the data that How-weird used to sell Buy-A-Lots on renewing. And convincing them to open up an umpteenth new store in Lancaster County."

"You had words with How-weird?"

"Because he'd hawked sample data. It was bogus. And he knew it," Norman said, and he took another swig – bigger this time – of his beer. And coughed. He got attacked by a group of well meaning slaps on the back from Vito.

"Data, schmata. I don't get it," K. whined.

"Garbage in, garbage out," Ma said, and chewed another olive.

Norman continued. "The data that's used to test new algorithms is a fairly steady, representative sample. No outliers, no data surprises. That way we can see how the algorithm is working without having data quality issues to muddy up the works."

"Algorithm?" Aunt Muriel and Vito asked. They looked at each other. Vito beamed. Muriel scowled.

"An algorithm is a mathematical equation that provides the statistics we're looking for," said Norman, coddling his new friend between his hands. "EEJIT's applications use various algorithms to determine various outcomes, using various sets of data. The data is varied – always contains some kind of minor flaws – because it's refreshed periodically, and from various sources. So we need to ensure the algorithm's stability before using it against actual data."

"Oh. Sos it's kinda like testing a recipe but making sure all the food is good, and not rotten. Or making sure you're not testing a chocolate cake recipe using brussel sprouts," Vito said.

"I like brussel sprouts," Ethel interjected.

"Hey, me too!" Vito beamed. He was followed by a chorus of, "Shh!"

"Anyway, the recipe analogy is pretty good," said Norman easily. A little too easily. I wasn't sure if Norman had ever had a whole beer before. I was beginning to hope he would make his excuses to Janice and stay nappily at Bauser's place. "Anyway, Howard insisted on using the test data for presentation to Buy-A-Lots. I warned him it would present like a Buy-A-Lots Utopia. I also warned him about using a disclaimer about the sample data. He didn't. "

"So?" asked K.

Norman sighed. “We sold them the actual package using virtual data, before the actual data was incorporated. So Buy-A-Lots ran their marketing programs – and budgets – with the test data. Which is bad, because the actual data we sent them, to replace the virtual data, was almost a year old. Either way, the test data predicted plenty of future Buy-A-Lots all over.”

“What's so different about that?” Bauser asked.

“No, I mean, like right on top of an existing store. Or, say, in the middle of the Susquehanna.”

“Would make for one hell of a fishing department,” Bauser retorted.

“I suppose opening retail stores don't use a restaurant row concept?” asked Ike.

“Similar, but not exactly,” Norman said. “According to Buy-A-Lots' market analysis, they don't want to be the only Buy-A-Lots in a county, but at the same time they certainly don't want to out-convenience their own convenience. Like building right next to an existing store.”

Trixie’s “Huh?”came out muffled, through a mouthful of Raspberry Brownie sandwich.

“The thing is, Buy-A-Lots ran with the whacky data. And How-weird knew it. They made a lot of corporate decisions – and investments – based on bogus assumptions.”

“Oh. Like Iraq?” asked K. We all nodded at him. He was getting it.

“Then, when we gave the data update, with the real data, that blew their forecasting out of the water. So now How-weird is trying to figure out a way to make the bogus data seem actual, and the actual data seem somewhat bogus. But incrementally, because we have to wean their system off the fake whacky data and onto the real whacky data, but without too many whacky results.”

“How do you know all this?” I asked.

“Because How-weird's making me do the tweaks. He's finally realized he can't shift the blame to the real data, so he's shifting it to development. And of course, he'd never shift the blame by admitting a mistake, or the truth,” Norman said. “Which means every time I ‘fix’ something, to try to get the actual data to give similar bogus results, I'm meddling with years of research. And development.”

Gack. So that's why Norman kept getting corralled into weekends. Eeek.

“So that's why I've been running tons of backups. Assuming, once all's said and done, Howard wants the king's men to put all the bits and pieces together again.” Norman took another swig of beer. I made another hash mark in my napkin. This might have made three or more whole swigs of beer he had taken. Maybe in his whole entire lifetime.

“Anyway, the system started to get real funky when Norman ran the data re-runs,” Bauser said. “So awhile back I did a concurrent live time monitor while Norman ran a fake run.”

“And?” I asked.

“Someone is monitoring each and every run of Norman's, but only against the sample data,” Bauser said.

“How can you tell that?” asked Ike.

“Because I put out packet sniffers,” replied Bauser.

“Huh?” we all asked.

Ma clapped a hand to her forehead. “Of course!” I looked at her and winced. Ma and Bauser looked around at the rest of us, and realized we were clueless. “A packet sniffer is a program that is able to go out across a network and tell you who's sending out what – whether it's an email or FTPing data. The more sophisticated ones can even tell you who's packet sniffing you back,” she explained.

Bauser blushed. “Well actually, not more sophisticated – more like modified.”

Ma looked at him like she'd just discovered chocolate. If Bauser kept playing his cards this way, he'd be out of EEJIT and in New Jersey with Ma's firm before the ink was dry.

“Anyway, we still can't pinpoint who's spying on my runs,” Norman explained.

“How come?” asked Vito.

Bauser said, “Too many sales reps logged into EEJIT from too many outside locations.”

“So that's why I ran concurrent runs against the sample data,” Norman said, with another swig. “I haven't done that before, mostly because I was afraid it might hang the system while other data runs were going out. But the fire was the perfect opportunity. I figured most everyone was logged out, and mine would be the only programs compiling. I'm hoping the concurrent behavior will get the Watcher to launch multiple tracking. Which is easier to be sloppy with, and maybe give us a clue."

"Mina, I'm impressed that you work with these guys," Vito said.

"Work with us? Heck, she just hangs around and gets konked on the noggin," Bauser joshed. I tossed a breadstick at him. Jim caught it mid-flight.

Suddenly we were all chatting away with different people and different conversations about the same thing: whodunit? When at last we came to a lull, Trixie piped up, as she looked out the window.

"Gee, Vito, I'm surprised you didn't bring your niece over with you."

Vito flushed, Aunt Muriel choked on some melted ice cubes and Ma cleared her throat. "Oh, Annie, you mean," Vito said, smiling and showing off his bridgework. "Oh, well, uh, she had to go back home to, uh, Virginia."

"Really?" Trixie asked, still looking outside.

"Yeah, uh, that boss of hers, he's got her doing lots of stuff for him," Vito said. He mopped his brow with a crumpled napkin.

"Gee, does she live close to the Beltway?" Ike asked.

"Huh?"

Now it was Ethel's turn. "Vito, does your niece live in Northern Virginia?"

"Oh, yeah, sure..."

"Gee, where? We live in Springfield."

"Where does she work?" toyed Trixie.

"Uh, D.C., I think..."

"Then don't you think it's kind of funny that she's been parked across the street from us for the past two hours?" Trixie asked.

Vito gulped and looked a lot like Vinnie when he's about to cough up a hairball. I looked over at Trixie. She had a very determined look on her face. I suddenly felt very, very sympathetic for Appletree or any other prospective boyfriend she might have.

Everyone, including Vinnie, Jim and the Ratties, dove to the living room windows to gape at Vito's niece, Annie, sitting parked across the street from my house. Except for Trixie and Vito. I didn't move because I couldn't. My head felt like cement. Besides, K. was using my shoulders for a perch.

"So, what is it?" Trixie asked Vito.

"Hey, Trix," Vito began.

"You wanna see your little doggie again? I heard what you did from my old boyfriend George at the animal shelter."

CHAPTER 6

(Tuesday Night)

Vito's lip quivered and he began to cry. It started out with his back turned then went into a full soaker hose drenching. During the course of which everyone got distracted from the windows.

"Sos I called the animal shelter and says I want to adopt the little fella," Vito sniffed. "But they says they can't adopt a dog out what's not theirs. So I had to turn him in."

Aunt Muriel exchanged glances with Ma. Ma dove into the kitchen and got the roll of paper towels and handed them to Auntie. Aunt Muriel broke off two towels, handed one to Vito, and they blew in unison. Vito smiled wanly. The rest of us grabbed our napkins and blew.

"So now what?" cried K.

"I gotta leave him there for 72 hours, on account of he could be licensed to someone who might be looking for him. The dumb jerk. Who could let a little fella like Stanley run around, anyways?"

"Stanley?" we all parroted.

"I had to call him something! Besides, it's a very historical and dignified name."

"Only if you're a rabbit," said K.

"No, that's Harvey," Aunt Muriel corrected.

"Do you mean like Stanley the Great, of Poland?" asked Ike.

"Exactly!" Vito smiled. Ethel hung her head.

"Well, he might actually have been lost. It could have just been an accident," Ike said. Ethel elbowed him.

"So what happens after 72 hours?" Norman asked.

Vito wiped his nose and blew. "I get to go in and get him," he said. "Unless he does have a previous owner, and he claims him before I do." He looked at Trixie and sniffed.

"Oh, for Pete's sakes," Trixie said. "You already put dibs on him. You don't think they want another doggie for their collection, do you?"

"No, no. I guess not."

"Hey, what time is it?" Trixie asked.

Bauser checked his wristwatch – which has the accuracy of the Hubble Space Telescope – and said it was 10:11:04:0000567 p.m. Since Vito had turned the gnawing Terrier in at a little after 9 a.m., we assured him he was over twelve hours into what was going to eventually be the home stretch. Only 59:49:56:0000033 to go. In layman's terms, another two and a half days. Another two dinners. Another three bird fluffed lunches. Yikes. I set my shoulders and jaw line into the ready position for the upcoming dyspepsia and associated Swifferings.

"Don't you think we should invite her in?" asked K. "I mean, after all, she is his niece – she can't possibly stay out there all night!"

"Who are you talking about?" Norman asked.

"Annie," he answered.

Vito leapt across the room and stood in front of the door. "NO! NO! NO!" Ma and Muriel shrieked.

"She probably just forgot something. Or maybe she's counting change," Vito added.

"You could at least offer her dessert," Trixie said levelly.

"Look, I've really gotta go. I could bring her a brownie on my way out, and let her know she's welcome to come in and join you," Norman said.

After some micro-debate and some more NO-NO-NOing from Vito, Ma and Auntie, K. packaged up a brownie in a tin foil swan a la doggie bag and sent Norman trudging across the street toward Annie's car. Vito stood by the windows, looking out and sweating a lot. I checked my AC. Yup, it was working. Do senior guys get hot flashes?

Ethel, Ike and K. started cleaning up. Oddly, Aunt Muriel and Ma hovered around Vito's window watching.

“I thought they gave you today to decide about being on the Plan,” I said, and let Bauser in about Lee and her crew. He shrugged.

“Either I'm on the Plan or I'm out of work,” he said. “But even if I'm out of work, EEJIT still owes me a boat load of back vacation pay,” he finished

“How? I thought they bought you out already? Isn't that why you bought the wall-to-wall TV?”

“They bought me out some, not all. Part of my strategy for job security, with the corporate takeover. I figured they would hate parting with a full payout.” I nodded. I had to hand it to Bauser: he was pretty smart.

There came the sound of squealing tires, and a car sped away from the curb. Vito looked out the window. “See, she was probably just counting change, after all,” he said. “She's got a long drive ahead of her, don’t forget.” He sat down and mopped his brow.

A firecracker went off outside. Then some cursing and shouting in Vietnamese went off. The doorbell rang. I opened the door and saw Mrs. Phang. “This yours,” she snarled and pointed.

“What?” I asked.

“Man in driveway!” she huffed at me.

I went down the front path and saw Norman sitting at the bottom of the driveway at the curb, holding his forehead in his hands and bleeding. Apparently, Norman got shot.

After some shrieking and more shouting in Vietnamese and various regional American accents, we got Norman inside while Trixie cleaned him up and gave him the once over.

“You're lucky; it just grazed you,” she said, cleaning his wound with vodka and making him wince. Ma and Aunt Muriel winced, too, but I had a feeling that was more about Trixie using their Absolut. Bauser came back into the house with Norman's towel, and held it out to him. Norman slung it over his shoulder, and pressed a cold beer to his forehead.

“Well this is just ridiculous!” K. pronounced, hands on hips. “I mean, really, what is this neighborhood coming to?”

Vito tsk-tsked him. “Hey, this neighborhood's good. This shooting is a very unusual happenstance,” he said.

"I think we should call the police," Trixie said, getting all slitty eyed.

"No!" Vito and I shouted, and looked at each other. Clearly, we both had very different reasons for wanting Trixie to never call the police.

Trixie pouted. "He did get shot at, you know. And it wasn't exactly a hunting accident."

"You make too much big deal," Mrs. Phang said.

"Over a gunshot wound?" Ike asked. If his voice rose any higher, Ethel would have to pull him down off the ceiling.

"Just accident. I miss." Mrs. Phang shrugged.

"YOU SHOT ME?" Norman asked.

"NO ON PURPOSE! NO ON PURPOSE!" Mrs. Phang screamed. "MAKE MISTAKE! YOU NO HURT!"

"I know I'm going to regret this," Norman began, after taking an enormous swig of his new beer – which had been opened by Bauser, this time – "but I have to ask: if you weren't aiming at me, who were you trying to shoot?"

Mrs. Phang threw her arms up in the air, and sat down. She looked at Vito. Vito shrugged and sat down next to her, and patted her on the shoulder. We all winced and thought him brave.

"The least you could do is offer me a drink, Muriel," she said in perfect, unaccented English. "It's pretty much over, anyway." Vito and Ma nodded.

Aunt Muriel whipped up a drink, and the rest of us made ourselves ready for a good story. K. dug out the brownies and cheesecakes. Vinnie snuffled peacefully in the corner. The dogs all sat pretty.

"A few years ago, my husband wanted to retire and move to Lancaster, to be near his sister," Mrs. Phang said.

Trixie yelled, "Your husband?" She was the only one of us ballsy enough to ask what we all thought: Mrs. Phang was just too mean to have a husband. She was the type that probably killed her husband immediately after mating, just like a praying mantis.

"Yes, yes, my husband. Cong Phang. We were married for thirty-five years," she said. Her face softened. She looked down and spotted Trixie's handbag, and her Swank's. She looked around. "May I?" she asked.

"Sure," Trixie said, handing her the cancer sticks. Mrs. Phang moved to sit near the screen door. Ma made her tight lipped face; she hates smoking. But she hates missing a good story more.

Mrs. Phang lit the cigarette and blew a puff of smoke outside. She smiled. "First one in twenty years." Then she continued with her story: "My husband owned a small hardware store in Hackensack. I worked in the hospital. I helped patients sort out their medical billing crises after they got through their health crises.

"Cong wanted to retire. The store had made a decent profit, I'd been working steadily, and we didn't have kids. We couldn't." Vito nodded his head in sympathy. "Besides, another Buy-A-Lots was opening up, and it was getting harder and harder for him to compete with the big box stores.

"So I retired from Tri-County Hospital. Cong sold the store and we sold the house. Cong moved here ahead of me, to scout out the area while staying with his sister and her family. Less than a month later, he died of a heart attack."

"Oh jeez," Trixie said, and helped herself to one of her own cigarettes.

"It gets worse," Mrs. Phang continued. "You see, Cong stayed with his sister to help her and her husband out with their business. It was failing." Mrs. Phang let out another puff. "After the funeral, I found out he'd let his life insurance lapse. I also found out he'd 'helped his sister out' by investing the sale of the hardware store, and our house, into Lickety-Split Laundry."

"Oh dear," Aunt Muriel said, and found her way to the kitchen and the Absolut.

"With Cong gone, my brother-in-law, Fu, had a lot more stress, with all the workload back on him. That's why my sister-in-law, Fen, thinks he drove off Route 283 in the delivery van. He must have fallen asleep at the wheel," she finished.

"But why the phony accent?" I asked, and added, "And why all the yelling?"

"It was easier getting legitimate customers in and out quickly that way. I'm not really retail-oriented." She shrugged. "So there I was, stuck with no real home and no job. I went back to the hospital, but they'd already hired for my old position. And since I'd removed myself from the pecking order, if I started back there again, it would be almost like starting all over. Complete with getting 4 weeks vacation whacked back down to 1."

"Ouch," Bauser said sympathetically.

"My sister-in-law was in similar straits, and we talked about living together. But we couldn't figure out if it would be better for her to sell the business and move up with me, while I hopped back on the bottom rung at the hospital, or for me to move here and try to help her out."

"Well, you're here... so things worked out, right?" Ma asked.

"For the most part, now. But in the beginning it was pretty tough. Especially while I was trying to figure things out, and stuck with the apartment in Hasbrouck Heights," she said.

"Hasbrouck Heights?" Ma and Aunt Muriel asked.

"It was a 6-month rental, after we sold the house, while Cong was looking for a place here. But when all those plans went kaflooey, I needed some kind of income, just to pay the rent and eat until I could think." Mrs. Phang stubbed out her cigarette. "That's when I started working at the Bagels 'n' Borscht."

Ma and Aunt Muriel looked at Mrs. Phang with pity and awe. Ethel and I nodded. Ike was still trying to wrap his head around bagels, much less borscht.

"It wasn't so bad. And it turned out to be a good thing. I used to get my lunch there a lot when I worked at the hospital. The Bagels 'n' Borscht was right across the street," she explained. "Anyway, I wandered in for lunch one day and told my tale of woe to Rachael, the gal who worked there, and it turned out they were hiring. So there I was."

"So Lickety-Split Laundry must be a success, right?" K. asked nicely.

"It's getting there. But when we were bleeding all the cash Cong invested, along with most of the income, it was pretty frustrating."

"Start-up costs?" Norman asked.

Mrs. Phang shook her head. "Gambling debts. It turned out that Fen, my naïve sister-in-law, was paying off my nephew's online gambling debts with the investment monies. And our income."

"Isn't that illegal?" Trixie asked.

"Nope. Online gambling is legal if you're over twenty-one. And his mom was willingly paying off his debt." Mrs. Phang sighed. "But he's all grown up, with a great paying sales job. He lives on the Mainline in Philly," she said. "So I had a down and out with him, and told him he'd have to help us out of this mess. And then I cut up his credit cards."

"You did?" Ethel asked, with a nervous glance at Ike. I opened my mouth, then closed it. I didn't want to know.

"Excuse me, but what exactly has all this got to do with shooting me? Accidentally, I mean," Norman asked.

"I thought you knew the redhead. I've been tailing her for a few days. I saw you bring out a silver squash to her, so I figured you were friends."

K. jumped in and explained about the leftover brownies and cheesecakes and the superiority of foil swans vs. doggie bags. Mrs. Phang agreed and helped herself to a cheesecake. Then we shushed him.

"She pretended to be some good Samaritan looking for part-time work to my sister-in-law, on the one day I went out," she said. "I wasn't expecting any pick-ups or deliveries, so I figured I was in the clear."

"Oh dear. An entire day without one customer dropping off dry cleaning," K. tsked.

"No, not dry cleaning. Prescriptions," Mrs. Phang said. We all looked at her with a collective question mark. She rolled her eyes. "My gambling-prone nephew, Fa, is a pharmaceutical sales rep."

"So?" Ike asked.

"Look, Fa got pulled out of debt, but with my retirement money. I explained to Fa that he had to repay me, and his mother."

Ethel frowned. "I don't understand." Clearly, her head was spinning too. And it wasn't just because of the late night beverages or sugar overload.

"Fa gets tons of free samples. Most of which just sit in the extra bedrooms in his condo, because a lot of the meds need to be kept in climate controlled spaces. He had so much stored there, he got bonked on his noggin when a box of steroid inhalers fell on his head. And that's what gave him the idea."

We stared blankly at Mrs. Phang in unison. Except for Trixie, who shouted, "Oh!!" and clapped her hand to her mouth and hopped up and down. "You're selling prescription samples!" Mrs. Phang touched the side of her nose with her finger.

"But how the... who the... where... huh?" I asked, none too coherently.

"Of course you know, prescription medicines, especially for retired seniors, are so very, very expensive," Mrs. Phang began.

"YOU'RE SELLING STOLEN SAMPLES?" I screamed not too nicely.

"They're not stolen. They're... redistributed," Mrs. Phang replied.

"BUT YOU'RE TRAFFICKING PRESCRIPTIONS?" I asked.

"Umm... no dear. You are," Aunt Muriel explained.

"You know, I'd like to hear more about this, but maybe we could talk about it in the morning. Late morning. Don't you think we should go home?" Ike asked as he stood up. Ethel glared. Ike sunk back onto the sofa and sulked. Both Ratties scurried up to offer some slobber and sympathy.

"So how long has Mina been a mule?" Bauser asked.

"Well, it didn't start out that way," Aunt Muriel began. "We all used to take turns. But then there were the mix-ups..."

"WHO IS WE?" I yelped.

"Well, the church choir; the Brethren Breakfast crews; some of my neighbors; some of your neighbors; some of their relatives – and our online teams of course – and sometimes your mother..." Aunt Muriel trailed off.

"I'm the Jersey connection," Ma added. I hung my head.

"I got concerned that the laundromat was being watched," Mrs. Phang said. "And then, if a real customer was around, my sister-in-law would get flustered and mix things up – she's such a goodie-goodie. So someone expecting high blood pressure medicine sometimes wound up with decongestants, and that wasn't good. After all, we're trying to help these people, not kill them."

"Excuse me, but, at the risk of again regretting asking this, what does this have to do with shooting me?" Norman asked again, bandaged head held in his hands.

"I wanted to scare you, not shoot you," Mrs. Phang answered. "Besides, it's only a BB gun. For the life of me I can't figure out how you got hurt." Trixie heaved a huge sigh of relief. I guess she was glad Norman's gunshot wound wasn't really a gunshot wound.

"I figured you could tell me who the redhead is since you were bringing her a doggie bag," Mrs. Phang said matter-of-factly.

K. mumbled something about, "Swan. It was a foil S-W-A-N. Not something you bring home to feed Ratties..."

"Well, anyway, the stupid thing went off in my hand by accident and scared the crap out of me."

"Oh. Sorry," Norman said.

"No problem," Mrs. Phang replied. Norman sighed.

"The redhead poking around the shop, especially at the end of the month, clued us in," Mrs. Phang said. "Her posing as cheapo help was pretty cheeky."

"You see, we used to have a little problem with everyone's re-order dates winding up on the end of the month," Aunt Muriel explained. Oh, yes. Of course. It was a clear as mud to me now.

"Anyway, one day while Muriel and I were trying to improve deliveries, in walked Vito with a gym bag full of dry cleaning, and a bottle of Lipitor. It was supposed to go to Eric Glassbaum, but wound up with Vito's shirts by accident."

My curiosity bit. So did I. "So?"

"Well, luckily I recognized Vito from the Bagels 'n' Borscht." Mrs. Phang smiled nostalgically. I wondered whether happier times were ahead, or far, far behind us.

"Yeah, that was some coincidence," Vito said. He grinned. "I used to be a regular."

"Anyway, we got to feeling each other out, and we found out that actually Vito is very simpatico about deep discount prescriptions for retired seniors. And he's been a great help," Aunt Muriel said. "We charge a fee, of course, but not nearly the mark-up the drug companies do. And we're not cheating them; after all, if these companies can afford to give it away for free, it's not missed income."

"So you're reselling samples. For profit?" Bauser asked. Aunt Muriel and Vito and Mrs. Phang nodded. Bauser blew out a long, soft whistle. "Umm, you know, this is kind of a very illegal thing to do."

"I know, I know," Mrs. Phang said unhappily. "But we were really in a jam. And it's not forever; just until we put the money back that Fa and Fu bled from the business."

"How's Vito helping?" I asked warily. All of a sudden I sensed the end of the world.

"He matches the requests with the orders. He's Logistics. Vito makes sure the right prescription gets delivered to the right person."

"So how does Logistics deliver?" I asked, rubbing my forehead. I had a feeling I already knew the answer.

"Well, dear, you do. You deliver the prescription orders in the pocket of a shirt in some dry cleaning in Vito's gym bag," Aunt Muriel answered. "Mrs. Phang exchanges that for a box chock full of prescriptions, along with a clean shirt or two, to muffle any rattling sounds the pills might make. And you bring it all back to Vito. Then he makes his delivery rounds."

"And this was working great, too, until that stupid redhead started hanging around," Mrs. Phang grimaced. "And we were so close, too. I figured by next month Vito would be delivering 'Thank You' promotions to all our customers, to let them know the dry cleaning business was really going into the dry cleaning business. We even printed out $10 dry cleaning gift cards to distribute." She smiled proudly.

"Well, Vito should have been able to tell you who the redhead is," I said. "She's his niece, and her boss is a U.S. Marshal. I guess she's his assistant or something."

Vito clapped his collective hands to his forehead. The rest of us looked at each other. All except for Ike; he snored.

"Uh, maybe I better explain. Geez, this is awkward. I think I might have kind of have a confession to make," Vito said to Mrs. Phang and Aunt Muriel. They both suddenly resembled gargoyles. "But ya know, it is pretty late." He glanced uneasily over at Ike and his chorus of ZZZs. Ethel walked over and flicked Ike's nose. He stopped snoring. Vinnie started.

"Maybe what we need is some coffee," Ethel said.

"Okay," I said, automatically digging out my party percolator to brew coffee for thirty people. Bauser talked with Norman, who nodded. Norman phoned home, and after a lot of Mhming said he was going to stay over at Bauser's because of working late. "It'd be hard to explain the gunshot wound this late at night, anyway," he said limply after he'd hung up.

The coffee was brewed and passed around. We pulled some chairs into the dining room – away from Ike's and Vinnie's snoring – and sat around Vito. He began.

"You see, the reason I was a regular at the Bagels 'n' Borscht was on account of my late wife, Marie," Vito said, then started to sniff. Ma rolled her eyes, went into the kitchen and came back with the roll of paper towels. Vito took a hunk and blew. "You see, my sainted Marie got poisoned by what we think was some bad pierogies. We got her to the hospital, but not soon enough. The poisoned pierogies really did a number on her system, so she was in the hospital on IV's and stuff for a couple months. Then, just when I thought she was gonna get discharged and come home, she dies."

We all offered our condolences and sympathies, but really there was very little we could say or do. Marie was gone, and I now lived in the 'Hers' portion of their townhouses. This we knew. But a little birdie fluttered through my head. Apparently Marie must have died before she picked out the His 'n' Her townhouse. Or purchased it.

"Vito, I thought I bought Marie's half of the His 'n' Her townhouses?" I asked.

"Yeah, I know."

"So?"

"I lied."

"Oh."

Vito sighed. "You see, I couldn't tell yous the truth. And I'm not so sure I can now. Look, it's like this," he said, leaning in. We all leaned in too. "I'm kind of in a witness protection program," he said.

"Oh, that's so nice, Vito. I didn't know you protect Jehovah's Witnesses. These days they probably need all the help they can get," Aunt Muriel said sleepily. Ma pinched Aunt Muriel and hissed in her ear. The penny dropped. "Oh!" Though I wondered about any remaining spare change.

"You see, Toots," Vito said, looking at me and nervously licking his lips. "My name's not exactly Vito. I mean, it is now. But before it wasn't."

"What do you mean?"

Vito took a big breath, and exhaled. Then he took another and exhaled again.

"Do you think he's hyperventilating?" Trixie whispered at me. I politely shushed her by waving my hand in her face.

"My real name is Vladimir Pryzchntchynzski," he exhaled, and looked around expectantly.

"God bless you," Ethel said sleepily.

The rest of us looked at each other. Crickets chirped. Someone shuffled their feet. Vito stared at the floor. Nothing. Then we looked over at Ma, Aunt Muriel and Mrs. Phang, and their literal open mouths.

"Oh my gosh – oh my gosh – oh my gosh," Mrs. Phang spluttered. "Of course! That's why you looked so familiar when I met you at the Bagels 'n' Borscht – it was all the pictures in the paper!"

Pictures? Paper? Huh?

"Oh dear, yes, yes," Aunt Muriel tsked. Ma shook her head. "Well, who'd have thought? It's not everyday we have dinner with a genuine Mafia Don."

Don Mafia? Who's he? Huh?

"Ummm, pardon me, Vito. I mean, uh, Vladimir," Norman began.

"No, no – it's Vito now. Really. No problemo."

"Of course. I don't mean any, erm... disrespect... but, ermm... should we know you?"

Vito smiled. "Not if I was doing my job right. Which I was, mostly. But some operations, which didn't go exactly as planned, got picked up in the local news."

"Oh," Norman said, nodding like he understood.

"You see, I'm third generation. I wasn't exactly planning on this as a career. But then Tatuś – my dad – got whacked. And I loved my Grandfather, who took us in, and I didn't want to disappoint him. Besides which, I couldn't." Vito cringed. "Just before Marie got sick, I found out some young Turks were trying to merge our family with some Italian New York family – and drugs. I got mad. I said I'd rather rat them out than see drugs come in through the Family. For chrissakes," he sighed, "that kind of garbage was what Pop said the Family kept out of our neighborhood. Back in the day, it was about protection. These days, it's all about money. It's all gone down the drain."

"So, umm... who's your Family?" Bauser asked. He took out the pain pill I'd given him earlier and swallowed it.

Mrs. Phang looked at Bauser like he'd just crawled out of a cave. "Why, Vladimir Pryzchntchynzski ran the Moils, the Jewish Polish Mafia, out of Bumville," she answered.

Jewish Polish Mafia? So that explains all the kielbasa. I wondered if kielbasa was kosher.

"Oh," the PA contingency said.

"Oh!" Aunt Muriel exclaimed, thrusting out of her chair and up onto her feet. "You're Jewish?"

"Uh, yeah, Toots. It kind of goes hand-in-hand with the Jewish Polish Mafia thing."

"Oh, well then that explains everything," Aunt Muriel said, smoothing her headband back over her charred bangs and sitting down. Vito stared at her.

"Oh!" Vito exclaimed. "You mean about the wine and cookies at St. Bart's?"

"We call it the Eucharist, Vito," Aunt Muriel corrected. "After all, if you're going to pretend to be an Episcopalian, you'll have to know these things."

Ma and I exchanged looks. Aunt Muriel was on her way to garnering yet another Episcopalian for St. Bart's. Even if he was Jewish and in a witness protection program.

"Well, I didn't want to be impolite," Vito explained sheepishly. "I thought I was supposed to drink the whole thing, lest I offend. I never been somewhere where everyone passed the same glass. Hey, you think that's sanitary?

Aunt Muriel assured him it was.

Bauser asked, "Where is Bumville?"

"It's kind of lodged between Lodi and Carlstadt," said Ma. "It's a pretty small town."

"With a bar on every corner," Vito beamed. Somewhere, far, far away, I thought I heard a ka-ching from a remote corner that housed a barstool in Bumville.

"Anyway," Vito said. "After I ratted these punks out, I was offered witness protection. They said I had to pick between Tampa or Lancaster. I really don't like the heat. So I came here."

I recalled Vito's orange neck. Yup. Florida would definitely not work out for him or his fake hair.

"And everything was going great too, until Red started hanging around Mrs. Phang's. But then we came up with another system, and I thought we were fine. But since I found out she's with Mike it makes things a little awkward."

"But why would your niece visiting you be awkward?" Aunt Muriel asked. Ma picked up Auntie's coffee mug, sniffed it, and put it down.

"Oh. Well, uh... Mike's kind of like my U.S. Marshal godfather. He said he stopped by because it turns out that the Young Squirts I got put in the pokey have been talking about getting even. I guess they stood to lose a bundle with those deals not going through. It was heard they paid someone on the outside to make an impression on me."

Gack. Didn't Vito have to go home? Wasn't my townhouse up for sale any minute now?

"So Mike's probably going to be hanging around for awhile, off and on. Which is kind of stupid. So long as it's obvious he's hanging around, no one's gonna really make a move. But I had no idea Red – Annie – was with Mike. Until today," Vito finished and gulped some coffee.

"But, now that we know who you are, doesn't this blow your cover?" Norman asked.

"Yeah, it probably will. That is if Mike and Annie think it's blown," he said.

"How do you mean?" Bauser asked.

"Look, yous alls are my friends. Heck, Mina's like family." Vito shrugged. I silently wondered if I'd become kosher by osmosis with all the cooking Vito – Vladimir – had burnt in my kitchen. And as fake-family, I also wondered if I was destined to be marked for fish food. "Unless any one of you is going to put me in the news, or write a book or something, I can't see it being that big of a deal. Unless, of course, you blab to a cop or something," Vito said, looking pointedly at Trixie. "Which would not exactly be in your best interests," he added.

"Nope, nope, nope... what happens in Mina's kitchen stays in Mina's kitchen, ha ha," Trixie stammered. Well, whaddaya know. So much for impersonating a cop's girlfriend. Huh.

Aunt Muriel furrowed her brows. "Well, what are we going to do now?" she asked.

Ma yawned. "I suggest we all go nighty-night." She yawned again. Which was catching. Because then we were all yawning.

The coffee mugs got collected and stacked in the sink. Ike lay passed out on my sofa with the Ratties. Trixie checked Norman's noggin again and gave him a cleanish bill of health. Then she checked mine, got out a package of frozen peas and thumped them on my forehead. "You better hold this on there for awhile. You're gonna have quite a lump." Great. I hoped it wouldn't clash with the other lumps.

Trixie started telling Bauser about waking Norman up every couple hours. Bauser said that wouldn't be a problem, since they would probably be up in a couple of hours, anyway. We all shuffled to the door to say our final goodbyes, and took turns patting the various pets goodnight.

I opened the front door and saw a large object sail through the air, land on Vito's front porch and explode into flames. A car skidded away.

Vito's porch was on fire.

Honestly, if it wasn't for bad luck I wouldn't have any. I sighed in resignation: there would be no sleep for me tonight. Except for Ike and Vinnie. And the damn Ratties. I felt like pinching them all.

"Yes, that's right, you heard me correctly," Trixie was saying into her cell phone. "FIRE! The address? It's, uh, next door to Mina's. 3041 Clovernook Lane."

While Trixie was on the horn, Bauser and Norman were fumbling with untangling the garden hose that lay disconnected on my front porch. They were just about to turn it on toward the flames when Vito stopped them. "Just a minute, fellas," Vito said, turning off the water spigot. "You don't wanna do that when you don't know what the fire's made of. Some kinds of fires get made worse if they're put out by regular water."

"How'd you know that?" Bauser began. Vito stared at him. Bauser exchanged glances with Norman. They put the hose back down.

Pretty soon, my neighbors were leaning off their various front porches, wondering what the early morning wienie roast was all about. Someone walked over to see if we were okay. Someone else ran over and did the same thing. Another neighbor came over and asked if we should bust Vito's door down, to rescue him. We introduced him to Vito. A new voice piped up, and said I should be ready to get Vinnie and Marie out of the house, in case we caught fire, too. Or because of fumes. Ethel and I gasped. I didn't have a carrier for Vinnie, I admitted. Ethel went inside to check on our respective furry and feathered kids. Including Ike.

Another neighbor went back across the street to get me her cat carrier to borrow. "Make sure it can fit a really, really large turkey," I yelled after her thankfully. She swiveled and gave me a funny look, and then went home.

Ethel came back outside. All our pets – feline, canine, avian – were slumberous. And not because of fume inhalation. Ethel had got the Ratties' travel gear set up and Marie's cover and supplies handy. She put a large laundry basket of mine in the foyer. Along with a large, wooden carving board and a roll of duct tape I'd forgotten about.

"What do you want me to do? Wash and fold him?"

"No, stupid. Put him in the laundry basket, and duct tape on the carving board for a top. We can get him to Aunt Muriel's in about 15 minutes. It wouldn't be so bad."

"Oh."

Herb Nelson's son, Ned, was visiting for the weekend. He was also a volunteer fireman back home in Des Moines. He was the one who brought over Herb's emergency kitchen fire extinguisher. ("Don't you know every kitchen should have one of these? There are some fires you make worse by putting out with water," he said.) Ned had the flames out in a few minutes just as the fire trucks arrived. And the police.

After some assurances that neither one of our homes would be ablaze again that night, Bauser took Norman and Jim home. Aunt Muriel commiserated with Mrs. Phang about the late night activities and Mrs. Phang's dopey sister-in-law getting on her nerves. So Aunt Muriel invited her for a last minute sleepover. Mrs. Phang accepted, popped open a cell phone, said something in Vietnamese – the tone of which was familiarly unfriendly – hung up and smiled. The girls were off for their slumber party. Ma pouted. Then Aunt Muriel invited her. Ma packed up her NJ kit bag with what was left of the Absolut and my individual cans of tomato juice and left. Ethel and I furrowed.

"How come they make everything into a party?" Ethel asked. "I mean, even a fire, for Pete's sakes." For Pete's sakes? Either Ethel was moving to Lancaster, or she'd lived with the von Trapp family too long.

"I dunno. It's better than worrying about it, I guess," I said.

Ethel sighed. "No, we do that."

"Well, look at the bright side," I said, "at least we know where they are."

Ethel smiled. We had the same childhood memory of the weekend when Ma and Aunt Muriel decided they needed a girls' night off. This was after Dad had mangled his toes in the lawnmower and Uncle Albert (husband #1) had mistakenly put his fist through the closet door when he was reaching for Auntie's credit cards. Or was it her throat? Probably both.

Ma and Auntie swore up and down they told us all where they were going. But they hadn't. Ethel and I wondered. Mostly about dinner. Dad and Uncle Albert worried. Mostly over Dewar's. Then Dad worried about how he was going to get to the bathroom without Ma; he wasn't about to lean on two teenage girls. Uncle Albert worried more matter-of-factly and called the New Jersey State Troopers. Which was why Ma and Auntie and Ma's cousin Patsy got busted and interrogated alongside Englebert Humperdinck in Atlantic City. Apparently they'd decided they were due for a casino romp at Patsy's suggestion. So they watched the show and got invited back to Englebert's dressing room 'for a beverage'. To this day, neither Ethel or I want to know how they achieved this. Ma and Auntie came home very cranky and very unhappy that their one night as late blooming groupies was a bust.

"Was it Tom Jones, or Englebert Humperdinck?" Ethel asked. "I always get them confused."

"Englebert Humperdinck," I said.

"How'd you remember that?"

"Dad kept yelling about 'the Dink' until Christmas that year."

"Oh."

"You think that's why they split up?"

"No. Maybe. I dunno."

"You think that's why we found Dad's presents on the curb?"

I sighed. “Maybe.”

“I always thought it was because we didn't leave the Manhattans out for Santie Claus that year, like usual. I figured Santie got mad.”

Vito and Trixie and K. came up behind us. “Hey, Toots, we, uh... moved a few things over to your house, for safe keeping.” Vito winked.

“Huh?” I asked.

“Umm... some supplies and such.”

Trixie stared at me, and then nodded back to Vito's house and the multiple entering and exiting policemen. “For SAFEKEEPING,” K. shouted understandingly.

“OH!” I nodded and whirled right around into Archie Daley.

Archie Daley had hoisted his girth up my front path. He was an even less cheerful or convivial Fire Marshal after midnight. “Oh, you again,” he huffed.

“I live here,” I said.

“Huh. Where's the owner?” he asked, nodding his head toward Vito's charbroiled front porch.

“Right here, sir,” Vito piped up dutifully.

“Well, looks like you've got a theme here,” Daley said.

“Huh?”

“A theme. With your neighbor.” He nodded at me. “You work for EEJIT, right?” Daley asked.

I nodded miserably. “Yes.”

“That's the place that got torched with dog poop.” We all nodded mutely. “And it looks like your porch got put ablaze here with some fecal flambé.” I looked at Vito. Vito looked at me. “Burning poop,” Daley clarified, shaking his head.

“Doggie poop?” Trixie asked.

“Probably.” He shrugged and leaned over to Vito's porch and sniffed. “It's pretty stinky.”

A car pulled up quick and parked at the bottom of my driveway. Appletree hopped out wearing 101 Dalmatians jammies topped off with his police officer’s cap, and huffed up my driveway and toward my front porch. I glanced at Trixie and hoped she wouldn't rearrange her cleavage in front of mixed company again. Trixie's fingers twitched, but she held firm. Her self-control was probably helped by Appletree's being mostly out of uniform.

"Archie. Mina. Vito. Trix," Appletree said. I introduced Ethel. "Heard the address on the radio, thought I should look in," he explained.

"Hey, that's real nice of you officer," Vito beamed back at him. "It being pretty late and you're being off duty and all. But it looks like I'm okay here. We was all getting ready to head in, anyway." He stretched and faked a yawn.

"We were?" K. asked. Vito pinched him. K. yelped. Clearly he was hoping that the all night party was going to be an all night party.

"There's been an awful lot of burning poop getting thrown around lately," Daley said.

"Hey, yeah, you know, you've got a point about that," Appletree dully realized. We looked at each other and then quickly away to avoid any further eye contact. An ancient black Hyundai hatchback pulled up short and parked at the bottom of my drive, double-parking Appletree's car.

A guy who looked an awful lot like he might be a reporter got out. Vito shook his head. Then a WLOL-TV van pulled up, and double-parked next to the reporter's Hyundai. Then came another, which parked on the opposite side of the traffic island, and got immediately flanked by two WLOL-TV SUVs. The cul-de-sac was starting to look like a matchbox car line up made by a media happy 4-year-old.

Before we knew it, lights from a TV camera were blinding us, and a bleach blonde anchorwoman was saying something she obviously thought was profound whilst occupying most of Vito's and my conjoined driveways. I looked over at Vito. Or, rather, where Vito had been: he was gone.

"Vito?" I whispered. Trixie poked me, and I looked over at Vito's front door, where two firemen and a policeman were being helped out of Vito's house by Vito's very own paws.

"Thanks lots, fellas. I'll sure remember yous all when you're selling barbecue sauces next fall, ha ha," he said, and closed and locked the door behind him.

The blinding light got hotter and more intense, as the WLOL anchor woman invited herself up to my porch and thrust herself and her microphone in our faces. "And these – these must be the neighbors of, ummm..."

"Vito!" cried K. happily, only too glad to be the center of attention. Trixie pinched him.

"Tell me, did your neighbor's porch also get set on fire by a flaming bag of feces?" the anchor woman asked with therapist-like intensity, shoving the microphone at me. My head hurt.

"Umm, well, you know, I don't know. He likes kielbasa..."

After a few more non-sequitors, the anchor woman groaned and drew an invisible line across her throat to the cameraman. "What's going on here? Don't you people even know that your neighbor's house was on fire?"

"Ummm..."

"And who's this? A slumber party reject?" she asked, pointing toward Appletree.

Appletree puffed up and readjusted his cap. "There's a fine for double-parking in this neighborhood," he said simply, and started walking toward the squadron of TV vehicles.

"Hey!" the anchorwoman called, trailing after him with her cameraman trotting behind.

I yawned. Ethel and K. and Trixie yawned back. "C'mon, K.," Trixie said. "Let's go back to the big city." K. nodded and looked wistfully after the TV van driving away from my neighborhood – taking with it his 15 minutes of fame – and made his way to his curbside car. Ethel and I shrugged, and went inside for what we hoped would feel a lot longer than a midsummer night's nap.

I closed and locked the doors. I turned up the AC and hoped it would take some of the smoked dog poop smells out of the house.

The phone rang. "Sorry I had to run out on yous, Toots," Vito's voice apologized. "I had some other, uh... priorities what come up."

"Sure," I yawned back.

"And don't worry about the stuff in the basement. I'll get that off your hands real soon."

"Uh huh. Okay."

I hung up and yawned again. I looked in the living room. Ike and the Ratties had slept through it all, the bums. So had Vinnie, who lay splayed out on his back in the middle of the living room floor, his legs sprawled wide open and his belly rising softly up and down in the AC breeze, his right paw hooked over his nose.

I heard water running upstairs and figured Ethel had found some jammies and a spare toothbrush. I went into the kitchen for a glass of water, looked at the clock and winced: it was 3:00 a.m. I looked at the basement stairs and sighed: Vinnie's litter box. I wanted to put it off – but realized I hadn't cleaned it since early that morning. And I really didn't want him exploring alternative options. So I down to the basement I trudged.

I got halfway downstairs and stopped. The room was stacked from floor to ceiling with boxes. Great columns and piles of medical sample boxes lined the entire room. I sighed, weaved through the maze in search of Vinnie's litter pan, cleaned it, and repositioned it to the bottom of the stairs. I figured at least this way he wouldn't get clobbered by an avalanche of boxes during a private moment.

When I finally got back upstairs, Ethel was in my bed laying on my side. I got in my jammies, washed up, and poked her. "Slide, Clyde," I ordered in a loving sisterly fashion. Ethel mumbled something I was pretty sure I didn't want to hear and moved over. "I need the side near the alarm clock. I still have to go to work tomorrow morning. I mean this morning," I explained.

"I wanted the side nearest the bathroom. I don't feel so good," she sniffed back. We looked at each other and switched sides again. "Do you think you have anything for a rumbly tumbly?" Ethel asked quietly.

I thought about the pharmaceutical factory in my basement. "It's a possibility," I said.

"Good," she said as she got out of bed and went into the bathroom and whoopsed. So much for gourmet pizza dessert buffets. Or sleep.

After Ethel whoopsed again I investigated my own medicinal arsenal, because I was afraid of the stockpile falling on me in the basement. "Okay, we've got Tagament, Pepto-Bismol, Rolaids, Mylanta, Maalox, ummm... some Zantac and something that looks like a mini Tums," I said, holding out the tummy wares to my pukish sister. Ethel peered at the stash I'd put on the bed next to her. She picked up the mini Tums.

"This isn't a mini Tums. It's a button."

"Well, suck on it."

"Sure. You try."

"I'm not nauseous."

"It's your button. You suck on it."

"Okay, I'll suck on the damn button if you just take something and stop puking!" I half-shouted.

Ethel glared at me, grabbed the bottle of Maalox and took a swig. I sucked my button but forgot and swallowed. Ethel fumped back down on the pillows. Then she put a leg outside the bed and onto the floor.

"Whirly beds?" I asked.

"I think I have a fever. I'm burning up. Is your air conditioning on? And working?"

I sighed and padded back downstairs and checked. It was a cool crisp 70 degrees on a balmy 101 degree night.

"Can you turn the air conditioning up a bit?" Ethel called down. I sighed and lowered the temperature setting to 65, then went back upstairs and covered Marie's cage and shut the vent in her room. I found my winter bathrobe and my heavy socks and lay back down in bed next to Ethel in the dark. I was going to ask her if she felt any better when I heard her snoring. I sighed one last time and closed my eyes for what I hoped would be an almost whole two and a half hours sleep.

CHAPTER 7

(Wednesday morning)

I hate it that I dream in smells. Most people dream in color – but not me. My dreams are like smell-a-vision. A turkey fryer fried turkeys feverishly in my garage (try saying that fast!). I kept running up and down Mt. Driveway carrying trays and trays and trays of food. The more full trays I carried down the driveway the more empty trays I returned into the envelope slot in the door at the back of my garage. Sort of a pet door for hors d'oeuvres trays. This apparently had some kind of exponential effect. It was a lot like the Sorcerer's Apprentice but with canapés. Every time I thought I had delivered enough full trays to the waiting vans below, more drove up and honked horns. At the same time, I was taking one turkey out of the fryer and immediately replacing it with another.

That was when I smelt burning kielbasa. I turned and saw Ma and Aunt Muriel and K. applauding my efforts on Vito's front lawn. Another van drove up. This one was Ike and the Ratties. But he didn't have the Ratties exactly. Ike had stuck them in the middle of a deli tray each as garnish centerpieces. The trays were the size of sleds. The Ratties were bound with grape vines and gagged with plum tomatoes in their mouths.

A taxi drove up and Ethel got tossed out on the curb. She looked like she was pregnant with a baby elephant. But she kept yelling at me to get her Ratties away from 'That Man'. That was when Ike tossed the antipasto Ratties onto the lawn while Ma, Auntie and K. applauded in lunatic unison.

I awoke to Ethel tossing her cookies. Again.

"Do you remember Dad's aftershave?" she asked after she'd rinsed her mouth for the 73rd time with a forgotten bottle of Lavoris I kept under the sink for special cookie tossing occasions.

"Umm, no..."

Ethel took another swig of Lavoris and spit. "I think it was something called, 'That Man'."

"Mmmphfmph."

"You know what?"

"Mmmphfmph?"

"I remember really disliking that cologne."

"Mmmphfmph..."

"And the name."

"Mmmphfmph."

"You know what else?"

"Mmmphfmph?"

"I think I'm a little pregnant."

I sat bolt upright and pinched myself. Ow. Yup, definitely awake. "Are you sure? And what do you mean 'a little'?"

"I don't know," Ethel sniffed. "I kind of lost count. I think a missed a few periods."

"How few?"

"Maybe like four?"

I mentally smacked Ethel on her forehead. "So, what do you think it is," I sighed, "a Hansel or a Gretel?"

Ethel sniffed a little. "I don't know. And I'm not having Ratties. I mean Yorkies. But if I have them – it – Ike will make me give up the Ratties. I mean the Yorkies. I mean Hansel and Gretel." She was well on the road to wailing now.

"Huh?" I asked.

"Ike said we could get Hansel and Gretel when it looked like we couldn't have kids," Ethel sniffed. Ike said we could? Apparently my sister's relationship with Baron von Trapp was a lot less Sound of Music-like than I'd imagined. "Ike doesn't approve of the dogs and kids together thing," she explained weepily.

I thought of a zillion Kodak commercials with kids and puppies and thought another zillion unprintable thoughts about Ike.

"Well, why don't we find out if you're really pregnant before we really worry about it?" I volunteered helpfully. "After all, you could have a medical problem that's making you miss your period. And be nauseous. Hey, maybe you have a tumor!" I said brightly.

"Hey, yeah, you're right!" Ethel smiled.

After some logistic discussions about buying pregnancy test kits – my suggesting Ethel buy her own kits, her suggesting I buy them because she didn't think she could buy them without Ike since he insisted on driving her everywhere in 'his baby', my suggesting she buy them because I didn't want to run into anyone I knew who might actually think that I might be the Pregnant One, her asking what was wrong with that, my pointing out the obvious, etc. – I got stuck agreeing to buy her stupid pregnancy kits. I finally got myself washed and dressed. I waved good morning to Ike on the sofa. I got Vinnie, Marie and the Ratties fed. And sneaked Ethel some saltines and tea while Ike washed up. Then I nuked a gallon of last night's leftover coffee for the morning's shift of unannounced visitors. Vito would probably be over any minute now with some other house's jelly donuts. And he was.

"Sorry, sorry, sorry, Toots," Vito said, letting himself in and holding a large white paper bag. "I got a little side tracked with some... ummm... errands this morning. But I got yous some jelly donuts and stuff. I figured after last night yous all could use them." Truer words were never spoke.

"Jelly donuts?" Ethel called wanly from upstairs.

"Not for you," I shouted back kindly.

"But I love jelly donuts," Ethel sniffled. Yeeshkabiddle.

"Why can't Ethel have a jelly donut?" Ike asked. He looked at me. I looked at Vito. Vito looked at me. So did Vinnie. And the Ratties.

"She, uh, had... too much party last night. Yeah, that's it. Too much party last night," I lied.

"BUT I'M FINE NOW," Ethel yelled down pointedly.

"Okay," I said. "If you're really feeling up to it, then you come down and get it." I was definitely not going to deal with anymore tossed cookies, much less tossed donuts. If Ethel could pass the staircase vertigo test, then she was cleared for donuts.

"Ikey, could you bring me up a jelly belly?"

Ike got caught with his arm halfway inside the bakery bag. Ike laughed nervously. "Of course. That's just what I was just doing," he said. He placed what looked like a jelly injected powdered pillow on a Dippin' Donuts napkin and went upstairs. Vito and I grimaced. Hansel and Gretel and Vinnie immediately gathered around the open bag vying for sniffing privileges.

After wrestling the bag away from the pets, I put the goods on the kitchen counter out of reach of the Ratties and Vinnie. Vito had actually sprung – instead of his usual scrounging various neighbors' houses – for freshly baked goods: jelly donuts, Bavarian cream donuts, apple fritters, honey buns, crullers and crumb buns aplenty. I was impressed. I hadn't seen a legitimate crumb bun since moving to Lancaster.

"Where'd you find crumb buns?" I asked.

"I got connections. Besides, I figured I owe you some storage rent," Vito said with a gaping smile. On account of because he hadn't put his bridge in yet. But the day was young. It was only a little after seven.

"Huh?" I asked around a mouthful of apple fritter, while I poured coffee.

"For the, err... storage space in your basement," Vito explained.

"Your house was on fire, Vito. One night isn't a big deal."

"Actually, it kind of might be more than one night."

"Like, how many?"

Vito shrugged. "Until I can convince Mike I'm in the clear, and all is safe amongst us Amish."

"A – we're not Amish."

"I know. But after I moved here, I found out that's all people outside of here think about us. That we're all Amish."

"But you're not Amish."

"I know. But I'm Polish. And I'm Jewish. That's some ish-es. And sometimes I'm a little kosher-ish, too."

Oy vey.

Ike ran downstairs and into the kitchen, grabbed my fritter from my fingers and flung it in the sink.

"What gives?" I cried.

"THE DONUTS ARE BAD! ETHEL'S PUKING!"

I squinted. "Who said the donuts are bad?"

"Ethel," Ike said.

"There's nothing wrong with the donuts." I retrieved my flung fritter and blotted it with a paper towel. I figured the 5-second rule applied. "I told you: Ethel had too much party."

"Oh. Great!" he said, and reached for a crumb bun.

Vito caught his hand in mid-help-yourself. "I think maybe's you owes Mina a apology. What for flinging her fritter and all."

"I'm not going to apologize to Mina for – OUCH!" I looked at Vito with newfound appreciation. "Uh... YEAH... uh... sorry for the misunderstanding, Mina," Ike winced. Vito let go.

"There, that's better," he said, and helped himself to the crumb bun Ike released with his sprained hand.

"Vito, I have to ask you for a favor," I said.

"Sure, sure, sure, Toots. Go ahead. Name it," he said, brushing his crumb bun crumbs off his tummy and down to the appreciative audience of Hansel and Gretel. And Vinnie. Who knew?

"Umm... I'm pretty sure I need a ride to work."

"Your car broke?"

"It's still at the garage at work. From yesterday. Trixie couldn't find my pocketbook, remember?"

Vito nodded. "Sure, no problemo. I mean problem. Hey, how's your head..." He fell short once he actually looked at my noggin. On top of my usual Technicolor nightmare, I was complete with a melon on top. Any more colors or bumps and I'd look like I'd escaped from a Star Trek convention.

I stared at Vito. He shrugged. Ike chewed. I poured some more coffee and the three of us clinked mugs absentmindedly. The upstairs toilet flushed again and we heard water running. I turned to Baron von Useless. "I have to go to work. It's Wednesday," I explained. Ike looked at me blankly. "It's a school day. I have to work. I'm not on vacation," I tried.

"Oh," he said and munched on what looked like a life size replica of a chocolate covered tire. What kind of bakery did Vito go to? The Flintstones?

"Vito's gonna drive me. I'm gonna leave," I explained to my insulin challenged brother-in-law.

"Uh huh."

"Ethel's gonna need some things. Like Pepto-Bismol, and Maalox and stuff."

"Uh huh."

"She will probably need to eat something later."

"Uh huh."

"Like chicken soup. And saltines."

"Uh huh."

"And I wouldn't give her any more jelly donuts, if I were you."

Ike shivered and swallowed some coffee. "I still don't see how she could get that sick from last night's party. I'm fine," he said, and reached for another crumb bun. Vito slitted his eyes. Ike opted for a Bavarian Cream.

I shrugged and said, "It's a mystery."

I sipped my coffee. I could practically feel the caffeine zinging through my veins. Even though science has disproved it, there are real-life honest-to-traffic-jam commuters who know for a fact that huge amounts of sugar and caffeine directly compensate for miniscule amounts of sleep. Especially if it's double-strength black coffee and a humungous apple fritter. Even if it was a little soggy.

I went upstairs and checked on Ethel. She was lying in bed, at rest and perfectly green.

"Don't puke in my bed, okay?" I asked. She nodded.

I emptied the bathroom wastebasket into an old grocery bag, tied a knot and made ready for La Garbage. I put the empty wastebasket next to my greenish sister. "Just in case," I said.

"Okay," she said back.

"Do you want anything?"

"Just a few dozen pregnancy test kits."

I sighed and nodded and took the trash downstairs.

Vito was sitting on the sofa, holding the Peaceable Kingdom at bay by feeding the Ratties and Vinnie individual crumb bun crumbs. Ike sat in the club chair, clutching the remains of what looked like a white icing covered raft, staring off into space.

"Okay, Vito, I gotta roll," I said. I dodged into the garage, deposited the trash in the garbage pail and came back in through the hallway. Vito was still doling out onesy-twosies crumbsies, and Ike's eyes drooped while the raft o'icing leaned precariously toward the floor. I took the vanilla icing donut from Ike into the kitchen and signaled for Vito to dismiss his subjects. I automatically went to the newel post for my pocketbook. Then I remembered it got lost. I wondered how I was going to buy Ethel's pregnancy test kits. Or get into EEJIT. Or drive my car. Or get back into my home. Well, at least I had company to let me in.

Vito and I walked across our driveways and got into his car. That is, I got into his car after we moved a medium sized dog bed, leash, collar and bags of kibble, wet food, treats, toys and a 'How to Teach Your Dog Smart Tricks' book to the back seat. Then I got in. I looked at Vito. He shrugged. "For Stanley," he said simply. I took a deep breath and buckled my seat belt. I hoped that Stanley, or a really good Stanley lookalike, would be available for adoption in less than 72 hours.

We drove along in amicable silence and moved easily and non-stoppedly past only green traffic lights all along Manor Street. I frowned and silently cursed my red traffic light mojo.

Vito looked over at me. "You want I should pick up some groceries or Pepto-Bismol for Ethel?" he asked.

Now that I remembered I was without my pocketbook, bank card or checks, I nodded yes. I grimaced while thinking about spending the better part of the day on the phone with the police, the bank, credit card companies, the car dealer and a locksmith. "That would probably be a good idea," I said out loud, regarding the locksmith and all. I also wondered if it would be too personal to ask Vito to pick up a few dozen pregnancy test kits. "Would you mind if I borrowed a little cash?" I asked. "I have some... umm... personal things I have to pick up."

"No problemo," Vito said, preventing me from divulging any personal information by holding up a hand. He pulled up to the drop-off at the Chestnut Street entrance, parked and reached for his wallet. It was stuffed with wads of monopoly money. Except this was genuine cold, hard cash. Well maybe it was a little warm, but that was only because Vito had been sitting on it, right?

He pulled out four fifty-dollar bills and handed them to me. "Just get what you need, Toots."

"Thanks again, Vito," I said. I opened the door. My leg was inches from the ground when Vito stopped me.

"Hey, Toots." I turned around. "What time you think you'll be done work? When should I pick you up?"

Oh. I'd hadn't even thought about a ride home. And I hadn't really thought about thinking about how long I would actually be at work – that is, if I had a job left.

I shrugged. "I'm not sure. I call you."

Vito nodded and put his mirrored specs back on. As he pulled away and waited for a break in traffic, I thought I saw him look in the rearview mirror and insert his bridge. I shuddered and held up a virtual hand inside my brain to halt that image: I just didn't want to know. I trudged off to the Armstrong Building entrance and entered.

What greeted my arrival were wafts of burnt electrical fumes and taped up 'Out of Order' signs across the bank of elevators. Great. I'd have to walk up the seven flights of stairs to EEJIT. Again. And work in stale smoke. Again. With How-weird. And possibly getting konked on the noggin. Again. I wondered which was worse.

I walked over to the vacant reception desk, and let myself in behind the counter. I found the phone set and dialed Howard's extension to ask him to let me in once I climbed Mount Staircase. No dice: I got his voicemail. I hung up. I dialed Bauser's line and got his voicemail, too. Same for Norman. Since I knew Norman would rather be anywhere, even EEJIT, than home with his step-daughters, I wondered if Effhue, Ltd. had actually closed EEJIT officially for the day.

So I tried calling EEJIT's main number, and got a new outgoing message. "Hello and welcome to the voicemail system for EEJIT. Our Lancaster location is temporarily closed due to maintenance difficulties. If you know your party's extension, please dial it at any time to leave a voicemail message. If this is an emergency, please press 2 for Howard Blech. Thank you for calling, EEJIT."

I hung up the receiver and blinked. Number one: the outgoing phone message was ordinarily left by me, as part of my duties as office manager. The last time I changed it was last February because of a snow emergency. Number two: not only was the outgoing message voice not mine, it was Lee's, which brought home that she was obviously 'in the loop' and I was not. Lastly, number three: if Lee was performing one of my duties, that couldn't bode well for the rest of my job description.

I decided to call Bauser's apartment to see if he and Norman were still there. The phone rang four times. I was about to hang up when Bauser answered.

"It's me," I said.

"Hey," Bauser said back. "Isn't it great? A paid day off after all!"

"It would be great if I had known," I said.

"How couldn't you know? You're supposed to leave the outgoing message," he said.

"I didn't. Lee did."

"Crap. Hey, Norman." I heard the two of them conferring in the background. Then Bauser came back and said, "Norman said he thought How-weird got Lee to do it because of your getting konked on the noggin and all."

"Nope."

"Crap."

"Well, Norman called in to check for both of us. But I stopped by early this morning to make sure, and saw the signs on the doors."

"What signs?"

"The notices taped to the entrance, Mina."

I looked over at the glass doors to the Queen Street entrance, and saw two letter-sized leaflets taped to the doors. I sighed. "I came in the Chestnut Street side. Vito drove," I explained.

"You mean you're in the lobby? How'd you get in without your ID?"

"I opened the doors and walked in."

"Mina, the building should be on off-hours security. The lobby doors should be locked. That means you had to have your ID to get in. Where are you calling from?"

"The front desk."

"Where's the guard? Can I talk to him?"

"No guard."

"Maybe you should leave."

A shadowy realization slunk behind my forehead and I began to understand I was probably risking another bonked noggin. "Yup," I answered, hung up, and hustled out the building and across Chestnut Street. Mostly because I heard an elevator bell ding from the allegedly non-functioning elevator bank just as I exited the lobby, stage right.

I walked across Chestnut Street, shaded my eyes and looked toward the office building's glass lobby walls – but I couldn't see a thing except reflections. Well, now I had a predicament. All paid off and no place to go. Especially with no car and no pocketbook. I winced, realizing there was probably another dry cleaning ticket in my wallet that needed picking up. But, since the jig was up, and Mrs. Phang admitted she was really from Hawthorne and not Vietnam, she probably wouldn't be as persnickety about my not having an actual ticket. Especially as she might not have to fake an accent in front of me anymore. Unless, of course, a real dry cleaning customer was present.

I shrugged. The sun was shining, the air was clear, and only fluffy white clouds floated in the clear blue sky. A real break in the weather. I decided to go window shopping at the artsy stores along Queen Street. I couldn't remember a day this perfect. What could go wrong?

I traipsed along Queen Street, feeling halfway between playing hooky and summer break. I thought about calling Howard at home and asking, "What gives?" about Lee's leaving the outgoing message. But I thought better about it, held my breath and counted to ten. There was no point in ruining a perfectly legitimate bonus day off. Anyway, I'd probably find out soon enough at work tomorrow. I highly doubted that Effhue Ltd. would sanction a second paid day off, fumes or no fumes.

I reached the corner of Queen and Lime, just across from the House of Happy. Across Lime there was an actual payphone. But then I realized I had to have actual change. But maybe I'd get lucky. I fingered the change slot, just in case – and found a forgotten quarter! Was this my lucky day, or what? I popped the quarter in and dialed Bauser's.

"Hello?" Bauser answered.

"It's me," I said.

"Mina, jeez, where are you now? What happened?" Bauser asked.

"Corner of Lime and Queen, at a payphone." A mechanical woman's voice broke in and advised we had thirty seconds left to our conversation. "Hey, Bauser, can you call me back? I was just lucky and found a quarter to call you."

"You can't call back payphones anymore. Drug dealers. Talk fast." The woman's voice interrupted again and told us we had ten seconds left. "Why don't you just stop by? You're not that far away," Bauser said.

I was about to answer when the mechanical female voice broke in again and pleasantly advised our conversation was terminated. I banged the phone a few times with the receiver for good luck and hung up.

That was when a remodeled Volkswagen bug careened the wrong way up Lime Street, cut a right onto Queen and headed straight for the payphone. And me. It ran up over the curb and onto the sidewalk and splashed a few weeks worth of stagnant puddle sludge on me. As I jumped back, it did a U-turn to go the right way down Lime and pulled up to a stop at the traffic light in front of me. The driver's head looked like a pumpkin. Mostly because the driver wore a Halloween pumpkin head rubber mask. As the light turned green, Pumpkin Head looked at me, waved, and sped off. As the Bug screeched away, I decided to accelerate my stride and my arrival at Bauser's before I got attacked by another vegetable.

Bauser lives in an oddly split shotgun-style apartment on Water Street, off of Chestnut Street, fairly close to both St. Bart's and EEJIT. The building's front door opens off Water and into a trim closed off hallway that once served as a fairly impressive foyer. The door on the left is Apt. #1A, a small studio. That apartment had seen a former life as a small dining room with a butler's pantry. A rotating squad of art school students, mostly guys, lived here for a few semesters until the next art student moved in.

Apt. #1B is at the end of the hallway, and is a large efficiency with a normalish sized kitchen, and is the home to a retired shoe salesman, Harry, who's mostly out of town between rotating visits to his two daughters in Indiana and California. Which means it's usually empty. Which is good for Bauser when he wants to blast his retro-punk records, since his apartment is directly overhead.

The next first floor apartment is to the right of the entrance. It's another studio, and houses a male nursing student no one's ever seen because he works nights as a bartender in-between days studying physiology and medicine. But he's definitely real, Bauser says, because his mail and newspapers get picked up.

Bauser's apartment #2B is on the second floor, up a once grand mahogany staircase, and occupies most of the second floor. It even boasts a 'deck' on top of the kitchen to Apt. #1B. Bauser's 'deck' is adorned with a portable screened in gazebo that you enter and exit via a zippered flap.

I knocked on Bauser's door, and Jim answered.

"A-WHOOO-WOO-WOOO-WO-WUUU," Jim bellowed neighborly. I winced and hoped the folks on the other side of town didn't mind the racket. Then I heard scuffling, some admonishments from Bauser, and tumblers opening. Bauser opened the door with one hand, holding Jim back with the other.

"Hey, come in," he gasped. He let go of the door and wrapped both his arms around Jim's neck. It looked like he was trying to saddle a small long-haired pony. Which was not a bad feat for a large dog with only three legs.

I let myself in and closed the door behind me, and Bauser let loose of Jim. Jim jumped up on his leg and put both paws on my shoulders in greeting. He tried to hop back down but his foot skidded on the wood floor and he slid sideways. His shoulder hit the floor, he shook his head, scrambled up, and grinned up at me sheepishly while wagging a slightly embarrassed tail. I patted him on the head and he trotted off to his spot on his recliner. It was the 'His' match to the 'His' and 'His' recliners Bauser had bought for them from the White Elephant thrift shop. Which was just as well, since they both were a little worse for the his 'n' his wear.

I looked past the shredded recliners, the huge flat plasma screen TV on the facing brick wall, and into the 'porch' tent at Norman, who lay sprawled out on a plaid, folding pool-side chaise lounge circa 1955, with 'Nerd World' magazine spread across his chest and his eyes closed. I looked at Bauser. "He's actually been up since about 4:00," he explained. "He got on the phone to coach the girls through feeding the horses and mucking the stalls."

"Haven't they ever done that before?" I asked.

"Yeah, but I got the impression mostly as observers. I think they mostly participate by IMing."

"Huh?" I asked.

"Text messaging," Bauser spelled out while rolling his eyes at me. Bauser might live in the past as far as music is concerned. But he's on the bleeding edge with the rest of technology. And he loves to needle me about my vinyl.

Bauser looked at me funny and sniffed. "Is that you?" he asked.

"I got splashed by a Pumpkin Head," I said.

"Pew."

I sighed, went into the kitchen and mopped myself off with some paper towels. Bauser handed me a clean Steelers T-shirt and I went into the bathroom and washed up and got out of my stinky puddle top. "You want a beer?" Bauser asked when I was out.

"It's ten a.m.," I said.

"It's Saturday," he said.

"Huh?"

"Getting an extra, unexpected paid day off is like getting an extra Saturday. So, it's Saturday-II," Bauser said.

"It's still ten a.m."

"It's five o'clock somewhere."

I thought about it. It had been a pretty eventful morning so far. "What kind of beer?" I asked.

"Krumpthf's" he said.

I winced. Krumpthf's is a local beer, bought only by locals. That is, really cheap locals. Or 'frugal', as Bauser continually tries to correct me. Legend has it that Krumpthf's was created by a farmer during prohibition after the birth of his 13th child. After trying it once, I figured it was created as Amish birth control. It tastes like dirt even after you strain out the leaves and twigs and stuff. I shook my head and opted for an A-Treat birch beer instead.

I popped the lid open and woke up Norman. Norman yawned, sat up, and looked at his wrist watch and shrugged. He reached over and drank from a tumbler of tomato juice. "Cheers," he said and toasted. I sipped my soda and frowned.

"Hey, Bauser didn't offer me a Bloody," I said to Norman. "That would have been acceptable at ten a.m. Even on a Saturday-II."

Norman sipped. "It's not," he said. "I mixed my Krumpthf's with some leftover V-8 he had in the back of the fridge." I shuddered. "No, really. It's not so bad. I mean, after you strain the leaves and twigs and stuff."

I walked out to the 'porch' and sat down on the floor in a beach chair, and stretched out my legs. Jim came bounding in and leapt onto my lap. I felt the circulation in my thighs shut down. Bauser came in with a fresh Krumpthf's, booted Jim off my legs and reclined in an inflatable club chair. The clubhouse was complete.

"Nice to see you," Norman said thoughtfully. "How was EEJIT?"

I filled them both in about the status of the non-secure lobby, and the functioning non-functioning elevators. And the near miss phone booth. And Pumpkin Head. Bauser and Norman exchanged glances. Jim put his head on the floor and covered his eyes with one paw.

"We've got something to tell you," Bauser said.

Apparently, what with the package sniffer thingy, Bauser and Norman had finally deduced that whoever was sniffing Norman's runs was not sniffing within EEJIT. And not even within any kind of Effhue corporate network identification. This pointed to a bonafide, complete outside source hacker.

"But why would a hacker be interested in Norman's runs?" I asked.

Norman shrugged. "Money," he said. "Buy-A-Lots is pretty huge. Taking a piece of their action would be pretty significant."

"Yeah, but would it be worth the risk?" I asked. "It seems pretty high school."

"It could be. And it could be high school kids. That's one scenario," Bauser said.

"Or it could be just plain dumb," Norman said.

"Huh?" I asked.

"Consider the obvious. Myron, Lee, How-weird, Ken..." Bauser mused.

"The usual suspects," Norman finished. "They all have motives. Even if they're lame ones."

I sighed and sipped my lukewarm A-Treat and wished Bauser kept his soda in the fridge. If only. His sacred frosty space was reserved for Krumpthf's and Jim's Whoof-O wet food.

"So now what?" I asked

Bauser shrugged. "Nothing. We wait."

"For what? Another package sniffer readout?" I asked.

"For someone to konk you on the noggin again," Norman said happily.

"Or another fire. Or, maybe another drive-by fecal flinging!" Bauser added enthusiastically.

"Huh?"

"There probably isn't a person alive who doesn't think it's not some kind of retributional karma if Buy-A-Lots gets ripped off."

Norman nodded. "Karma," he repeated sagely. I winced. "But the thing is," Norman continued, "is that you can't keep getting konked on the noggin. Or your office smoked out."

"It's not my office," I said defensively. "It's EEJIT's."

"Yes," Norman continued, for the very slow to follow. "But you're the common denominator where the most damage has occurred."

"And don't forget Vladimir's – I mean Vito's – house getting set on fire the exact same way," Bauser said.

"You mean the flaming bag of feces flinger?" I asked.

"Exactly," Bauser said, like this explained everything.

"Huh?"

Bauser and Norman looked at each other and grimaced. Norman drank more of his curdled V-8. "What if last night was a mistake?" Bauser asked.

"Huh?"

"What if last night the perp really meant to fling the flaming feces at your house?" Bauser asked, all CSI style.

"How'd you mean?"

"The common factor between all the fires, including Vito's, is you," Bauser said matter-of-factly.

Oh. Great. So Bauser and Norman got it. I was hoping it was mostly the Krumpthf's that was talking. But the nagging feeling pounding the lining of my tummy thought otherwise.

"So what do I do?" I asked.

"Like I said, nothing," Bauser answered. "You just go on business as usual. But using the buddy system."

"Huh?"

Bauser sipped. "Norman and I have it all worked out. Then we called Trixie. We called Vito, too, but he was out driving you to work," he said. "We're going to buddy you up until the flaming feces finishes," he said.

"And your mom and sister visiting is really great," Norman said, smiling. "This way we can make sure you're okay at home, and that your home is okay while you're not at home."

I pursed my lips and frowned. “Look, this is really, uh, a high tech philosophy you've got going here,” I started.

“Not just high tech, but accurate,” Bauser boasted. “After we called Trixie, she emailed Officer Appletree. He said he was forbidden to respond to evidence regarding an official investigation, especially one he wasn't assigned to, but he also told her she wasn't barking up the wrong tree.”

No, just the wrong Appletree, as well as barking mad, I thought.

“Okay, well, look, that's great. It'll be a lot of fun having all your company all of the time,” I said, trying to edge out of the mesh tent. “But I need to run some errands now.” I started to the door, but Jim was splayed out across the threshold, blocking my escape route.

“Great!” Bauser said. “We'll go with you!”

“We?” I replied weakly.

“Sure! Jim needs some air. And so does Norman,” he said, looking at Norman, who was starting to suffer another bout of lounger lag judging by his blinking eyes.

I sighed, accepted my fate, and helped rouse Norman back from the visions of Krumpthf's in his head.

We pounded down the stairs from Bauser's and paraded out onto Mulberry, Jim wagging ecstatic. Which is a little embarrassing because every time Jim wags ecstatic he wags himself over where his other leg isn't. So we picked him up a lot. We piled into Bauser's Aspire, cheek to fuzzy jowl, including Jim's.

“Okay, so where's the first stop?” Bauser asked.

“Umm... you can just drop me off here,” I pointed to the corner of Lemon and Prince.

“In front of the drugstore? No way. We're supposed to stay with you, right? We'll go in with you.”

“Umm... you know, this is kind of personal...do you all have to come in with me?”

“No. Sure. We don't all have to go. I'll go in with you,” Bauser said.

“Well, I don't want to sit out here with your dog in my lap,” Norman complained. Jim groaned a ‘Same to you, buddy,’ and shifted around to put his butt in Norman's face. I sighed.

"Okay, okay, we'll all go in. But I'm not sure Jim can go into a drugstore," I said. They looked at me. "Only dogs for the handicapped can go in."

"Well, Jim's handicapped. And he's a dog. That counts," Bauser said.

I sighed again and counted to ten. Bauser parked on the street between a Humvee and a taxi. Who lives in Lancaster and can afford a Humvee? As it was, there seemed to be a literal epidemic of them lately. And if you could afford a Humvee, why would you park on Prince Street? I hoped we wouldn't come back to an Aspire accordion.

We got out. "C'mon, Jim. Drugstore, Jim," Bauser said. Jim looked at him blankly. "Limp," Bauser instructed. Jim wagged understandingly and smiled. Then he started down Prince Street, his right paw upheld and limp-hopping on his only hind leg. After a few practice steps, he turned, looked back at us, and coughed for the nice audience. Jimmy Camille O'Bauseman. Great. Nice Irish Setter.

Off to the drugstore we trooped, Jim practicing various fake infirmities, including his canine impersonation of hacking up fur balls as we went. At the entrance, I stopped. The parade stopped next to me.

"Uh, thanks, guys. This is great. But really, err... I think I really need to do this solo," I tried.

"Negatory. You are part of Buddy Buds. You have been assimilated. We do not disengage," Bauser replied. I glared at him and cursed his Star Trekiness. Jim whoofed. I glared at Jim. He smiled some more while slobbering on my toes through my sandals. Norman stared up at the sky.

"Look – I have to get girl stuff, okay!?" I cried.

Norman's gaze came back. "Oh, you mean Tampax. And pads. I've bought those before. Which do you prefer? Regular or Pearl? Mini or maxi?" he asked.

I closed my eyes and swallowed hard. Norman's females had him completely trained.

I looked at Bauser but couldn't read him through his wrap-around vintage punk rock sunglasses. Then I looked back at Norman, who actually didn't look unhappy. I guess feminine hygiene was a comfort zone for him. Which was TMI. So I looked down at Jim. He was smiling and wagging his tail at someone's grandpa coming out of the drugstore. Jim leaned over on his only hind leg, giving full display of his amputee-ness, coughed, and then pretended to struggle to get up. The someone's grandpa handed Bauser a dollar and patted Jim on the head. "Get your dog to a vet soon, son. That's no way to treat a crippled guide dog." Bauser nodded and folded the dollar into the pocket of his shirt.

"Okay. You can accompany me. That means no talking. And especially no helping." This last remark I said pointedly to Norman. He and Bauser exchanged looks. They shrugged.

"No biggie," Norman said, and held the door open for me. And Bauser. And Jim.

I slunk into the drugstore amidst the pitter-pats of various male feet. Aggravation got the better of me and I turned around mid-scowl to find Jim peering at something near someone else's gramma. The gramma was opening a bag of doggie treats off the shelf and feeding them to Jim. I looked for Bauser and Norman to catch their attention to Jim's telepathic shoplifting. Norman was comparison shopping men's athletic protection, while Bauser appeared to be engrossed in a 'Smut and Smuggin's' girly/PC magazine. I blinked. Then I blinked again. But they were all still there. In living color.

While they remained oblivious, I hustled toward the pharmacy at the rear of the store and the pregnancy kits kept by the counter. There was a large selection. But apparently there was a pregnancy epidemic in Lancaster, because all the stock – except for the Instant Speedo Econo Pregometer ('Like 2 kits in 1!') – were all sold out. And there were only two of those left. Which I guessed meant that they could count as four kits. But that still didn't exactly come close to Ethel's requirements for a dozen or so. I wondered if not getting the wished for kits, during high anxiety level, would upset her stomach enough to kick in her preggo puke reactors again. I sighed and picked up the last two Instant Speedo Econo Pregometer kits and plunked them down on the counter for the pharmacist to ring up.

Except the pharmacist was busy being a pharmacist. And an upbeat, college-age clerk was busy training their newest cashier, Evelyn. Evelyn of Breakfast Wars fame. Yikes.

“Hello, did you find everything you needed today?” the part-time manager sang out too brightly in his attempt to be a stellar employee example for Evelyn, even though she was about a thousand years older than him. But then I figured it was probably for the store manager, who kept grunting and glaring at him from behind the glass window in the office above the pharmacy.

Nonchalantly as I could, I examined the ingredients on the back of a pack of gum to avoid Evelyn, and willed her to not recognize me. I finally looked up. She blushed.

“Well hello, Mina! Well, you know, a girl does need something to do. And this does give me some pocket money,” she added, all smiles, while both her painted eyebrows waved in opposite directions in agreement. I nodded. I completely understood. After all, when it comes time for me to collect Social Security, there won't be any. So Evelyn had it lucky. And at least her boss didn't holler at her.

I plunked the two Instant Speedo Econo Pregometer (‘Like 2 kits in 1!’) kits down on the counter. Evelyn picked one up and scanned it according to the part-time manager's smiling encouragement. No beep. She scanned it again. It didn't scan. Then, our boy, Hal, instructed Evelyn about key entering the barcode numbers manually, yada, yada, yada. Which of course came up boopkas. That was when the overly helpful trainer instructed Evelyn to request a price check using the loudspeaker system.

It was when Evelyn's clear, Breakfast Wars announcer voice rang out, “Price check in Pharmaceuticals for the Instant Speedo Econo Pregometer pregnancy test kit,” that she registered that I was trying to purchase not one but two pregnancy test kits (or four, depending if the marketing statements of the Instant Speedo Econo Pregometer were truthful.)

Evelyn looked at me and gaped open-mouthed. Then Hal looked behind me and asked, “Can I help you gentlemen?” Which was when I looked behind me and saw my motley crew.

“We're with her,” Norman said.

Bauser nodded. Jim wagged.

Evelyn's eyebrows flew upside her forehead so high they pushed her wig back. I did the only thing I could do in a situation like this: I stared back blankly. Norman coughed. I shot him the Look. He looked down at his shoes.

Bauser cut the silence by interjecting, “We're not sure,” and indicating the pregnancy test kits. I mentally slapped him in the forehead. Too late. Evelyn looked from me to Bauser then Norman and landed her gaze on Jim. Jim jumped up, put both paws up on the counter, schlurped Evelyn and fell backward.

$34.72 later we had the two – or four - pregnancy test kits in our clutches. My clutches, that is. Oddly, Bauser and Norman didn't ask me about them. Which I wasn’t sure whether to be thankful about or not; they weren’t asking. But then, I wasn’t the potentially pregnant one. Sigh.

We got into the car.

“Where to now?” Bauser asked.

I gulped. I figured he wasn't going to like this. “Umm... I need a few more, err... test kits,” I muttered.

“THAT'S COMPLETELY UNDERSTANDABLE!” Norman shouted from the front, since I'd opted for the back with Jim, hoping for fewer questions as well as less Bauser/Norman contact.

“Sure! Your first pregnancy! You want to be sure before you start nailing the guy for a paternity suit!” Norman said, nodding. Ugh.

“How many tests were you thinking of?” Bauser asked. My head swam. I really wanted to explain the Ethel thing but also really didn't want to rat on my maybe preggo sister.

I sighed and answered, “A dozen or so, I guess.”

“I know just the place!” Bauser shouted triumphantly. I wondered briefly how he knew this, then sidelined the thought. Why Bauser had this kind of information was not something I wanted to know.

A few minutes later, we were on Fruitville Pike and pulling into the Wagon Wheel Shopping Center. We shoved ourselves – collectively and individually – out of the car. Bauser started walking into the Bag o' Bucks Store. Norman and Jim and I followed. A store clerk shouted at Jim in Spanish, and pointed toward the door. Jim pretended to herd me like a blind person and knocked me into a display of sunglasses. I put a pair on and made like Stevie Wonder.

Jim led us up to the counter and POP displays where, what to my wandering 'blind' eyes should appear, several hundred preggo kits for $1, my dear. I put $12 down and picked up 12 generic pregnancy tests.

At least Ethel would be relieved. Especially after she peed 16 times on 16 different kits.

CHAPTER 8

(Wednesday afternoon)

Bauser pulled up Mt. Driveway. We all got out and were greeted at the screen door by oil scented wafts and sizzling. I pulled on the door handle. It was locked. I shook my head and rang the bell to be let into my own home.

Vito greeted me holding an in-use Swiffer one hand, and my cordless phone in the other, while pressing one foot against Hansel to keep him from escaping. Hansel gnawed at the tassel of Vito's loafer and growled in response.

"Sure, sure, sure. I gotcha, Mrs. K.," Vito said, then hung up and opened the door for me. "Hey, Toots, I didn't expect to see yous so soon. I was just cleaning up a little," he said, blushing and coddling the Swiffer.

Bauser and Jim sniffed. "Wow, you cook for Mina, too?" Bauser asked. Vito clearly looked pleased, and I just didn't have the heart. I was realizing that cooking in some circles might be an indiscriminate term. I guess some folks figure if they ate what used to be food, and survived, it was cooking.

"Only just lunches. On account of Mina's so busy and all. And it gives me some practice," Vito answered.

Bauser and Jim looked at me with accusing eyes. "Geez, do you live the life, or what? I'd kill to have someone clean and cook for me," Bauser said. Jim sighed in agreement.

"Careful, kids," Vito warned. "I used to know some peoples what did."

"Hey, are these pot stickers?" Norman asked. Apparently the scent of Vito's cooking and a tummy full of Krumpthy Marys carried Norman into the kitchen ahead of us. Well, at least we were spared seed hulls and fluff since Marie lived upstairs now.

"Are you kidding? These are homemade pierogies!" Vito ambled down the hall toward the kitchen with Hansel, Jim and Bauser trotting along behind him.

I wasn't so sure about Vito and his pierogies, especially after the Johnny Mazerotti's a la Vito Spaghetti. Also, I remembered eating store-bought pierogies from the frozen food section was a lot like eating mashed-potato stuffed raviolis. Except more revolting.

"But these don't look like pierogies. They look like pot stickers. Their skin is so delicate," Norman said, peering over the sizzling pan.

Vito rested his trusty Swiffer, picked up a spatula and inspected his creations. "That's what real homemade pierogies look like," he explained. "The dough takes forever. All the kneading, and the rolling. It's really an art."

"Wow, you did all that just this morning?" Bauser asked.

Vito shrugged. "Not really. I'm not exactly a dough person. And I didn't have the time. So I stopped by the Chinese grocery store for dumpling wrapper dough. They're the right kind of thin, and dough is dough."

"Oh. So that explains why they look like pot stickers," Norman nodded.

"What are they stuffed with?" Bauser asked, leaning over the pan and inhaling.

I leaned against the door jamb and wish I'd had the Krumpthfs at Bauser's when I'd had the chance. And I also started to wonder when anyone would notice I had four large plastic grocery bags stuffed with pregnancy test kits. But Vito's culinary instruction was just too weird not to pay attention to it.

"Traditionally, pierogies are stuffed with little morsels of leftovers," Vito explained. "Sliced mushrooms, maybe mashed potato and cheese, or sauerkraut. The idea is like mini-casseroles made from leftovers."

Leftovers. Huh. That would assume one ate, and cooked, food at home. And didn't eat all of it. Or let it grow fuzz. Go figure.

"I like to put my own spin on things," Vito continued to his attentive pupils – all two-legged, three-legged and four-legged varieties. "But I also feel sensitive about keeping with tradition," he added. Bauser and Norman nodded. "So I use non-traditional leftovers, in the leftover tradition, of course. I made use of our party leftovers from the other night: pizza, olives, pepperoni, cheeses and relish."

"Relish?" I asked. I knew I shouldn't but I had to. I didn't remember relish from the Mediterranean feast.

"You had it in the fridge," Vito answered.

My relish. My fridge. Let's see... I bought the house about a year ago. I think that's when I remembered buying relish.

Bauser and Norman did all but sit pretty and wag their tails for their share of the putrid pierogies. Speaking of, I hoped that it wasn't Vito's pierogies that poisoned his sainted Marie. I suddenly felt like lying down next to Ethel. "And I even made some dessert pierogies," he said brightly.

"Dessert pierogies?" I asked. I couldn't help it. It just fell out of my mouth. Like I expected the pierogies and their contents soon would.

"Leftover jelly doughnut fillings!" Vito beamed.

Bauser and Norman looked impressed. And hungry. Which could only mean that Krumpthfs has a lot more alcohol content than is published on their label.

"You wanna try some?"

Jim barked. Hansel tried to sit pretty – but his belly was too big and he wobbled over instead. "Hey, we got plenty. I was just fixing some more for Ethel," Vito went on.

"More?" I asked.

"Yeah. After I dropped you off, I came back here, of course. Your sister didn't look too good. I figured she could use something solid in her tummy."

I wondered if a bambino counted.

"She ate this?" I asked. Vito and Bauser and Norman snapped a look at me like I'd coughed up a hair ball on their dinner plates. "I mean, she was so ill when I left for work I just figured she wouldn't want anything else to eat," I tried. Vito relaxed. Bauser and Norman relaxed more: Vito shuffled some pierogies onto plates for them.

"Sure. When your tummy's empty like that, it can make you feel very nauseated," Vito replied sagely. "So I figured a good, hot nosh was just what she needed. And it worked. She's up and perky and made your bed with clean sheets, and now she's taking a shower," he said. "But now Ike's down with it. Must be some kind of 24-hour flu thing."

"Ike's sick?" I asked.

"Well, he hasn't actually been sick, but he said he feels like he could. So I figured I'd fry him up some pierogies and get his insides on the mend, too."

I looked around. "Where is he?"

"He went upstairs to lie down with Ethel. In your room," Vito said. Well, that was just peachy. How was I going to surreptitiously hand Ethel 16 pregnancy test kits in front of Ike's prone body? I sighed.

"Whatcha got in the bags? You go shopping?" Vito asked.

"Uh, yeah," I said brightly.

"Ohhh, yeah, right," Vito added. "Now I remember. Your personal shopping." He winked. Then he leaned toward me and whispered, "You need more money? You have enough?"

Bauser and Norman stared open-mouthed.

"Uh, yeah, thanks. I'm covered, Vito."

"Geez," Bauser exhaled. "And he gives you an allowance?"

Norman said, "Some people have all the luck."

I shook my head and stashed Ethel's stash in the hall closet.

Back in the kitchen, Vito, Bauser and Norman standing around and nibbling pierogies. Just my luck I'd get a lunchtime kitchen party. A collar tag tinkled against a bowl. I looked down to see Hansel, Gretel and Vinnie gnawing on pierogies too. I pursed my lips and hoped that Vinnie's share wasn't stuffed with pepperoni.

"Here, Mina, I made a few for you," Vito said, handing me a plate with three crescent-shaped pot sticker pierogies. I sighed. There was absolutely no polite way to get out of this now.

I faked a smile and prayed I hadn't won the relic relish pierogies. I cut one in half with my fork, edging toward the sink. Maybe I could pretend to slip and hurl it in there? Or fake an epileptic fit? Or just drop it near Hansel? He had to be good for something. Besides, with his girth he could do with a little food poisoning.

I looked down at my plate, and saw a small rivulet of jam ooze out. Oh. Okay. This must be the jelly donut pierogies. I nibbled. Gift wrapped sautéed jelly donuts wasn't so bad.

"See? Not bad, huh?" Vito grinned. "Those ones I like to think are reminiscent of bite-size mini blintzes."

I swallowed. Nothing happened, so while Vito kept staring at me I figured I should pretend to keep on going. At least until he looked away.

Ethel wandered into the pierogie party. "Good morning!" she sang.

Norman and Bauser grunted and chewed.

"Hey, look at you. You look like you're on the mend," Vito said, patting Ethel on her shoulder. Ethel smiled back at him. I furrowed. I hadn't really expected Vito to adopt Ethel, too.

"Yep. Completely cured. You were right, Vito," Ethel said, helping herself to a glass and my fridge and pouring some milk.

"Is that my milk?" I asked. Only because the last time I remembered buying milk was about when I'd bought the relish.

"You were out. And Mrs. Rivera had extra, on account of she was supposed to have her daughter's twins visiting her, but they got sick with ear infections," Vito explained.

"Mrs. Rivera?"

"The end unit up for sale on Daisy Petal Court. She just settled last week," he explained.

I wondered how Vito got this much information, and simultaneously willed myself not to ask. Some things are better kept under wraps. Like my relish should have been.

"Anyway, once I got a little something in my tummy, I felt lots better, just like Vito said," Ethel beamed. In fact, she was positively glowing. Uh oh.

Vito blushed. "Aww gee, don't mention it," he said, and went back to sautéing. Ethel leaned over to watch.

"I especially liked the pickle ones," she said hopefully.

I pushed the remaining pierogies around on my plate.

"Those were actually relish," Vito explained. "But Mina only had a little. I used it up," he apologized. I exhaled in relief. At least my family and friends would only be a little poisoned.

"Oh, okay. They were all good," Ethel said.

"Thanks."

"I was going to bring some up for Ikey. He doesn't look so good," she said.

"Sure, sure, sure. Coming right up, Cookie." Vito stared down at the board at the pot sticker pierogie dough. "But I think I'm running out of stuffings. Hey, Mina's the real gourmet around here. Can you think of anything?" he asked me.

"Toothpaste?" I suggested. Ethel scowled and opened a cabinet. I shrugged.

"Here, use this, Vito," she offered happily, presenting Vito with a can of refried beans. Huh. I didn't remember buying those. Ever. Maybe it came with the house?

"Hey, that'll work! We'll just add a little processed cheese on top and ole!" Vito grinned. Oh boy. I actually started to feel sorry for Ike. And my plumbing.

Vito started opening the fossilized can and began concocting away.

Bauser stared into my fridge. "Got any Krumpthfs?" he asked.

"Nope. Sorry," I said.

"Bloodies?" Norman asked.

"Sorry. I used the last of my tomato juice trying to wash Flower off of me," I apologized.

"Hey, ya know what would go good with this kind of a brunch?" Vito offered. I saw what was coming and silently wished I could put my hands and feet simultaneously over Bauser, Norman's and Ethel's mouths.

"What?" they asked.

"Hawaiian Orchids," Vito said.

We looked at him blankly. He shook his head and threw the rest of the Mexican pierogies into the pan, handed Bauser the spatula and decorated him ceremoniously by draping the dishtowel over his shoulder. Bauser nodded at the responsibility bestowed upon him and stood vigil over the stove. "I'll be right back," Vito said, and slipped his girth out the door. For a tubby guy, he could actually be pretty nimble when he wanted to be. And invisible. Well, at least the Moils had given him some legitimate skills.

After Vito had gone, Ethel said to me, "Oh, by the way, your boss called you."

"You talked to my boss?" I asked.

"No, I just listened. He called while I was putting your sheets in the dryer, and the machine picked up," she explained.

"Vito didn't answer?" I was incredulous. Vito always answered my phone. Even when I'm here.

Ethel shook her head. "He went out to pick up some milk for me when I went into the shower," she said. "By the way, I think you're out of shower gel." Well, that was probably true. I had used up most of my bathroom products and some of my kitchen products trying to de-skunkify myself the other morning. "And your shaver could use a new razor. And you need shaving gel. And cream rinse. And don't you use anything besides dandruff shampoo?" A sharp pinching sensation started inside my shoulder. I gave Ethel a look to match. "Oh. Sorry. I forgot about pinched nerve thing," she said. "Haven't you seen a doctor about it?"

"Yeah, last winter," I said.

"Didn't he give you anything?"

"She. And yeah. A couple of creams."

"Didn't you use them?"

"Yeah. Sort of. I went back in for a re-check and she asked me about them."

"What did you say?"

"I said they made my skin itch and burn a lot."

"Eech. What did she say?"

"She asked if the itching and burning was unbearable."

"What did you say?"

I shrugged. "I guessed no. I mean, unbearable has to be pretty bad, right?"

Ethel pursed her lips. "I'm no doctor. But I'm guessing something that's supposed make you feel better shouldn't itch or burn. You're not still using them, are you?"

I shook my head.

We listened to sizzling and watched Bauser domestically flip the beaner pierogies.

"Maybe you should see a homeopath," Norman piped up.

"She's friends with K.," Bauser huffed.

Norman sighed. "A homeopath. Not a homo."

"Oh."

I shook my head and stopped. A sharp crick in my shoulder shot down my arm and straight into my fingers. Youch. I wondered if this kind of pain would be considered unbearable. I mean, is unbearable like completely distracting, or can you still grocery shop but just be a bit grouchier standing in line? Besides, what was the alternative to unbearable? Drop dead?

"Anyway, why was How-weird calling Mina at home?" Bauser asked.

Ethel winced. "Umm... it's not real good. And he's mean," she said.

"Why do you say that?" I asked out of habit rather than any real reason. After all, he's my boss. Isn't mean a part of every boss' job description? Except for Ethel's boss, who's really more like her fairy godfather. Ethel's boss Ralph let her work from home the first week they adopted the Ratties and apologized for not being able to swing the time as FML instead of re-paid comp time.

"It kind of sounded like Howard fired you."

Bauser got caught in mid-flip and flopped a pierogie on the floor. Vinnie, Hansel and Gretel immediately surrounded the renegade pierogie, sniffed, and burnt their respective noses. They licked their chops, and sat around the steaming beaner in wait.

"Oh crap," Norman said. But not about the pierogie.

The pinch in my shoulder tightened in the opposite direction, pulling a nerve in my butt that throbbed all the way down from my neck to my heel. A quintessential tension headache was brewing. I tried to take a deep, cleansing breath and hiccupped instead.

"Okay, HIC, why do you think HIC-oward fired me?"

"Because he ended the message by saying 'YOU'RE FIRED'."

I sighed and started to go upstairs to listen to How-weird's apoplectic missive. Maybe Ethel misheard? After all, she could be preggers. Don't hormones affect your hearing? On the other hand, if it would scare my hiccups away then Howard's message might actually be useful.

"Mina, you might not want to listen to that alone," Ethel tried.

"HIC?"

"He was pretty mean. Even if all the things he said you didn't do aren't true. It didn't sound like he was just venting." I nodded and hiccupped upstairs.

"Here!" Bauser said and thrust the spatula and towel at Ethel. He lifted a chin to Norman to follow. Norman sighed and trudged." Just when you think you have a bonafide hooky day," he mumbled.

"Wait a minute. Where are you going?" I asked.

"We're going to listen to How-weird's missive. We'll give you a full report."

"Uh, don't you think I should listen to my own messages?"

"No," they said in unison, and thumped upstairs.

Fifteen minutes and another lifetime later, they were back downstairs in the kitchen, while Ethel and I had practiced the ill-advised art of El Hombre pierogie production. There were about four dozen pierogies heaped on the platter in front of us.

I, at least, felt more relaxed. Bauser and Norman looked a little grey. So did Ike, who'd followed down after them.

"Geez, your boss is mean," Ike said. I shrugged. Then he added thoughtfully, "Well, at least he's not your boss anymore," and helped himself to a heaping of pierogies on a plate. "Hey, got any salsa?"

I looked at Bauser and Norman. Norman looked down. Bauser shrugged. "You're probably not alone, if it makes you feel any better," Bauser said.

"Huh?" I asked.

"He made reference to your 'slacker buddy'," Bauser said. "Me."

"So?"

"And how you're out on your ass. Like me."

"Oh."

Vito waltzed back in the door with a large tray and a grin. But one look at us and his entire face fell. "Geez, who died?" he asked.

We filled him in on the casualties.

"Ugh," Vito said. "The slob. Who needs him, right? Ya know, just the other night your Ma and Mu and me was talking about how you were too good for that job anyways."

"The other night?" I asked, then mentally pinched myself. If I really didn't want to know anything, I had to stop being so damn inquisitive.

"Yeah, I thought I should go over to Mu's to see how the girls were doing after the fire and all. And we had a nice time looking at paint swatches," he said.

I-don't-wanna-know, I-don't-wanna-know, I-don't-wanna-know, I mantra'd to myself and banged my heels together three times. Planet pain came back into focus and shot the taut nerve in my heel back up to my shoulder, neck and noggin. But I was still here, and actually wishing I was in Kansas. Ouch.

"I've always felt Mina's talents were wasted at EEJIT," Norman said simply. "I'll miss working with you, and How-weird's an ass. But you'll be happier," he finished.

I thought about it. "Yeah, I'll be happier without How-weird," I said. "But I doubt I'll be happier without a paycheck."

"Details, details," Vito said. "If money's your only problem, you ain't got no problems."

Spoken like someone who'd never had to eat Insta-Noodles to pay the rent. But I was grateful for the nods of encouragement and mazel tovs at my termination.

"Well, looks like I got this stuff just in time," Vito said, settling his tray on the counter. "Nothing like celebrating the prospect of a new venture than with a Hawaiian Orchid."

He lined up a bottle of medium-okay champagne, a can of crushed pineapple, a can of mango nectar and a small jar filled with what I feared could double as turpentine. He gave the champagne to Norman to open. Bauser took it away. Then Vito dug around and pulled out my mini-Cuisinart which I hadn't used since I tried to curb the catering disorder.

"HAWIANN ORCHID – a little something what helps to take the taste of termination out of your throat," Vito said. Here goes:

1 can crushed pineapple

8 oz. mango nectar

8 ice cubes

1 bottle okay-ish champagne (don't waste the good stuff on this)

1 sugar cube per glass

1 dash Angostura bitters per glass

1/8 tsp rosemary

Rum

Put 1 sugar cube per glass. Drop Angostura bitters. Dash tsp. rosemary. Mix in 1 shot rum. Muddle. Combine pineapple, mango nectar and ice cubes into food processor/blender and mix until frothy. Pour about 2 shots fruit blender combination onto rum mixture. Mix gently. Pour in champagne and mix gently. Toast and drink to the past tense of a dead end and ALOHA to the future. Note: the drink probably will look a lot nicer in an actual wine or champagne glass, as opposed to the coffee mugs we used.

"Looks like it's the beginning of the beginning," Vito said.

"Or the end of the end," Norman said.

"Well, here's looking up your address," Vito said, and we all clunked our coffee mugs together. Except for Ethel, who clunked her glass of milk. I made a mental note to point her toward the hall closet and her pregnancy test kits quick, for the next time she had to pee. Which I hoped would be soon. And often.

"You know, I bet these look a lot nicer in glasses," Norman mused.

"What happened to the classy glasses you had the other night?" Vito asked.

"K.'s," I answered.

"That explains it," he said and sipped. "So now what are you gonna do?"

"Apply for unemployment, I guess," I said.

"No, I mean what are you gonna do about the Burning Buy-A-Lots?" he asked. I shrugged.

"Nothing," I said. "Except I'm going to have to get these insurance papers back to EEJIT."

Bauser stared. "Actually, ignoring EEJIT's and Buy-A-Lots mutual problem probably is not an option," he said. "Remember what we talked about before? Whoever's burning Buy-A-Lots has probably been konking you on the noggin."

"And burning my house," Vito added. Bauser nodded.

"Assuming this is a reasonable deduction," Norman began, "Mina should be somewhat safe now. Since whoever connected her with EEJIT and Buy-A-Lots will realize she's out of the corporate picture, they should shift their sights. Unless of course it's some kind of personal vendetta." Great. Personal vendettas. Am I lucky, or what?

"Well, ya know what they say. The only thing worse than getting a punch in the mouth is waiting for it," Vito said, finishing up his drink. "So there's no use in worrying about something until it happens."

We all clunked mugs again and agreed. After all this clunking, I was kind of glad my nice glasses were a thing of the past.

I leaned against the threshold to my kitchen and wished some genius computer nerd had invented an 'undo' button for life. Except that I'd probably end up smacking 'undo' back up to the day Ma first saw Dad. Goes to show ya. I readjusted my stance and tried to make my attitude shift along with it. Ethel looked me over.

"You know, you really need to do something about how you deal with stress," she said.

I glared back at her warmly. "That's why I go to Snappy Hours," I said.

Ethel opened her mouth, thought better of it, and closed it. Ike chewed on more beanie pierogies. "Hey, these aren't half bad. And I do feel better. Thanks, Vito," he said.

Vito looked Ike up and down, looked over at Ethel and shrugged. "No problemo. A person can't be all lousy if they're Hansel and Gretel's dad," he said.

"Well, I still have to get these papers back to EEJIT," I said, rifling around the dining room for where Ma or Mu had stashed them. I found the envelope tucked inside the bookcase. "And I still need to talk to the police about my purse. And my car. And the insurance people. And the credit card people. And get a new driver's license. And bank card. And..." I trailed off: the day was mostly gone and I still had a few hundred people or so to argue with. And I still didn't have a car. I mean, I had my car, but I didn't have my keys. And that also meant whoever had my car keys, in my pocketbook, also had the keys to my house. Great. Just what I needed. More unexpected guests.

I was tossing around the options of asking Bauser or Vito for a ride, when Trixie rushed into the kitchen. She tried to give us the heads up, as Appletree strolled in right behind her.

"Hey, are we celebrating or mourning?" Appletree asked, eyeing the empty champagne bottle and pitcher of Hawaiian Orchids. He shook his head. "Looks like an Irish wake." Then he continued, "But I got good news, anyway," and held up my purse.

Vito, Bauser, Norman, Ike and Ethel contributed individual cheers, with and without Hawaiian Orchids. Vinnie grred a, "Gratch-laash-ions," and the Ratties sat pretty.

I took my purse and looked at it. It looked really, really clean. "We had to dust it for fingerprints," Appletree said. Oh. Well that explained that, then. But everything, including my wallet and its contents were there.

"You think I'm okay to use everything as is?" I asked.

"Yep. Because we got it right off of her," he said.

"Her?" Bauser, Norman and Vito asked collectively.

"Yep; got her down at the station right now. Mina, do you know a Helena Pryz... Prychnitch... Pryzchntchynzski?"

"Gezundheit," Ike said.

We all looked at each other. Except for Vito, because his eyes rolled back in his head and he fainted in the middle of my kitchen floor.

Luckily for Vito, he had a crowd around him; otherwise he would've joined the Konked Noggin Club. Unluckily, Bauser and Norman and Ike broke his fall and kind of got a little squished.

Trixie rummaged around in her handbag and pulled out a tube of smelling salts and held them under Vito's nose. After a few dozen seconds he came to, looked around and blinked his eyes. "What happened?" he asked, rolling over. The fellas scrambled out quickly.

"Well, I was just about to ask Mina if she knew the gal we caught with her purse. Her name is –"

"Not important," Trixie cut across, eyeing Vito's face as its color began to drain all over again. He looked close to another faint. "After all, Mina's got her purse and wallet and stuff back, and none of it was used, right?" Trixie leaned into Appletree.

"Well, yeah, but –"

"And that's the main thing, right?"

"Well, that and assuming Mina is pressing charges," Appletree finished.

Vito rubbed his head. "Is that really necessary, officer? I mean, Mina's got her stuff back. Maybe it was just a case of mistaken identity," he said.

"Nope, there's no mistake about it. Her ID has Helena Pryz... Prychchitch.... Pryzchntchynzski all over it."

"Bless you," Ike said.

Vito swallowed hard. "Actually, I meant the identity about the handbag. Maybe this kid has one that looks just like Mina's?"

Appletree stared at Vito. Trixie rolled her eyes.

"Yeah, well, uh, maybe," she said, whilst simultaneously backing down the hall and toward the front door. "Hey, I almost forgot; I'm late for something," Trixie faked. Appletree stared back at her. "Would you mind moving your cop car? You're kind of parked behind me," she said.

"I thought you just got here?" Appletree asked.

"Yeah, but I forgot something that I'm late for now," she fibbed.

Appletree shrugged and handed me his card. "Give me a call in a couple hours, so we know where we're going with this. I have to know if we're hanging onto this kid, or letting her go," he said, and exited, shaking his head.

Vito sat up and put his head in his hands. "That's it. I'm cooked," he sighed.

"How do you mean?" Bauser asked.

"Helena's my niece."

"So?" Ike asked, munching on another pierogie. We all looked at him. Then I realized he'd been asleep during Vito's midnight confession. I looked at Ethel.

"I'll fill you in later, Ikey," she said. Ike shrugged and chewed.

"If she spills the beans about me, I'm toast," Vito said.

"Why would she do that?" Ethel asked.

"I'm guessing she's pretty sore at me. On account of I'm the one who put her boyfriend in jail."

"Her boyfriend?" I asked. I had to – some things you just can't help.

"Yeah." Vito sighed. "Mickey the Mouse. He was one of the young Turks I fingered."

"Mickey the Mouse?"

"Yeah, on account of he really likes a good cheddar. And he was also a bit of a pest," Vito said. "Anyway, Mickey the Mouse wasn't a bad kid. I guess he wanted to make a name for himself, but there was no way he was gonna fit into our family."

"You mean he's not Polish?"

"Worse: he's Irish." Vito shook his head. "If he'd wanted to really join the mob, he should have gone with his own family into politics." We all nodded in agreement. Clearly, Mickey O'Mouse was confused. "We should have taken him under our wing. Instead we kept trying to get him into something legitimate. Like shoe sales. You have any idea how much dough is in ladies shoes?"

Ethel and I nodded energetically. Our personal shoe hero, besides Ma and Mu, was Imelda Marcos. All legends.

"Next thing you know, he's talking big about the New York Italian family. It all went down the sewer pipe from there.

"I always thought Helena had a thing for Mickey, ever since their first Halloween in kindergarten. Helena got all dressed up as the Good Fairy and she wanted a wand. So I made one for her out of a 3/4" dowel, and jigsawwed a star out of plywood. Painted it silver with glitter and everything. We stopped by Mickey's house for tricks or treats – you know, just to be polite and all. And because Helena kept bugging me. Mickey shows up at the door dressed like a little devil, with plastic red horns and a little red tail. Helena tried to whack him, straight off." He smiled.

Ethel gasped. "Your niece tried to kill him?"

"No, no, no. She whacked him with her wand. Which probably kind of hurt on account of the dowel and wooden star and such," Vito answered. "Why would you think she tried to kill him?"

"You said she whacked him."

"You've been watching too much TV," Vito tutted. He took a pause and sighed. "Yup, those were the good old days, back when I knew my little Helena-noosh loved her Uncle Vlad. I mean Vito." He sniffed. I rolled my eyes and grabbed some paper towels and forked them over to him. He nodded thanks and blew his nose. "Anyways, when Mickey got into trouble, Helena got pretty upset. Then my brother sent her off to visit our dead aunt in Vermont."

Ethel stared at Vito wide-eyed. "You mean her family sent her away?" she asked.

Vito shrugged. "Pieotre, my brother, wasn't all that keen on Mickey either. Especially as he'd been seeing a lot more of him hanging around Helena. I can't says I blame him," he said. "Mickey could really be a pest," he added. Not to mention the extra supply of cheese, I thought.

“Anyways, that was the last I heard of my niece before I left. And I don't know why, but Pieotre was pretty much avoiding me.” Vito grimaced. “Which was pretty unlucky on account of having to leave town unexpectedly, sort of planned for like and all, because I couldn't get the chance to tell him goodbye.” He sniffed again. I handed him the full roll of paper towels. “I always worried about leaving him with sore feelings and such.”

Bauser got up and handed Vito a half a mug of Hawaiian Orchid. Vito nodded thanks and gulped. Norman held out his towel, which Vito took for comfort, eyes tearing up again. “Yous sees what I means? You kids are really swell,” he said sniffily, and sipped some more. I was just glad he didn't blow his nose in Norman's towel.

“Okay, so now what am I supposed to do about Helena and Officer Appletree?” I asked. “It's not like I’m going to press charges against Vito's niece. I mean, I got my purse back, that's the main point.”

Vito shook his head. “It don't matter. Charges or no charges, Helena's gonna blab. I'm pretty sure of that. And Federal protection or not, there might be a few outstanding, err... disagreements I've had with the police. In the past, I mean,” he added quickly. “Then again,” he continued, “if you changed your head and decided to press charges, that could get pretty bad too.”

“How do you mean?” I asked.

“Well, you might have the Moils out of Bumville after you, along with the flaming fecal flingers,” he said. I made a puzzled face at that; Bauser pointed his index finger at his temple and pulled his thumb-trigger to make sure I understood. Oh. Yikes!

“You know, maybe this was all some kind of family misunderstanding,” Ethel said. “After all, Helena has no connection with Mina and she obviously wasn't trying to steal anything. Maybe it was a desperate cry for help, to her uncle?” she asked with a misty-eyed look.

“Hey, ya think?” he asked. “I always was her favorite uncle. Even if I am the only one. That is, I was her favorite uncle until I got Mickey put in the pokey. I heard she was pretty sore at me about that.”

“Well, maybe the best thing is for Mina to go downtown and talk with her,” Ethel offered.

"Huh?"

"Well, you have to go return the insurance papers to EEJIT anyway. Isn't the police station right across the street?" Ethel said.

I sighed. She had a point. Even if it was at the top of her head.

Vito looked at me hopefully. "You'd do that, for me?" he asked all watery-eyed.

"Sure. What the heck," I said.

"But what if she blows Vito's cover at the station and starts yelling and stuff?" Norman asked warily. He quickly added, "Not that I think your niece is the yelling kind." I looked over at him. He had an over-stocked knowledge about female yelling, between his two teenage stepdaughters and his wife. I gulped.

Vito shook his head. "You're right. And she is," he added meekly.

"So what's our plan B?" Bauser asked.

Vito folded Norman's towel and handed it back to him. "Throw in the towel, of course," he said. "That's what Mike and Annie are for. Let's just hope we don't have to use them. Because I don't think I'm ever gonna fall in love with Tampa." He sighed. I shuddered, remembering Vito's hair-stained shirt.

We got the pierogies and pots and pans cleaned up, and mixed together a game plan, even if it was half-baked. Bauser and Norman filled Vito and Ethel and Ike in about the buddy brigade for me. I looked on hopefully – but unfortunately they all agreed and my privacy dissolved. So, Bauser, Norman and Jim were going to escort me back to EEJIT and to the downtown police precinct, hopefully while Appletree was still on duty. We figured Appletree left a wider range of maneuvering. Especially since I could hold Appletree a virtual hostage where Trixie and his wife were concerned. Ike was going to take the Ratties and Vito out to the dog park. And maybe also have a quick peek on Vito's would-be terrier, Stanley, in the hopes Stanley's former owner remained at large. Ethel was gonna stay at home and keep an eye on my house, Vinnie and Marie. She was also going to call Ma and Aunt Muriel to check up on them, and make sure their sleepover hadn't morphed into another Atlantic City escapade.

On my way out with the boys, I made sure to lovingly hiss in my kid sister's ear that maybe she might want to try out the numerous pregnancy test kits that were hiding in my closet. She gulped her milk and nodded.

I crammed into the backseat of the Aspire next to Jim, with Norman sitting shotgun and Bauser driving. We led the parade with Vito and Ike bringing up the rear. We turned right on Millersville Pike, heading downtown, while Ike and Vito made a left toward Rohrerstown Road and the animal shelter. Part of me nervously hoped Ike wouldn't get inspired to dump the Ratties there, if we found out that Ethel was actually pregnant.

Bauser pulled up to the Chestnut Street entrance and parked. Which was a big no-no: there's a ten minute limit for loading or unloading stuff.

"Ummm," I said, looking at the sign.

"We're unloading," Bauser said. I looked at him. He shrugged. "We're unloading insurance papers. Sort of." We trudged through the glass doors, with Jim hopping along, while Bauser carded us inside.

"Can I help you?" an anonymous uniformed security guard asked at the front desk. Huh. Where the hell was he when I was getting konked on the noggin?

"EEJIT," Norman replied, nodding his head upward.

The guard looked at us. We nodded. Even Jim. Then he shrugged. "IDs, please," he said.

Norman and Bauser produced their badges, and I produced mine – albeit after digging around in my very clean purse that still held the same old crap. After flipping some coupons, a Tylenol and a Tampax onto the counter, I withdrew the badge just as the guard waved me off. "Lady, I believe you, I believe you," he said. I shrugged.

The guard looked at Jim. "He's with me," Bauser said.

"Is that a dog for handicapped service?" the guard snapped.

"Yup," Bauser said. Well, at least he was only half lying. Jim was handicapped.

I looked at the elevators. They were sans 'Out of Order' signage today. "Is it okay to use the elevators today?" I asked.

"Sure! What's wrong with the damn elevators?" the guard barked.

"Uh, nothing," I mumbled, and shuffled toward the elevator bank and pressed the up button. I looked sideways from Bauser to

Norman and down at Jim. They each exchanged peripheral raised eyebrows at me. The elevator bank binged and all three elevators opened. I sighed and looked at Bauser. He pulled out a quarter.

"Call it," he said.

"Tails."

Bauser looked. "Heads," he replied, and held open the middle elevator door. We all shuffled in. Bauser pressed '7'. The doors closed.

"What would you have called if it had been tails?" Norman asked me.

"Individual elevators, with Jim using the stairs as backup," I said.

"Wow. You really do have a paranoid thing about these elevators."

"That's only because they hate me."

"Oh," Norman said, and rubbed at his non-gunshot wound.

EEJIT's lobby seemed to be back to normal. There were no more mega fans blowing smoke through the lobby's glass doors. In their place instead was a lot of stale, smoked fertilizer-esque smells.

We held our breath and our noses while Bauser carded us through the glass doors. Inside was worse. A lot worse. "Cripes, haven't they heard of air ionizers?" Norman coughed. "Or Air Fresh?"

"Aah, there they are, on time as usual," Howard cried.

We looked down the hall and realized we'd stepped into the middle of something, and it wasn't flaming feces. It was a company meeting, which Howard liked to hold in the main corridor. Howard thought this was a brilliant management technique because it made everyone stand up and force them to be succinct. This might have worked really well if anyone else but Howard talked. As it was, How-weird's various elevator speech narratives usually morphed into full-blown water cooler treatises.

Norman pushed his baseball cap back from his forehead. "Oh boy," he said. Bauser and I gulped. Since Bauser and I were already fired, we didn't really have much at stake. But Norman usually slid under the being-late radar mostly because he normally works about 75 hours a week – and is pretty much incredibly indispensible. But How-weird was in a full-blown mode of some kind.

"As I was saying," Howard sneered at us, "it's obvious we're not working in ideal conditions. But we're not a charity, either," he added. I looked around and saw a sea of folded arms, deadpan stares and thin lips. And I saw Lee, taking notes, sitting on a chair next to Howard.

Hey, wait a minute. Sitting?!? I never rated a seat, even back when I had to run that stupid 45 minute slideshow presentation of Howard's: 'Toilets and You: The Bottom Line on Restroom Hygiene'. Which, of course, we all had to watch while standing.

"Now, just to clarify," Howard smirked, "it's perfectly understandable if you have documented medical reasons that prevent your working in the office until the landlord mediates the, uh, air quality issues."

"That explains it," Norman whispered. "They didn't spring for renting air cleaners because they're foisting it on the owner of the building. They really are that cheap."

"However, unless you have bonafide work which can be done from home – and of course approved by your manager –" Howard all but winked at the managers a.k.a. his golf buddies – "well then your time is not considered HW – Home Work," he finished. He put his thumbs under his make-believe suspenders – his armpits – and waddled down the center of his employee lineup. "Now, of course, we are all professionals, and most of us, luckily, are able to do some work at home."

"Except for the golf course," an anonymous voice grumbled from behind a cubicle wall.

Howard heard. "Ha ha ha. Well some business meetings are more pleasant than others," he said.

Uh oh, I thought. Howard didn't break into a rage. He actually tried to be pleasant. This was going to be pretty bad.

"However, EEJIT's policy is an Effhue policy," he continued, "and in these circumstances, especially as our corporate offices are going through similar difficulties, the HW policy has changed. From now on, an HW day does not count as a full working day. An HW day will now accrue 5.6 working hours. This means that if you enjoy an entire work week of HW days, you'll owe EEJIT – and Effhue – 12 working hours for that week."

I was starting to feel light-headed. I couldn't believe my ears. Was this kind of Dickensonian stuff legal? Where was Bob Cratchit when you needed him? Or Father Christmas? Then again, it was only August. Wrong time of year, I supposed.

"Also, HW days will now accrue 0.435 benefit hours, and not the 0.63 hours of an office working day." This prompted a buzz of mumbling and a lot of expletives in various languages. 'Dirty dog of a flea bitten llama' in Hindu was the only one I recognized.

"Now, now," How-weird said, and smiled, "we also know many of you, as salaried business professionals, occasionally work over the appointed 40 hour work week. And while many of you take this in stride, some of you feel your 'extra time' should be compensated." Howard's smile drew even wider. I noticed he had spinach in his teeth. Probably from gnawing on a vegan programmer. "In these instances, you are encouraged to discuss comp time with your manager."

There was a lot more mumbling and more 'dirty dogs' about that. Everyone knew How-weird didn't hire or appoint a manager who didn't buckle under his fat little thumb.

"Also, ALSO," Howard shouted, trying to break through the now very loud non-mumbling, "comp time will no longer be a day for a day. If you work the entire weekend, your manager can approve one day of comp time to you," he said.

Silence. This was bad. Very, very bad.

"Of course, with a two weeks request notice," he ended.

I heard some rustling behind me, and then heard Achmed hissing at Mohammed in Arabic. Out of habit I hissed back, "Huh?" at them while keeping my eyes straight forward.

"I have said, that even while working in the times of the Tyrant, the hours of our lives were respected more during imprisonment," Ahmed hissed back.

"Or terminated gracefully," Mohammed whispered back sagely.

"I work in kabutz more sympathetic to hard work," grumbled Tevloh.

I shrugged philosophical. "Well, at least it's no worse than phone sales," I said.

"You have done the phone sales?"

"Were you that desperately poor?"

"You were prostitute of the phone?"

"Did they arrest you?"

"Did you sometimes wish to kill yourself?"

"Yes, yes and no, no no! " I answered. "Hey, I paid my way through college with that job," I said.

Some muttering and clucking went on behind me in Arabic, Hindi, Israeli and what I think I recognized as Norwegian. Then I felt various pats on my shoulders. "You should be very much impressed," the anonymous hands patted, while we all maintained eyes forward. I nodded thanks and felt very, very proud indeed.

CHAPTER 9

(Wednesday afternoon)

"Well, seeing as we've all broken out into our little side bar conversations, I guess our new policies are clear to everyone. So quit wasting time and get back to working," Howard hollered.

I looked and saw Chandtishe Pakashakaswyswaami's cane plunk smack dab into the middle of How-weird's foot. Chandtishe is about 1,000 years old, has a limp, and was literally counting the days toward his retirement a.k.a. Emancipation from EEJIT. Thanks to EEJIT's legal system, it had only taken about 10 years for him to receive a bonafide green card. 15 years later – just last year, actually – he had attained U.S. Citizenship through EEJIT's legal counsel, after working an additional sixteen months of twelve-hour days. Now, at long last, he was due to retire in February.

I smiled and waved to him. He smiled and waved back, and leaned down hard on the cane, piercing Howard's instep. Howard gritted, picked up Chandtishe's cane and removed his shishkabobed foot. Chandtishe faked an elaborate apology and then gave me the thumbs up as How-weird turned and bent over his foot. Chandtishe had always liked me. I figured How-weird was in for a lot more sore piddy's once Chandtishe got wind I got fired via answering machine.

I watched How-weird grit his teeth at Chandtishe and start to limp our way.

"Hey, Norman, you might want to get lost now," I whispered at him.

Norman rocked back on his heels, pulled his cap down and folded his arms. "You know, I've been thinking," he said slowly. "I've been thinking that maybe Betty's girls are old enough to get their own jobs."

I looked carefully over at Bauser. He was as wide-eyed as I was. Jim wagged his tail back and forth at us all and fell over again.

"Well if it isn't the two Losers," How-weird jeered. I gulped. I was already fired by proxy, which was bad enough. Now I had to get fired in duplicate? Publicly? Yeeshkabiddle.

"Just give us our paperwork, Howard, and we're out of here," Bauser said.

"We just came to give you these back," I said and handed over the envelope with the insurance papers. Bauser rolled his eyes at me. I stared back at him and shrugged. What was I supposed to do, eat them?

Howard snatched the envelope from my hand. "You're welcome," I quipped. Well... sort of quipped. Kind of.

"What have you done with these papers? Nothing! That's what!" Howard shouted at me, and that's when Jim, for the first time ever, growled. Howard took a step back.

"Actually, Mina's contacted the insurance company, forwarded the accident information, and you're due to be inspected by an insurance claims representative any day now," Bauser said.

I looked at Bauser, amazed. I didn't know I'd done all that. Maybe the konk on the noggin made me more productive? Not likely. So I figured Bauser had done it, since he had worked at EEJIT since Day One. And I was okay with him talking to the insurance company and saying he was me, unless he used falsetto. "Mind you, an arsonist is at fault. However, the contract you signed says that if EEJIT is in non-compliance of just one code requirement, Mid-Atlantic Liability and Culpability, PLC can default for breach of contract," Bauser added.

"Yeah, sure," Howard shrugged.

"Which means they won't pay a plug nickel," Bauser explained.

Howard spluttered.

Norman chimed in, "Yup, even if the fire was caused by an arsonist or act of war or terrorism. Apparently, some EEJIT representative signed, and continued, a contract with these limitations."

"Which, by the way, Howard, was you," Bauser finished.

I made to shoot him a worried glance, but held it at bay. Was he bluffing? He certainly was acting very melodramatic movie-like. But he was still wearing his shades.

"Ha ha, Bauser, that's a good one. Let's just see," Howard smirked, and pulled out the 4-inch thick tome of contract negotiations between EEJIT, Effhue and Mid-Atlantic Liability and Culpability, PLC. I sighed. We would be standing here for years. Even if Howard could read.

"Page 558, paragraph 7, item AAAA.aaaa.iiii.09.iv.aa.4," Bauser responded confidently.

Yeesh. I guess my concussed head had me knocked out so long that Bauser got bored enough to read through all this stuff.

"Okay, well, let's just see here," Howard muttered, riffling through the pages.

Norman peered over his shoulder. "Page 558 comes after page 555," he said. "Here, let me help you."

So, for what I guessed was our brief flash of glory, Howard stood there semi-publicly humiliated with some proverbial egg – a la flaming feces – flung at him. Norman read out loud, "Paragraph seven, item AAAA.aaaa.iiii.09.iv.aa.4 clearly states, 'In the event of any kind of fire, by natural or unnatural events including arson, war, terrorism or insanity,' " (yes, it really said that – I figured whoever drafted the document had met Howard) " 'Mid-Atlantic Liability and Culpability, Ltd. will hold this contract null and void. Also, this contract will be non-negotiable and void upon inspection and proof of non-compliance of all and any applicable local or national fire and electric codes.'"

Howard started sweating. "So? What does this prove?"

"I've been telling you for six years now that the server room and cooling units don't comply with code," Bauser said.

"Yeah, well, uh....you never gave me the particulars," Howard faked.

"Yes I did, Howard. I emailed them to you, and copied in Effhue. I'm sure you'll be able to find them in your past emails. I know I've kept my copies." Bauser smiled. Which was more than a little disturbing. Because I had never, ever seen Bauser smile before. Not a real toothy smile, anyway. For the first time I noticed the very large gap between Bauser's front teeth. It was wide enough to spit through. Ack.

"Heh, heh, heh, well jokes on me," Howard said awkwardly. "Hey, listen, we've all been under a lot of stress lately. How about I treat you to a nice lunch? Say, uh, the Fiesta Flamingo?"

The Fiesta Flamingo is a sandwich shop that is adored by Lancastrians for serving really huge Southwest style sandwiches really cheap. A real big spender move on Howard's part.

Bauser said, "I don't think so, Howard. But thanks anyway." Jeez. He really did fit into Lancaster; he was even nice when he was getting the heave-ho. "How do we get our termination papers processed?" he asked. "I mean, normally we'd go to Mina. But you fired her, too," he said.

"Hey, wait a minute, you know I was only joking. I panicked," Howard said.

"I know. You panic a lot."

Howard stared into Bauser's mirrored shades for what seemed a long time. His image stared right back at him. "Fine, fine!" he yelled at last, throwing up his hands. "I've had enough of the Mod Squad anyway. Just go see Lee. She'll take care of you!"

He backed up, bumping into Lee. "Ah! There you are!" he squealed. "Great! Just take care of these losers and process their termination papers," Howard shouted, pointing at me and Bauser. Jim growled again at Howard and barked. Howard leapt backward on his stabbed foot, and then hopped off onto his good one. I started to think that for my next job interview, I should probably take Jim along. He'd be able to sniff out in a few minutes what would probably take me a few years to figure out about the next crazy boss.

"Of course, Howard," Lee said. "My pleasure." There was a cruel edge to her voice. Clearly, she wasn't from Lancaster. "Follow me," she said over her shoulder as she started waddling down the corridor. Bauser and I looked at each other and shrugged.

"C'mon, Jim," Bauser said, and we started to walk away.

"And where do you think you're going?" Howard bellowed as Norman followed us. We both turned around. Norman stood shaking his head and opening up his backpack.

"Here," he said, handing various notebooks, papers and CDs to Howard. He zipped his backpack up and started away.

"Hey, I don't need you to babysit those two. I need you to work out the algorithm faults," Howard called after him.

Norman turned around. "There are no algorithm faults. There are data faults. And no thanks, Howard," he said.

"This isn't a request, moron. This is a directive!"

Norman stopped and turned back once more. "That's nice, Howard. But directives only apply to employees. I quit," he said, and walked toward us, smiling.

This was scary. Aside from the obvious, it was more than a few times in just a few days I'd actually seen Norman not unhappy.

"Dude, are you out of your mind? You can't get unemployment if you quit," Bauser whispered.

"Maybe you can un-quit. You know Howard needs you," I stammered.

"Yeah, then all you need to do is just screw up on purpose and get him to fire you. Then you can collect," Bauser added.

"It's okay," Norman said. "I never needed their paycheck, anyway."

"Huh?"

"Look, besides my Masters in Software Engineering, I've actually got a PhD in Astronautical Engineering."

Wow. "Really?"

"Yeah, I don't like to talk about it much. It's a little embarrassing." Bauser and I looked at him. "Rocket doctor jokes," Norman explained. We nodded. "So the work here was pretty interesting, and everyone used to be pretty friendly. And it got me out of the house. But after Effhue took over, it seemed like things just kept spiraling downward, all across the boards. And without both of you in the picture, that's a lot more ugly than I can handle." Bauser and I looked at each other. I knew we were both wondering if the BB-shot wound had caused more damage than we'd realized. Or the Krumpthfs.

"Umm, dude, that's cool, but like, what are you going to do to get paid?" Bauser asked.

"Like I said," Norman continued, "I never needed the paycheck. Haven't either of you wondered about my last name?"

"You mean Mudd?" I asked.

"So?" Bauser questioned.

"Like Mudd of the Mudd-Tee teabag. That TeaWorld, Inc. bought," Norman finished.

"Isn't TeaWorld, Inc. owned by another huge company?" Bauser asked.

Norman sighed. "Doesn't really matter. My old man was Manny Mudd. He was really into food engineering. One day he came up with the design for the Mudd-Tee teabag, and made sure to patent it. "

"Designer teabags?" I asked.

Norman sighed. "For the design of a one of a kind teabag. I found out after he passed away in 1992. Back then he was worth over $400,000,000."

"Four hundred million dollars?" Bauser gasped, like I'd wanted to. My mouth worked, but no sound was coming out. I get a little speechless when the words 'hundred' and 'million' are used in the same sentence as 'dollars'.

"Yup. Since dad passed away, I've never needed my EEJIT paycheck," Norman added. "Mostly I've used my EEJIT salary for charitable giving, or the girls' allowances," he said.

"Jeez, you mean you could afford to actually hire someone like Vito to clean and cook for you?" Bauser asked jealously.

"Yeah, I could. But my wife would kill me."

Bauser shook his head. "Well, I better get processed out of here. Jim's Whoof-O dog food alone definitely needs my unemployment comp," he said.

I sighed. "Agreed," I said, thinking about my 25-pound mountain lion cat and my cockatiel's sometimes freakish calcium dependency.

Norman shrugged. "Let's go," he said.

We walked to my old cubicle just in time to find Lee sitting in my chair and tweezing a hair out of the mole underneath her chin. Bauser, Norman and Jim collectively cringed backward. But I thought nothing about it and grabbed for the bottom file drawer.

"Hey, what the!" Lee stammered, hastily trying to shove her tweezers and compact mirror out of sight.

"Under 'U' for 'Unemployment Comp'," I answered, yanking the drawer open and into her shin.

"Excuse me," Lee yelped, "but these are the papers you need to fill out." She shoved a wad of EEJIT bureaucracy at me.

Bauser grabbed the papers and sorted through. "There are no Unemployment Compensation forms in here," Bauser said.

Lee smiled. "Oh, they'll send that to you in the mail." Bauser looked hard at her. She sighed. "Look, an Unemployment Rep will call you, at about the same time they send you their papers," she answered.

"Oh," said Bauser. "Since when did you become the HR rep?"

"Since they merged Mina's position with mine. And part of your IT duties." Lee smiled again.

"Wait a minute," Bauser said. "You're going to do my job, Mina's and yours?" he asked.

"Well, uh, no. Not really. Howard said just portions of them," Lee said.

"Well, I hope you're getting paid portions of our paychecks then," Bauser said.

"Well, no. But I'm promised a big raise at my review next November."

"Huh. Good luck with that."

Bauser tucked the papers under his arm and gave me and Norman and Jim the high sign to exit. We all turned together and walked down the hall.

"Just make sure to tell the Unemployment rep it's a 'mutual resignation'," she sang out after us.

Jim whined. "C'mon, Jim," Bauser said, and we shuffled into the elevator lobby.

"What's the matter with him?" Norman asked.

"He needs to let loose, pronto,"

It was at that moment that we heard Lee gloating around the corner to someone about having 'termed those losers'.

We looked at each other. Jim wagged his tail pleadingly. Bauser motioned to Jim to follow him, and marched back down the hallway and made a right turn toward Lee's former cube. Norman and I followed. We reached the outside corner of her old cube, which it was undoubtedly, judging by the state of packed files on the floor around her desk. Bauser pointed. "Here, boy." Jim gratefully and dutifully obeyed and emptied both tanks in the middle of Lee's cube. Then we high-tailed it for the stairs and exited pronto.

Seven flights later, we let out a collective whoop. Even though Bauser and I realized it was ridiculous for us to do so. Being unemployed and looking for a job stinks. But working at EEJIT really stank. Especially after the poo-poo pyro. I might not have been sure what was in front of me, but I sure knew what was behind me. And it greatly resembled what Jim left behind in Lee's cube.

Norman took his papers and dutifully put them in an appropriate section in his backpack. Bauser and I looked at ours and contemplated hurling them in the trash bin next to us.

“No,” Norman said. “Listen to me. You will fill this out. And you will await your call from your Unemployment Rep,” he said.

Bauser and Jim and I collectively gulped. I'd never seen Norman adamant about anything, except maybe the end of the world. Maybe that was why he was adamant now. “Okay,” Bauser and I agreed.

“So what now?” Bauser asked. Jim barked at PizzaNow!.

“Jim's right,” Norman said. “We need a slice and a beer. I'm buying.”

Jim barked in agreement and followed Norman, dragging Bauser up the entrance steps. I shrugged and followed. What the hey? We all know everyone at PizzaNow! loves Jim.

“Hey, Jimmy boy,” Joey sang out from behind the order counter.

Maggie cried and came out from behind, leaving a line of waiting customers in limbo. “Who's my boy? Huh?” she squealed, hugging Jim. Jim tried to reciprocate and fell over. “See, see? This is what happens to neglected pets!” Maggie shouted at the line of customers. Sheepish looks abounded amongst pet owners who had left pets alone all day long, with nary a radio on. Maggie seized the opportunity. “Guilt relief here,” she said, holding up her collection jar for the animal shelter, next to the check out register. Various hands released small piles of change. Could she sell or what? And she wasn't even from Jersey.

Maggie winked at us. “Pretty good, huh? Hey, what brings you here? Late lunch? Early dinner?” she asked.

“A wake,” Bauser said.

"We're celebrating," Norman corrected.

"Hungry?" I ventured.

"Huh?" Maggie asked.

"We lost our jobs," Norman explained.

"Oh my GOD! Oh my GOD!" Maggie shouted. "Here, take this table. HERE! Natalie – WATER! HERE! NOW!"

Norman held up his hands in effort to stop her flurry of waitressing. "Look, it's really okay. We're not that upset, honestly," he said.

"UPSET? UPSET! OF COURSE YOU'RE UPSET! YOU'RE IN SHOCK!" Maggie screamed, and went off in a stream of Sicilian phrases I wasn't quite sure about but pretty much guessed meant MAYDAY.

We sat down around the table, after we found a chair for Jim, just to make sure he didn't get knocked over by passing patrons or appear out of place. And also to make sure a passing patron didn't find himself suddenly relieved of his order. Natalie rushed over with a water pitcher and a bowl for Jim. Then she set us up, throwing a slice of lemon in each of our glasses, and passing around some menus. She finished by taking a doggie biscuit out of her apron pocket for Jim.

"Okay, okay, you take all the time you want. I'll bring over a small pie, just to get you started. On the house," she added, patting Jim on the head, then rushing back toward the kitchen.

"Wow, they really like Jim here," Norman said.

"We eat here a lot," Bauser said.

"I thought you mostly ordered take out?" I asked.

Bauser shrugged. "Jim likes to get out on weekends."

Natalie came back with a small pie – 8 large slices with everything on it – and a bowl of kibble. Jim stood up on his chair and wagged his tail hard in appreciation, and then fell toward the pie. Bauser caught him. Natalie patted Jim on the head. "You're welcome, sweetie."

We said thanks, too, and began to tuck in as we scanned the menus. When I looked up, the pie was almost gone. "I'm really surprised how hungry we are, considering," I wondered out loud.

Norman swallowed. "Disappointment does that."

"Oh," I said, thinking that was probably as good reason a reason as any for explaining the increasing national reports on obesity.

Maggie came over with a pitcher of beer. Bauser looked at it suspiciously. She set the pitcher down on the table, along with frosted beer mugs. "Look, I know you like your Krumpthf's," she said to him, "but that stuff is oogy. It has leaves and twigs in it. Besides, this is on the house, too" she added. Bauser looked a little put out.

"Well, okay. Thanks. Just so long as it's nothing fancy," he said warily.

"Nope; just plain old beer," she said.

Wow, real beer. Without twigs in it. I started to feel a little happier.

"Natalie will come back for your orders real soon. I gotta get back to the take out counter." And she rushed back as the line of customers backed up into Chestnut Street.

"Wow. That was real nice," Norman said, pouring out the lager.

We looked at each other. Norman was really becoming quite the drinker. Huh. Jim thumped his tail.

"Well, here's to us," Norman said, and we clunked our mugs together.

We studied the menus we'd read a thousand times before, and placed our orders with Natalie. Norman ordered Lancaster Lasagna (without the ham), Bauser ordered the Meat! Meat! Meat! & More Meat! Personal Pie! and I ordered the Triple Decker Eggplant Parmesan. Our entrees arrived, and after Natalie served us, she replaced Jim's kibble bowl with a small bowl of Whoof-O dog food. Bauser also fed Jim some of his steak and kidneys off of his plate, carefully excluding any bacon, ham or sausage that would be bad for doggies.

We'd just polished off our plates, when Natalie returned. "Some dessert?"

Bauser tried to hold in a burp.

"Uh, I think we're kind of full," Norman said, looking around. Bauser's burp burped, I nodded and Jim yawned. Jim was right: it was definitely nap time.

Natalie smiled. “Sure, sure. After a big shock like that, it's normal for your appetites to be a little off,” she said. “But you'll be back on your feet in no time. You'll see.” She smiled at us and hustled away with our empty plates. I rolled my eyes. If this was considered peckish, maybe my catering disorder might actually fit into Lancaster.

Norman reached for the check. Bauser went for his wallet. I started to rummage through my pocketbook. Norman held a hand up to both of us, and waved away our contributions.

“Wow, thanks, Norman, really,” I said.

“Yeah, thanks a lot. This is really decent of you, man,” Bauser said.

“Like I said, my treat,” Norman replied. “Besides, I didn't think anyone could handle meeting Vito's niece on an empty stomach – especially after Howard's tantrum.”

“Oh my gosh, I almost forgot,” I said.

“I didn't,” Bauser replied and helped himself to the last piece of pizza. Norman shrugged and we got up to pay at the register. Joey rang us out.

“Thank you. That'll be $46.46,” he said. Norman opened his wallet and pulled out a hundred dollar bill. Joey blanched. I blanched. Bauser blanched. Even Jim looked a little piqued. But maybe that was maybe because he was still digesting his share of the Meat! Meat! Meat! & More Meat! Personal Pie!

“Oh jeez, hey, I'm not allowed to change anything higher than a fifty, pal,” Joey explained.

“Not a problem,” Norman said. “Keep the change. It's a tip.”

Joey brightened up considerably. “Hey, pal, thanks! You're alright! I'll make sure Natalie and Maggie get covered.”

I rolled my eyes. While I knew Norman could probably afford this generosity, I secretly hoped I didn't share a happy hour with him any time soon. I really didn't want to get shamed into a 150% tip. Especially now that I had joined the masses of the unemployed.

We yawned and waddled out of air-conditioned PizzaNow! and out onto the furnace that was Chestnut Street. The heat blasted up at us from the sidewalk like the inside of a PizzaNow! pizza oven. The sky had become a hazy shade of dinge, just like any other U.S.

city during a hazy U.S. summer. Except that Lancaster sparkles a bit; it doesn't do dinge.

Jim panted hard. Bauser's and Norman's glasses were fogged up. We turned and made a blind lurch toward the new police station at Chestnut and Prince streets. We entered the lobby and were greeted by giant blasts of chilled air and gigantic black granite columns, floors and an elevated black granite reception desk. Granite? In a police station? This is how nice Lancaster is. Who wouldn't want to get carted off the street into a grand hotel-esque lobby in the middle of a heat wave? We stood in front of the reception desk, and Norman shoved me forward in front of the great and powerful Officer Du Jour. The female police officer on duty looked down at me. The main thought scampering across my brewski and Italian feast fed brain was: surrender Dorothy.

"Uh, hi," I tried, "Um, we're here to see Officer Appletree. Is he on duty?"

"Officer Appletree, huh? That's Detective Appletree, now. Just one minute," the Great and Powerful police officer said and ducked behind the granite wall. We heard muted voices and some Mhming. She popped back up. "He's here. Said he was expecting you," she said, and darted back down again. Expecting me? I hadn't even told her who I was yet. Yeeshkabiddle.

We shuffled around the lobby. Jim yawned and sprawled out in the middle of the granite lobby, parting pedestrian traffic. Which was a little awkward for some of the handcuffed folk. The officer popped back up. "Is that your pet? Or a service animal?" she barked.

"It's okay, Shawna; he's handicapped," Appletree answered, appearing in front of us.

"Huh. Okay..."

Appletree motioned us to follow him – quickly – past Shawna's watchful post.

"Hey, wait! He's not supposed to be handicapped: one of them is," Shawna yelled after Appletree.

"We're working on it," Appletree called back.

"Just you make sure he don't tinkle on them granite tiles!"

Well, it was at nice that she was looking after our taxpayers' interior design investments, after all. Then again; we're in Lancaster…

Appletree led us down a pristine non-granite hall and through some double-doors that opened onto a typical office space: a gerbil's nightmare of cubicle mazes. With the exception that each of the cubes were inhabited by combinations of uniformed or plainclothes police officers. At this particular time, it was mostly uniformed officers. Like an army of dark blue ants.

Even though I've never done anything illegal in my life, with the exception of aiding and abetting Vito and Mrs. Phang with their pharmaceutical sample ring, being around this many uniformed police officers made me nervous. I blinked and swallowed and promised myself I would never tell Trixie about this. However nervy this many uniforms made me, I was pretty sure she would have an equal and exponentially opposite pheromone reaction.

Appletree led us over to his pristinely empty cube. I looked around and was disappointed. Pictures of Detective Friday, Dirty Harry and Barney (the cop, not the dinosaur) swam around in my head. Appletree's very organized and very generic gray cubicle was not exactly the stuff of NYPD Blue.

Appletree motioned for us to sit down. Jim wagged his tail, hopped up in the chair and complied. I shook my head at Bauser, leaned on the edge of Jim's chair on one cheek and faced Appletree's modular desk. Bauser leaned against a counter stacked with files. Norman unpacked his towel, unfolded it neatly on the floor and sat down.

Appletree pulled out a file from his desk drawer. "Okay, so all we need you to do is sign this form," he said. "It states that we caught Helena Przy... Helena Prishnish... Proshchinsk..."

"Pryzchntchynzski," called out a male voice from the next cube.

"Bless you!" another officer sang.

"Thanks, Gus." Appletree grimaced. "Anyway," he continued, "we found her with your stolen purse."

I gulped. This was definitely a lot more official than I expected. And where was Helena? Did they have her in a dungeon? I started to have very, very guilty thoughts about wasting all that time consoling our unemployed stomachs at PizzaNow!.

I looked down at Norman. He shrugged at Bauser. Bauser looked at Jim. Jim smiled and pooted.

"Whoa, whoa, whoa," Appletree spluttered, waving the forms at Jim and digging around in his desk drawer and pulling out a can of Air Fresh. "I gotta work here, ya know." He whispered, "You have any idea what it's like to work in a cube farm? You can't even have a personal phone call without the whole force knowing what you're supposed to pick up for dinner."

"Yeah, I used to," I commiserated. "When did you get promoted?" I figured Trixie should at least know that much.

"Just this morning!" Appletree beamed. "Good things come to those who wait, right?"

"Hey, Appletree, quit cutting the cheese over there," a gruff male voice called over from another cube.

"See what I mean?" Appletree whispered. "Here, Mina, sign these before your eyes start to water."

I looked at the papers with Helena's name all over them. I looked down at Jim. Jim pooted – a silent and more deadly version this time. My eyes watered. Appletree hooked his hand around his face; Norman placed his baseball cap over his mouth.

"Look," I said, holding my nose and covering my mouth with my hand, "I'd like to talk with her."

"What?"

"I mean, how do you know she stole my bag?" I asked.

"Because we found her holding your bag," Appletree answered.

"Right. But that doesn't mean she took it from me," I said.

"Or konked Mina on the noggin," Norman said. "After all, that's the main point, Detective."

"How do you mean?" Appletree asked.

"Because whoever actually stole Mina's bag has to be the one who knocked her out cold," Bauser said, unwrapping a piece of gum and putting it in his mouth. Huh. No wonder he could drink Krumpthf's. And didn't mind Jim's poots. Bauser had no nose-buds.

"Okay, okay, we know all that. And that makes sense. And as much as I shouldn't do it, I'll let you talk to her – with me present," Appletree said.

"So we're thinking like detectives then, huh?" Norman asked from behind his baseball cap.

"Maybe. I don't know. I don't care. My cube is completely polluted – we gotta get out of here before Jim's fumes reach the whole department." Appletree waved the way toward the holding cells. "I'll never hear the end of it. My first day as detective. Geesh."

As we filed out of Appletree's stinky cube, we began to hear little spots of verbal recognition about Jim's freed fumes: "Pheeew!" "Who brought in the Amish fertilizer?" "Who got a nervy perp?" "Hey, where's that can of Air Fresh?"

We picked up the pace and trotted down the hall toward an elevator. We got into the elevator and Appletree kneeled down to talk directly to Jim. "Look, elevators are very confined spaces. So just squeeze your cheeks together until we're out, okay?" Jim smiled at Appletree and schlurrped him chin to forehead. Appletree pressed the letter 'D' (for dungeon?) and down we went.

When the elevator stopped, the doors opened onto a far less grand version of the front desk. It was still elevated, but instead of being covered in granite, this reception desk was just plain old Formica, surrounded by a clear kind of plexi-glass, which I guessed was bulletproof. Appletree stepped up to the desk and pressed a buzzer. The two officers manning the desk looked up from their monitors. Appletree took his ID and placed it in what looked like a drive-up ATM receptacle. One of the two officers retracted the shelf, opened it up, peered at Appletree and returned it back through the slot. "Who you here to see?" the reception officer asked.

"Helena Proz-crink.... Helena Proz-chink... Helena..." Appletree stumbled.

The other officer rolled his eyes. "You mean, Helena Pryzchntchynzcky. Man, I've been through half a dozen labels trying to get her file straight," he said.

"Babe needs to buy a vowel," the other officer grimaced. Appletree shook his head.

"Who you got with you?"

"Victim. Gal whose purse she stole," Appletree answered. The reception officers looked at each other.

They shrugged. "It takes all kinds," they said.

"ID please," the second reception officer directed me through the plexi-glass.

"ID?" I asked. "I'm not a cop."

Appletree hung his head. "Your driver's license, Mina," he said, rubbing his forehead.

"Oh," I said, and went through my newly recovered handbag. Which was when I noticed how much neater my wallet was since my purse had been recovered. And re-organized. Even the coupons in my wallet were folded up, not crumbled and shoved in like I usually kept them. It was good to know the police treated victims nicely, too. But I guess they had to; it's Lancaster, after all.

I found my driver's license and gave it to Appletree. Appletree put it in the slot and the reception officer mechanically grabbed it. He looked at it, and then at me. He nodded at Appletree. "Okay, you can go in," he said, putting my driver's license in some kind of a receptacle beneath the counter. I looked at Appletree.

"You get it back after you come out," Appletree explained.

I looked over at Norman and Bauser.

"We'll wait here with Jim," Norman said quietly.

I followed Appletree around the encased reception desk. A buzzer buzzed, unlocking the steel door in front of us. Appletree opened it and held it for me. For a lot of people, this probably seemed like pretty stringent police security. But it gave me a cozy feeling. It reminded me of when Ethel and I visited Gramma Maude and Grandpa Lester's apartment in the Bronx.

We walked through the door and into yet another reception area. Instead of having an elevated reception desk, though, there was a normal counter with a fairly normal officer behind it. Behind him was an open hallway with a series of closed doors.

"Go ahead, we'll bring her in," the officer informed Appletree. "Room A2."

We walked down the hallway, and Appletree opened another steel door – with a window in it – to the room labeled A2. It was small. One table that was about six feet long stood inside. On one of the long sides was a single chair. Opposite that were two more chairs. Appletree showed me into one of them. He sat in the other. We stared at the empty chair across from us.

He reached into his pocket. "Gum?" he asked.

"Oh. Okay. Thanks," I said.

Appletree nodded. "PizzaNow! is pretty good. But sometimes you wind up leaving smelling like garlic. Or beer." He winked. Great.

"It was sympathy beer. And it wasn't that much," I said.

"It's okay. Sounds like you guys have had a pretty tough day." I looked at him blankly. "Trixie," he clarified. "She called you at work, and got Lee. And the news."

Oh. Fantastic. Not only did I get my own unemployment news secondhand; now it was getting broadcasted to the police. Crap.

Appletree and I waited. Then came the sound of the tumblers unlocking on the other door. It swung open, and there stood a somber female police officer and a very weepy Helena Pryzchntchynzcky. The officer rolled her eyes, dug around in a pocket and handed Helena a tissue.

"You stole a handbag; you didn't kill someone. Get over it," she said kindly. Helena wailed a bit and nodded and gulped and blew her nose. The officer rolled her eyes again and rummaged for another tissue. "You keep on like this and they're gonna accuse me of dehydration abuse. Hold on." She darted away from the doorframe and returned with an economy size box of tissues, which she thrust at Helena. "Here. I'm not planning on having a cold or a boyfriend anytime soon."

Helena Pryzchntchynzcky stood weepy and fragile with her newly bestowed box of tissues cradled in her right arm and several drippy used tissues clutched in her left hand. I looked her up and down and was grateful – for her sake – that she didn't look a thing like her Uncle Vladimir. Vito. Whoever. Helena Pryzchntchynzcky looked like a porcelain doll: she was about five feet tall, probably weighed about 90 lbs. soaking wet and had wavy, platinum blonde hair that hung down past her shoulders and incredibly huge, jade green eyes. If it weren't for the fact I'd come to help her and her estranged uncle, I would have hated her. Nothing personal: just on principle. Helena was an exception to my usual rule of thumb of hating females who look perfect without even trying. That was because her huge jade green eyes were red rimmed and puffy from crying.

Appletree stood up. "Ms. Prochin... Ms. Prayzyn... Preztal..."

"Bless you," Helena snuffled.

"Helena, please, sit down," Appletree finally got out. He motioned to the chair opposite us.

Helena crept forward and slunk into the chair, hugging her box of tissues. I looked at her. She stared back and her face crumpled again. "I didn't do it," she wailed. "I just found the stupid handbag. I was just going through it to find some tissues," she cried.

"Well, that's understandable," I said, grateful that Vito's – Vladmir's – niece came with a ready-made excuse because I had yet to concoct one on my own. Appletree kicked me under the table. "Ow!" I replied.

"Sorry," he lied.

"Look, Ms...Helena," I said, "why don't you tell us what really happened?"

Helena sighed and blew. "I don't know why. I've told these morons about a zillion times, to a zillion different people."

"Erm… sorry. But at least we're new morons to tell," I said, and kicked Appletree back.

And that was when Helena Pryzchntchynzcky launched into the Bumville version of Alice's Restaurant, complete with the 8 x 10 color glossies with notes on the back and having to be put in the holding cell with the mother lovers and litterbugs. "So you see, I just came across this handbag. I figured someone must have dropped it. Which I thought was lucky, because I was having a real allergy attack. I saw some tissues on the top, and helped myself. I was about to call the police, when I got surrounded and yelled at and thought I was gonna get shot," she sniffed. "I was just trying to do the right thing."

Lie or not, this rationale seemed reasonable enough to me. Besides which, if I didn't get Helena out of jail, Vito might get sent on a one way ticket to Tampa. Or worse.

"Well, that's good enough for me," I said, getting up.

"Wait a minute, wait a minute," Appletree said. "We caught her with your purse."

"And I believe she was honestly trying to return it to me, and was interrupted by very, very diligent police officers." I smiled politely. "Besides which, look at her. She's tiny. She couldn't knock me out. She couldn't be strong enough to lift anything that could knock me out," I said.

"You got knocked out?" Helena asked.

"Yeah," I said.

"With your own purse?" she asked.

I shrugged. "Not sure."

"Well, it is kind of heavy. You have a lot of stuff in there."

Appletree looked at both of us like he was visiting inmates from the asylum. He shook his head.

"Okay, let me get this straight," Appletree said, rubbing the back of his neck at what I guessed was going to be a whopper of migraine by the time his shift was over. "The victim is not going to press charges?"

"Right," I said.

Appletree looked crestfallen. "This is going to be a long first day," he said.

He stepped around the desk to the door Helena came in through and pressed a buzzer. The door opened, the kindly tissue matron greeting him. "The victim's not filing charges. There's plausible doubt. The department's not pressing charges at this time," he said.

"Well thank goodness. Any more tears and we'd be calling in the Army Corp of Engineers," the female officer replied. "Bring her up to the front," she said and closed the door.

Helena sniffed and blew into another tissue. The wad she had in her hands had now grown to the size of a volleyball.

"Here," Appletree offered, and held up a wastebasket. Helena tossed the ball in. It landed with a thud. Appletree and I cringed.

"Thanks," Helena sniffed.

"C'mon."

We followed out the way we'd come in, but this time we took a detour to a back room with a table, chairs and a large mirror. I guessed this was an interrogation room. Appletree left Helena and I alone, disappearing after telling us he needed to get some forms.

For a few minutes there was just quiet, punctuated by her irregular sniffs.

"Thanks for believing me and not pressing charges," Helena said at last. She took another tissue from her box and blew.

"No biggie." I really didn't want to have too much conversation with Helena while Appletree was watching from the other side of the 'mirror'. If Helena started chatting about her Uncle Vlad – Vito – this would get a lot stickier, for both of us.

After several more minutes of non-productive quiet, Appletree came back in with a clipboard and some forms and a report with Helena's statement about finding my purse at the corner of Prince and Orange Streets.

"Just outside the Lickety-Split Laundry," Helena nodded helpfully.

"Mina, you sure?" Appletree asked. I nodded. He shook his head again. "Okay, you can go on out. I'll process Helena out of here," he said.

"Thanks," I said, wondering how I was going to hook up with Helena afterward without tipping off Appletree. I waved bye-bye to Helena, and went back to the reception area and rejoined Bauser and Norman and Jim.

"What now?" Bauser asked, while Jim slobbered my arm in greeting.

"Uh, well, I guess we go home," I faked brightly.

Bauser looked at Norman. The officer behind the desk opened the drawer/chute thingy, and offered me back my driver's license. I took it and tossed it in my purse.

"Yup. Let's go. Our work here is done," I sang, and led the parade toward the elevators. I pushed the button, the elevator arrived, and we got it.

"Mina, where's Helena?" Norman asked.

"Shh."

"Huh?"

I rolled my eyes and hissed, "The ears have walls."

"Huh?"

I led us out of the elevator, into the hotel-style public lobby and outside. Bauser's and Norman's glasses fogged back up immediately. Jim led us lopsidedly up the street to Bauser's car. We were almost legitimately handicapped for a few seconds. That probably explained why Jim was so happy.

"What's the game plan?" Bauser asked.

"Well, first, we can't let Appletree see we know Helena," I said.

"Oh jeez, that's right," Norman agreed.

"But we can't let her wander around Lancaster and maybe blow Vito's cover," Bauser said.

"Right. So maybe we wait for her and offer her a ride somewhere?" I asked.

"Right, and then what? Kidnap her? Escort her out of state?"

"I have no idea," I said. "But maybe if we offer her a ride, she'll tell us why she's here. Maybe she's just doing the tourist outlet thing?"

Bauser shrugged and pulled out his keys. His car sat waiting – with a ticket stuck to the windshield. He detached it with a sigh, and put it under his window screen visor. Norman let Jim and I in the back. Then he pulled the ticket out of the visor, opened his wallet and pulled out some cash, and placed it all back.

"Hey," Bauser began.

Norman waved him off. "You're unemployed, remember? When you're gainfully employed again, you can buy me some Krumpthfs," he said.

"Thanks, man," Bauser said.

"No problem, dude."

I hunched down in the back, grateful they didn't break out into some, "I love you, man," stuff, and also trying not to think of how many, many cases of Krumpthfs a traffic ticket's fine would actually buy you.

We pulled away from the drive-up, drove around the block, then parked across from the police station. Norman got out to put some change in the parking meter.

Bauser turned to me. "You know, I'm a little worried about Norman," he said in a low, almost conspiratorial kind of voice. I nodded. All this spending, no matter how loaded he was, was pretty uncharacteristic. "I just hope he doesn't go into shock or something." I nodded again.

We waited. We sweated. We unrolled the windows and hung our heads out. Sitting with 3 people and a large doggie in an Aspire in August gets pretty close. Especially with a pooting pooch.

After a few thousand years, I saw Helena walking out the front entrance of the police station. "There she is," I said.

"Right. Got it," Bauser said, restarting the car and pulling away from the curb. He drove slowly behind Helena, following her, and made the left onto Queen.

I hung my head out. "Hey, Helena, need a ride?"

Helena looked startled. “Oh, well. That's very nice of you. Especially since you thought I stole your purse,” she said. And she started to cry. Again.

“Oh jeez. I hate it when women cry,” Norman sighed. “I completely cave when my wife or the girls start.”

“Deal with it,” I muttered. “It's not like she's going to hit you up for an allowance.”

We shoved Jim over and Helena squeezed in.

“Sorry about Jim,” I apologized.

“Oh, what a cute doggie!” Helena gushed.

I looked across Jim at Helena while we sat sqooshed in the backseat, Jim panted, wagging his tail, and decided it was appropriate to lie flat on his back across both our laps for a belly rub. Luckily for Helena, she got Jim's head and shoulder portions. Not so lucky for me, since I got the vice versa. “Uh, Jim, ya know,” I said, trying to shove him on his side.

“Oh, him is a nice doggie woggie, isn't him?” Helena gushed some more, scratching Jim's ears. I looked up and saw Bauser's reflection in the rearview mirror. I was pretty sure Bauser was wishing he was a nice doggie woggie, too.

“So, where to?” Bauser asked.

“Uh, well, I don't know. I've only been in Lancaster for a few hours. That's when I found the purse and got arrested,” she said, starting a fresh brew of tears.

I pushed on with, “Well, all’s well that ends well,” and handed her another tissue from the almost empty box. “You here for the sales? We could drop you off at the outlets,” I fibbed.

“Actually, I'm trying to look up some family,” Helena admitted. “My boyfriend Mickey asked me to find my uncle,” she said.

“Your boyfriend Mickey?” I nearly shrieked.

Helena sniffed. “Well, sort of. He's my daughter's father, anyway,” she said.

“YOUR DAUGHTER'S FATHER?”

Norman turned around in his seat. “You'll have to excuse her, miss. Mina's pretty traditional. She's not used to the having children before boyfriends thing,” he faked.

“Oh, that's okay. Me either. It just kind of, well, happened. And we do want to get married. That is, once Mickey's out of prison,” she spluttered. And then broke off into another fresh wail.

"Oh. That's, uh, nice," Bauser said, nearly driving into the car in front of us – his gaze had been fixed in the rearview mirror at Helena.

"Uh, hey, uh, would guys mind if I, uh... stopped here at this store and grabbed a paper?" I lied.

"Nope," Bauser said, and pulled over.

"Norman, could I borrow some change?" I asked.

"Sure," he said, digging around in his backpack and handing me a couple of pounds of quarters. Yeesh. Didn't his shoulder hurt him?

"Great. Thanks. Anything I can get you while I'm in there, Helena?"

"Oh. Well. Maybe, if you don't mind, a box of tissues please," she said, digging around in her Dooney & Bourke handbag for her wallet. I waved her off.

"I got it. On me. Well, really Norman. Welcome to Lancaster, ha ha," I said, and got out of Bauser's car quick and hurried into the store in search of a payphone, stat.

I dashed into the store, grabbed a newspaper and a box of aloe vera tissues – I figured Helena's nose had to be pretty sore by now – and looked around for a phone.

At the rear of the store was some poor sad soul who was obviously down on his luck. "Thank, thanks a lot, man. I appreciate that," he said, hacking up a lung into the receiver, and hanging up. I cringed. I began to realize the appeal of cell phones and regretted my technophobia.

The man left, wheezing goodbye to the clerk. The clerk gave him a nod, then continued reading his book from behind the counter. I walked to the phone, opened the box of Klean'ums, picked up the receiver with a tissue covered right hand and wiped the mouthpiece off with another wad wrapped around my left hand. I dialed the keypad with my hands wrapped inside tissue mittens. I called my house, looking for Vito.

"Kitchen Residence," a jolly voice answered. It was Vito. He sounded very happy. He was probably Swiffering.

"Hey, Vito, it's me. Mina," I said into the phone, holding the receiver about fourteen inches from my mouth.

"Hey, Mina, where you calling from? The bottom of a well? I can hardly hear yous," Vito said.

"I'm calling from a payphone," I said.

"A public phone? That's not too sanitary."

"I know. Believe me, I know. Listen, Vito, we've got Helena with us."

"You're kidding? You do? You mean she actually wants to talk to me?"

"Uh, well, in a manner of speaking. She doesn't know we know you."

"Oh. So why's she with you?"

"We thought if we offered her a ride, maybe we could find out why she was here in the first place. We were hoping she was outlet shopping."

"Oh. That makes sense. Was she?"

"No. She's here because her boyfriend wants her to look up her uncle."

"Boyfriend?"

"Mickey."

"It figures."

"Actually, sounds like he's more of a fiancé. He's kind of promised to marry Helena once he's out of prison. Mostly because he's her daughter's father."

I heard a thump, and then silence. "Vito? Vito!?"

For a few long seconds, nothing … and then panting.

"It's alright, I'm alright, I'm alright, Toots. Just lost my balance for a minute, that's all."

"Well, what do you want me to do?" I asked.

I heard Vito sigh. "Just bring her home. I'll take care of this," he said.

"But what if, umm... this means you have to relocate?"

"Hey, there are worse things. Tampa might not be so bad. Besides, my niece is my niece. You just bring her home so we can get this all sorted out straight," he answered.

"Yuppers," I said and hung up, shaking my head. Maybe Vito was right. Tampa isn't so bad. Besides which, it couldn't have many more senior citizens than Lancaster.

I paid the kid behind the counter, who rang me up, took the change and gave me a receipt without taking his eyes off of his book. "Good book?" I asked.

He shrugged without looking up. "It's okay," he said. "But nobody's got whacked yet," he added. I winced.

"Shame about that poor guy," I offered. The kid looked up at me like I'd landed from Pluto, the outcast non-planet. "The guy at the payphone," I explained.

"Oh, him," the kid shrugged. "He just comes in here for cigarettes and to use the payphone sometimes," he said.

"That's a shame, especially for someone down on his luck like that," I tried.

"Are you kidding me?" the kid yelped. "That's our landlord. He owns this building, and the two parking garages behind it."

I cringed and walked out the door toward Bauser's car, and saw Jim splayed across the backseat with his head on Helena's chest, and looking up at her in complete adoration. I opened the door, picked up his one hind leg and sat down. Then I passed Helena what was left of her box of tissues. She looked at the opening. "Allergy attack," I fibbed.

"Yeah," she said.

"Well, where to now?" Bauser asked, looking into the rearview mirror at me.

"Actually, I think maybe Helena would like to meet my neighbor," I said.

"Really? Why's that?" she asked.

"Because he's your uncle," I said simply. Bauser nodded and we drove off, while Helena began to sniffle again.

CHAPTER 10

(Wednesday afternoon)

"You just don't understand," Helena sobbed. "Wujek will kill me," she wailed.

"Uh, no, I don't think he's going to kill you," Norman offered.

"Of course not. What for?" Bauser added hastily.

"B-b-because I had a BABY!" she wailed.

"Well, these things happen," Norman offered.

"And the father's not even POLISH," Helena continued. "Or JEWISH."

"Well, nobody's perfect."

Norman shrugged. Helena blew. Jim bayed a la beagle in support.

"Jim bays?" I asked.

"Who knew?" Bauser shrugged.

Huh. Figures. Just like every other guy I ever met, Jim has a thing for blondes, too.

"When I got pregnant, Pop sent me to a group home in Vermont for wayward shiksahs," Helena explained. "He wanted to shame me because the baby's half-Irish. But a week later, Ma showed up and bailed me out. We took a cabin on Lake Champlain for the summer," she added wistfully. "That was a real happy time. Ma was nice to me. It was a real first." I nodded empathetically.

"So Ma and I decided to rent a condo in Burlington, near the hospital. At that point, neither of us was speaking to Pop, anyway. Especially after he told us Uncle Vlad had Mickey locked up."

Helena started to sniffle again. The wad of used tissues in her lap grew from the size of a ping-pong ball to something more like a baseball.

"I had a beautiful baby girl, Marie, named after my Auntie Marie, may she rest in peace," she ended.

"So where's your kid now?" Norman asked nervously.

"Not to worry; she's with her Gramma and Grampy back in Bumville," Helena said.

"I guess you patched it up then?" I asked.

"Sure; right after Marie was born, when I moved back. I didn't really want to, though." She paused and blew again. "But I had enough of Vermont. I really hate snow. And skiing. I completely don't get the downhill thing," she said. "Bu the time I came home, Uncle Vlad had just – poof – left. And Pop wouldn't say a peep." Another tissue joined her growing collection. "Later I visited Mickey in prison with the baby, and he told me all about Uncle Vlad testifying against him in court."

"Jeez, are you sure you want little Marie to, umm... visit Mickey in prison?" Bauser asked.

"He is her father," Helena sniffed. "And I don't understand what the big deal was about, anyway. Don't you think it's a little extreme to put someone in jail over some lousy unpaid traffic tickets?" she asked.

Traffic tickets? "Umm... yeah," I said. Oh boy

Bauser forced the Aspire up Mt. Driveway, tugged at the emergency brake and shut the motor off. The car lurched back. Norman and Bauser got out, and hauled me and Helena and Jim out of the gulch what was Bauser's backseat. We shuffled to the front door where Vito was already waiting, dressed up in a dark blue Armani suit, light blue silk shirt and paisley tie. He was even wearing his bridge.

Helena gulped a breath, stepped forward, and sobbed into her basketball of tissues. Vito hurried down the steps and engulfed Helena and her snotty ball in a big Uncle Vlad bear hug.

"Moja mała mysz," Vito said to the top of Helena's platinum flaxen head. We weren't sure what that meant, but it was obvious it wasn't something bad.

"Oh, Wujek!" Helena wailed.

Vito – Vlad – held her and patted Helena on the back of her head. We all sniffed a little, too. I sniffed mostly because Helena was snotting all over the lapels of a perfectly good, and rarely used, expensive Armani suit. Ma and Aunt Muriel would have had a fit.

Ethel came out red-eyed. Either she was watching the same thing we were, or peeing on her Instant Speedo Econo Pregometer ('Like 2 kits in 1!') pregnancy test kits took a lot more effort than I'd reckoned. Vito turned around as the screen door shut, and noticed the rest of us.

Vito mopped his brow with a meticulously folded handkerchief. It turned orange. "Well, listen, Cookie," Vito – Vlad – began to his niece, "I think we should talk. But in private like; not here out on the lawn."

Helena blew into another tissue and added it to her mucoid medicine ball. She looked at me, then Vito, and nodded. "I guess you don't want to talk about family stuff in front of your neighbor," she said.

"Hey," Vito replied, "Mina's more than just a neighbor. Her and her aunt kind of took me in, like. As far as I'm concerned, she's family."

I felt a tug at my heart. Then I realized Jim was sitting pretty with his paw on my chest.

I also felt the usual crimped nerve in my spine. I can't help it. Public displays of familial affection make me a little nervy, unless there's shouting involved. The crimp pinched with a vengeance. I rubbed my butt.

Helena started sniffling again. Wasn't she getting dehydrated? Vito winced. He must have been thinking the same thing. Or maybe he was wincing because Helena had crumpled his very expensive Armani handkerchief and merged it with her soggy wad.

"C'mon, Cookie," he said. "Let's go inside, have a bite to eat, and catch up."

Helena sniffed and nodded. She turned to look at us, and then she started bawling again.

We waved bye-bye at Helena and Vito. Then I herded all my escorts into my house.

Vinnie grrled and stretched hello at me. Clearly things were not so uptight at my house that Vinnie hadn't been able to nap.

Then again, I had yet to find too many situations that Vinnie couldn't nap through. Jim greeted Vinnie by sniffing his butt. This made Vinnie spring upward, fur sticking up in all directions, especially his tail. Hello, Afro Cat.

"What's wrong with her?" Bauser asked, thrusting his chin toward Ethel, who was blowing her nose in the corner.

"Uh... cramps," I lied.

"Umm... your, uh, little boys room is down here somewhere, right?" Norman asked.

"Yup," I said, and showed him the powder room.

"And another's upstairs, too?" Bauser asked.

"Uh, yeah, right off my bedroom," I said to Bauser's sneakers heading up the stairs. I guessed Krumpthf's has diuretic effects. At least, I hoped that was it, and not the effects of Meat! Meat! Meat! & More Meat! Personal Pie.

I walked into the kitchen to find the counters lined end to end with pregnancy kits. "What the?" I asked.

Ethel sniffed. "Well, there wasn't enough room in the bathrooms for them all."

"Okay," I said. "Well?"

"Every friggin one of them says I'm yùn fù."

"Huh?"

"I had to look it up on the internet. Yùn fù is Chinese for pregnant woman," Ethel said.

"Oh. Well, that's great," I said. Ethel started to cry some more. "Look, I'm sure Ike was speaking in the figurative about Hansel and Gretel. He'd never get rid of them. Especially now that this is a real situation, not a hypothetical one."

"I guess. I don't know. They'd be too nervous in a foster home!" she wailed. "Hansel's on a very strict diet. It's expensive. Most people wouldn't take care of him like we do." I gulped. I wasn't going to tell Ethel about the donut crumbs if nobody else did.

Norman came out of the powder room. "Mazel tov!" he said.

Ethel sniffed. "Thank you, I think..." she gulped.

"No, really. This is great news. You must be relieved all the tests had the same results." I stared blankly at Norman. "The pregnancy kits in the powder room are all positive," he said. I looked him. "Yùn fù is Chinese for pregnant woman. Our neighbors own the Rising Sun Chinese Restaurant. We've had Dim Sum there every Sunday for years."

I shook my head and looked at Ethel.

"Well I wasn't going to line them all up in the kitchen," she said.

We heard flushing from upstairs and then Bauser bounded back down. "Congratulations," he said matter-of-factly to Ethel. Ethel nodded and cried some more.

"Where's Ike? What does he think?" I asked.

Ethel shook her head and blew. "Ike just dropped Vito off. He said he wanted to go to Pets-A-Million with Hansel and Gretel to look for new winter sweaters for them, because they're on sale..." She trailed off, trying to stifle a sob.

"Uh, well, that's nice," I said. Ethel sniffled some more. "What is the matter with you?"

"They have adoption groups at Pets-A-Million... What if he gives Hansel and Gretel away?" she wailed.

I grabbed some paper towels, wet them with cold water, and threw them in her face. "Stop it!" I shouted neutrally. Ethel wiped the cold wet towels across her face, took a big breath, and then exhaled.

"Now don't be so stupid," I said. "Ike's not that bad. Let's just give him a little time. He's probably just stocking up on Hansel's diet food," I said.

"Okay," Ethel sighed.

"And if you're wondering about how to tell him you're pregnant, leaving these test kits scattered all around the house sure would be a hint, even if you don't speak Chinese," I said.

The other shoe dropped. "Oh!" she said. Then she moved into hyper drive collecting up the kits and throwing them in the garbage.

Bauser grabbed a trash bag. "I can't stand family fights," he said simply, and pounced up the stairs.

Norman shrugged, grabbed another garbage bag and went into the powder room.

Before long, all of the kits were disposed of, and we breathed a collective sigh of relief.

Ike walked in later with the Ratties. The very, very fluffy Ratties. Hansel and Gretel looked like they had been given bad perms and tumble dried. They were also spectacularly dressed for some unknown occasion. Gretel had a large dopey red-sequined bow fastened to the top of her head. Hansel sported a matching dopey sequined bow-tie around his neck. They both looked equally humiliated.

"Hey, the Lancaster Pets-A-Million is great," Ike said with a grin, taking Hansel and Gretel's leashes off of them. The dogs immediately began tearing at their respective bows. "They've got a doggie day spa and everything. I got Hansel and Gretel manicures and pedicures, and a Fluff 'n' Phoof volumizing pooch wash. Don't they look fluffy?" he asked proudly.

Hansel lay down and put his paws over his head. Gretel growled at Ike.

"Uh, yeah," I said.

"It's really neat," Ike went on. "They've even got doggie hair dryers."

"Really? What are those like?" Bauser asked. Jim growled.

"They look like people hair dryers," Ike said. "But they say 'just for dogs' on them." Gretel growled some more. "What's wrong with her?" Ike wondered aloud.

"Maybe her bow's on too tight?" Norman asked.

"Hey, has anyone heard from Ma?" I asked, trying to switch gears. Ethel said she had, and that the girls were having a girls' day at Aunt Muriel's. "Great! I mean, uh, that's nice," I started, "so we'll just go have a look in on them, right guys?" I hinted at Bauser and Norman.

"Oh, right, yes," Norman said, picking up his backpack and slinging it over his shoulder.

"OH! Right, yeah, need to stop by," Bauser continued, catching on.

"Great, we'll follow you," said Ike.

"NO!" Norman, Bauser, Ethel and I yelled at him.

I said, "I mean, I'm sure you and Ethel haven't had a quiet moment together since you got here. And you just got Hansel and Gretel back from the puppy spa thingy. You wouldn't want all this humidity to defluff them, would you?"

"Why don't you just call her?" Ike asked practically.

"Uh... we have to drop some things off to her anyway," I said, as Norman and Bauser walked toward the door with Jim.

"Like what?" Ike asked to our backs.

"Us," Bauser said, and we all exited stage center, pronto.

We piled back into Bauser's car and slalomed off Mt. Driveway, dodging the traffic island and careening across the cul-de-sac. We turned onto Millersville Pike.

"Do you really think Ike will make Ethel give up the Ratties?" Bauser asked.

"Naaa, he's just blowing smoke," Norman said. "All guys say stupid stuff like that before they have kids."

"But if he did, I bet Vito would foster them until Ethel could get a divorce," Bauser added brightly.

I slumped down in the backseat. My conversations with my friends were getting stranger and stranger.

We drove into the Mansion District that once housed turn-of-the-century manufacturing moguls. We crossed Wilson, passing the 'dream house' I spied when I first moved to Lancaster.

"Still think they'll adopt you?" Bauser asked, meaning the family who owned my favorite mansion.

"No," I sighed. "Looks like they already have kids."

"Maybe they need an old kid," Norman offered helpfully. "You know, to babysit and serve canapés at bedtime or something?"

I shrugged. It was just a silly game we played a lot.

We crept onto Marietta, then Good Drive, and finally onto Aunt Muriel's street. We drove up the driveway and parked in the side lot she had paved for guests, next to a dark grey mini-van. The garage door was open, so we walked in through the unlocked back door, across the mud room and into the kitchen.

"Hello, Goils," I called out as I motioned Bauser and Norman and Jim in through the kitchen. "Hey, Aunt Muriel, I brought some company with me..."

I trailed off as I entered the living room and saw Ma butt naked under a sheet with someone who was definitely tall, blonde and handsome standing over her. And thirty years younger.

"AGGGGGGHHHHHH!" I screamed.

Bauser and Norman rushed in behind me to see the affronting vision. "AGHHHH!" they agreed.

"AGHH!" Ma yelled back.

Tall, blonde and bemused just stood there shaking his head and smiling.

"What the?" I asked.

Ma sighed. "Well, so much for the soothing effects of massage," she muttered.

"Huh?" I said.

"Muriel's treating us to a mini spa day. James is a massage therapist."

"Oh, uh, sorry," I said, walking backward and onto Jim's hind foot. He gave a little yelp and fell backward. "Sorry, Jim," I said, stumbling over him, as Norman and Bauser followed my lead and we backed up into the kitchen.

"Oh for Pete's sake, he was done anyway," Ma said.

James said politely, "Just lie there please, Mrs. Kitchen. You need some privacy to drape yourself."

"Oh please," we heard Ma puff as she got off the table and walked into the kitchen with the sheet wrapped around her, toga style.

"Remember to drink a lot of water, Mrs. Kitchen, to wash away the toxins," James called out after her.

"Toxins, right, okay," Ma said, and pulled a Brita water pitcher out of the fridge and a bottle of Grey Goose from the pantry.

"So where're Aunt Muriel and Mrs. Phang?" I asked.

"We're in here, dear," Aunt Muriel called.

I left Ma with Bauser and Norman. I went into the living room, where James was folding up his table, and nodded a sheepish 'hi' to him. He gave me a big smile back that I wasn't sure wasn't altogether not laughing at me. I proceeded into Aunt Muriel's bedroom and found Aunt Muriel and Mrs. Phang in their trousers and bras with plastic grocery bags over their heads.

They each slipped short sleeve pastel silk pullovers over their grocery bag heads, and carefully removed the bags from their faces. They looked at themselves in the mirror.

"You're right!" beamed Mrs. Phang. "Your hair stays perfectly in place this way!"

"Hello, dear, how are you?" Aunt Muriel asked.

"Uh, okey dokey. Just thought we'd stop by to say hi..." I trailed off. I figured I shouldn't tell them that the real reason we stopped by was to let Ethel tell Ike she had a bun in the oven that was almost half baked. “So, uh, Ethel said you ladies are having a girls’ day?” I tried brightly.

“Oh, yes!” Aunt Muriel beamed. “Your mother and Tina and I just had the most wonderful massage. James is a miracle!”

“Wow. That's great.”

“Now your mom and Muriel get to go to Paws 'n’ Claws,” Tina – Mrs. Phang – added with a sigh. “I have to go home. My dopey sister-in-law text messaged me about 50 times this morning.”

“Paws 'n’ Claws?” I asked. Did the girls want to adopt some pets, too?

Aunt Muriel nodded. “Oh yes, it's supposed to be the best salon in Lancaster,” she said. “And I can’t wait to get these bangs fixed!” She emphasized by tucking her singed hair back up under her headband. “Luckily Tina's been there; she recommends it!”

“Yes,” Tina/Mrs. Phang nodded. “The service is great. The name – not so much.”

“I've even heard of them. They got a write up in the Ledger,” Ma said, coming into the bedroom and carrying a glass filled with ice and a clear beverage that I hoped was mostly Brita water. She wandered into Aunt Muriel's ballroom size master bath, and we heard water running in the whirlpool bathtub. Clearly, Ma was taking the spa day verbatim and making ready for a good relaxing soak. “The Ledger said that for special customers, they even give you a Mai Tai!” she called out happily from the tub.

“Really?” I asked Mrs. Phang.

“Sure.” Mrs. Phang shrugged. “You just have to tell them you're Korean.”

“Mina, dear, are you all taking a late lunch? Can I get you something?” Aunt Muriel asked.

“No thanks; Norman bought us lunch at PizzaNow!” I said.

“That's nice of you to stop by then,” Aunt Muriel said, slipping on a pair of pink sandals that matched her knit top.

I flopped down in confession mode on top of Auntie's bed. “I got fired,” I sniffed. “Twice!”

“We know, dear. Your sister called us,” Aunt Muriel said.

I rolled my eyes. I'm the only person I know whose life gets scooped by others.

“You didn't like that job, anyway,” Ma called out from the whirlpool.

"I know," I sniffed. "But I'm not going to like looking for a job a lot less. And I didn't dislike my paycheck."

Ma splashed around some. "I keep telling you, if your only problem is money, you don't have any problems."

"No, my other problem is not paying my mortgage and losing my house," I said.

"Phhhffff," Ma raspberried back. "That's not going to happen. Do you think me or Muriel would let that happen?" she said.

"No," I answered, and started to cry.

"There, there," Aunt Muriel said. She handed me a few hundred tissues. I sat up and blew my nose a few dozen times.

"I feel like such a failure."

Ma came out of the tub re-draped in a large pink towel. "You're not a failure; they are," she declared. I sighed and nodded my head. I knew better than to contradict Ma when she went Greek on me.

Mrs. Phang patted my shoulder. "You're a smart gal. You'll find something. You just have to start networking."

I sighed in agreement.

Ma sat down next to me and wiped my face with a corner of her terrycloth toga. "First you need to rest. You haven't had a good night's sleep this whole week. Or more, judging by the look of you. No wonder you're weepy."

"I'm just feeling a little anxious, I guess," I said.

Mrs. Phang and Aunt Muriel and Ma all agreed and reassured me how normal that was, that I would find another job that I liked soon, that I was better off this way and all the other nice lies you tell someone unemployed you feel sorry for and worry about. But it made me feel a little happier, all the same.

"But don't Bauser and Norman have to get back, dear?" Aunt Muriel asked.

"Nope," I said, and told them about Bauser getting canned too, and about Norman's quitting his job, and his newly divulged extremely great financial situation.

"What's his last name?" Ma hissed intently.

"Mudd," I said.

Ma smacked her hand to her forehead. "Oh, for heaven's sake. I read about his father years ago," she said, nodding. "So, you see?

The worst thing that could possibly happen is that you have friends and family to owe," she said. "If you must."

Mrs. Phang stood in front of Aunt Muriel's mirror and put on turquoise and gold dangly earrings that matched her silk top. She turned to Auntie. "Thanks lots, Muriel. It's been a long time since I had a girls' night out," she said, and hugged Aunt Muriel. "Or a spa day!"

"My pleasure," Aunt Muriel hugged back.

"Bye, Louise," Mrs. Phang said to Ma. "It sure was fun meeting you. And, Mina, you just take it easy. Something will turn up soon."

Aunt Muriel walked Mrs. Phang out of the bedroom, and to the back door. The sounds of them laughing with James drifted up to us. Then Aunt Muriel called out, "Byee!" and we heard the back door close. Then we heard Aunt Muriel talking with Bauser and Norman.

Ma patted me on the head. "Don't worry about the job search this week. Save that for Monday. You need a little R&R," she said. I sighed. She was right. And my new buddy system wasn't doing a whole lot to relax me. It was getting on my nerves. But I didn't want to tell Ma about it, and worry her, especially after she just got her back kneaded and whirlpooled and all.

Ma got dressed and fixed her hair. "C'mon, let's go see what the boys are up to with Muriel," she said, and led me out and into the kitchen.

We came in to see Aunt Muriel and Norman and Bauser sipping long, tall glasses of Brita water, nodding and talking quietly. Jim lapped at his own Brita water from a large crystal salad bowl on the floor.

"Mina, dear, I hope you don't mind, but I already have your mother and I on the wait list for Grazings," Aunt Muriel said. "I thought we should go tonight; weekends are just impossible."

I shrugged. "No biggie."

"Hey, I've heard about that place," Norman said. "Isn't that the tiny BYOB place that only serves you standing at the bar? And you can only get a seat if the cook likes you?"

Aunt Muriel took a deep breath and exhaled slowly. "Grazings is a very upscale restaurant run by the famous Chef Bernard, who trained at the Sorbonne," she explained. "And they rated a New

York Times review," she added. "They do not do reservations. They have a call list. If Chef Bernard deems it appropriate, he offers you a seat at the bar. But only if you've brought a wine that he approves of." Aunt Muriel sighed. "It's almost like being in an uptown restaurant."

"Well, I don't think we should leave Mina alone the first night that she's fired," Ma said.

Aunt Muriel looked at me doubtfully. "Would you like to go with us, Mina? It really doesn't matter that I left a request for two on the call list; they're certain to ignore it."

I shook my head. "Thanks, but I'm not really in the mood for having my wine rejected."

"Well, I'm not leaving you alone," Ma said.

Aunt Muriel furrowed. Clearly she had been looking forward to being stood up at Grazings.

"It's okay, Mrs. Kitchen. Jim and I will hang out with Mina," Bauser said.

Ma relaxed a little. "Are you sure?" she asked me.

I looked thankfully at Bauser. "I think I'm up for a quiet night at home. Besides, we had a huge lunch," I said.

"Yeah, we did," Bauser agreed. "We should probably just grab something light like a Calzone or lasagna or something."

Aunt Muriel glanced at the clock. "Oh! C'mon, Louise! The time!" Ma looked up at the clock and gulped and dashed for her purse. "Sorry, kids; we're going to miss our mani-pedi if we don't hurry!" Aunt Muriel called from the hall above the jingle of her car keys.

I shook my head. There are few things in this world that put Ma and Mu into first gear than the possibility of being late for a nail appointment.

We collected Jim and hurried out and smooshed back into Bauser's car, and pulled out of Auntie's driveway. Muriel backed out right after us, pointed her car into position and all we heard or saw were squealing tires and dust. Bauser stomped on his accelerator, the Aspire spluttered, and we all leaned forward to help it down the hill and out of Auntie's development.

Back at my side of town, Bauser parked behind Ike and Ethel's car. We got out and stood around the front yard. I was wondering if Ethel had broken the news to Ike or not yet. Norman slung his backpack over his shoulder and walked to his Echo parked at the curb. He pulled on the handle and burnt his hand. He carefully opened the car door with his baseball cap and started the ignition and rolled all the windows down, and walked back to us.

"I better go home and break the news to the girls," he said.

"How do you think they'll take it?" I asked.

Norman shrugged. "They'll probably want to get even with me by enrolling in their favorite equestrian camp in Montreal," he said. "And my wife will probably want to recover from the shock with a trip to Provence."

"Wow. Tough break," Bauser said.

"Yeah. It is. I'm not so keen on the France thing. Even though we still have Dad's villa. But Janice will make me go with her. And she'll probably make me go with her to visit the girls in Canada, too," he sighed.

"Too much traveling?" Bauser asked.

"Shopping," Norman answered glumly.

Jim sat pretty for Norman and held out his paw. Norman shook it and Jim leaned into Norman's thigh with a hug. We waved bye-bye as Norman pulled away.

Ethel and Ike came out on the front porch with the poofy Ratties dressed up in full walking gear.

"I thought I heard you out here," Ethel said. Hansel and Gretel yipped in agreement.

"We just pulled in," I said. I looked at the newly poofed pooches in their matching twin wear. They reminded me of the Star Trek episode about Tribbels. Except these were much larger and wore sequins. "Going for a walk?" I asked.

Ethel nodded. "Ike found a doggie friendly sidewalk cafe. We thought if we went now, we'd get a better table than at dinner time."

Ike said, "Some guy in the dog park told Vito and me about it. Gave us directions and menu tips and everything. He even said there's a doggie menu. People sure are nice around here." He added, "It's creepy." I nodded in agreement. It took some getting used to.

"Do you guys want to go with us?" Ike asked.

I looked at Ethel to see if the proverbial cat-what-wasn't-Vinnie had been let out of the bag. Ethel shook vigorous but tiny 'no' movements.

"Uh, actually, we had a really huge lunch," I said, while Bauser and Jim sat back down in disappointment.

"Hope you don't mind letting us out?" Ike asked Bauser. Bauser had their car blocked in.

"That's okay... Mina and I need to get back to my place and pick up some Whoof-Os for Jim, anyway," Bauser said to me pointedly, opening the door for me. Jim leapt in. I sighed. Clearly I was no longer allowed in my own house alone while the buddy system was in full force.

I walked up the steps to lock the front door. Vinnie grrled hi to me. "Later, buddy. Be back soon. Promise."

"You know, we don't have to go all the way across town to your apartment for Whoof-Os," I said.

"Oh?" Bauser asked.

"Why don't we just go to the grocery store right here in The Plaza?"

"Are you okay to go into grocery stores these days? What if you have a recipe relapse?"

"Sure, I'm okay," I fibbed. I figured the best thing to take away the feeling of failure and termination was cooking up a little something for a hundred or so. After today, I figured I could use all the help I could get. Besides, cooking is cheaper than therapy, right?

Bauser parked his car at the Barn Mart. We all got out. I looked at Bauser, then looked at Jim. Then back at Bauser. "Well, it's not like I can leave him in the car," Bauser said. "It's a zillion degrees out."

"You can't bring Jim in a grocery store," I pointed out.

"But he has a disability."

"No, he has the ability to con little old ladies into feeding him straight off the shelf."

"Oh. You have a point. Well?"

Actually, my point was I didn't want Bauser to chaperone my shopping. Besides, I reasoned, I had company visiting, right? And I'd just put out a few buffets.

"You need anything besides Whoof-Os?" I asked brightly.

Bauser narrowed his eyes. "No. Just Whoof-Os. The only aisle you need to wander down is pet food," he warned.

"Yup. Got it." I smiled.

Bauser sighed and handed me ten bucks. I skipped and waved bye and raced toward the market. "I'm timing you!" I heard him shout to my back as the door automatically opened for me and my shiny new red grocery cart. New carts! Was this is sign, or what?

I pocketed Bauser's ten bucks and went down the first aisle – bakery goods – towards produce. While in bakery goods I circled like a hawk over the mini stuff: mini brownie bites, mini cheesecakes, mini muffins, mini cookies – and threw them all in the cart. From there I went into produce and picked up bunches of cucumbers, red onions, mushrooms and the usual vegetable crudités things – carrots, cauliflower, celery, cherry tomatoes. Bags of lemons and limes were on sale; I bought them. Fresh herbs were on sale; I bought them. I checked out the deli and took advantage of sales on Italian smoked turkey, roast beef and provolone. Then the meat aisle had a two-for-one-sale on family packs of lovely Delmonico steaks. I tossed them in. And about eight London broils. And a family pack of boneless chicken breasts.

I hadn't visited the condiment aisle since I bought the lone jar of relish. Now it sported fancy gourmet olives and marinated mushrooms. There were sales on roasted peppers. And lovely salad dressings (are they a great shortcut or what?). Luckily the tunafish was at the end of the pet food aisle, or I might have forgotten Jim's Whoof-Os. I threw them in the cart along with some sale cans of solid white albacore, smoked oysters and anchovies. The fish department had lovely jumbo prawns; I got five pounds. I also threw in a couple of frozen pizzas, cheese tortellini and a couple more boxes of Frothy mix for cocktails. I have company, right?

I topped off the cart in the dairy section with sour cream, plain yogurt, milk (Ethel's preggers, right?), hummus, four different kinds of cheeses, a container of 18 eggs and a few rolls of Pop'ems biscuits. The ice cream section had also gotten fancy in the last year: mini-chocolate éclairs, Bavarian crème puffs and phyllo pastry abounded. I rescued them from the frozen cases and balanced them on the top of my piled cart. I remembered I needed more mixers and put some seltzers and tonics on the bottom rack under the cart since I'd kind of run out of room. I grabbed a box of POP doggie treats for Jim on line to the cashier. I was about the tenth person in line when I'd realized I'd forgotten vital ingredients. I made my apologies to the guy behind me and got a sworn vow from him to keep my place in line. I hightailed it back through the store grabbing up various spices and oils I'd forgotten. Plus the kitty litter and bird seed and Finicky Fare I'd also forgotten, which should have been in the cart with Jim's Whoof-Os.

I got back to find the guy behind me loading my stuff onto the conveyor belt. "Wow, sorry," I panted.

"No problem, honey," the nice elderly Hispanic man said to me. I nodded and said a sincere thanks.

"Don't you need my Barn Mart discount card?" I asked the cashier.

The kid behind the register shook her head. "Nope; your friend here used his," she said.

"Wow, thanks a lot, mister!" I said.

"De nada," he replied and smiled. I keep telling you, are these Lancaster folk nice, or what? "You have a big family, yes?" he asked smilingly.

I shrugged. "Only when they visit."

"Oh, you have party!" he answered. I smiled back sheepishly. "No wonder you nervous!" I nodded. He was right. There was nothing like a party to make a girl nervous. "And you have gatos, perro, and the ave!?" he asked incredulously.

"I've got the gatos and the cockatiel; my friend Bauser's got the pooch," I answered. "He drove me here to get dog food. I guess I got a little carried away." I smiled, hugging myself inside. There is almost nothing that gives you a false sense of safety and security than a completely jam packed fridge and freezer. Ha!

"Ahh," he said and nodded knowingly. "Ride is better than the bus." I nodded in sincere agreement. "Me, I have the gatos."

"Really?" I asked nicely. After all, the guy had held my place in line, used his discount card for me, and hadn't treated me like a complete simpering idiot. Or growled at me.

"Yes, I have ocho gatos," he said proudly.

"Ocho?"

"EIGHT. I have EIGHT gatos."

“Wow,” I said, impressed, now looking into his cart and seeing his two thirty-pound boxes of Pew-Be-Gone kitty litter, boxes of Kitty Cookies and crates of Finicky Fare.

“Si. These cats, they find me. I think I save them, but they save me.” Who was I to argue with karma? He explained, “My apartment, she catch on fire last Christmas when I sick. These cats, they wake me. But I not leave them. We go out to fire escape and wait for help.”

“Ohmygosh – you were lucky. Were they all okay?” I asked. I mean, I had to ask, right?

“My neighbors, they help. They pass the cages – the carriers. I pack them together and the firemen, they carry them down.”

“Wow, you were lucky. What happened to your apartment?”

The man smiled broadly. “The slumlord get served. Another one buy the property. I have the renters insurance; my daughter, she make me. I get the money. The new landlord sells for condos. Now, I own condo! With everything new! Stainless steel!” He grinned. “The Lord, He answers your prayers,” he said sagely.

I thought about EEJIT and the burning Bu-A-Lots and losing my job. Yup, God does answer. Sometimes strangely, but He answers.

“That'll be $336.84,” the cashier said. I pulled out my bank card and swiped. I signed my receipt and she handed me back the five-foot long ticker tape receipt. I shoved the receipt into my pocketbook after folding it I don’t know how many times, waved bye-bye to my new grocery store buddy and heaved the hundred pound cart smack into Bauser.

“Woah, woah, woah!” He yelped from behind the mountain of groceries. He peered around. “Mina, is that you?”

“Yip,” I said.

“I thought you said you were okay solo in the grocery store?” he asked.

“There were sales,” I replied defensively.

Bauser came around to the front of the cart. He looked at me and shook his head. “C'mon. Let me help you,” he said, and hefted the cart forward with a grunt. “What did you buy anyway? The entire cow?” he asked.

“No, not actually,” I said, but realized I probably shouldn't elaborate.

We came up to the security guard who was babysitting Jim. "He's a great dog, mister," he said. "And that story about his losing his leg in the line of action, damn, that just made those punks disappear." He patted Jim on the head.

"Yeah, especially the part about how he can't sit pretty or he gets real mean," Bauser added. "Later, dude."

"Later, man. Damn, I gotta get me a three-legged dog."

We got back to the now very small looking Aspire. Bauser looked at the cart, then at me. "Mina, how is all this going to fit?" he asked.

"I got it all figured out," I said. "Just put all the perishable groceries in the back seat, and crank the AC. The dry goods can go in the trunk. Jim sits in front, so he doesn't eat the groceries."

"And where do you go?"

"Jim and I can share the front seat," I said, then worried. "He doesn't have to tinkle, does he?"

We lurched out of the parking lot, back up Millersville Pike and toward home. Once in the driveway, I extricated myself from underneath Jim, and opened the front door. Vinnie was lying in cockroach position, but asleep and snoring. I patted him and he stretched and smacked his chops a few times. "C'mon, buddy," I said and herded him toward the basement stairs. He blinked at me sleepily. "Groceries," I explained. Vinnie yawned in understanding and trotted down the steps. I closed the door. It had been a long time since I'd unloaded any serious groceries through the garage, but clearly it had made an impression. I pressed the button to open the garage door and motioned Bauser to pull his car inside.

After parking, Bauser herded Jim inside, four bags of groceries clutched precariously in his grip. I followed behind with six more bags.

Once I'd crammed everything into the fridge, Vinnie shook the basement door with both paws. I let him back up, then he re-met Jim. Vinnie looked roundly at him and smacked him on the nose. Jim licked Vinnie. Vinnie shook his head and sauntered off muttering something that I could only assume was not repeatable.

Bauser came in. "So, what's for dinner?" he asked.

I looked up. It was six o'clock. I handed Bauser Jim's Whoof-Os and a bowl. Vinnie ran back in at the sound of rustling, and looked at me aghast. “Jim's company,” I told him defensively. Vinnie pounded his fists on the counter while I offered him this evening's choice, Hammy Hinds or Guppy Guts; Vinnie picked Guppy Guts. I gave him his dinner, then went downstairs to check his kitty box. While I was down there, I made effort to keep my eyes averted from the drugstore den that was now my basement, lest I paused to marvel.

I came back up to the kitchen to find Bauser staring into the open fridge.

“Repeat: what's for dinner? I know better than to help myself when you're Menu-Aholic,” he said.

I opened the freezer and pulled out some boxes. “Frozen pizzas,” I said.

“I hope they're not gourmet or anything fancy,” he said and turned on the oven.

We got the pizzas ready. I found a beer for Bauser. He retreated into the living room; half a minute later the sound of a ball game entered my ears. I took out one of the roast beefs and washed and seasoned it, getting it in line after the pizzas came out. I washed and peeled and chopped the cucumbers and celery and carrots and all the other crudités veggies. The kitchen was alive with garlic and pizza and fresh veggie smells. Life was good.

Bauser found a ‘Doom 'n' Gloom’ sci-fi re-run and I went back happily to putting the roast in the oven and moving on to making canapés and other goodies for the Freudian Tapas I'd been concocting. I was almost finished when a knock came from the door. I washed my hands and went through the hallway. Bauser peered out from behind the living room curtains.

“It's Vito,” he hissed. This was unusual. Why hadn't he just used his key? “And he's got Helena.”

I held my breath and opened the door.

“Hey, Toots, how you doing?” Vito said shyly.

Helena looked small and red-eyed and red-nosed and clutched a new box of brand name tissues in her hands.

“Come on in, Vito,” I said.

Vito motioned for Helena to enter first, and he followed. Vinnie sauntered up the hallway, took one look at Helena and sat pretty and trilled for her.

"Oh, what a sweet – uh – lion cub," Helena said and rubbed Vinnie's head. Vinnie grabbed her hand with both paws and showered her with kitty kisses. Either she had just trussed a chicken, or Vinnie had Jim's hankerings for blondes, too. The bums.

"We was just headed out for a bite," Vito said. "But I thought we should check in on you, to make sure yous was okay."

"Except for getting canned, we're great," Bauser said, looking brightly at Helena.

"Yeah, I heard about that. That's too bad," Vito said.

"You heard about that?" I asked.

"Sure. Trixie called here after you guys left." Great. Scooped by both my sister and my best friend. Everyone was a step ahead of my life, except for me. I was going to have to speak to the author about this.

"Hey, instead of going out, why don't you dig into what Mina's been cooking?" Bauser asked hopefully, looking at Helena.

Vito looked at me. I stared back at him.

"Look, I've got a lot of company here this week. I got a little nervous," I said.

"Okay by me," Vito said, and wandered into the kitchen and opened the fridge door. He let out a long, soft whistle. Then he looked around at the 5 platters of cold hors d'oeuvres lining the counters. He whistled again. "Mina, you sure knocked yourself out. You want we should save this for your Aunt and your Ma?" he asked.

"No, go ahead. I'm planning on making some salmon mousse and liver pate for them in a few minutes," I answered.

"Gee, that's great. Come here, Helena. Look at all this!" Helena started to sniff. "Now what are you crying about?" Vito cried. Clearly Helena's waterworks were getting to him, too. Either that or he was running out of tissues. Which could happen – and it wouldn't take very long to happen, either.

"I'm a terrible cook. I can't cook anything," Helena wailed.

I rushed over, held up a platter and poked a canapé at her. "These are not cooking. These are canapés. You don't cook anything. You just assemble. It's like a kit," I said. I held a shrimp and guacamole and roast pepper canapé at her lips. Helena dutifully opened her mouth and I shoved it in. She chewed. Then she started crying again.

"I could never arrange all these flavors together. They're won-der-ful..."

Vito rolled his eyes, walked over to my sink and grabbed a few yards of paper towels and shoved them at her. I sighed. I wish I had invested my 401K in paper products.

"Sure you could," I said. "It's just a matter of trial and error. When you make a mistake, you just don't do it again."

Helena blinked more tears and chewed. "That's very philosophical." She chewed some more, then added shyly, "Thanks, these are really good."

"No biggie," I said. "It kind of helps me out to cater like this sometimes."

"How so?"

"I like to make food stuff when I'm a little nervous. After today, I felt a little, uh, worried about losing my job and all."

"Oh. I've never had a job. What's it like?"

Vito hung his head. Helena looked at him. "Lint," he lied, pretending to wipe invisible fluff from his trousers.

"Oh."

We all herded into the living room, along with more trays of canapés and several Mugs O'Merlot. For a while we flipped through the channels, before finally settling on the local news.

Bauser turned to Helena and asked, "So, uh, how are you liking Lancaster?"

"It's very nice. Even the police were nice to me," Helena said and reached for a paper towel. Vito ripped one off for her. "I'm sorry, Uncle Vlad – I didn't understand," she wailed.

Vito sighed. "There, there, my moja mała mysz, no harm done..."

"So I guess you two had a lot to talk about?" I asked carefully.

Helena nodded. "Oh yes. Uncle Vlad told me all about what happened between him and Mickey," she added.

"Oh?"

"Yeah, I figured Mickey was fibbing about the traffic tickets and all. But I didn't think it was this thick," she said. "You see, what Uncle Vlad didn't know was that Mickey was set up. He didn't know he was running drugs. He thought he was scamming bogus Dooney & Bourke bags." She blew her nose. Vito ripped off another paper towel and held it out to Helena.

"There, there," Vito said patting Helena's head. "I told Mickey he should stay away from that crowd, if he knew what I meant. But he didn't," he grunted. "He thought he was gonna make big points by acting like a hot shot. And after all that, alls he was was a mule."

Helena nodded. "Mickey thought he was just passing off fake Dooneys as real ones, and getting a percentage of the difference," she said.

"Percentage?" Bauser asked.

"Why sure, they promised him a piece of the action," she said.

"Yeah, he got a piece of the action. Right inside prison," Vito answered. Helena responded with a sob. Vito handed her the last paper towel. Bauser sighed and got up and came back with a new roll of paper towels for later.

"He was going to make this a one time thing. Ladies' accessories aren't really his schtick. He just wanted to get some cash under him, to impress my dad. And then, he was going to take some classes," she sniffed.

"Classes?" Vito asked.

"Real estate!" Bauser and I exchanged glances. "Uncle Vlad knew about the New York family's drug activities, so he figured Mickey was into something bad. But there's no talking to Mickey once he gets an idea in his head. Even when told me he didn't understand what a bunch of thugs wanted buying ladies' purses for top dollar, at the pier," she said.

Vito shook his head. "Those bums had PixieDust sewed in the lining of every other bag in a shipment," he said.

Helena nodded. "It's true. If Mickey had any idea it was drugs and not Dooney's he was dealing, he'd never have gotten involved. That's why he wanted me to find Uncle Vlad and explain. See, if Uncle Vlad forgives him, Pop will too, and let us get married." She let loose another sob.

"But moja mała mysz, the guy needs a job. Where would you both live until he got settled?" Vito asked.

"With Ma and Pop!" Helena sang out happily. "After I moved back, Pop had the basement converted into an apartment. It's worked out great."

Vito sighed and rubbed his head with his hand – vigorously. Which turned his fingers orange.

“Oh, hey, that's great,” Bauser lied. “But what's Vito going to do? Now that your cover’s blown, I mean.”

Good point.

“Only if I want it to be blown,” Vito said. “And from what Helena tells me, even though Mickey might be getting out sooner than later, those other mugs aren't. I'll be pushing daisies before I have to worry about them.”

“So long as you're not pushing daisies because of them,” Bauser said.

Helena sniffed. “I'm sorry, Uncle Vlad. I didn’t know. I thought if Mickey knew where you were, especially with his being in prison and all, it was common knowledge.”

“It probably is,” Vito – Vlad – said. Helena blew her nose. Vito rolled his eyes. “Hey, the worst that happens is I get taken off the protection list. I don't get babysitting visits from Green or Annie no more, and that would be a good thing, right? They're not exactly subtle.” He grimaced.

“So who would you be?” I asked.

Vito picked up a cucumber and smoked salmon and sour cream with capers canapé. “Everybody around here knows me as Vito. So I'll stay Vito. No point in changing tradition.”

The doorbell rang; I got up to answer it. It was Annie. “Hi there, Mina. It's Annie, Vito's niece.” I looked over at Vito.

“Hey, Annie, c'mon in. I'd like you to meet Helena, my real niece,” he said.

CHAPTER 11

(Wednesday afternoon)

After a few awkward introductions, we got Annie settled down with a mug of wine and her own platter of canapés. She sat and sniffled. Helena held out one of the new box of tissues that Vito brought back from his house, since my supply was leaning toward extinct.

"So you see, if you're not in the protection program, I'm going to get kicked back to desk work or worse – filing..." Annie trailed off in tears. Helena patted her on the shoulder and offered her another tissue.

"Hey, it's not your fault, Annie," Vito reasoned. "Green told me from the get-go that it's my call about staying a protected witness. If I change my mind, I don't get no protection, that's all. Now it looks like I'm okay to take my chances, just like any other Joe."

"No you're not," Annie said. "The New York family is mad their kids got busted."

Vito shook his head. "No they're not. They're just saying they are to keep their kids' tempers in line. They're actually glad I'm the fall guy on this, and not them," he said.

"How do you know that?" Annie asked.

Vito looked at her and tapped the side of his nose. "I have it on good authority. Believe you me: I'm protected."

We each looked at each other and shivered. I wasn't so sure about the nature of Vito's protection. But for the time being at least, Vito was convinced it wouldn't let him get whacked. Or fed poisoned pierogies.

We heard a car pull up. Bauser looked out the window.

"It's Ethel and Ike," he said.

"Is Ethel crying?" I asked.

"Probably."

I opened the front door carefully as Ethel and Ike walked up. Both Ratties lay prone and stiff in Ike's arms. I gasped.

"Sorry," Ethel said, eyes moist.

"Yeah, it's not like we planned to do this," Ike said.

The Ratties lay still. "Murderer!" I screamed and slapped Ike upside his head.

"Ouch!" he yelped.

Hansel opened his eyes and nipped Gretel's ear. Gretel responded by leaping out of Ike's arms and chasing Hansel.

"They're alive!" I cried.

That was when everyone kind of looked at me funny. Hey, Ethel was afraid for the Ratties because of the whole preggers thing, right? So it stood to some kind of reason to think Ike had taken some things into someone else's hands. To me, at least.

Ethel walked over to me and slapped me up the head sisterly-like. "Never take a pregnant hormonal mommy-to-be seriously." She exchanged a smile with Ike and the yapping Ratties. "After we ate at the Canine Cafe, we went to the doggie park and let Hansel and Gretel run around. And that's when, and where, I told Ikey," she said happily. "We had a long, long talk. And a long, long walk. Hansel and Gretel got worn out and fell asleep so soundly in the backseat on the way home, we didn't have the heart to wake them up."

"Yeah, that's it," Ike said, rubbing his head.

"Oh. Sorry," I said. Ike shrugged. Ethel gave me a hug.

"If he'd really done that do you think I would have brought him back with a pulse?" she asked. I looked at Ike. Ike blanched. Clearly, Ethel was spending way too much time with Vito.

"What's going on, Cookie?" Vito asked.

Ethel hugged Ike, and he hugged her back. "We're going to have a baby," she announced.

Helena sniffed, "Oh, that's wonderful! You're so lucky to be married to the baby's father. Especially since he isn't in the slammer." Vito shook his head and gulped his Mug o'Merlot.

"Hey, what this heres calls for is a celebration. I got just the ticket," he said, and hurried out the door and back to his house. I saw Bauser and Annie exchange glances, and watched as they followed Vito.

I led Ethel over to the sofa so she could sit and cry with Annie and Helena. Ethel looked at the platters and smiled. "I was wondering when you'd start acting like you again," she smiled.

"What do you mean?"

"You like catering. You like cooking. That's a part of you," she said.

"I know. But I can't get it right for less than a hundred," I complained.

"So?"

"So what?"

"Sew buttons," she answered. "Okay, so maybe you have some volume issues. Big deal. Who doesn't?"

She got up and gave me a big hug, and I noticed we were a little farther apart then usual. We looked down at her belly. "Well, maybe it was more than four missed periods," she said.

"Listen, Ikey's kind of mad about that. Preggo vitamins and that kind of thing. So he wants us to get back home tomorrow and to the obstetrician pronto," she said.

"You have an obstetrician already?" I asked.

"Sure. Ike was on the phone the moment I told him," she answered happily. "We have an appointment for Friday morning."

"What you need is a good nosh," Helena said. "C'mon, look here. Look what's in Mina's kitchen." She led the way into the kitchen where we all stepped carefully over Jim and Vinnie, who lay snoozing.

Helena opened the refrigerator door, and she and Ethel gazed at the three remaining canapé platters like they'd found the Holy Grail. "Oh, you made my favorite!" Ethel squealed and grabbed a platter from the bottom shelf. "Look, you have to have one of these," she said, and handed a fully loaded toothpick to Helena, while munching on one herself. "Simple, robust, delightful: a full complement to an adult cocktail with a reminiscent nod toward childhood play."

"What'd ya have?" I asked her.

"Bologna pie."

I nodded. "But with a twist," I explained. "I used layers of Mort Della, spread with chived cream cheese mixed with some plain low fat yogurt, and added some mini capers and olive tapenade."

"It's wonderful, very upscale," my sister said. "But actually, I prefer plain old bologna pie. No offense," she added, helping herself to another.

Bologna Pie was the hors d'œuvre of choice Dad's folks entertained with in the Bronx back in the day, with a full complement of bathtub gin on the side. Bologna Pie consists of spreading cream cheese on top of thick slices of baloney, layering them, and then putting the pie into the icebox to chill. When company comes, you cut the pie into small wedges. When Gramma wanted to be fancy, she served them with cellophane fringed toothpicks. Gramma said everyone thought she was very clever. As kids, Ethel and I thought so too, although that line of thought wasn't about toothpicks.

The Ratties stumbled in hungrily and inspected Vinnie and Jim's bowls. Boopkas. They looked up at Ethel and yipped melodramatically.

"I know-ums you-ums want-ums grown-uppy food," Ethel said sappily, "but this would make-ums my Hansel-pudding and Gretel-pie sickey-wickey."

I rolled my eyes and wished for a really strong drinky winky. I was going to be sickey-wicky with all this goo-goo speak and mug-in-a-box wasn't going to cut it. Then I realized how much worse Ethel and Ike's baby-speak would get once Junior stumbled onto the scene. I cringed.

Helena spotted Jim's Whoof-Os on the counter. "Can't they have some of Jim's cereal?" she asked.

Ethel read the box and furrowed. "Well, it's dog food. Sort of," she said, and poured some out into two soup bowls for Hansel and Gretel. "Honestly, what's the matter with Bauser? This is about as bad as feeding your kids cheese doodles for dinner." Ethel put the bowls down for the dogs. They yipped and twirled thanks, tucked their heads in and crunched happily. Which woke up Jim and Vinnie. So Jim got some more Whoof-Os. Which was why Vinnie stood up and pounded his mitts on the top of the kitchen counter bar-keep style. Ethel and Helena stopped and stared at Vinnie.

"Yeesh, he really is a big cat," Ethel said.

"Actually, I think he's kind of small for a cougar," Helena answered.

I sighed and gave Vinnie some more Kitty Cookies, after Ethel insisted on vetting the ingredients on his bag, too.

The front door opened and Vito and Annie and Bauser shuffled in. Vito held a large tray of grown-up looking glasses and a pitcher of something that might have been Amish Cosmos, because of the leaves and twigs and stuff in it. My grown-uppy drink prayer might have been answered – sort of – after all.

As soon as Vito put his tray down, the doorbell rang. I opened the front door to find Ma and Aunt Mu. They did not look happy. They stood there clutching bottles of Grey Goose and Absolut. Huh. Maybe God gets a little delayed with His responses. But it was starting to look like he was making up for lost time.

"Well, you're not the only one who's been severely disappointed today," Aunt Muriel sighed as she entered the hallway.

Ma shrugged. "That jerk wouldn't know a White Burgundy from a Beaujolais," she said.

"I guess you didn't get into Grazings?" I asked simply.

"Oh, we got in alright. We got to pay the $75 prefix, got shuffled to the back, then finally got approval from Chef Obnoxious to sit at the bar," Ma said, with a big emphasis on the 'aw' in bar.

"We were all settled in, talking cheerfully with everyone around us," Auntie said.

"We were even nice to the people behind us, even though they weren't nice to us when we were behind them," Ma said, as she rummaged around my freezer for some ice cubes.

"Suddenly, just as we were served our 'Primo' tasting of spam stuffed mushrooms, the bartender complained to Chef about us!" Auntie finished.

"Spam?" I asked.

"It's very 'in' now," Aunt Muriel said. Ma shrugged.

"Chef served Medallions of Salmon ala Stroganoff, which he felt should only be accompanied with a Pinot Noir," Auntie explained.

"And we did bring a Pinot Noir. But a white one," she said. "Well, for heaven's sake, it was in a blue bottle," she continued. "Anyone with any sense knows red wine never comes in a blue bottle." She sniffed. Helena and Ethel held some tissues out for her. Auntie took them and blew.

Ma rubbed at the crick in her neck. "What a complete waste of a perfectly good massage," she muttered.

"How'd you like the salon?" I asked, noticing my godmom's new doo.

"Do you like my new haircut?" Auntie asked. I nodded.

"Oh, it was very posh!" Ma sighed.

"Did you get a complimentary beverage?"

"Oh, yes. Tina phoned ahead for us. They gave us very nice Manginis."

"Manginis?" I asked.

"Yes. It's new. It's like a Balini but with mango juice, rum and champagne," Ma explained. She rubbed at her neck some more. "If I'd known I was going to get that aggravated, I would have asked Mu to schedule James for tomorrow. What a bunch of fluff." She winced.

"I've never felt so humiliated," Aunt Muriel added.

Wait, I thought. You're in my house. And the night is young.

"Well here's a little something for what ails you, Muriel," Vito said shyly, holding out a martini glass with foamy pink liquid in it. Aunt Muriel sighed, said thank you and looked grateful.

Vito nodded and handed out glasses to everyone – except for Ethel, who got sparkling cider. We toasted. We sipped. Then we all stared at our drinks.

"Uh, what are we drinking, Vito?" I asked.

"My own invention!" Vito grinned. "I mixed some Galliano, frozen strawberry daiquiri mix, tequila, orange juice, Chambord and banana schnapps. And then I added some prune juice for oomph!" he said.

Great, I thought. Somewhere behind the rainbows of the Pink Squirrel and the Rusty Nail, Vito had slipped us Rusty Squirrels.

Vito smiled, and together he and Bauser shuffled off into the living room to offer the other victims their own colon cleansing cocktails. As soon as they were out of sight, Ma and Mu and I quietly poured our drinks down the sink. I got out the cranberry juice and a lime and Muriel and Ma mixed it all up pronto with their own vodkas. Aunt Muriel genuflected and added several drops of my left-over coffee to each glass, so our drinks would sort of match the color of the poison ones Vito made. No one was the wiser.

We shuffled into the living room with a new platter of canapés from the fridge. "Well I'm glad you had some company tonight, especially after today," Aunt Muriel said, looking around at the usual crowd.

Vito waved her off. "This here's not company. It's all family. By the way, this here is my real niece, Helena. And you remember my fake niece, Annie, right?" Vito asked.

Both Helena and Annie exploded into tears.

"Now what's wrong? What'd I do?"

Helena and Annie blew into dueling wads of tissues while Ma and Mu served up the econo size box o'tissues.

"I feel like such a failure," Helena sniffed. "What kind of a girl has a baby with the father in jail?"

"Well then I'm a double failure," Annie said and blew into her wad. "I can't maintain a subject's cover, or surveillance, and I almost lost Mina's cat," she said tearfully.

"Huh?" I asked.

Annie sighed. "I know you're gonna think this is kind of funny, or really not so funny," she began, "but my boss was afraid that Vlad – Vito – was starting up some maybe too noticeable sideline activities."

"How'd you mean?" Vito asked carefully.

Annie blew her nose. "He thought maybe you might be into some kind of money laundering scheme, because of all your trips to Lickety-Split laundry. Especially since your niece is involved with Mickey the Mouse," she said. She took a deep breath and continued. "Mike told me to keep a steady watch on you, that it would mean a real promotion for me. And I guess I got a little overzealous."

"Huh?" I asked again.

Annie hung her head. “I pretended to help out at the dry cleaners, thinking I could find an angle there.” Bauser, Vito, Ma, Mu, Ethel and I exchanged furtive glances and took long collective swigs from our beverages. Helena and Ike nodded from their respective corners of oblivion at Annie.

Annie took another tissue and dabbed at her eyes. “I couldn’t find anything there. I guess I got a little frustrated. I really needed to find something, anything,” she said, looking at me. “So when I watched Vito coming and going from your house, I figured you must be involved with whatever he was involved with.” She sighed. “That’s why I broke into your house while you were at the polo match with your Aunt.”

Vito looked at her levelly. “Annie, you means to tell us you're the one what let Vinnie out?”

A giant light bulb clicked on above all of our heads.

“Good Lord, you made all that mess?” Aunt Muriel shrieked.

“I know, I know! I told you I was a worse failure,” Annie cried, and sniffled into a new wad of tissues. “But I didn't know you had a cat, or a bird. That part was really a series of bad luck,” she continued, and took a gulp from her prune daiquiri. “Everything was fine until I got upstairs. Your bird started shrieking. So I popped my head in quick to look at her, and saw she had her toe stuck in the cage door. I couldn't leave her like that. So I opened the door a teensy, weensy bit – and she flew right downstairs. That was when I saw Vinnie in the hallway.”

As if on cue, Vinnie sauntered into the living room, and sat in front of Annie neatly cleaning his paws and stared at her. Detective Purr-o.

“Vinnie growled at me and chased me into the kitchen,” Annie sniffled. “I wanted to shoo him into the basement because I was afraid of leaving him out with your bird. But he roared at me.” Annie shivered. “So I slipped out the back as quick as I could. I figured it would be alright since you would be in the house any minute. But he chased after me.”

We all looked at Vinnie. Vinnie looked around at his court with an exceedingly self-satisfied look on his face.

“Wow, feline security. Whaddayknow?” Vito said.

Vinnie turned and stared at Annie to demand the rest of her confession.

Annie sighed. "I didn't want to have anything happen to him, even if he did growl at me," she said. "But he chased me all the way back to my car. I managed to get him inside by giving him my leftover Buddy Burger. Then I drove to the nearest pet store, and got a carrier. I went back to your house, and waited. But then your Aunt came over. And Vito. And your friend Trixie shows up. Then the police arrived. Crimaney – your house is like Grand Central." I shrugged and nodded. What could I say? She was right.

"I finally found a moment after Appletree left. I would have carried Vinnie inside, except he's too big. So I hid with him behind some shrubs, and then shoved him in through the back door once you finally looked away."

Bauser blew out a whistle. Jim came trotting over. The Ratties followed and sat pretty.

"Well, yous was decent enough to look after Vinnie, so I guess you ain't so bad," Vito proclaimed.

"Well, we never would have expected that. There's not much that can top that," Ma said.

"Actually, we might be able to top that," Ike said.

"Yes, we can," Ethel agreed, and proceeded to tell Ma and Mu they were soon to be a grandmother and a great-aunt.

After Ma and Aunt Muriel stopped shrieking, everyone went around and gave each other little hugs and got cried on a lot.

The phone rang. "Hello?" I asked.

"Hey, Mina, it's me, Trixie."

"Are you on your cell? You sound kind of funny," I said.

"Yeah, I'm on a break. Can't use cells inside the ER. Or smoke," she puffed. I was glad that as a health professional she followed the rules.

"I thought you only worked nights?"

"Louella called in, so I picked up the second half of her shift," Trixie said. I had to hand it to her: the girl sure had stamina. I barely handled an 8 hour working day at EEJIT, much less a 12 hour shift on my feet. And here was Trixie was on another 18-hour shift marathon. Well at least her patients had continuity of care. A few poor souls could count on being treated by the same worn out grouchy nurse who admitted them earlier this evening until tomorrow morning.

"Well, at least you'll get her breaks, too," I said hopefully.

Trixie grunted. "Yeah. I got halfway into my first break when some drunk fraternity prankster puked all over," she said.

Eeeeeeeew.

"But the thing is," she continued with another puff, "they got TVs on in the ER waiting room. Just in case any of the gunshot victims want to see if they made the news."

"Oh. That's nice."

"Yep. Anyway, Channel 13 was showing the new Buy-A-Lots – the one that got you in so much trouble? It got set on fire again. The same way."

I sighed. "Well, at least that's not my problem anymore."

"I'm not so sure. I just treated some of your senior Breakfast War gang for multiple burns."

"Huh?"

"Your egg slinging buddy Ernie, and the one you said you're all afraid of, Evelyn," she said. "They both claimed barbecue flare-up incidents, but I'm kind of doubtful."

"Why?"

"Because they both had dog doo all over their shoes."

"Yick!"

Trixie sighed. "Listen, you didn't hear this from me. I'm honor bound to report anything funky to the police like gunshot wounds, stabbing, contusions, or anything else that can be associated with a crime – including dog poop."

"Right." I sighed and rubbed my forehead. It was going to be another long night.

"Look, they both insist they were barbecuing. I'm gonna say, they're old. And since they were barbecuing in their backyards, it makes sense that they wandered into doggie poop while they were on fire, right?"

"Oh. Right!" I said happily. Good old Trixie!

"That's my story and I'm sticking to it. But the thing is, they can't do it again. You or your aunt are gonna have to have a long talk with them."

"Oh, right..."

"Okay... anything new on your end? You've got ten seconds."

"Ethel's preggers!" I said quickly.

"That's great! Is it a Hansel or a Gretel?"

"Dunno."

Trixie sighed. "Okay, I gotta go. I have a minute and 35 seconds left to pee. Bye."

"Bye bye."

I hung up and went into the living room and turned on the news to watch flambéed feces on Fruitville Pike – again.

"Geez, is that Buy-A-Lots on fire again?" Vito asked.

"Yip," I answered. I looked over at Bauser. He hung his head.

"Well, at least you're not konked on the noggin again," he added glumly.

"Hey, yeah!" That was good, at least. It was getting to be too much of a habit.

"And now reporting to you live, from the future Buy-A-Lots site..." the announcer droned.

Bauser leaned over and turned the volume up. A young blonde, who looked directly related to the older blonde who accosted us on Vito's porch, orated. Jim yawned. I patted his head in agreement. Suddenly the screen 'split' as Channel 13 showed off its new technology. The older blonde, seated at the TV studio desk, broke into the young blonde's reporting from a small screen on the lower right hand corner of the TV set.

"I'm sorry to interrupt you," the older blonde lied, "but we have some late breaking information from a tipster that we'd like to play for our viewing audience."

"Great, thanks," the younger blonde woman fibbed back, sweating in the summer heat and smoldering burnt poop. "It'd be great to have a tip on this series of heinous, heinous arsons."

Bauser smirked. "She just likes to say heinous because it rhymes with anus," he grinned. The rest of us gasped and stared at him. He shrugged. "She dated my brother in high school," he answered. We all exhaled. Except me. Bauser had a brother?

"And now, live from our newsroom, is the recent information from a tipster," the anchorwoman said. She nodded authoritatively in the direction of the camera and said, "Okay, Artie, let her roll." The younger blonde held her ear piece closely to feign attention.

"Now I don't want to get a body in trouble or nothing. Or caught with the law not on their side. But I just can't live with myself knowing who's been starting these fires. Now, I know he's a church going soul, but seriously – a body could get hurt.

Including Henry. So I figure the best thing to do is to make this here anonymous phone call, to make sure he behaves himself. I mean, just nobody barbecues that much. This is not Texas. No, sir, I said to myself, Norma Jean Brown, you just sit right down and use that anonymous tipster hotline and... OH!" Both blonde TV women both stifled smirks.

"Well, I guess we'll be having some more information later this evening from our 'anonymous' tipster," the anchorwoman said.

"To be sure," the younger blonde woman beamed back at her. "And that's our live coverage about the latest Buy-A-Lots fire in Lancaster, Pennsylvania."

Vito and Aunt Muriel smacked themselves on their foreheads. Vito wandered out into the kitchen and dispensed another drink for himself. Muriel and Ma followed and retrieved their bottles of vodka from the freezer.

"I knew those two had to be finks," Vito said.

"Who?" I asked.

"Norma and Ray. After all, who works in a kitchen and don't sweat? It ain't natural. In summer, no less!"

Muriel clanged some ice cubes into her glass. "Goodie goodies," she muttered.

Annie wandered into the kitchen. "Do you mean to tell me that you know who's behind the burning Buy-A-Lots'?" she asked, wide-eyed.

"Well, not all of them, of course," Vito said matter-of-factly. "Just the local ones, I mean, pretty much."

"Vlad – Vito – this is a national level case," Annie replied. "So I-don't-hear-you I-don't-hear-you," she said, pretending to hold her hands up to her ears.

Aunt Muriel rolled her eyes. "Oh, please. Who doesn't want to burn a Buy-A-Lots?" she said and took a swig.

I shrugged and did what I do best when I'm stressed. I whipped up some sausage and peppers and onions and eggplant to go over some nice risotto. Then I dug out some hearts of Romaine lettuce from the fridge and tossed a Caesar salad. I sliced up the roast, laid it on a platter and dressed it in its own juices. I placed it on the impromptu buffet table along with salad, potatoes, butter, sour cream, chives and some cream cheese for good measure.

A short while later, my family and friends were more calm, reasonable, and slightly more sober. While they helped themselves to the largess, I zipped around making sure my crazy cockatiel and cat were taken care of. And I remembered to throw the mini-bakery stuff on the banquet pyre, too.

I re-entered the living room to a chorus of, "Chestnuts roasting on an open fire." Apparently Ethel found my 'Yuletide Harmony – The Sounds of Christmas' video. It features a 'live' Yule log burning in 'real' time, while Christmas carols play in the background. Ethel loves it. I do, too. Just not so much in August.

"Uh, chilly?" I asked Ethel.

She shrugged. "I figured we could use something calm. Too bad you don't have a real fireplace," she said.

I nodded, but wondered when Ethel's hormonal thermostat thingy would stop acting whacky.

Vinnie settled down in front of the TV Yule log. Jim settled alongside him. Everyone else settled sleepily and stared blankly at the screen. Julie Andrews began to sing 'My Favorite Things'. Why is that considered a Christmas song? I've always wondered about that.

After Ike began to snore, I poked them all awake, hoping that visions of leaving would dance through their heads. As my slumberous herd yawned and stretched, the doorbell rang. I grimaced and opened the door bravely, fearing another visitor. A woman clad in party wear greeted me. "It's alright! They're not dead!"

Ordinarily I would have figured this was just another visit from an enthusiastic Jehovah's Witness. For some reason, Jehovah's Witnesses visit my neighborhood a lot. However, this evening-wear version was a new breed. She was clad in a hot-pink silk jacket and electric green slacks. Her eyes were smeared with lots of lime green eye shadow that matched the streaks in her hair. She also sported an air-brushed beach-scene manicure, and wore about as much gold jewelry as a small third world nation.

Vito lumbered up behind me, yawning and stretching. "Hi ya, Miriam," he said sleepily.

Miriam. Oh. Yeah. Right. Miriam. Didn't recognize her with the green streaks. Last time I saw her, they were fushcia. Then again, that was last Christmas.

Miriam's my neighbor on the other side of Vito. Miriam Gladstein, the Happy Widow. That's how she introduced herself to me when I first moved in, while I was holding the bottom half of a mahogany dresser: "Miriam Gladstein – the Happy Widow! Pleasure to meet you, I'm sure. My husband died eight years ago. He was a cheap S.O.B.. Never let me have a nickel. After I scraped together enough cash to get the carpet washed, that's when I found $50,000 under it! No wonder it was hard to vacuum. The kid cleaning the carpet found it! Lucky for me that kid was real honest. So I tipped him a hundred bucks! Altogether we found $358,625 stashed across the house! The ceiling, the box spring, behind the medicine cabinet, the garage – you name it. Saul would have bust a gut to know I'd found that money, or tipped anyone a hundred dollars! Ha! I sold that old dump, moved here, and got an African Grey, a parakeet and two Conjures. Did I mention I love birds? He never let me have none of them. I found a special vet for mine, too – it costs lots. Ha!" In the time it took for Miriam to introduce herself to me, I had lugged the dresser all the way upstairs, placed it, and packed it full of clothes.

"Oh, Vito, I was hoping you were here!" Miriam cried.

I looked at Vito. He rolled his eyes. "Well, you know, I do live next door, ha ha," he said.

"Of course, of course, ha ha!" Miriam agreed. "I saw Muriel's car here, and figured she'd want to know the news, seeing as Henry goes to St. Bart's and all." She looked around. "I hope I'm not interrupting a party or anything," Miriam said in a hopeful voice that told me she hoped exactly the opposite, clearly glad she was all decked out with some place to go.

"Sorry, no, not at all; please come in," I said.

"Actually, Mu's got some news tonight," Vito grinned.

"Really?" Miriam asked hungrily. She was unable to resist the lure of neighborhood gossip.

"Yeah, Muriel's gonna be a great-aunt!"

Miriam pursed her lips and stared at me.

"No! No! It's not me! I'm not pregnant!" I yelped quickly, holding my hands out in front of me.

"I am," Ethel called out from the living room.

"My sister Ethel; my brother-in-law Ike," I introduced quickly. "And Ma," I added.

"Louise," Ma clarified.

Miriam nodded and walked around the room, pumping hands. "Miriam Gladstein, the Happy Widow..." she began. I went back into the kitchen to refresh my drink, and whip up a batch O'Brioche. After all, I knew I had the time.

I came back into the conversation a lot more buttery but no less informed. "So, Ethel, you are the one who is expecting?" Miriam asked.

"Yup," Ike beamed back for both of them.

"Mazel tov!" Miriam said, "This calls for a celebration!"

Vito held up a hand. "Just a second, just a second – we got just the thing, Miriam," he said, and went into the kitchen to dispense a Rusty Squirrel for the newest guest. I looked at Ma and Mu. They shrugged.

"Well, I guess you've been too caught up with your news, what to be watching the TV news and all," Miriam sipped.

Then the TV sang out joyfully, "We wish you a Merry Christmas! We wish you a Merry Christmas! We wish you a Merry Christmas! And a happy New Year!"

Miriam looked around at us, opened her mouth, and closed it. That was the extent of her trout impersonation. She shrugged and took a really big sip from her Fleet Cosmo. She came back up with a pinkish frothy mustache. In keeping with the incidental Hallmark Christmas theme in my living room, she looked a bit like the Little Drummer Boy with his painted on smile.

"Well, it turns out Henry's just about burned his fingers off. Involved in some kind of arson, according to Norma," Miriam said with a dismissive smirk. "What an imagination. It's getting so a person can't even barbeque a brisket around here without being accused of some goofball scheme," she said. "Remember when she forgot she signed up for call waiting? And thought the call-waiting beeping was her wire being tapped?"

Aunt Muriel, Vito and I collectively rolled our eyes and nodded. It had taken Aunt Muriel the better part of a weekend to walk Norma through those instructions. And a proportionate volume of Absolut to recover from administering the call waiting tutorial.

"Anyway, he and the Mrs. got taken to the hospital on account of the flare up," Miriam continued, and sipped.

"Are they okay?" Aunt Muriel asked.

Miriam shrugged. "Except for their eyebrows, I think they'll be fine," she said.

"What happened to their eyebrows?" Ma asked.

"Singed right off. They probably look like a couple of peeled eggs.

"Anyway," Miriam continued pointedly and turning to Vito after another long slurp, "I know how you have plans to have, uh... coffee with Henry like usual tomorrow morning. You know, like you do every third Thursday of the month? But since I heard the news, like I just told you about, Henry might not be feeling so up to it, on account of being so crisp and all," she said emphatically.

Vito nodded blankly. "Oh, jeez, sure. That's completely understandable."

"But if you like, I could give Henry the book you keep meaning to give him. I mean, I'm sure he'll miss it," Miriam said breathily, flushed and pleased in thinking she might possibly be involved in some kind of dramatic secret mission.

Vito thunk hard, then dropped into a chair. Along with the penny. "Oh, yeah! Sure! Right!" He beamed. "Actually, I got it right here. I put it in Mina's basement here for, uh... safekeeping," he said and then went thumpity-thump like downstairs. For a big, round guy, Vito always surprises me at how swift of foot he can be. But I guess that had its plusses in his former career.

I looked at Aunt Muriel. She invited Miriam into my make-shift banquet hall to partake of the repasts. I just hoped she'd leave soon after, before all the effects of her cocktail kicked in.

We all settled back down with our various reinforcements of food and drink. "...five G-O-L-D rings!" sang sappily from the flickering tape. Miriam looked at me. I shrugged. She shrugged back, and chewed. Miriam had it right. What you don't know can't burp you.

Vito came back up the stairs waving a plastic grocery bag crammed full with a lot of stuff that did not look in any way, shape or form like a book.

"Here you go!" he said happily, coming in through the dining room and holding the bag out to Miriam.

"What kind of a book is that?" Annie asked.

Vito looked around. Ma looked at the floor. Aunt Muriel's eyebrows shot up and waved in place over her head. A thin orange line trickled along Vito's shirt collar.

"It's a Book Club book. Vito gets it in installments," Bauser lied.

"Oh," Annie said, and nestled back down into her corner of the sofa.

Vito nodded his head up and down a lot and smiled. "Yeah, that's it!" He grinned. "Here, Miriam, I'll just show yous out here."

And he hustled her out the front door. She flushed and handed her glass and fork to me on the way out. From the front porch, we heard Vito bidding Miriam farewell. We heard Miriam bidding Vito farewell. Then we heard what sounded like a lot of boxes tumbling all over my front walk. So we all went over and looked out the windows. About two dozen boxes of prescription samples lay littered across my walk and tumbled onto the lawn. Vito and Miriam were picking them up and shoving them like Easter Eggs into Miriam's beach bag size purse. Vito looked up at the audience in my living room windows. He waved and pointed to the ripped grocery bag he held in his other hand.

That was when Miriam clapped her hand right over Vito's mouth. "My purse broke. I keep all my samples in here. My doctor insists I try samples for weeks before he'll prescribe the real McCoy," she shouted. We all nodded back in acknowledgment.

"Well, I guess it's getting to be that time," Aunt Muriel said, giving Ma the 'high sign' to get Annie away from the window. "Let's help Mina put some of these things away."

Everyone agreed – including Ike, who stayed on the sofa and put his feet up. I looked back out the front window and saw Miriam and Vito gesticulating loudly, their hands crammed full of samples. I looked closer: one of the samples was labeled 'Viagra'.

"It's always a surprise, isn't it?" Annie asked, standing right next to me. I jumped. I thought she'd followed Aunt Muriel into the kitchen. "Sorry," Annie said, looking out at Vito and Miriam. "Didn't mean to startle you."

"Oh. Yeah. Right. No biggie," I lied

"But you have to agree, it's pretty surprising," she said.

"What's that?"

"The lengths people will go to for medications."

A dim roaring started to pound in my ears and I realized it was either all the blood in my body rushing to my head or away from it. I didn't blame it. I figured that most of my blood cells didn't want to get caught by a U.S. Marshal's assistant, either.

"Well, you know, she is older…" I stalled.

"That's why it's always surprising. Who'd have thought an old gal like that would have a boyfriend on the side, with, ermm... issues?" Annie asked matter-of-factly. "Nice of Vito to cover for her," she added.

The pounding started to fade. I realized I had been holding my breath for a few months, then exhaled.

"I wonder if Vito's jealous?" Annie mused. I stared at her, afraid to ask about the basis for that convoluted logic. Then, indicating the platter of half-gnawed canapés she'd been holding, she asked me, "You want another one of these?"

"Uh, no thanks," I said.

"Suit yourself." She shrugged, popping a slice of bologna pie into her mouth and heading toward the kitchen.

I looked out the window to see Miriam waving bye-bye to Vito, her purse bulging open with its contraband contents. I sighed. That was as close to federal entanglement as I wanted to get with Mrs. Phang's pharmaceutical folly. Then I shrugged. It could have been worse. It could have been Ma's or Aunt Muriel's pocketbooks full of Viagra.

All the food got put away, as well as divvied up, since I basically had enough food left over for a small wedding. Everything else got washed and cleaned and put away.

I went into the kitchen to find Ma and Mu arguing.

"Yes, I am," said Aunt Muriel

"No, you're not," Ma replied.

"Yes – I – AM!"

"AB-SO-LUTE-LY NOT!"

"What's the matter?" I asked stupidly.

Aunt Muriel rolled her eyes at me. "I told your mother that I would schedule another massage for her, to make up for what got undone tonight, and she's refusing."

"I told you, I'm fine!" she said, rubbing her neck.

"Then why are you rubbing your neck?" I asked.

"You see!" Aunt Muriel cried.

Ma turned her head and glared at me. “Don’t be such a helper,” she hissed.

“Sorry,” I mumbled.

Ma looked at me again. “I know! I'll get a massage, if Mina gets one! She could use it!” I felt the tiny twinge pinching my right cheek again. That is, the cheek that's not associated with my face.

“Well, Mina? Your mother's spine turning into a pretzel or not is completely up to you,” Aunt Muriel warned.

I sighed. I wanted to say no thanks, thought about the impending guilt and then thought again. My cheek pinched again. Maybe this wasn’t such a terrible idea.

After some more bickering about when Aunt Muriel should schedule the next round of massages, she herded my family out of my house. Annie bid farewell, in search of a motel since Vito's real niece had displaced her guestroom privileges. Bauser agreed to take Jim and leave me without supervision, since he'd been convinced that Vinnie was a bonafide guard cat, thanks to Annie. Helena went back to Vito’s, to call her folks and check on her mini-Marie.

“Hey, I gotta get going, Toots,” Vito said. “We’ve got a big day tomorrow!” He flashed a wide, gappy grin; his bridge was out. I glanced carefully down at the coffee table, sofa and end tables. No toothies. I hoped he'd had them in his pocket and Vinnie hadn't hid them away as a treasured cat toy.

“Huh?” I asked politely.

“Tomorrow’s Thursday! The 72 hours will be up! I’m gonna adopt Stanley!” he beamed, and practically skipped out the door.

I looked at Vinnie. Vinnie looked back at me. We shrugged. I hoped that Stanley was still unspoken for, and that everything would work out for both of them. I supposed things would, so long as Stanley didn't eat any of Vito's cooking.

Vinnie trilled at me and threw himself on his back for a belly rub and purred. I went along and gave him his well-deserved scritches. Another silent-but-deadly poot wafted up at me while Vinnie lay back looking smug and happy. I coughed and got up ‘butt’ quick.

“Pew! Man, oh man, oh Manischewitz. No more pepperoni for you!” I said, waving my arms at him.

Vinnie trilled something back at me which didn't sound exactly complimentary.

CHAPTER 12

(Thursday)

I dozed off on the sofa. Again. Which meant waking up to *Beevis and Butthead* at about 4:30 a.m. fully clothed, with sandals. Me, not them. But apparently I pass out neatly since my feet were dangling nicely over the sofa arm and asleep.

Meanwhile, my right arm rested painfully on Vinnie's belly. The pinch in it spread down through my right butt cheek and proceeded to whip up a Charlie Horse. Ouch. I tried to roll my shoulder. It rolled back at me. Vinnie lay on his back, snoring contentedly, his paw hooked across his nose.

"EEEK! EEEK! EEK!" screamed Marie.

Oh crap. She'd been left to watch the 'The Muppet Movie' running in repeated loops all night long. After her all night movie marathon, she probably thought 'The Muppet Movie' was more like 'Gremlins XXIV'

I staggered upstairs and found out I was right, of course.

Marie hissed at me. "I know, I'm sorry," I agreed. I turned the Muppets off. "Here, have an early breakfast and a long snooze," I said, petting her head then closing her door.

I looked at my bedroom. My bed sat waiting, neatly made and inviting. I sighed. No point getting in it; I was up now.

I shuffled downstairs awkwardly and uncomfortably to make some coffee. While the coffee perked, I went into the powder room. That's when the front door opened and I heard Vinnie trill at someone.

"Shhhh, shhh, Vinnie," I heard Vito say. "Let Mina sleep."

I shook my head, took a deep breath and came out.

"Oh, hey, I didn't think you'd be up this early," Vito whispered. I yawned, shuffled into the kitchen, and squinted at the clock on the stove. It blinked 5:00 a.m. I groaned. "I gotta whole bunch of deliveries I gotta make this morning, before I take Helena to the train. And before I go and adopt Stanley."

I shrugged. "It's okay, Vito; you don't have to whisper. I'm awake."

"Oh, hey. That's right!" He brightened. "Hey, I'll just be a minute, okay?" he said and ambled down my basement steps.

"Help yourself."

Vinnie trilled and trotted after Vito. I was going to stop him, but remembered his kitty box was down there. But there were still a ton of Vito's prescription sample boxes down there, too. Well, at least if Vinnie would let me know where Vito was if he got pinned under an avalanche of drug samples. And vice versa.

I started to pour some coffee, and heard what sounded like the kitty box being scooped out. I was so tired that at first I thought it was good of Vinnie to finally learn how to clean up after himself.

Vito came up with a laundry basket full of medical samples, and a wrapped up bag of kitty stuff. He looked at me and blushed.

"Well, since I was down there and all any-who," he said.

I nodded thanks and poured two mugs of coffee. Vito lumbered out through my front door, laundry basket and kitty stuff bag in hand. A lot of single people say it's a drag living alone. I still wonder what it's like.

Vinnie came back into the kitchen, rubbed against my shins and licked my knee. "Yup, let's get your breakfast," I responded automatically.

Then Vito came back through the front door, holding up a pristine white bakery bag. I looked longingly at it. Vinnie banged his paws on top of the counter, waving me on, demanding his cookies.

"Noooooooooow! Nooaw! Now!" Vinnie urged.

"Yes, you're getting your breakfast now," I said, and placed his bowl in front of him, per his instruction. Yeeshkabiddle.

Vito stood in the hallway, holding the bag and shaking his head. "Boy, Vinnie sure is one big cat," he said for the one zillionth time.

"Yup," I said back.

Vito held up the bag. "Crumb buns!" he announced.

I was impressed. Again.

"So who's your crumb bun connection?" I asked, getting some plates.

"I cannot divulge a bakery source. Let us just say someone with New Jersey origins continues to owe me a pretty big favor," he said. I shrugged.

"So my plan's this," Vito said seriously. Which was tough since his mouth was covered with powdered sugar. "I've gotta finish up this month's... deliveries."

"Right," I said, biting into more of my crumb bun and gulping more coffee. But it didn't seem strong enough. I seriously wished stores would label coffee with ratings: WAKE UP!; OMG – YOU'RE LATE!!; and READY TO PAINT THE LIVING ROOM TWICE. Times like these, the last one wouldn't go amiss, I thought.

"That should give folks about a month's warning to look for their, uh... product somewheres else," Vito added with an exaggerated wink. He looked like he had something stuck in his eye.

"What are you going to do with the rest of the stuff in the basement?" I asked.

"Huh?" Vito said, jiggling crumb bun crumbs from his shirt and onto his plate.

"The rest of your luggage in my basement?" I asked loudly.

"Oh! Like I said, I'm going to finish up this month's deliveries. I should be finished in a couple days."

"You mean all that stuff in the basement is just two days' worth of deliveries?"

"Well sure; you have no idea how many prescriptions doctors write for older persons," Vito said, biting into his crumb bun again.

I rubbed my neck. Dim visions of Vito, Aunt Muriel and Tina in fluorescent orange prison jump suits throbbed through my head. My butt twinged. I rubbed it. Vito looked at me.

"Maybe yous wanna sit down, or have some alone time or something," he said and blushed. I nodded and sat down on the floor.

Vinnie came up and sniffed at my crumb bun, then looked up at me. His muzzle was dusted with a snowy coating of powdered sugar. I moved to wipe it off but he hissed at me and stalked away. Apparently he had a thing for crumb buns, too.

"So this morning I got it alls worked out to make some urgent deliveries first. Then I'll take Helena to the train station. I offered to drive her back to Jersey myself, but she wants to talk to my brother first, and kind of work things out like. But I'm pretty sure he's figured out where she's been and all."

"How come?"

"Because when she called to check on the baby, she said she was staying at Uncle Vlad's," he said. I smacked my forehead with my hand just like Ma and Aunt Muriel, forfeiting any claims of individuality from my genetic cesspool. "Hey, but this could be nice!" Vito said quickly. "Maybe they'll come visit. We could barbeque," he mused. I stared straight at him, which he returned with a blank, sappy gaze. I rolled my eyes. Before Vito got descended on by his family at large, most of which probably was at large, I was going to have to whip up a batch of chutzpah and ask for my spare key back. Or pretend there'd been a drive-by lock changing by an OCD locksmith.

"Then, after I drop Helena off at the station, I'm gonna adopt Stanley!" Vito went on brightly. "Hey, you wouldn't happen to have an extra box of tissues, would you, Cookie?" he asked.

I clambered back to my feet and looked around the living room. The remains of one of Vito's Econo-size tissue boxes was perched on the coffee table. I grabbed it and put it next to his crumb bun bag.

He nodded and brushed his remaining crumbs off into the sink. He took the tissue box and walked toward the front door, then stopped. "Don't worry, Toots. Even when I have Stanley, I'll still make time to Swiffer for you. After the crowd you've had these days, your floors sure could use it," he tsked, shaking his head and leaving.

I looked into my coffee mug, and toward the liquor cabinet and pictured the bottle of whiskey I wish I had and knew I didn't. Well, it's the thought that counts.

I hopped in the shower, and was just getting out when the doorbell rang. I dripped and swore, brushed Vinnie away from trying to climb into the tub with me, threw on my bathrobe and headed downstairs. I opened the door to find Bauser and Norman and Jim. Jim sat up pretty and leaned. Bauser propped him up with his knee.

"Uh, hi," I said, opening the door. "Isn't this a little early?" It was just after six o'clock.

Norman sighed. "I've been up since three, anyway," he said, walking in, followed by Bauser and Jim.

"The horses?" I asked.

"Cat wrangling," Norman yawned. "The horses sleep in until five. So I figured I might as well finish painting the side of the barn. Then I got to some weeding, watered the vegetable bed, vacuumed and made breakfast for the girls."

I shuddered. No wonder Norman took naps on his towel at lunchtime. Clearly married persons with families have lots more chores than I ever imagined. While I, on the other hand, remain chore challenged and am becoming increasingly dependent on Vito's Swiffer addiction.

"We've got a clue," Bauser said. He stepped into the kitchen with Jim, and his eyes immediately fell upon the crumb buns. I made some more coffee, dug out some more plates while Bauser, Norman and Jim nosed around inside the bag.

"So what's the clue?" I asked.

Before they could answer, the doorbell rang again. I rolled my eyes and went to answer it. It was Trixie.

"How're you doing? You want some coffee?" I asked her, at the same time wondering why none of my friends used telephones.

Trixie rolled her eyes. "I'd rather have a shot and a beer." She sighed. "What a night! You wouldn't believe."

I nodded and agreed, while my right butt cheek winced with another shot of pinch de jour.

I looked around at the accumulating breakfast crowd. Well, at least no one could accuse me of living in isolation. Trixie looked around the kitchen, then at the powdery sugared muzzles of Jim, Bauser and Norman.

"Sorry," Norman gulped. "If we'd known you were coming we wouldn't have let Jim have the last crumb bun."

Trixie waved him off. "That's okay. I'm not much for sweet stuff, anyway," she said.

"I guess not, if you're up for a bump and a beer for breakfast," Bauser said.

Trixie shook her head. "What a night," she repeated and sighed. I felt sorry I didn't have any beer for her.

"I can give you a Mug o'Merlot? Or a Bloody, I think... well, sort of..." I trailed, realizing I hadn't re-stocked tomato juice, or vodka, even with my mega marathon grocery extravaganza.

Trixie squinted at me, considering. "What do you mean, 'Bloody, sort of'?"

"I don't have any tomato juice. Or vodka. But I do have some wine, and some canned spaghetti sauce," I answered.

Everyone winced. Including Jim and Vinnie. "Yuck," Norman said.

"Just a minute here," Bauser piped up, and jogged out the door. The rest of us looked at each other and shrugged.

Trixie had her head inside my fridge, trying to figure out what she wanted me to make her for her third shift dinner-breakfast, when Bauser strolled back in carrying a cooler. He plopped it down on the counter and opened it to reveal two six-packs of Krumpthf's. He broke open a can for Trixie and handed it to her.

"You might want to use a strainer or a coffee filter first," Norman advised.

Trixie looked at the can and winced. "Krumpthf's," she sighed. "It's come to this. Krumpthf's."

"I like Krumpthf's," Bauser said.

"That's because you're cheap," Trixie replied, opening the can over the sink and grabbing a mug and a coffee filter.

"Frugal," Bauser corrected.

"What are you doing with a cooler of Krumpthf's in your car? Are you guys going fishing or something?" I asked.

Bauser looked at me. "I always travel with my own six-pack," he said. "Besides," he added, "would you believe there are actually some beer distributors that don't carry Krumpthf's?"

I winced.

"It's actually not so bad, if you mix it with some tomato juice," Norman offered, while eyeing the remaining cans in the cooler. "But you don't have any tomato juice at all, right?" he asked me hopefully.

"Just spaghetti sauce," I replied.

"Too bad," Norman said.

Trixie finished straining her Krumpthf's, took a sip and sighed. She reached for her purse and brought out a new pack of Swank's. "You mind? I can go out back on the deck," she asked.

I looked around at the fellas. I didn't know quite what to say, since I was recently guilty of succumbing to the nicotine nasties myself when I thought I'd lost Vinnie. I motioned to Trixie and opened the back door to the deck. Trixie nodded and took her purse and we left the fellas inside.

"So what gives? Why are you scrounging beer for breakfast?" I asked.

Trixie took a short swig of her Krumpthf's, made a face and then took a long drag of her cigarette.

"First of all," she exhaled, "it's Krumpthf's, not beer. And this isn't breakfast for me. More like supper," she said. She took another swig, made a face, and then took another really long drag from her cigarette. "And second, my shifts – plural – sucked."

"What happened?"

"Well, after your aunt's church pals Ernie and Evelyn admitted themselves in for barbeque burns, in came the other church buddies, Henry and his old lady Caryl. They all fill each other in about why each other is there, comparing barbeque mishaps and all, when Henry and Ernie start shouting and shoving each other. Eventually, one of the clinical assistants and I got the fellas calmed down. But the next thing you know, the two old girls are hollering at each other and having at it. By the way, did you know Evelyn wears a wig?" Trixie asked.

I balked. I was still trying to wrap my brain around the fisticuff images Trixie had just pasted inside my head. Fighting? Ernie? Henry? Cat brawl? Evelyn? Caryl? None of this made any sense. It certainly wasn't very Episcopalian, with the espousing tolerance thingy and all.

"Anyway, the next thing you know, we're admitting herds of senior barbecue burn victims. It was weird," she said.

"They all had barbecue burns?"

"Not only that, but they all claimed to be Episcopalian. And you didn't hear that from me," she said, taking another drag. "I can't tell you whether or not they attend St. Bart's, but their admission forms all had 'Episcopal' written in for religion. And apparently they all knew each other. One minute they're all watching the news calmly. The next minute all hell broke loose." She put out the stub of her cigarette and lit up another.

"Some old bag thunked her walker on top of some old guy's foot, then the next moment someone's toupee went flying. Two other old guys were pointing fingers into each other's chests so hard that they both claimed to be having chest pains. So then we had to admit them both, just to rule out angina. Then we had the wheelchair babe cruising down the aisle and knocking people down with her sister's cane." Trixie shuddered. "Then," she continued, "Appletree comes in, because of the previous brawl being called in and all, with none other than the Mrs." Her face downturned in a grimace. "You know, I know the whole freaking town knows about me and Appletree. I get that. But it was pretty embarrassing when I found out the unit secretaries were taking bets which brawl was gonna be next: me and Herself or the sizzled seniors." She added, "I'm okay with the I-was-the-other-woman thing, mostly. I'm just not so okay about getting beat out by a 4-foot, 200 pound troll with no make-up and bad hair."

I sighed. I'd heard this before. But I figured it must have been especially painful when encountered in person with the 200 pound troll.

"That's okay," I said, patting her head. "You don't want Appletree, anyway. He's not much taller than a troll, either," I said.

She sighed. "I know. I guess it's just the uniform thing."

"Oh!" I cried. Trixie looked at me. "I forgot to tell you, he got some kind of a detective promotion recently," I said.

Trixie shook her head. "That explains it. He kept babbling about Eve driving him around, because his car was in the shop. I thought that was weird since he wasn't in uniform, coming directly from work and all. And in a suit, no less." She sighed.

"His wife's name is Eve?"

"Ycah."

"But isn't Appletree's first name Adam?"

"Yeah, so... oh!"

"You never thought of that before?" I asked again, incredulously. "You tried to break up Adam and Eve?"

Trixie grinned wildly. "Hey, I never thought about it like that!" she exploded and we both collapsed.

We stopped gasping and sat grinning stupidly at each other.

"You know, I think you could actually find a single guy, of normal stature, that you might actually like," I offered.

Trixie shrugged. "I know. I guess it's just the uniform thing," she answered.

"You liked Mike, the U.S. Marshal guy, until you found out he was gay," I suggested.

"Yeah, but U.S. Marshals are a whole other bag of wax. I mean, the suit is their uniform."

"Oh."

"But you're right. I'll try better next time. Especially about the not married thing and all."

"Well, if you found a guy that was more normal, and single, and had a job and all, couldn't you just ask him to dress up? Like, maybe try it out around Halloween or something?"

Trixie seemed happier with that thought. "It's not quite the same thing as a real uniform. But I like the idea of finding someone single and solvent," she agreed.

"RentalRama's right on Prince Street," I suggested.

"Yeah," Trixie replied, with a far off look in her eyes. I sighed. I began to worry about the poor unsuspecting cubicle working dolt who would soon find himself in for tricks or treats, no matter what the season.

Trixie took a final drag from her cigarette. "Cripes, even menthol doesn't help this swill," she said, finishing another swallow of the Krumpthf's. "You got any weeds out back you want killed? I'll pour it on them."

I nodded toward one of the zillion thistles crawling up the hill that I'd yet to outsmart. Trixie walked toward them and poured. I swear I thought I saw them tremble as she approached. They soon wilted after she poured the remaining contents of her can on them.

"I've still got some Box O'Burgundy," I offered.

"Anything's better than this," she said. "Besides, it's stinking hot out here."

We wandered back inside to find the fellas watching 'Guys! Cook! Now!' They sat transfixed. Even Jim sat upright. Trixie and I looked at each other and shrugged, wondering what cooking show could capture the attention of four non-culinary males.

After a few seconds, we got it.

"The Cowboy Special, huh?" I asked.

"Geez, would ya look at the size of those steaks?" Bauser asked. Jim panted. Norman nodded. Vinnie stared. The 'Guys! Cook! Now!' dude was rubbing some kind of chili salt and sugar rub onto what looked like the size and thickness of Mastodon steaks. "And don't forget the homemade coleslaw," he added hypnotically.

The camera panned onto a family size serving bowl piled high with shredded green, red and Savoy cabbage, along with shredded carrots, fresh green peppers and pineapple chunks. The highlighted single serving looked like, roughly speaking, enough fancy coleslaw for thirty.

I stared at Norman. He was texting notes on his Crackberry to himself.

"I do all the cooking at home," he answered automatically.

"Shhhh, he's getting ready to actually cook the steaks directly on the coals!" Bauser hushed.

Vinnie scrunched down and watched the screen transfixed, too.

I shrugged and went to the freezer and took out two of the eight London Broils I'd bought. Then I began to rustle Trixie up a three-egg Greek style omelet with some fresh spinach, feta cheese, mozzarella, sliced black olives, green onions and tomatoes.

Trixie and the fellas were back in the kitchen as soon as they heard sizzling. They all looked at me. "For Trixie," I replied.

"Oh," Norman, Bauser and Jim sighed dejectedly. Vinnie muttered something derogatory and sauntered downstairs to the basement.

"You guys are hungry?" I asked, getting ready to thaw out the steaks in the microwave.

"Well, it's just the damn cooking show. All they ever talk about is food," Norman answered.

I shrugged. "I took some steaks out. Do you want them now or later? Or omelets? Or subs? I picked up some rolls and cold cuts and stuff."

"Subs! With Krumpthf's! Wow!" Bauser said. Jim whoofed.

Trixie dumped out her Burgundy and poured some coffee. I served up Trixie's omelet while the fellas plunged into a free for all sub frenzy. They all stood around, chewing happily while Trixie explained to them about her sizzling seniors shift. They explained to Trixie and me about their new Burning Buy-A-Lots' clue.

“So what is it?” Trixie asked.

“Well, I started running the packet sniffer at home,” Norman started.

“How could you do that? Haven't they shut you out of the system yet?” I asked. “I mean, wouldn't it make sense for EEJIT to lock you out of their data systems after you quit?”

“Apparently that hadn't dawned on them until early this morning. I was in all last night,” he yawned. “Anyway, I set off another run after I launched the Pocket Snatcher.”

“Pocket Snatcher?”

Bauser nodded emphatically. “Norman came up with it on his way home last night,” he said.

“Basically the Pocket Snatcher gets activated anytime a Packet Sniffer starts to nose around. It not only follows the activity of the Packet Sniffer, but it snatches its unique location ID – kind of a pick-pocket rogue.”

“Did it work?”

“Theoretically, yes,” he said. “I got a unique internet address tied to a specific computer. But the best I got from cybering around my usual haunts, and not being a Fed or something, is that we're getting packet sniffed from a user somewhere in Bangladesh.”

“Well, that narrows it down,” Trixie said.

“Now what?” I asked.

Norman shrugged. “Don't know, because now I am locked out of EEJIT's systems.”

Bauser swallowed some Krumpthf's and looked worried. “But whoever's doing this was probably the one who konked Mina on the noggin,” he said.

Norman shrugged. “Perhaps.”

“I don't get it,” Trixie said. “What does this have to do with the burning Buy-A-Lots?”

Norman sighed and ran a hand over his head. “Buy-A-Lots will blame EEJIT for damaging their company and associated insurance costs, not to mention lost revenue from the delays in opening the new store locations. So they'd cancel the current and future contracts and probably also sue EEJIT."

"Right, I get all that," Trixie gulped. "What I don't get is the why." Norman, Bauser and I looked at her blankly. Trixie shook her head. "Boy, you all would make lousy cops," she said. "First, the obvious question is: who stands to profit by Buy-A-Lots – and EEJIT – losing?"

The three of us ex-EEJIT types looked at each other blankly.

"Yikes, who wouldn't profit by it?" Norman asked. "I mean, any time a Buy-A-Lots opens, a lot of other smaller stores are displaced. There's usually not a lot of benevolence toward a new store," Norman asked.

"Well, if these fires are all connected to new store openings, why don't you just use the software you have now to predict where the next fire is going to happen?" she asked.

Bauser nodded. "After the very first fire, EEJIT worked with the Lancaster police to launch a pretty high tech security system over the entire construction site. But the only thing caught on tape was when a rabid squirrel that gnawed through the wires and got zapped." He grimaced.

"Well, I sure would like to know why a bus load of senior Episcopalians all got burned barbequing last night," Trixie said. "And I'd especially wish I knew what the heck was on the news that got them banging each other with their walkers," she added.

"Oh, I remember what was on last night's news," Bauser piped up. "A whole bunch of fires got started at a bunch of Buy-A-Lots."

"What?" the rest of us asked collectively.

"Yeah, you know how they have lots of barbeque grills sitting around outside the store entrance for people to gawk at?" he asked.

"Yeah?"

"That's where all the fires happened; lawn and garden," he said, then shrugged. "I guess it'd be pretty easy to do. People are always driving up and waiting to unload passengers or load up merchandise, so a waiting car really wouldn't be too noticeable. Anyway, no one thought the fires were too weird at first because they were all in the grills. Until they realized they were new grills that were for sale. Then some of the grills exploded. Luckily no one got hurt. The police were actually chalking it up to some lousy publicity stunt. But the newscaster was speculating about tying the fires to the new store arsonist."

"Why?" I asked.

"There were burnt up bags of doggie doo-doo in all of the fired up grills. Along with baby food jars filled with gasoline. Which I guess explains the explosions. And the smelly entrances."

Trixie gritted her teeth. "Did the news mention the store locations?" she snarled.

"Yeah, probably. It's probably in the papers this morning," Bauser answered.

"Why?" I asked.

"If the fires were at various Lancaster County locations, it would be very unusual if my senior burn victims lived near all the locations, right?" she frowned.

"Unusual, but circumstantial," Norman said thoughtfully.

"Besides, it was probably just a fluke thing; probably some kids doing dare-you mischief," Bauser added.

Trixie shook her head. "You better hope so. And you better hope your newly appointed Detective Appletree doesn't come to the same conclusion I do."

"But why would a bunch of old folks want to burn bags of doggie doo-doo inside barbeques at a bunch of Buy-A-Lots?" I asked.

"Are you kidding? You should hear the way they go on. Last night their major complaint was that their four hour wait in the E.R. took less time than checking out of a Buy-A-Lots."

Ah. Well, that was a good point.

The doorbell rang. I thought about issuing a secret password, but I answered it anyway. It was Ethel and Ike, with Hansel and Gretel sporting another new his-and-her matching bowtie and hair-bow accessories, this time in coordinating fushcia and orange polka dots.

"We thought we'd stop by and take you out to breakfast. Ma and Aunt Muriel are on their way over, too," Ethel said.

I hugged Ethel, above Gretel's growls, and let them both inside. They put the Ratties down and Jim hopped over to greet them.

Ethel sniffed. "You've been cooking!"

"Just breakfast kind of thingies," I replied defensively.

She went over and sniffed at Trixie's plate. And sighed. "The good old faux Greek omletey thing." She sighed again.

Ike rolled his eyes. "You just had some bagels. And a yogurt. And a banana. And cereal. And a not so mid-morning breakfast pastry snack," he said. Ethel focused her newly acquired maternal death beam directly onto his forehead. Ike winced. "Maybe we should feed her now. After all, she's eating for two. Or a litter. Or something."

We went back into the living room, where Bauser and Norman and Jim tried to talk me into cooking the steaks while Trixie tried to talk them into going to a beer distributor and buying a case of anything but Krumpthf's.

The doorbell rang. I went to answer it. Forget the password idea. At this point I needed a toll booth.

There stood Vito with a bandaged nose, holding a small, snarling terrier in front of him. "Thmanks, Twoots," he said nasally. "I whud of yuthed my key, but got my awms full here."

I looked at Vito, who was smiling ear to ear. I looked at Stanley, who was baring fangs from ear to ear. I kept the storm door closed.

"Uh, sure. Uh, just a minute, huh, Vito?" I said, making sure Vinnie was still in the basement. I gave Bauser and Ethel the high sign. "Uh, you might want to hold onto the pooches for a few minutes," I said. While I appreciated Vito's Swiffering, I really didn't want too much blood on my kitchen floor.

I went back down the hall and let Vito and the rabid looking terrier inside. Vito put the dog down, who immediately seized Vito's trouser leg between his jaws and began snarling and pulling.

Vito shrugged. "I thwink he'th a widdle upset about gedding put in duh pound," he said.

"Are you sure this is the same dog?" I asked.

Vito nodded. "Him wath vewy, vewy good to Tatchi, whathn't him?" he asked Stanley's third person. Stanley growled back at him from his trouser cuff and shook it vigorously up and down. Vito shrugged. "We wuth fine until we got inside the cawh. Then he godda widdle exciteable," he explained. "I think he thwinks car wides are bad things now, poor bubby."

He stooped down to pet the terrier. Stanley snarled back. Vito snatched his hand away and put it in his pocket.

"Did he do that to you nose?"

"Yeah," Vito sighed. "I thwink he did not wike his wabbies shot," Vito said. "Good thwing I had sample gauz pads and tape wid me."

I shook my head. Stanley growled some more.

"Can you whatch him sos I can ged set up at home for him?" Vito asked.

"I could, if you could detach him from you. And if he doesn't bite."

Stanley wagged his tail at me. Then he looked up at Vito and growled and chewed on his pant leg some more.

"Thur, thur, thur, Twoots," Vito said. "Him will be a good ogey-wogey." He bent down, patted Stanley's head and put the leash to his collar. "Just take the weash and walk him inthide," he directed.

I took the lead and really wished I was wearing something more than slippers and my bath robe. I pulled gently and started to walk toward the kitchen. Stanley looked up, stopped snarling and trotted over and sat pretty for me.

"Thee?" Vito said. "He just hath a widdle grudge. He'll ged over it."

And he went back out the door to get Stanley's supplies from his car, gingerly fingering his nose.

I looked at Stanley and shrugged. "Maybe you're just hungry?" I asked the terrible terrier. He yipped a yes, and we went into the kitchen to join the rest of the crowd and scrounge up some goodies for him, too.

After a bowl of instant oatmeal and some deli roast beef, Stanley was a far less terrifying terrier. Vito came back over and sat on the sofa, with Stanley panting happily by his side, and nuzzling, not nipping, at his hand. I'd finally made it back upstairs, while everyone else kibitzed, to put some clothes on and brush my now strangely dried hair.

The doorbell rang, and I heard Vito and Stanley answer it. "Well, hi there, Muwiel!" Vito shouted above Stanley's yaps and Jim's baying. Hansel and Gretel yipped the chorus.

"Nice to see you, too, Vito," Aunt Muriel shouted back.

"How's it going Lou-weese?"

"GREAT, THANKS," Ma hollered back.

I sighed and joined the din.

"Well, dear, we didn't think we were interrupting anything," Aunt Muriel said. "We thought we'd all go to breakfast, before Ethel and Ike go back home today."

"We're going to the Canine Cafe," Ethel said, smiling. She looked around at my pals. "Your friends can bring Jim and Stanley, too."

"Ah'd wuv too, Twoots," Vito said. "Bud I dunno about Thanley gedding bag inthide a cawh any time thoon," he added. I nodded. Bauser and Norman grimaced.

Trixie yawned. "I've had enough breakfasts for one day, thanks," she said. "And actually it's time for me to get some shut eye. Especially working these vampire hours they got me on."

Vito waved bye-bye to the rest of us and took Stanley back to his new forever home. Trixie beeped her Jeep goodbye at us as she sped down the street. I let Vinnie back up to tell him the coast was clear.

I stood in the driveway, contemplating the consequences of sitting the backseat with the Ratties, versus sitting in the backseat of Auntie's Lexus and getting lectured about paint swatches. So I wound up in the backseat of Bauser's car with Jim on my lap.

The last breakfast was nice, too. We all had our assorted pancakes, breads, omelets, layered bagels and fruit salads arranged in front of us. Hansel and Gretel and Jim dove into their Doggie Ice – a sort of ice cream for doggies that I'm pretty sure is mostly frozen lard.

Afterward, Ike and Bauser gave Hansel and Gretel and Jim their walks before their respective car rides to their respective homes. And Ethel took her fourth potty break. Then, we all made sure Hansel and Gretel were strapped into their puppy protective car straps correctly, and waved bye-bye. Ethel and Ike pulled out of the Canine Cafe parking lot and out of my current tense. I sniffed. I always miss my sister before she's gone. Jim pawed my butt in sympathy, then fell over.

I tumbled back into the back seat of Bauser's car with Jim, where my eyes watered a little.

"You and your sister are really, tight, huh?" Norman asked.

"Yeah," I answered. "And Jim should never, ever have Doggie Ice again. Phew!"

It took a few minutes with the windows rolled the entire way down – and my hair looking slightly more Bellevue than I'd wished – for Jim's aromas to dissipate.

Heading back down Orange Street, I asked Bauser, "Hey, you think you could drop me off at the parking garage? I still need to get my car."

"Sure, I can drive you up, if you want," he said.

"It's okay, you really don't need to," I replied.

"Yes he does," Norman chimed.

"Why?"

"Your car's been parked for a few days now, and you don't own an active EEJIT card pass anymore. But you do have an affluent friend to ransom your car back for you," he said.

I then realized I probably owed close to a hundred bucks for several days of parking, which I probably couldn't blame on snow emergencies. Yeesh. "Thanks," I said, and meant it.

We drove up to the top level, where I'd left my car parked near Bauser's usual rooftop spot. But as we got within sight we noticed some security guards and police cars huddled around my van. Along with the 'new' Detective Appletree. I groaned and slid back down in the backseat next to Jim, poots or no poots.

Appletree walked over and leaned in the window. Then he backed away, waving at Jim's fumes with his hand. "Hi, Mina," he said, about two feet from the Aspire, with a handkerchief over his nose. "Was wondering when you'd show up. Not like you to leave your van like this, right?"

I sighed. "Nope; didn't have my keys after my purse, uh, didn't get stolen," I said, and rubbed at the twinge that was tapping inside my shoulder.

Appletree sighed. "C'mon out. I think you'd better take a look at this."

Bauser cut the engine and we all climbed out. Appletree led me over to the Doo-doo. He pointed to a broken window at the backseat.

"Oh, great," I muttered. Why is it when the Unemployment Fairy visits, she dumps expensive accidents on you, too?

Appletree shook his head. "Not just the broken window. Look inside."

I peered in and saw what looked like hundreds of neatly folded, filled brown lunch bags, wrapped up and piled high on the seats and even in the way back, along with a small container of gasoline. And rags. And fireplace matches. And a plastic recycle carton full of glass coke bottles.

With the broken window open, the stench of cooking doggie poop was unmistakable. Norman and Bauser looked in and held their noses.

"Look, I was nowhere near this van until just now," I started. Appletree waved me off.

"Relax; you're not a suspect. Knowing you, if you tried to be an arsonist, you'd set yourself on fire." He pulled a smile. I looked back at him flatly. "And besides, whoever put this stuff in here broke your window to get into your car. It's not exactly like anybody would break into an old van to steal doggie poop out of it. And it also looks like somebody was getting ready to barbeque your van."

Appletree pointed beneath the van. I knelt down and peered. Several waiting Coke bottles, filled with gasoline and stuffed with rags stared back at me. This I did not like. I don't like the Doo-doo, but she's mine. It wasn't fair that someone would break in and put doo-doo in the Doo-doo. The thought of someone torching it – for whatever reason – was akin to pet abuse.

"We'd like to tow your van back to the station, and get it dusted for fingerprints. It's going to take some time. Your car insurance should pay for a rental."

Car insurance. Great. When you're driving a 1996 Dodge Caravan, you pretty much don't have a two-hundred and fifty dollar deductible. Try, like, twenty-five hundred. So now I'd get to treat myself an early Christmas present of a new window and a rental car.

My butt twinged and I rubbed at it absentmindedly. Appletree blushed. "Hey, maybe you wanna sit down or something? Or have some, uh, time to yourself?"

I nodded and sat down on the hot floor of the parking garage roof. Jim sat next to me.

"Here's my card with my new contact information," he said, handing me a rather official police detective business card. "You call me Friday afternoon and I'll be able to let you know when you can pick up your car. You'll need your I.D. with you."

I nodded, took his card, and itched my butt with it before throwing it in my purse. Appletree shook his head. Bauser and Norman shrugged. They picked me up off the ground and packed me back inside the backseat with Jim and we headed back toward my house.

The drive back was quiet. I was deeply immersed in not irritating the little black cloud that kept floating serenely over my life.

We drove up to my house but had to park at the curb, because the fire truck was in my driveway. Also, the firemen were blocking the entrance to my front door.

After screaming at them that I had two pets who I did not want to be barbequed, I dragged out my driver's license and they let me through.

Billows of smoke were coming out my front door. Vito and Miriam sat on my front porch, chit-chatting with a couple of firemen and shaking their heads.

"What happened?" I screamed.

Vito shrugged. "All I wath doing wath trying to leave a thwank you. So I braised a brithket for yuth," he said. "Then I thought I'd make a tweat for Thanly," he added.

"A treat?"

"I was trying to thmoke pigs' feet. Anyway, Mirwium thwings by, and we got to talking, and next thing I knows the pan's a widdle too hot."

"There was smoke!" Miriam said defensively.

"There'th supposed to be smoke!" Vito yelled back. "I was thmoking pigs' feet!"

I rubbed the back of my neck; as my headache creeped down my spine.

"You were burning brisket! And the pigs' feet! You're supposed to smoke food outdoors! With water! In a pot! " Miriam cried.

"I TOLD YOU! DO NOT BE AFWAID OF CARBONIZATION!"

I interrupted, “Carbonization?” Vito nodded his head up and down. I sighed. “I think you mean carmelization,” I said. “Where's Vinnie? And Marie?”

After dealing with and apologizing to the firemen, and checking on Vinnie and Marie – now housed in separate bedrooms upstairs in Vito's townhouse, away from all the smoke – and after borrowing a half dozen fans to blow the smoke out of my house, it was a little after four in the afternoon and I was mad. Vito knew it.

“I wath justh twying to thay thwank you,” he stammered. “And I got dithtwacted.”

“Why were you cooking in my house?” I asked simply.

Vito shrugged. “I gueff it's kinda wike a habit now. And bethides, you got real good pots and dings. I dunno know how to shop for that kinda thutff,” he said, gingerly fingering his nasal injury. I looked pointedly at the burnt out cast iron pan, and the burnt out stockpot – the culprit – on top of my stove. “Ah guess ah should have athked you,” he said sheepishly.

“Look, I'll take you shopping soon and we'll get you your very own set of good quality pots and pans that you can burn out happily in your own kitchen,” I said.

“You mean id? And spitheth?”

“Yes,” I sighed, “and spices.”

CHAPTER 13

(Thursday into Friday)

Downstairs was still pretty smokey, so we got Vinnie and Marie arranged upstairs. Then Aunt Muriel called to let me know she'd made dinner reservations at Conestoga Cabana for her, Ma and me for seven o'clock. It was five-thirty. She asked me if I wanted to come over and have a drink first, which I certainly did. But after the way today had gone, I was afraid I wouldn't stop. Plus, I was still without a vehicle. And I still needed to shower, dress and make another vain attempt at cosmetics. We then began the logistics negotiations.

That was about when the migraine in my posterior voiced a loud and angry salutation. I kept nodding and uh-huhing into the phone at Auntie while I walked over to the freezer and took out a bag of frozen peas and held it against my butt.

Ten minutes later, I was still reminding Auntie I was without a car.

Vito waved at me. "Yeth you do, Toods," he whispered, dragging out a large, heavy golden key chain from his pocket. "You justh take my Towncawhr," he said. "I'd dwive you over, if we weren't airing oud your houthe. Id's the weast Ah can dew."

I motioned for him to throw me the keys. I dropped the peas, caught the keys, and told Aunt Muriel I'd meet her and Ma at the restaurant.

By now the clock said it was a quarter to pretty late. I got Vinnie's food ready and carried it upstairs. He was ensconced across my bed, one paw hooked over his nose, enjoying the most of it. Really. He took up the whole bed. Beside him was a Recipes Quick! magazine I'd left on my night table. Apparently he'd dragged it onto the bed for perusal. I shrugged. Maybe someday he'd show me a 5-minute feed-and-clean-the-pets-and-shower-and-dress-and-get-your-ass-out-the-door-in-time-for-work recipe.

Vinnie woke up, stretched longer and yawned. I put his dinner down in front of him – Chicken Toes-es with Fishie Noses – then left and closed the door to repeat the parallel process with Marie across the hall.

I went back into my room, looked in my closet and saw a bundle of fresh dry cleaning waving at me. Sorting through the plastic wraps, I found a favorite silk shirt set that I'd completely forgotten about. Wow. It was as good, if not better, than getting a new outfit for free. I remembered the Capri linen pants that went with it, which by some miracle were hanging up clean and not bunched up in the dirty laundry.

I lay everything out on my bed. "Okay, Vinnie, no pre-fluffing my good duds, right?" I asked.

"Aw-kay!" Vinnie yipped in response and leapt on top of the bed to guard my clothes from the 'mysterious other cat' who is usually responsible for shedding on them.

I grabbed a quick shower, then threw back the curtain to find Vinnie sitting vigil in his usual spot – just outside the tub – and immediately began chatting me up with a diatribe of cautionary tales while I toweled off. Did I know what happens to humans who get deliberately wet; this was how pneumonia and disease are spread; you wouldn't catch him doing that sort of thing, etc.

I threw on my clothes and some make-up and opted for my usual wet ponytail since I'd run out of blow-drying time. I gave a goodbye pat to Vinnie, poked my head into Marie's room so she could hiss me farewell, and clopped downstairs.

Vito looked up. "Wow, Twoots, you wook gweat!" he shouted above the fans. I rubbed at the nerve that was starting to twinge again deep inside my right buttock. Vito winced, then handed me his keys. I patted Stanley on the nose and headed out the front door toward Vito's driveway and his waiting Towncar.

Air conditioning. In a car. Ahhh. And silence! I suddenly realized just how noisy my household was these days. I exhaled in relief, blasted the AC, and changed the radio station from WPOP (Polkas of Polska) to an FM station I can't pick up in the Doo-doo. Mostly since the Doo-doo only picks up AM. Not that she doesn't have a normalish radio. It's just that she refuses to pick up FM. Unless it's some kind of religious talk show, or Christian rock.

I headed out Vito's driveway and checked in the rearview and almost ran over top of Mr. Perfect, aka Bruce, as he walked David past the driveway. He waved back good naturedly. It figured. Now that I was all dolled up, and know Bruce is gay, of course I'd run into him when I wasn't looking crummy.

I stopped and pushed the button to unroll the driver side window. The trunk flipped open. I tried again. The gas cap opened. I tried again. The windshield wipers washed. I sighed. I pressed the last of the Chinese takeout buttons on the driver's side door and the front passenger side window rolled down. Bruce loped over with David, shut the trunk, closed the gas cap, then leaned in the opposite window at me and turned off the windshield wipers.

"Hi!" he beamed. "Wow, new car?" I shook my head, explained about the Doo-doo and needing to borrow Vito's car to meet Aunt Muriel and Ma at Conestoga Cabana. Bruce nodded enthusiastically. "You'll have a fabulous time!" he said. "And you'll be able to check out the menu before the Conestoga Cabana Cup at polo this Sunday!"

"Huh?" I asked politely.

Bruce explained that the restaurant sponsors a competition game each summer, and that invitees only gain admittance to the private party via invitation. Which was only issued to regulars. The feast is served while the guests pretend to watch the polo match. "It's a lovely, lovely time," Bruce advised. "Your aunt is such a regular at Conestoga Cabana; I'm sure she's invited. She must bring you!" he declared. Or I thought I heard him declare. Well, I certainly didn't declare – I'm born well north of the Mason Dixon line.

But I gulped and felt a little panicked. "Umm... well, maybe I should skip it this year, and try next year, after everyone's forgotten about the Chukker Tent getting set on fire," I mumbled.

Bruce waved me off. "Oh, that's nothing," he said. "You should have been there when one of the patrons used a mini-propane grill to win the tailgate competition – inside his trunk!" David woofed in agreement. "They were invited not to bring a hot meal ever again!" Bruce added. I gulped again. "Look, I'm sure they sent me an extra invitation so I'll stop by to see if you need it – that is if your aunt hasn't already received hers," he offered.

I blushed. Gay or not, Bruce is waaa-aaay cute. And very nice. But then again, he is from Lancaster.

I smiled, said thanks again, patted David on top of his giant head – which he was hanging through the passenger side window, slobbering down Vito's side panel. I made a mental note to feign complete ignorance about that when I returned the car, and hoped Stanley wouldn't bite too much.

I waved bye-bye, then pulled out of my development and onto Millersville Pike, and started my trek toward Conestoga Cabana.

After I was well into Manheim Township, I made a left at the used car place that housed the 'Conestoga Cabana – This Way!' billboard above it. I followed the arrowed signs that led to it, driving across the small wooden covered bridge and up a long driveway.

Finally, I entered through the iron gates that welcome visitors to Conestoga Cabana and parked under one of the many trees in the parking lot. Which was unusual, since most establishments don't asphalt around trees for their parking lots. But this one did. It also sported over-sized paintings on the restaurant's exterior walls. Done by the owner himself, or so I'd heard. I always wondered what made him trade a brush for a spatula?

The digital temperature screen in Vito's car told me that inside the car was a wonderful sixty-eight degrees, which accounted for the goose pimples on my arms. Outside it was ninety-eight with 85-percent humidity. I braced myself, opened the door and stepped out. Walking to the front door, I tripped on a tree root and lost my shoe while tumbling into an exiting patron. I put my slightly damaged very best sandal (damn!) back on, and limped inside.

At the Maitre'D's desk, I was officially greeted by Gus, Armand's manager. "Good eee-ven-innng," Gus intoned. I nodded. It was best to spare as few words as possible with Gus, especially where poor Armand's work schedule was concerned. "Do you have a rez-errr-vaaaa-shun?" he creened.

He had to be kidding. Did I have reservations? Where should I start? I'm worried about everything. I wasn't even sure I should be here.

Armand appeared behind him. He didn't walk out from behind a partition or curtain or anything. I mean, he just appeared. Literally. He leaned over Gus from behind. Which was easy to do, considering Gus is vertically challenged.

"She iz weeth Table 12," Armand glowered.

Gus shot a daggered look back up at Armand, then shifted as he realized I was still in the audience. As well as the party of eight lined up behind me.

Gus looked back down at the reservation list. "Ahhhhhhhhhhh, yes of course, you would be joining the Mrs. Muriel?" he said. I looked at him blankly. The Mrs. Muriel? Did he think I was boarding a ship?

Armand answered for me. "That izz correct," he replied darkly.

I tried to warm the frost-bitten air. "Hey, Armand! Great to see you! Didn't realize you'd be working tonight!" I said.

"Yes," he replied darkly, looking directly at Gus. "It is Thursday."

Gus winced. Apparently Gus was living to regret putting the kibosh on Armand's weekend schedule status. Then Gus glowered back at Armand. He was nothing if not punitive.

Gus sniffed. "If you will pleeeese follow your waaaaaaaai-ter." And he gestured toward Armand's rapidly receding back.

I caught up with Armand at the home stretch as he held out a chair for me at Aunt Muriel's and Ma's table. "Sorry I'm late," I started to say, when Armand muttered, "Motherless dog of thieves," while seating me. Aunt Muriel's eyes bulged; Ma immediately picked up the menu she had obviously studied ad nauseum while waiting for me and re-read it with renewed gusto.

I faked a smile that probably looked a little like I had gas. "Aunt Muriel, Ma, isn't this nice? My friend, Armand, is our waiter tonight," I said.

"Oh, my!" Aunt Muriel said. "I remember you and K. telling me so much about him! Very nice to meet you, Armand." She relaxed and smiled. Ma copied. "My goodness, I've been here so often this summer, I'm surprised we haven't met before," Aunt Muriel offered.

Armand glowered and turned a kind of plum color. "You dine here on the weekends, yes?" he growled.

"Well, of course, yes..." Aunt Muriel began.

"It is Thursday."

After Armand took my drink order, and some quick unplanned replenishment drink orders from Auntie and Ma, I explained to them about the weekend mafia schedule. They nodded with understanding. Armand came back with our cocktails – Aunt Muriel's usual Absolut, Ma's Grey Goose, and my very nice Cosmo in a very, very nice glass – patted me on the shoulder and left with our appetizer orders.

For those of you wondering about how to make a very nice Cosmo for one, here goes:

COSMO FOR 1 RECIPE HERE: starting with 1 very, very nice glass (remember, presentation is everything).

- Vodka of choice; 2 shots
- Triple Sec; 1 shot
- 2 shots cranberry cocktail juice
- 1 shot water
- 2 tsp FRESH squeezed lime juice
- couple drops of angostura bitters

Mix in a small pitcher with a lot of ice. Stir well (I'm not good at martini shaker thingy... I mostly wind up with a Cosmo colored walls when I do this). Strain into a pretty looking martini glass. Top with an ice cube, and sip alongside a decent vinyl of Coleman Hawkins.

We heaved our glasses and sighs of relief, imbibed and exhaled. We chatted about Ethel and Ike and the soon-to-be junior. Or junior miss. Apparently it was already decided between Ma and Mu that I would be the godmother and accordingly would arrange the baby shower. Soon. Very, very soon. I sipped my Cosmo while visions of tubal ligations and vasectomies danced through my head.

Armand returned without a growl. In fact, he looked smiley. For Armand. He served us our appetizer orders: artichoke and spinach spread with house baked bread and a smoked fish sampler platter (smoked trout, salmon, roe caviar and sturgeon). Then he presented some unordered fare: seared sea scallop and artichoke kabobs, eggplant and olive tapenade with a bonafide San

Franciscan sourdough baguette, and twelve raw oysters on the half-shell, which he placed in front of Ma.

"I have remembered Mina has said the Mamma likes these especially," he said, his lips curling. Which almost resembled a smile. Sort of. I was impressed. And scared. I hadn't seen Armand in this good a mood since the local news divulged Conestoga Cabana's chief competitor achieved their tender melt-in-your-mouth prime ribs by salting them overnight in lots of MSG. I squinted up at him. Armand shrugged. "Apparently someone was not timely when picking up his orders. Your Aunt is one of our very best patrons, so of course I signed that it is the compliments of our manager," he said, sneering deliberately toward Gus.

"Ha ha ha," I faked.

"Enjoy!" he commanded, and departed as Ma slipped down her third oyster. Well, no complaints there.

We ordered our dinners, and chatted quietly and calmly. That was when I saw Armand talking to K., as K. was exiting the cocktail bar. Armand pointed toward our table, and K. waved excitedly. He came to our table, gave little hugs and kisses into the air next to us, then wagged a finger at me.

"Now don't forget we have our special dinner date out this Saturday, missy!" he warned.

Dinner? Missy?

"Huh?"

"The SUPPER CLUB!" he chimed. "My friend Gillian finagled reservations for us! For Saturday! Remember?" he asked.

Great. That meant a very long exodus to New York City in my van with no A.C. in August, and possibly leftover poo smells. I sighed. But I had promised. I just hadn't thought K. could actually swing it. Or remember. Rats.

"I'll call you tomorrow!"

He waved, skipped out the door and was gone. I wondered if I'd have my van back in time for this odyssey.

Armand came back with our dinners, placed my order of mussels marinara in front of me, and I sighed contentedly. I just love the smell of gahhhlic. I'd just have to worry about it tomorrow. The Supper Club, not the garlic, that is. And it might turn out to be a blessing in disguise, anyway. If the Doo-doo wasn't available, someone else would have to drive. Which might mean I wouldn't have to go. I felt a little relieved at that prospect.

Armand served Ma her roast duckling, and Auntie looked down happily at her sea bass. It looked back up at her.

I was about to ask about the polo cup thingy Bruce talked about, when Armand asked Auntie if she had received her invitations. Auntie nodded happily, said she had and that she and Ma had been talking about going, too, since Ma wasn't going back to New Jersey until Monday morning. After Armand's long stare in my direction, they assured him that I was going too, with or without a helmet and/or fire extinguisher. Armand nodded approvingly and vanished.

We continued to eat and chat, and declared we would not even think about looking at the dessert trolley. Which we did end up doing, but decided to assuage our guilt by sharing a single (but very large order, probably thanks to Armand) Chocolate Pecan Pie.

We said our goodbyes in the parking lot, and Auntie said she'd call me as soon as she heard from the massage guy tomorrow. I ambled my way back down Oregon Pike, through downtown Lancaster, and carefully back into Vito's driveway without grazing anything on Vito's car, or anyone else's, either.

I found Vito lying fast asleep on my sofa, Stanley splayed out asleep on top of him. I glanced at Vito's nose. It wasn't bandaged anymore, and had a distinct nip mark. It looked pretty bad, but at least it didn't appear to have been re-gnawed by the Terrorist Terrier.

The television blared. It was 'Frannie!', the Southern maven of refried, retried, bonafide and deep fried cuisine. If it wasn't fried, it wasn't Frannie's. Which included the Fried Alaska on the screen right now (instead of baking the ice cream in a solid meringue coating like a typical Baked Alaska, she fries it; it's faster).

I thought the TV screen looked a little dirty, then realized a few thousand gnats also thought Frannie's show, and Fried Alaska, were worth watching. Along with the very loud chorus of crickets serenading from outside. Or inside. I wasn't sure.

Then I heard snoring and saw Miriam passed out in the corner chair.

Stanley stretched and affectionately patted Vito's sore nose with his paw. Vito yipped, "OW!" and sat bolt upright, which threw both Stanley and Miriam off their seats. Along with the gnats, which swarmed away from the TV screen and hovered like clouds.

"Hi there, Toots!" Vito smiled, swatting the gnats. "How was your dinner?" he asked, while trying to poke a plastic grocery bag full of 'product' toward Miriam with his foot, which Miriam tried to smash down into her new 'purse', an over-sized beach bag.

"Good," I shrugged, and started up the stairs, trying to be nonchalant.

For some reason I was edgy. I figured I was just anxious about Vinnie and Marie. If Vito and Miriam had let this many bugs in, I wanted to make sure Vinnie and Marie weren't let out. Or covered with gnats.

"Hey, it doesn't smell like smoke, anymore, right?" Vito hollered up after me.

"Uh, no," I said, peering into Marie's room. Which was true, actually. Finally.

I went into Marie's room and removed the cricket serenading her in her seed dish and put him in my pocket to put back outside.

"See, Miriam here had a great idea..." Vito continued to shout up the stairs at me. Oh boy, I could hardly wait.

I checked out Vinnie in my room. He sat on the floor next to the threshold arranging his tally: 6 dead crickets lined up in a row, 2 lightning bugs and a box elder, with a last bug twitching on the end. I shuddered. He gave me the head nod and trilled. Clearly, Vinnie knows I do not want our home filled with bugs. Even crickets, who are supposed to be good luck. I am not Chinese, but I wouldn't care how much luck they bring even if I was. If I can scoot them outside, that's great. Otherwise, as far as I'm concerned, they're just cockroach cousins with big noisy elbows.

In spite of my repulsion at Vinnie's line-up, I was glad he caught them. And that he hadn't eaten them. I got some tissues and scooped up the carcasses – and the one that was now post-transit – and flushed them down the toilet. Vinnie accepted congratulatory petty-pets on his head.

I went back downstairs to find Miriam post-stretching and yawning and Stanley and Vito in similar stages and wagging their tails. Really. Never mind.

"Well, uh, thanks, Vito," I said. "Looks like the fans worked."

"Oh, no, Toots!" Vito said. I also noticed he no longer had a speech impediment. Guess that was because of finally losing the nose bandage. "Miriam here's the life saver! She said the screens would hold in the smoke, sos it was better to have them sit open. But what with the pets and all, she offered to sit with me to make sure no one got out." Vito beamed.

Miriam nodded enthusiastically, draped in what could only be described as a tablecloth with plastic gemstone fringe and gold embroidery sewn across it in an owl motif. But the complimenting black and purple headscarf, with a hot pink feather tucked rakishly in its front knot, underneath the plastic jewel, really did the trick.

"I know how conscious you are about your pets and all," Miriam twittered.

Conscientious, I thought. But maybe she was right. I resolved not to think again until I woke up tomorrow morning.

"Uh, thanks," I said.

"I read in Housework America that smoke leaves quicker when you have the screens up. But I know how worried you are about bugs and all, so the article said to rub some clove oil and fresh garlic along the window jambs," she said, nodding.

I closed my eyes and sniffed. No wonder I felt anxious when I walked in. My house was riddled with savory harbingers of Thanksgiving and Christmas holidays past. Those kind of memories always make me a little jittery. They conjure up traumatic visions of menus for six and winding up with leftovers for fifty.

After some prolonged faked exchanges, I shuffled Vito, Miriam and Stanley out onto my front porch, and then closed my front door. My guests dispensed with, I vowed, once again, to change the locks. I closed all the windows, shut all the fans and mercifully turned the AC in the house back on. I vacuumed up the gnats while they watched the end of their lives across the TV. I scooted a few more crickets out the back door, along with the one in my pocket. I tucked Marie in and let Vinnie out of his kitty jaildom. Then I poured myself a mug from the Box O' Burgundy, and settled down to watch the evening news. So did the chorus of crickets chirping peacefully in the background.

The phone rang. The crickets stopped. Huh. Well, that was an upside. Maybe I could get friends and family to call and hang up repeatedly. It might convince the crickets that being outside was a lot more peaceful after all.

I rolled off the sofa, mug in hand, and managed to answer the phone on the fifth ring.

"Hello, dear," Aunt Muriel's voice sang. She sounded really happy. Then again, it was late, after a very nice dinner, and I'm pretty sure she and Ma were having a very nice nightcap. "Sorry to call so late, dear," she offered, "but I just heard from our masseuse – he can fit us in at ten o'clock tomorrow morning!" She giggled. Somewhere in the background I heard Ma's voice complaining about nonsense, waste of money and lost time. I wondered if she was referring to me or the masseuse. Then I heard Aunt Muriel hold her hand to her receiver, hiss at Ma, and come back to me. "Well, then we'll see you about ten o'clock tomorrow morning, right? After all, if you want your mother to be able to walk normally again, you have to have a massage too, remember?"

I sighed and nodded. "I promise I'll be there about ten o'clock tomorrow morning," I replied.

"Good girl," Aunt Muriel said, and hung up singing a "Nighty-night!" to me.

I sat back down on the sofa and tried to go back to the news. Which was over. I flipped the flipper, and fell back to the cooking channel. 'Romantic Dinners Gone Wrong' was on, and I immediately got suckered. This was getting good. Then I started wondering when I'd ever serve a romantic dinner again. My non-existent social life was overrun by somewhat peculiar family, friends, pets and a pervasive theme of doo-doo. Nothing, oh nothing, about these social circumstances hinted whatsoever at finding a boyfriend.

The Twinge started up again, and a sharp pinch started in my ass and shot down to my toes. I panicked. I couldn't stand being this tense, with my nerves kicking me in my own literal butt. And what about the massage guy? Did he really laugh at me? He was cute. And OMG he was going to be feeling up my butt at ten o'clock tomorrow morning.

Another pinch. I winced. I had to do something to relax, quick.

I was up and on my cramping feet before you could say custom omelet for two. I grabbed the leftover loaf of French bread that was turning a slighter shade of stale from the top of the fridge. I sliced, beat eggs, fried bacon, grated cheese, found the lost Parmesan cheese and threw in various peppers, onions and the like. I got all these savory ingredients on top of the bread bits lying peacefully along the bottom of my good lasagna pan. I covered them up with wrap, and put them back in the fridge. Tomorrow morning I'd throw them in the oven for forty-five minutes and have a nice hot breakfast casserole to take to Auntie's. Ha! I'd impress that massage guy!

I was contemplating side dishes (ham? hash browns? fruit cup? muffins?) when the phone rang. Again. I looked at it warily and answered.

It was Trixie. "Hey, I just wanted to say thanks and all for dinner last night." Good old Trixie.

"No problemo," I said, smiling.

"Huh?" she asked.

"No problem." Seemed Vito-speak was starting to rub off on me.

"Also wanted to say thanks for the boyfriend pep talk," she said. "I think you're right. I guess I've just been a little low."

"No, no, you're fine. You know you've been working very hard."

"You're telling me. That witch tried to hitch me with a third second shift this week. I've already put in sixty hours and it's not even the weekend yet. And you know they're gonna call me because I'm single, have no kids, and now everyone knows that I have no boyfriend."

"Well, your track record's still better than mine," I offered.

"Mm. I guess it's not so bad being solo. Just lonely, sometimes," Trixie said. I gulped at some of my wine, jealously wondering what that was like. She added, "Sometimes when I'm feeling really lonesome, I just go and leave the toilet seat up before I go to bed. That way when I wake up in the morning, I feel like I haven't been home alone all night. And it really annoys me, so then I remind myself how much better off I am without a guy around."

You have to admire Trixie's logic. Or not.

"Anyway, how have you been? Anymore burning Buy-A-Lots news? How's your pinched nerve?"

I told Trixie about the morning massage. "Well, seeing a massage guy should be a good thing," she said. In the background I heard her rummage around and throw some ice cubes in a glass.

"What are you drinking?" I asked out of curiosity. And envy. The Box O' Burgundy and Mugs O' Merlots were getting old.

"Tom Collins," she replied.

"You're listening to Tom Collins?"

"No, stupid, Tom Collins is a drink mix. Tom Jones is the guy you listen to."

"Oh," I said.

"I can bring some mixer over for you Saturday, on my way into work, if you want to try it," she offered. I explained about getting roped into the NYC supper club dinner thingy. "Well, the massage is a good thing anyway, right? And your auntie's paying for it, right?" Trixie reminded me. Which was when I reminded Trixie I'd have to be seeing Ma and Aunt Mu en Toga in front of the hot massage dude. "Oh," she said. I heard her light a cigarette and exhale. "I see what you mean. But the dinner should be fun?"

I explained about being dubbed the chauffer.

"Well, maybe you can bake a cake or something quick tonight, to take the edge off? At least you might not show up all hunched over tomorrow," Trixie said.

I told her about the impromptu brunch casserole, and discussed accompanying side dishes. Trixie yawned.

"Sorry. Not the company; just the hour. Although I should be feeling awake now," she said.

"Yeah, how come you're calling me from home at night time?" I asked.

Trixie yawned again. "Split shifts. Short on nurses; so they asked me to split my shift Instead of working from three this afternoon until eleven tonight, I worked seven until eleven tonight. Then I go back in tomorrow morning to work seven to three."

"Ugh," I replied.

"Double ugh," she agreed. "They also put me on call from three p.m. tomorrow until seven."

"Well, at least you get to be in your own home before dawn for once."

"Yeah. Maybe I should get a pet..."

I coughed and gently reminded her about her stint with the several hundred house plants she'd installed last summer to create a faux-Solarium per instructions published in Lancaster Life magazine. All perished under her care within two weeks, per K.'s prediction. “You have to pass the houseplant test first,” I said.

“Damn,” she said, “you're right. I forgot about those plants.”

“How could you forget about palm trees?”

Trixie exhaled another of what I imagined was a menthol flavored plume of carcinogens. “Which is exactly the point,” she said. “I mean, you can't ever forget about a Fluffy or a Fido without some really major consequences, right?” I agreed. “Anyway, I don't think your brunch delivery is a bad idea. Especially since your auntie's paying for the massage party. It's the least you can do, right?”

I brightened a little. My catering disorder might actually come in handy!

“Yeah,” I echoed.

I began rethinking my unplanned planned menu. Suddenly the breakfast baked casserole with one side dish seemed paltry. I had to whip up something memorable – like breakfast shish kabobs, or a fruit boat. And maybe some homemade biscuits and barbeque sautéed shrimp, wrapped in thinly sliced something-fancy-I-had-to-figure-out-what-fast-because-I-had-no-proscuitto-on-hand.

I said a hasty goodbye to Trixie. She yawned. “S’okay.” And she yawned again. “I gotta go sleep for a couple hours so I can wake up in a couple hours.”

“Call me later,” I said.

She said “'kay,” over another yawn and hung up.

I opened my cupboards and took out essential and non-essential ingredients. Which basically means that I panicked and sprawled everything out on every available flat surface.

Within a couple of hours, I'd whipped up breakfast crepes, a lovely marinated seafood salad, some Artisanal bread and a show-off of unexpected fresh local fare – fresh peaches. In short:

- Spinach and feta crepes with Parsleyed Newberg sauce
- Shrimp, bay scallop and mussel salad
- Fast Artisanal bread
- Fresh Lancaster-county peach and shortbread custard torte
- Breakfast casserole

- Steak-fried hashbrowns

I pulled out my coolers and pre-loaded the ice packs and the food. All I had to do was get up in the morning. I could heat everything at Auntie's. I loaded the dishwasher with as many platters, mixing bowls, and anything else I'd gunked up. It began to hum happily. I sighed in contentment.

I made my rounds and turned the lights off. The crickets chirped happily again as I wandered upstairs in the dark.

I checked in on Marie; she was snoozing to a blank TV screen. I turned everything off; told her nighty-night and quietly closed the door. I looked into my room. Vinnie lay diagonally stretched across my bed with his paw over his nose, snuffling peacefully. I sighed, set the alarm and lay down on top of the coverlet next to him. There was no point in changing into jammies and trying to crawl into bed. I would have woken him up. Besides, there was no room.

The alarm went off about at 7:00 a.m. Which would have been fine, if I had gotten up when it went off. Unfortunately, repeatedly hitting the snooze button for additional zzzs doesn't make waking up on time a predictable activity. I think I hit the sleep button the first two times. I recall Vinnie hitting it once or twice, too. But I'm not sure. I was asleep. Fast, fast, asleep.

CHAPTER 14

(Friday)

The phone rang. It was K.

"RISE AND SHINE, MISS SCARLET!" I held the receiver from my face like a day old trout. "TODAY IS YOUR LUCKY DAY!"

"Huh?" I replied intelligently.

"I've rung GILL-I-ANNN!!"

"Gillian?" I ventured, dipping a virtual big toe into K.'s frenzy.

"GILL-I-AN! Of the HUSH-HUSH New York supper club!!!"

My mind rummaged feebly through the rank and file of stock excuses. Nothing fit.

"Remember? TOMORROW we will have our EXPERIENCE!!" K. squawked proudly. Crap. I thought about travelling three hours in each direction in the Doo-doo. Crap was a pretty good description.

"Who is 'us all'?" I asked.

"Well first, before I rang you – I know how grumpy you are first thing in the A.M., dearie," K. teased, "Armand is coming."

"You mean they still haven't put him back on weekends?" I asked.

"No, the bat rastards. But he feels the Supper Club is necessary professional research," K. replied matter-of-factly. "And of course I thought to include Ida and Walter, since Gillian's invitation is for five."

I sat up. "WALTER? YOU INVITED WALTER?" I asked hysterically.

Walter is a very, very nice guy (he's from Lancaster) and he's also very, very large. Walter is about 6'3" and weighs four thousand pounds. So, unsurprisingly, traveling with Walter can be … problematic.

"Well, he rang me up and I was so excited about our news... I was just so eager to tell someone... and he does appreciate a decent meal..."

K. has a good heart. I sometimes wonder what happened to his brains.

"K. – if it's not an 'all you can eat' you better make sure Walter's well advised. You know, fed, beforehand."

"Done."

"The Doo-doo doesn't have A.C."

"We'll open the windows."

I sighed thinking about the broken car window of my stinky van. K. dove into the silence of my non-response. "Saturday, 2pm-ish; you pick me up. Then we'll pick up Ida, then Walter. We should get into the city about five-ish; perhaps have a beverage? Our reservations are for six-thirty!"

I yawned. "What time is it?" I asked lazily.

"Oh, it's not too early. It's just after nine."

I felt my scalp catch fire. "Gotta go! Call ya later!"

I slammed the phone down and launched myself off the bed. Vinnie flew off beside me and raced me for the stairs. I checked the coolers – I was in luck, and very glad I invested in the brand name coolers that everyone told me I didn't need. I took care of Vinnie and Marie and threw myself into the bathroom for a light speed shower. Luckily, I landed softly. After that I dressed and quickly pushed my hair back into another wet pony tail.

I ran across my front lawn and banged on Vito's door to make sure hijacking his car was okay. He answered, wearing a fluorescent peach Hawaiian shirt, electric blue shorts and holding a newspaper.

"Hey, Toots," he beamed, bridge fully in place.

"Hey, Vito, mind if I borrow your car this morning?" I asked.

Vito sweated. "Hold on, Toots," he said, entering back into his secret lair and leaving me out on the front porch. I surveyed the damage post-flaming-doo-doo. The porch still had a freshly charred look to it. And smelled a bit like burnt doo-doo. Pew.

I stepped off Vito's front porch and waited on his walkway.

Vito finally stepped back out. "Sorry for keeping you, Toots." He beamed again. This time his bridge was gone. "I had to arrange for alternative arrangements," he explained.

"Oh, of course you can borrow Vito's car ANY-TIME! We're happy to help!" Miriam beamed as she exploded out the front door after Vito, clad in her previous evening's getup with her turban slightly askew. "Here, dearie." Miriam smiled, handing Vito his MIA bridge.

"Thanks, Vito," I said, running toward the safety of my garage. I thought I heard a distant "Toots," in the background, but it was muffled by sound of Miriam's giggles and the slam of Vito's front door.

I started loading Vito's car with the breakfast bounty. The phone rang. I looked at the clock, saw it was 10:15 a.m. and ignored the phone. It was probably Auntie. I shrugged. It was a massage party, right? So Auntie and Ma could go first, right?

I finished loading Vito's Towncar, cranked up the AC and I flew across town like a maniacal meals-on-wheels.

I got to Auntie's with one of Vito's floor mats slightly worse for the wear after baptism by salad dressing. The rest of the tubs and platters were a bit askew from the hairpin turns I inflicted, but otherwise they survived. I hefted out the first cooler, exceedingly proud of myself, and headed inside Auntie's house.

I found Auntie, Ma and the massage guy sitting at Auntie's kitchen table sipping coffee and perusing various editions of Meals and Deals magazines.

"Uh, hi," I said brightly.

They looked at me like as if I had Jell-O spouting out my nose.

"Picnic?" the cute massage guy smiled at me.

Aunt Muriel clapped her hand to her forehead. "Mina, you didn't!" she said, shaking her head.

"She can and she did," Ma answered for me. "What's for brunch?" she asked.

"Brunch? Hey, that's great," Massage Man beamed.

I stared at him. Pieces of the usual equation began to float toward the front of my mind and summed together: Gourmet cooking magazines + VERY good looking + very, very nice must = gay.

I shrugged and plunked the first cooler down. “Thanks. I'll be right back; I've just got a couple more coolers in the car,” I said, retreating.

Massage Man leapt up and was at my side in a culinary flash. “Let me, please,” he said, walking past me and opening the door to Vito's car.

“Ah, sure...” I said.

Before I knew it, he had the two other coolers out, and was hefting them together inside the house ahead of me. Wow. He could carry two coolers at one time. It was impressive. And useful. I looked down. A half dozen prescription sample boxes lay scattered at my feet, yelping for attention. I scooped them up, patted them, and put them back under the floor mats, locking the doors.

Massage Man set the two coolers down on the kitchen floor, right next to where Ma was unpacking the first cooler and spreading the contents out on the counters. Conversely, Aunt Muriel sat at the kitchen table with her head in her hands.

“You were just supposed to show up for a massage empty-handed,” she said. “This was supposed to relax you.”

“I know, Auntie, thanks,” I said, “but getting ready to get relaxed made me really, really nervous, so I just made a little something to calm me down.”

Massage Man coughed, put a hand to his mouth, and turned away. He turned back around, shaking his head and smiling at me. Again. I stared at him. He stared back at me. In the distant background I heard the theme from ‘Fistful of Dollars’ playing, accompanied by Ma shuffling plates and slamming things into the microwave.

“Are you making fun of me?” I demanded, hand on hip.

“Yes.”

I huffed, and thought about high-tailing it out of there. I didn't want some sarcastic massage mope putting his paws on me, congratulating himself that he was relaxing me when all he’d accomplished so far was making me uptight. And losing another night's sleep.

I huffed again. Aunt Muriel flew up and over the kitchen table and assumed referee position. “Mina, dear,” she began cordially, “this is James. He's your masseuse this morning, dear.”

"I remember," I said, trying not to pout at him. He smiled back brilliantly.

The microwave binged. Ma shuffled another plate inside and re-set it.

"James; Mina. Mina; James," Auntie continued.

"Not Jim? Or Jimmy?" I asked, accepting his outstretched hand – and then only because Auntie's glare made me.

"No. James," he replied, holding my hand in his cool, strong, smooth hand.

"Oh," I said, all noncommittal.

I looked down. He was still holding my hand. Aunt Muriel looked flustered. Ma banged several more plates into the microwave. We were still holding hands. That was about when I started blushing.

"So very nice to meet you, uh, James," I said, pumping his hand up and down.

"Brunch is ready!" Ma shouted.

The three of us looked over at the kitchen table. Ma had the table set with four places, and was working at fixing Bloody Marys at the counter.

"Muriel?" Ma asked, pouring multiple shots of Vodka into glasses.

Aunt Muriel surveyed the repast. "Really, Lou, all I usually have for breakfast are a few berries," she said.

Ma stared at her. "Right then, this one's yours," she answered, pouring more Vodka into Aunt Muriel's glass. "James?" Ma asked.

"Just tomato juice, thanks. I'm on the clock," he said, smiling at me.

I stared at him. I couldn't stand it. Way deep down, in his soft brown eyes, I wondered if he was laughing at me, or did I have spinach in my hair?

I heard Ma pouring out more shots and clinking ice cubes into glasses. "All ready," shc said, placing the various beverages on the table.

"Hey, you didn't ask me," I said.

"That one's yours." She pointed a finger at my place. "Sit."

"Woof," I answered and sat down and sipped. And coughed. My Bloody Mary looked a bit anemic compared to the rest of them. Apparently Ma had just waved the tomato juice over my glass as a blessing.

We ended our brunch on a much more congenial note than it began. Mostly because of the Bloody Marys, I suppose. But maybe because I finally relaxed a bit.

"Well, I suppose we better get started," James said, politely wiping his mouth.

I looked at him. "Huh?" I asked.

"With your massage, Mina," Auntie answered for me, rubbing her temples with both hands.

Rats. I thought I had obfuscated my way out of this one.

"The table is in there." Ma pointed toward Auntie's living room. "Take the sheet, get down to your skivvies in Muriel's bedroom, drape the sheet around you, lie down on the damn table and proceed to be relaxed," she ordered.

I stalled. "Someone's got to clean up."

Ma and Auntie were up in a flash, plates in hand and water running in the sink.

"We've got it; just go!" Ma yelled.

I looked at James. He smiled, took my plate and his and walked over to the sink.

I got up and peered around the corner. There, directly in front of me, stood the dreaded massage table. Waiting. On top of it laid a folded, clean, white sheet.

"Go!" Ma shouted again.

I trudged into the living room, grabbed the sheet and toddled off into Auntie's bedroom, none too eager to strip down to my skivvies.

I quickly realized I hadn't been too particular about my skivvy selection that morning, since I began my day shot from guns. I gazed at myself in the mirror, sans everything except for a dreary pair of faded flower print Gramma panties with a slight hole starting at the band. I suspected that there were nuns who wore panties more alluring than mine. And without holes. But if they had holes, maybe they'd be Holy panties?

Clearly the Bloody Mary was taking effect. Which was probably a good thing, since I couldn't imagine myself in a sober moment agreeing to scamper out into Auntie's living room wearing only tattered panties and a sheet.

I stepped out into the living room with the sheet wrapped around me, trying to pretend it was the most normal thing in the world. I sat on the sofa and draped an arm across the back of the couch. The sheet slipped off. I grabbed it and held on tight with my armpits like a junior high girl in her first strapless dress. Outside the living room windows, I watched Ma and Auntie sit at the umbrella table, looking at more magazines and catalogues together. The smell of crepes and casserole hung heavy in the air. Maybe they were still hungry?

I started to walk toward the kitchen and was met by James, water glass in hand.

"Here; this is for you," he said quietly.

"Oh," I said, taking the glass and holding it.

"You need to drink a lot of water after a massage," he explained. "It releases a lot of toxins in your body."

"Uh huh," I replied. It came out as an unintelligible babble.

"And that Bloody Mary," he added. "Those things have lots of sodium."

I shook my head and began to think sober thoughts. Clearly there was more to this massage thing than met the eye. Although James was certainly easy on the eyes. I sighed inwardly. Clearly, as usual, I was attracted to another out of bounds guy.

James helped me onto the massage table, explained the drill, the philosophy of massage, and within moments I was yawning. He turned on some new age music in his portable boom box. "To relax you," he explained.

"Oh," I replied, lying face down on my tummy.

"Do you prefer oil or cream?" he asked. I picked my head up. Huh? Were we having salads now? "For your massage," he clarified.

"Oh. Dunno," I answered.

"Right. Okay. Well, let's try this; a lot of people like this," he said and started rubbing my calves and feet with a warm oil that smelled like rosemary and lavender.

I woke up in the late afternoon light with Aunt Muriel asleep on the sofa to a Classics! movie re-run. I rolled onto my side. It looked like we were in the middle of 'African Queen'. Auntie snuffled softly in the foreground. I sat up, stiffish and all-over stickyish. I was still wrapped in my sheet. And almost every inch of me was covered in a lavender rosemary scented film. I looked around and saw James' boom box. It was still on the coffee table, with the water glass on it, and a note that read, 'Drink this.' Even though I wondered if I'd grow too big or shrink too small, I realized I was very thirsty and that this might be a good thing to do. I drank the water and wondered into which phase of Alice in Wonderland I would be propelled. Then I got up and shuffled the glass into the kitchen. The dishwasher hummed happily, and my casserole dishes and various serving pieces lay cleaned and drying on Auntie's kitchen counters. The clock on the microwave over the stove blinked 3:43 p.m. I got out a mini bottle of spring water from Auntie's fridge and drank that, too.

I walked back into the living room where Auntie was still fast asleep to Humphrey Bogart and Katherine Hepburn battling leeches. I shuddered. I hate leeches. I can't stand the sight of escargot because I'm pretty sure they're just French leeches in disguise.

I went into Auntie's bathroom and showered and dressed. When I came back out, Auntie was awake, flipping the remote control in one hand, with a mug of coffee in the other.

"Brunch was very good, dear," she said, still flipping. She landed on the local news recap.

"Thanks. I really didn't mean to go overboard," I said.

"I know. I just wish you didn't worry so much," Auntie said.

I sighed. "I don't mean to. It's just my stupid catering disorder."

"Stop it."

"I keep trying," I said.

"No, I mean I wish you'd stop referring to it as a catering disorder," Auntie said. I looked at her. "You know, your mother and I were talking after you passed out... I mean, were having your massage."

"I passed out?" Auntie nodded. I was horrified. "What did Ma put in my Bloody Mary?" I asked.

"Nothing more than the usual. But James explained that sometimes stress builds up so much in some people that when they finally relax, they sometimes pass right out. He said it's a lot like people suffering from sleeping disorders. They have so much sleep deprivation that when they finally get that first good night's rest, they sleep for days."

"Oh," I said.

Auntie sipped her coffee. "He felt very badly for you, dear," she said. I rolled my eyes. "Luckily you were his only appointment today, otherwise he would have had to wake you to take his table back."

"I was his only appointment? I thought you and Ma were getting massages too?" I asked.

Auntie sipped. "We lied," she said.

"Oh. Where's Ma?"

"Outlets."

"Oh. That makes sense."

"By the way, dear, James needs to pick up his equipment tomorrow morning, and I have a hair appointment. Would you be a dear and be here to let him in?" she said.

"Are you lying again?" I asked.

"No, I really do have another hair appointment. I'm due for my dye."

"Sure," I said.

"Anyway, your mother and I were talking," she began again, "and we think that you should get into some kind of restaurant business. Maybe take a job with something already established, to learn the ropes, and then branch out on your own."

I swallowed. "Auntie, you realize that starting out with no experience in that kind of a business basically means I'd make dishwasher's pay?"

"Well, it beats flippin' burgers," she answered. "Unless of course they're your own burgers," she added quickly.

A Botox commercial ended and the news came back on. The news anchorwoman – the same one who'd shown up at Vito's porch-burning – appeared on the screen.

"This just in: breaking news about the burning Buy-A-Lots," she beamed. "What do you have, Cecily?"

The TV screen shifted from the polished looking anchorwoman in the air conditioned studio, to another, much slighter version of herself, standing glumly in the middle of a rainy cow pasture. The rain drizzled off the top of her rain jacket hood and flowed steadily down in a mini-waterfall that drained between her face and her microphone.

"Thanks, Barbie. Just moments ago, Howard Blech, 45 of E-town, was arrested as an apparent suspect in this, what appears to be yet another arson attempt, at burning down a new Buy-A-Lot store. As fate would have it, Nature came to the rescue, ahead of the Adams County fire department," she said brightly, tipping her hood and showering her feet with fresh rainwater. The girl grimaced. "Live to you from Adams County, I'm Cecily Barns."

I gulped.

"Isn't Howard Blech your boss?" Auntie asked.

"Ex-boss," I corrected.

"Right. Well, maybe EEJIT will rehire you now?"

I looked at Auntie and rubbed my neck.

I left the various brunch booty and containers at Auntie's. After all, I'd be back tomorrow morning to let Massage Man in, right? I sighed. That was going to be embarrassing. I just hoped I hadn't talked in my sleep, or worse. What if I snored?

Outside, the late afternoon air was almost bearable. A wind picked up. I watched some dark clouds roll in. Apparently we were due for the same storm Auntie and I had just watched on TV in Adams County. Well, that's Central PA weather for you. If you don't like the weather now, just wait a few minutes and it will change. I got into Vito's car and headed home, back through the maze of upscale streets that led to my normal scale neighborhood.

I pulled back up Vito's side of Mt. Driveway and shut the car off. It looked like all was quiet at the OK Corral of my house. And Vito's. I wondered how long I could sit in the driveway. Probably not long. I opened the door, and clambered out. I felt a little stiff. Funny.

As I walked up my front path, I saw my door was open with only the screen door closed. I leaned my face against it until my forehead waffled. Again. I sniffed: no smoke. I peered into the living room windows. The TV was on. Vito lay on my sofa with Stanley curled up on the sofa arm, sleeping on his back, his belly rising softly up and down in time with Vito's snoring. Vinnie lay on the floor with his belly up and legs splayed in front of the TV. Marie screamed from upstairs. Another usual evening in my unusual household.

As I stepped inside, Vito sat up and yawned.

"Hey, Toots," he said, rubbing his eyes and patting Stanley. Vinnie rolled over and yawned at me. "Hey, did you see the news? Did you hear about your old boss?" Vito asked, wide-eyed. "Who'd of thunk it, right?" I shook my head.

"How was your massage?" he asked.

I told him the broad strokes polite description, careful to omit my passing out on the massage table part.

"Hey, you got a message from Appletree on your answering machine," Vito said when I'd finished.

"Really?" I asked.

"Yeah, he said you can pick up the Doo-doo anytime tomorrow; yous just gotta have a photo ID."

"Anything else?"

"Well, of course I'm happy to drop you off to pick up your van tomorrow morning."

"Great. Thanks. Might be kinda early though."

"Really? That's great! I mean, why?"

I gave Vito the thumbnail sketch about having to be at Auntie's house in time to let James pick up his gear.

The phone rang. It was K..

Vito waved at me. "I'll let yous have your privacy, Toots," he said, Stanley yipping in tow behind him, chasing his trouser cuff.

"Aren't you EX-CITED!?" K. cried.

"Sure," I lied.

"Alright, now what time did you promise to pick me up tomorrow?"

"Huh?"

"Tomorrow! The Supper Club!" K. yelped.

After getting chastised and then forgiven by K., we rearranged that I'd pick him up no later than one o'clock tomorrow afternoon, so we'd have more time to spring Ida from her tower and hoist Walter into the van.

I hung up the phone, and proceeded to take care of my pets. I gave Marie some water, seeds, and 'The Sound of Music'. Then Vinnie led me back downstairs. "Alright," I said, offering two cans of Finicky Fare. "Chicken Lips or Fishy Feets?" I asked. Vinnie put a paw on top of the can of Fishy Feets. I grimaced. "I hope you realize that I know that fish do not have feet," I said. "I don't name or make the stuff. So I make no guarantees." I shuddered to think what animal parts the pet food industry considered fish feet worthy.

I fed Vinnie, poured myself another glass of water, and sat down on the sofa to watch the remainder of the food show Vito and the boys were watching when I came home. Apparently, we were in the middle of something called 'Real Men Eat This!'

I watched in horror as some guy walked about various villages eating various forms of dung bugs. Yick. It seems they're called dung bugs for a reason. They looked like mushrooms on legs. That said, I considered where mushrooms grow. YICK.

The phone rang. I flipped the flipper before I sidled out of my chair. I didn't want to leave Vinnie with the dung bugs and spoil his Fishy Feets dinner.

"Hello," I answered, gulping my water in the hopes of washing away images of dung bugs.

"Hi, Mina, this is James," the voice on the other end said.

I swallowed hard down the wrong pipe, coughed and sprayed water across the sink backsplash.

"Hold on," I gasped.

I coughed into the sink. Well, at least it hadn't been wine. Burgundy splatters across my Anita Bryant orange kitchen would have looked like a deranged French child's first painting of a sunset. I looked at Vinnie. He glowered at me pointedly, indicating a faint rain of drizzle on his forehead. I wiped at it. "Sorry, buddy," I apologized. Vinnie responded with emphatic comments about stupid is as stupid does, and humans are much too aggrandized regarding thumbs. Then he resumed his meal.

A few thousand years after putting the phone down, I picked it back up.

"Are you still there?" I asked.

"Are you alright? Did I call at a bad time?" James asked.

"Oh, no, everything's just great," I fibbed.

"Okay. Hey, look, I left my stuff over at your aunt's today, and need to pick it up tomorrow morning before I see my next client. But your aunt said she's not able to be there; she has to get her hair done or something. She insisted I call you, to let me into her house tomorrow morning. Can you meet me over there and let me in?"

Clever Auntie. Made sure James had my phone number for purely business reasons. Right.

"Sure, I just have to pick up the Doo-doo in the morning," I said.

"Huh?"

"My van," I explained. "It's a long story. Sort of. Anyway, I'm planning on picking it up first thing in the morning from the police impound."

There was another long pause. Then, "How about you call me as you're leaving for your aunt's house?"

"Okay, what's your number?"

James gave me his cell phone number, admonished me not to be late because of his morning client, and we hung up. Well.

I no sooner hung up the phone when Bauser called.

"Hey, Mina, did you see the news? It was How-weird after all!"

"I know. Somehow, it just doesn't make sense. I mean complete sense," I said.

"Sure doesn't explain the IP address or the Packet Sniffers," Bauser mused. "Whatcha doin'?"

"Not much. Spitting into the sink," I answered.

"Want to get a pizza and watch some sci-fi?" Bauser asked.

"Yeah, okay. You coming over?"

"Sure. Hey, any word from Vito about his niece lately?" Bauser asked. Aha.

"No, why, you interested?" I asked.

"No, just curious."

We hung up, and I dialed PizzaNow! and ordered a Meat! Meat! Meat! & More Meat! Personal Pie for Bauser and Jim, and a thin crust veggie white pie for me. And some garlic sticks. And salad. And hot wings. And a cheesecake. After all, I wasn't sure how long they'd be here, right? And Jim might be hungry.

Bauser showed up in tandem with the PizzaNow! delivery guy. Really. There was a vehicular stand-off at the bottom of my driveway. I went out, waved Bauser up and then the pizza delivery guy. This turned out good because Bauser paid. But then I felt guilty. This is bad because guilty pizza is not tasty pizza. But free pizza is.

Bauser took the pies and walked toward the house. I pulled some cash out of my pocket.

"No problemo, Toots," Bauser said ala Vito. "I'm still rolling in Norman cash."

"Did you make him lose another bet about another one of his step-daughters?" I asked.

"Wasn't much of a bet," he said, shrugging.

We went up the front walk, and I was about to go inside when I heard hissing from the bushes.

"Psss! Psss!"

I looked around.

"Over here, Toots," Vito said. He was perched behind a holly bush. "Hey, Toots, ya think we can pick your van up extra early tomorrow?" he asked. "I got an, uh, errand to run over at Mrs. Phang's," he explained, wiggling his eyebrows. And his ears. Apparently they were connected.

"Uh, sure. What time?"

"Seven-thirty," Vito answered.

"Yikes."

"Sorry, Toots. You got big plans tonight?"

"Nope. We're just eating pizza and watching some science-fiction thingy," I answered.

Vito looked hopeful. I sighed. "Wanna come over?" I asked resolutely.

"Hey, sure! But I'm not so sure about leaving Stanley home alone again."

"Why?"

"Because when I was out, uh... visiting this afternoon, he gnawed a big hole right in the middle of the kitchen floor." I stared at him. He shrugged. "It's okay. He pretty much did me a favor."

"Why?"

"It's orange and olive plaid," he said.

Somewhere in heaven, Marie hung her head.

Vito brought over Stanley, and a blender full of cocktails, this time with an Asian theme. I identified Vodka and something ginger-ish. Bauser brought in his twelve-pack of Krumpthfs. Jim sniffed Stanley. Stanley snipped at Jim. Vinnie watched from an elevated position on the top of my head.

"Hey, Mina, c'mon, it's on!" Bauser said, flipper in hand, with Vito next to him on the sofa.

I sat down to ‘Ghosts R US’, our usual fare for spectator ghost hunting.

Vinnie tiptoed off of my head and onto the back of the sofa, keeping a watchful eye on Stanley

A little while later, and a few real (or unreal?) ghost stories the wiser, I said goodnight to the boys, and got myself ready for an uneventful evening's slumber. I actually went upstairs to bed. Maybe things were looking up.

CHAPTER 15

(Saturday)

The sleep I got was fitful, and interspersed with dreams of kidnapped Ratties, flaming feces, my pregnant sister (who gave birth to a litter of yapping Hansel and Gretels) and pierogies. Eventually I woke up, covered in a film of perspiration, and sat bolt upright. It was five-thirty. I sighed. I'd set my alarm to go off at six so there was little point in lying back down. So I lay back down.

I looked at the pillow next to me. Vinnie lay fast asleep, mumbling. I patted him and he chirped back at me. I yawned, stretched and lay flat on my back. Then I smelled bacon.

I opened my eyes. I still smelled bacon. Vinnie headbutted my chin. Apparently he smelled bacon, too.

I crept downstairs, flip-flops in hand, ready to clobber whatever bacon cooking intruder I found with foam rubber.

Looking in my kitchen, I saw bacon frying simply in a pan. I shook my head. Maybe I hadn't really gone to sleep? Was I sleep cooking? Maybe I had my very own sleeping disorder? I began to fantasize about hearing people murmuring about me in hushed tones, "Did you hear about what happened to her? She's got MinaKitchens!"

I looked around. Not only was bacon sizzling, but I also smelled and heard coffee brewing. Then a crash came from the basement. I heard growling. Then swearing. Vito came shuffling up the basement stairs with a laundry basket full of prescription samples, dragging Stanley along while he hung onto Vito's pant leg, as usual.

Vito got to the top of the steps and put the basket down. “Morning, Toots,” he said sheepishly. Stanley growled hello at me.

Vito leaned so close toward Stanley I was afraid he would get his nose bit again, so I put my hands over my eyes. Vito gave Stanley a directive – in Polish – and Stanley let go of Vito's pants and lay belly up, in contrition. Huh. I'd hafta ask Vito what he said. It might come in handy someday. Then again, maybe his past lifetime with the Moils had a legitimate use, after all.

“Sorry, Toots. I figured you'd be up to get your van and all. Just thought it'd be a good idea for you to start your day off with a nice breakfast,” Vito said.

I shrugged and yawned.

“Okay, thanks. Hey, what happened to your crumb bun connection?” I asked.

“Hey, a fella's gotta watch his girlish figure, ya know,” Vito said, cracking an egg into the pan.

Vito was blotting off the bacon with a paper towel while Stanley sat pretty. Vito pulled a doggie biscuit out of his shirt pocket, and held it out to Stanley. He took the biscuit, trotted off happily into the living room and began to crunch crumbs into the carpet. Vinnie came running down the hall and stared at me, appalled.

“I know he's a dog, but he's a guest,” I explained. Vinnie shook the back paw at me and sauntered toward the basement stairs. “Okay, how about breakfast?” I asked.

“Grrrrraht! Fwnks!” Vinnie trilled.

I got him his breakfast and threw some Tweetsy Weetsy treats on top, just to keep the peace.

“I'm just gonna make a couple of deliveries here, and I'll be back to take you to your van later, okay?” Vito asked, sipping his coffee carefully.

“Yip,” I said, drinking my coffee and wishing it wasn’t so very, very early.

Vito left, so I figured it was as good a time as any to get ready for the day and start running around like an idiot.

I washed and changed into a cute outfit and matching jewelry, and headed downstairs. A couple of game shows later, Vito was back and actually knocking at the front door. I answered.

"Hey, Toots! Wow, you look swell," Vito said. "You don't even look like yous has a tick or nothin'!" He paused, then smacked himself in the forehead. "Sorry, Toots; I know how sensitive and all yous are about your epidural challenges and such," he said.

"Huh?"

"Epidural challenges. Impressive, huh? Miriam made me a present of a vocabulary calendar."

"Epidural challenges?"

"Yeah, you knows. Challenges with your skin and such."

My eyes did a tumblesault in their sockets of their own volition.

"Hey, Vito... I think you might mean epidermis," I said.

"You sure?"

"Yeah. Epidermis means about your skin. Epidural is the anesthesia you get in your spine."

Vito blushed. "Sorry, Toots. Geesh. Hey, hows about I run some of my new words by you before I use them next time?" he asked.

I pictured a bleak Webster's Collegiate Dictionary future in front of me, and suppressed a groan.

"Sure," I lied. After all, I really do want to fit into Lancaster, right? It just seemed like the nice thing to do.

"Great! Hey, we gotta get going! I'm running late!"

Vito and I tumbled out into the hundreds of degree heat and humidity and quickly found our way into the air-conditioned Towncar. I looked over at Vito. Even the few moments of walking from my front door to his car had made his collar turn orange. I was going to have to talk with Auntie about the political correctness of discussing fake hair mishaps with Vito. He might be a pain in the butt. And some kind of fugitive. But no one wishes social humiliation on anyone. Except for maybe an ex-husband or two. That is, according to Auntie.

Vito pulled into the Prince Street parking garage and found a spot after we helped a Crown Victoria full of seniors from Saskatchewan navigate the parking ticket conundrum. We also advised them that it was best to travel in the same direction that the arrows pointed, and not the opposite.

After we helped the confused Canadians, Vito and I parted company. I looked over my shoulder as he exited onto Orange Street.

"Hey, Vito, umm... you gonna need any help bringing your, umm... dry cleaning... back to the car?" I asked.

Vito shook his head. "I got it all taken care of, Toots. I'm not expecting any new dry cleaning coming my way anymore, if yous knows what I mean." I sighed gratefully. Then coughed. "You okay, Toots?" he asked.

"Yeah," I choked. "Carbon monoxide kinda chokes me up sometimes."

"Hey, me too! Every time I have Pasta Carbonara it always backs up on me the next day."

I hung my head.

Vito toddled off to Madam Phang's. I toddled off across the street toward the fancy Marriott-style police station to claim my unfancy van.

I walked up to the Police Department of Oz desk. A policewoman peered down at me. "Who goes there?" she asked. Or at least that's how it sounded.

I replied, "It is only I, Mina the Meek."

It must have been the height of the desk.

"State your business," the policewoman instructed, ignoring my Wizard of Oz flashback.

"I've come to fetch the Doo-doo," I said, and kind of curtseyed. I couldn't help it.

"It's alright, Hazel," Appletree offered up, from just about Hazel's belly height.

"Uh," she grunted and hopped down off the imperial stool. "I got to go on break anyhow," she said, and sauntered her 3-foot wide girth toward what I guessed housed a break room. I wagered a bet with myself that the break room probably had a state-of-the-art cappuccino and espresso maker as well as a full-time barista. What else would fit in with the alabaster walls?

Appletree sighed. "It used to be a lot easier," he said. I shrugged.

"I'm here for the Doo-doo," I said.

"I know. Fill this out." He thrust a form at me that was only few hundred pages long.

Hazel's replacement came while I sat in the very nice waiting area, complete with Brazilian Cherry counters, filling out the form. I handed it over to Hazel II. Hazel II was the male version of Hazel I, complete with grunts and instructions. Well, at least they were consistent.

"Detective Appletree said he was taking care of this," I offered.

More grunts. Then ringing of intercoms followed by grunted telephone instructions. "Wait there," Hazel II commanded. I curtseyed again and obliged.

Buzzers buzzed, doors opened and Appletree entered the lobby. "C'mon," he directed, waving me toward the entrance doors.

I shrugged and followed him outside. The temperature out here felt like it was a thousand degrees. My sandals stuck to the pavement. I figured this was because they were melting. I checked, and scraped a wad of gum off the bottom. I followed Appletree around the corner to the chain-linked impound lot on the corner of Chestnut and Queen.

Appletree approached the manned kiosk and showed his badge. The officer in charge of baby-sitting impounded cars buzzed us in. Appletree showed him a ticket, with a number – which would hopefully indicate the location of the Doo-doo. The officer looked up the number in the kiosk records, read the description and groaned. "Oh, that one," he said.

I sighed. This did not bode well.

Appletree and I followed the attending officer to the back of the lot. By the time we walked back there, Appletree's neatly pressed detective shirt was completely wet across his back, neck and underarms. And I realized I wasn't much better. Ick. And there would be no air conditioning in the Doo-doo. Double ick.

"Here she is," the attendant said, gesturing to the Doo-doo. He produced a clipboard. "Sign here for the keys, please."

I did as instructed and got the keys for the Doo-doo. I swatted at the flies buzzing in and out of my smashed window

"I can give you a ride back to the station," I offered Appletree as I opened the driver side door. A blast of hot air rolled out at us that was scented with a thousand turds.

"Uh, no thanks," he said, fanning his hand in front of his face.

I held my nose and peered in. The Doo-doo was immaculate. There wasn't even any dust. "Ah dawnt undethwand," I said, still holding my nose. "Doo-doo's weeewy qween."

Appletree didn't respond.

I came back out of the Doo-doo and looked around. Appletree had backed several feet away, still fanning his face.

"I don't get it," I said, walking toward him. "The Doo-doo LOOKS really clean; spotless."

Appletree nodded. "She would; she was dusted for fingerprints within an inch of her vinyl," he answered.

"But why does she have the poopy smell?"

Appletree shrugged. "Hey, they remove evidence, not smells. It's not like you brought her here for detailing."

"But now the Doo-doo smells like her name," I whined.

Appletree shook his head. "Look, just roll the windows down and air her out. She was probably sitting in the lot for a few days with the poopy bags in her, until they got around to dusting her."

"You mean they left Doo-doo sitting here for days with poopy bags cooking inside her?"

"Probably," Appletree answered, holding his nose and rolling down the van's windows. I sighed and climbed aboard. Appletree closed my door. "Here, try this," he said, offering me a spray bottle of breath freshener. I took it and sprayed some in my mouth. He shook his head. "No, not for you. Here." He reached over and sprayed the breath freshener inside the van. I sniffed. Great. Now the poop was spearmint flavored.

I started up the Doo-doo and drove out of the lot. I waved bye-bye to Appletree who stood chatting with the guard at the kiosk. They both held their noses and waved bye-bye back as I exited and turned onto Queen Street. I made way back to Orange Street and toward Marietta Avenue, which would take me to Auntie's.

I pulled into Auntie's driveway and did my usual seventy-seven-point-seven turn to maneuver the Doo-doo around to face forward, and left room for Massage Man to park. A lone wasp buzzed toward the smashed window, hovered, then retreated hastily. Well, at least there was an upside. The Doo-doo's new aroma doubled as wasp repellant.

I got out and walked over to the garden gnome I'd given Auntie as a house present. I lifted off his cap and fished around for

Auntie's spare key. The gnome is a bit out of place with the rest of Auntie's décor, but it's a useful hiding place. Then again, there's no place like gnome. Ba-dump bump.

I opened up the front door, and walked inside. Auntie's house was cool and quiet and full of fresh cut flowers. As usual. I sighed. I love it that Auntie goes out and buys herself fresh cut flowers. Even if they are courtesy of Uncle Max.

I went into the living room and looked at the erect massage table. It reminded me of a people-size ironing board. How had I ever been comfortable enough to fall asleep on it?

The front door knocked. It was James.

"Good morning," he said nicely.

"Morning," I mumbled back, letting him into Auntie's foyer.

"How are you feeling?" he asked.

"Great, thanks," I said.

"Do you mind if I just..." He nodded toward his table.

"Oh, no, really, help yourself. It's all just where you left it. Except for me, of course, ha ha," I said, forcing a laugh.

James nodded at me and went toward the massage table and started picking up sheets and whatnot. As he started dismantling the table, I realized that this was a very transportable structure. And that James had incredible shoulders and back muscles. And a cute butt. And that he would shortly be leaving again. Very shortly.

"So, uh... sorry about falling asleep on you yesterday. It wasn't a criticism," I started.

"Actually, I took it as more of a compliment," he said. Huh.

"So, uh, what interested you to become a massage guy, anyway – I mean, masseuse," I asked.

"Massage therapist, actually" he answered. Then he stood up and smiled at me. Huh. James also had an amazingly brilliant smile. Oh-please-oh-please-oh-please-don't-be-wearing-a-bridge, I hoped. And please-oh-please-oh-please for my ego's sake don't be gay. I mean, it's perfectly alright to be gay. Except that my illusionary love interests are starting to show a distressing inclination toward exceedingly unavailable men.

"You know, if I had a nickel for every time someone asked me that, I could probably retire," he answered.

"Why?" I asked.

"Because the people who knew me in my past lifetime ask me that a lot," he said.

Past lifetime? Oh crap. Why was I alone with this nut?

"Oh," I said, nodding, hoping to end the conversation.

"You see, up until a couple years ago, I was a capital investments broker."

Oh. Investments. Okay, well that's pretty normal. "Pretty stressful, huh?"

"Not too bad," he answered truthfully. "Actually, the massage thing began as a hobby."

"Really?" I asked, hoping to continue the conversation until he asked me out.

"My girlfriend was getting kind of stressed out," he answered.

Girlfriend? I smiled brightly and was completely crestfallen. On the upside, I'd broken my tendency toward being attracted to gay men. On the downside, I'm apparently still attracted to unavailable men. Rats.

"Oh, really?" I smiled politely. I disengaged and put myself on autopilot.

"Yeah. She was a Victoria's Secret lingerie model." Lingerie model!? "It's pretty stressful. Mostly because she traveled a lot. You see, she's got a real fear of flying. So the only thing I could do to help her relax was massage," he said.

"Right, of course. Well, it's not like she can have an ice cream sundae to take the edge off," I answered smartly.

"Exactly," he answered. Well then. "And then the market got shaky about the same time as she was setting me up with her model buddies for massages. Then my investment buddies got word, and of course they trusted me with their families and partners, knowing that I'm not some kind of a nut," he said.

"Right," I replied, and regretted thinking him a nut.

"So I kind of started with a built-in niche," he finished. "It's not the income I had as an investment broker. But I sure sleep better at night." Huh. After massaging his girlfriend and her lingerie modeling buddies, I felt sure he did.

James left a few minutes later, and I sat in the middle of Auntie's living room deflated and at odds with myself. On the one hand, there was something about him that made me feel defensive.

On the other hand, I was starting a new trend toward being attracted to straight guys. Okay, maybe things were getting better.

The grandfather clock in the hall bonged. Crap. I had to get moving so I could get dressed up and pick up K. and crew. Double crap. Because that's what the Doo-doo smelled like. Transporting humans for several hours in a van with no air-conditioning to New York City in the summer was looking like a bad plan. The dinner, ride and the Doo-doo were now a trifecta of crap.

I locked up Auntie's florist shop home, and got back in the Doo-doo and held my nose. I wound my way back across town singlehandedly, acutely aware that not only did Auntie's side of town look more upscale than mine, it smelled better too.

I pulled up Mt. Driveway and jumped out of the Doo-doo panting, having held my breath for the last mile. Clearly there was no way I could transport anyone across town, much less across state lines. I wondered if there was an environmental law I'd get arrested for, like transporting stench without a license?

"Hey, Toots, how ya doin'?" Vito asked from his charred front porch. He had the newspaper in front of him and Stanley by his side, gnawing peacefully on a burnt porch spindle. I shrugged. Vito raised his eyebrows in return. "Hey, aren't you happy to be getting ready to go on your big night out and all?" he asked.

"Huh?"

"Yeah, I ran into K. at Madam Phang's, 'cause he was picking up his fancy dry cleaning and all for your Supper Club party tonight. He couldn't stop talking about it. Seems like you kids are in for a good time." Vito smiled. Complete with bridge.

I gulped. "Well," I started, and began to rehearse my explanation about the Doo-doo to Vito, and being sorry to let my friends down and all, but these things happen, etc., etc., etc.

Vito folded up his paper and came across to my side of the driveway, with Stanley snarling affectionately and hanging onto a new trouser cuff. I looked at Vito. "He has separation anxiety," he answered.

Vito came toward the Doo-doo and did a repeat action of the wasp at Auntie's. "Wow, twad's pweddy baaayd," he said, holding his nose.

Stanley hopped right inside and jumped in the way back, digging at the wheel well.

"What the?" Vito and I asked together.

I opened the doors to the back, and Stanley's attempts to dig toward China via my spare wheel storage. Vito said something in Polish and held his nose. He dug out a doggie treat from his front pocket. Stanley looked from the wheel well to the treat and back again. Clearly, this was a decision. Finally, as Stanley realized the doggie treat might be more appetizing than the vapors from the wheel well, he yapped and jumped down, taking the treat and crunching happily on the lawn.

Vito and I looked at the wheel well. And the almost visible cloud of noxious gases hovering over it.

"Didn't they fingerprint this at all?" Vito asked.

"Yes," I said. "They thed they dwid," I added, holding my nose.

"Amateurs," Vito said, shaking his head. "Scuse me, Toots." He crossed in front of me toward the back of the open van.

"Hey, Vito, you don't have to," I began, but it was too late. Vito was opening the wheel well.

He unscrewed the cover and took off the cap and we almost fell backward. "What the!?" he asked.

Curiosity got the better of us. We held our hands to our faces to check out the contents. Apparently, my spare wheel was missing. Dumped in its place was a huge stash of loosely bagged doody.

"Yeesth, no whanda your car thmelled," Vito said, holding his nose.

"Ugh-huh," I replied, holding my nose and hoping my eyelashes weren't melting.

Vito closed the back of the van. A fly came in through the back open window. Several zillion followed. I sighed.

Vito led me by the elbow back to his front porch. "Hey, Toots, I don't want to butt in or nothin', but I think I can help yous out here," he said. Visions of the Doo-doo going up in flames 'mysteriously' raced through my mind.

"NO! You are not going to torch the Doo-doo!" I yelled.

"Yeesh. You really have an overactive imagination, you know?" he said. I sighed. "No, seriously, I've got a buddy who does car detailing for rental car companies. You should hear what he's told me he's had to clean up. This kinda crap won't be nothing to him, literally." I looked at him. "Sorry, Toots, I wasn't trying to talk off color or nothin'. But we are talking about a lotta crap."

"Agreed," I said.

"Well, yeah."

"But I still have to let K. know I can't pick him up this afternoon."

Vito smiled. "No you don't, Toots; I'm not going anywhere, so why don't you just drive my car?" Vito asked.

The Towncar? Air conditioning? Wow. Things might not be so bad after all.

"Are you sure?"

"Sure I'm sure," Vito said and handed me his keys. "Besides, this ways I got an excuse for not showing up at Miriam's tonight," he said quickly.

"Oh?"

"Yeah, she's having one of those Majong things. I'm not too up on it." I shrugged. "Besides, she's getting a little territorial," he added, and blushed.

"How do you mean?" I asked.

Vito sighed. "She came over with an outfit for Stanley."

"An outfit?"

"Yeah, you know. She bought him doggie vest and bowtie. She made him wear it. He looked like a used car salesman," he said.

"Yeeshkabiddle," I said.

"Times two," Vito added.

I called K.. "Okay, I have good news and bad news; which first?" I asked.

"Oh no, please do not tell me you are without transportation this afternoon!!" he cried.

"Well, yes and no," I replied.

"Alright, alright... give me the news."

So I told him the bad news was we couldn't go in the Doo-doo. Which was actually the good news, since Vito was loaning the non-doo-doo smelling Towncar complete with air conditioning.

"Oh, this is wonderful!" K. bubbled. "Oh-my-gosh– you better hurry, girlfriend!"

"Huh?"

"You're supposed to pick me up in forty-five minutes, dearie!" he said and hung up briskly. I looked at the clock and rubbed my butt. Well.

After arranging an impromptu pet feeding schedule with Vito, I ran upstairs and made every attempt to look clean, upbeat and in style. I knew this meant a lot to K. Because we were going to New York, I made sure I wore all black and was slightly rumpled, to make sure I'd fit in.

I picked K. up at his Craftsman home, parking along the very tree lined and very reputable State Street. K. literally bounced out of his house as he opened his front door. I hadn't seen him this excited since his favorite big-box store opened a new branch on Lincoln Highway East.

K. had also costumed himself as a Native New Yorker: he wore a white shirt, black hip-hugging slacks and Ray-Ban sunglasses. I exited the Towncar and greeted K. tottering on my 3-inch strappy sandals. They elevated me to almost 6-feet tall, which was okay since this was definitely not a date. If ever a venue existed for me in which to display 'forbidden footwear', this was it.

We stood together for a moment on the walkway to K.'s front door. Together we resembled the ex-patriated wait staff of 'Tavern on the Green'.

K. gasped and sang, "Look at you, NEW YORK!! NE-EEW YORK!!"

I smiled gratefully and began to totter toward Vito's Towncar. Already my right pinky toe had started to protest. I wondered how long it would take for the rest of me to do the same.

"OMG! We have pimped our RIDE!! OMG!" K. squealed in delight. I hung my head. "Oh, it's alright," K. soothed. "Everyone will just think it's our ride, which is the same thing!" he bobbled. I nodded.

K. leapt into the Towncar swinging a clipboard, directions, maps, bottled water and a Tony Bennett CD. Figuring out how to play the CD wasn't too successful; I ended up spraying car washing fluid. But we finally managed and Tony was crooning just before we picked up Ida Rose.

Ida Rose lives with her very old and very rich Aunt Gladys in the very huge and very impressive Watt & Shand mansion on the corner of Marietta and President Avenues. That is to say, Ida Rose lives in a servanted mansion, as well as a genuine historic landmark. K. and I once visited for a poker game last winter. At some point during our poker tea (Ida's Aunt Gladys does not serve alcoholic beverages) I went to the powder room and got lost. By the time I found my way back, everyone had left. This was unfortunate as I have not been invited again by Ida's Aunt Gladys. I found out later that Aunt Gladys thought I had cheated at poker, because I was winning, and my being lost was interpreted as 'casing the joint' thanks to a female detective novel she was reading at the time.

So K. and I pulled into the U-shaped turn-around drive to the mansion. I looked at K. to get out and ring the bell for Ida. K. looked at me likewise, then returned to reading his map. I shut off the ignition and waited. It got hot. K. sighed, folded up his map and hopped out. I clambered out muttering under my breath at my toes to stop complaining or I wouldn't buy them fancy new attire ever again.

We walked up to the Citizen Kane-like front doors and stood staring at the huge entrance. K. tugged at the giant cord that served as the front door bell. BING-BONG. We jumped a bit. We always did.

"Don't you always expect Lurch to answer?" K. whispered. I nodded.

Instead we were greeted by Ophelia. That is, Ida Rose in costume.

Ida greeted us in the front doorway, fluttering in gossamer fairy skirts with shoulder caplets, with her hair done up in ringlets, all in a dusty blue. Her costume that is, not her hair. Her hair was its usual jet black. Ida sparkled in a cloud of fairy dust. Then she sneezed, which sent more fairy dust billowing. I wondered which of Aunt Gladys's long-ago social dresses Ida had dug up for this occasion.

"Gracious me, do come in," Ida drawled.

K. and I held each other's gaze in sympathetic unison. Ida Rose's favorite moment from way-back-when was when she played Blanche in her high school's production of 'A Streetcar Named Desire'. She usually resurrected this when she was feeling a bit blue. Her costume was clearly evidence that she was in

'Streetcar' mode. Someone needed to break the spell. I stared at the ceiling.

"Ida, dear, the dinner is in NEW YORK, darling, not TARA," K. teased, holding up the hem of her fairy skirt. Ida sniffed. Not good. I rubbed the back of my left calf with my sore pinky toe, to stop its whining.

"Are those new sandals?" Ida screeched, pointing at my pulsing feet.

"Yes," I said demurely.

Ida loves footwear and has wonderful taste in shoes. Which goes nicely with her humungous shoe budget and shoe closet. So, if Ida Rose admires your shoes, you've done very well indeed.

"Where did you get them? Whose are they?" she demanded.

K. looked beseechingly at me. We were using up valuable Walter-loading time: we both knew it would take luck and a crane to settle Walter into the car.

"Oh, I'll tell you on the way," I said, smiled, turned and did my darndest to sachet and not limp toward the car.

"Leaving now, Aunt Gladys – byeeee," Ida whooped, snatching a dusty-blue sequined clutch from an outstretched servant's hand (Lurch? Really?) and floating toward the car. K. did a multitude of nervous bows from his waist to an invisible Aunt Gladys and departed backward.

Ida Rose sat happily in the middle of the backseat. K. looked relieved. Clearly, he was worried that Ida might have wanted to ride 'gun'.

"Oh, Ida Rose, dear, thank you so much. I hope you don't mind sitting in the back," K. said.

Ida raised her eyebrows a few stories above her ringleted forehead. "Mind?" she asked.

"Not sitting in the front," K. explained.

Ida Rose giggled, all Blanche Dubois like. "You are a card, my dear K.. Why, Auntie dearest would never condone our sitting up front with the chauffeur; it would be considered vulgar."

I looked at K. K. frowned at Ida. I counted one-Mississippi.

"So, in other words, you do want to sit in the front, so long as we switch seats before we drop you back home, so your Aunt Gladys doesn't see you not sitting in the back?" I asked.

"Precisely," Ida whispered, nodding enthusiastically.

I pulled Vito's Towncar out of the mansion's driveway, making a right onto President's Avenue. We drove into the islanded residential area just before the intersection of President's Avenue and Harrisburg Pike.

"Oh, I just LOVE this neighborhood!" K. said, as he had a thousand times before as we drove through it. Ida Rose and I chirped in agreement.

"Oh, look what they've done now! I just love that Tudor-bethan," Ida said happily, sans Blanche Dubois.

"What happened to Blanche?" K. asked.

Ida frowned. "You are becoming worse at this. It wasn't Blanche; it was Maggie from the 'Cat on a Hot Tin Roof'." She pouted.

"Oh, you are much more appealing than Maggie, dearie," K. said.

Ida looked pleased. "Really? Well, so glad I found some hidden party duds then," she said, patting her dress. Little clouds of non-fairy dust poofed about the backseat. Ida coughed. K. became resourceful and used the automatic window openers to open all the windows, switching the AC onto full blast to help with the proceedings.

"Really, K.!" Ida and I both shrieked.

"Really, windswept is not a hairstyle statement," Ida Rose complained. "Besides, I hate that loose free feeling," she added.

K. sighed. "I know, dearie," he said, "but really, we can't have you posing a health hazard in an eating establishment, coming in just as if you've crawled out of a vacuum cleaner."

Ida Rose waved her fingers pointedly at K. as if she were casting a spell on him, smiled successfully to herself, and then the windows rolled up. Well.

By this time we had crossed Harrisburg Pike and Manheim Pike and came to Fruitville Pike. Yes, another Pike. A visiting friend once asked me why Lancaster has 'pikes' and not 'roads'. Dunno, was my response. Still is. Just go with it.

I weaved along toward Oregon Pike. During all this Ida Rose and K. played their usual 'I Spy' game which in particular focuses on drivers and passengers of cars around us rather then settings.

"I spy nose-picking," Ida Rose said.

K. looked about. "Yick, who doesn't?"

We drove past the Gass-up! gas station, and made the next immediate right into Armand's McMansion development, and pulled up to his front door. I have to say, once we entered Armand's neighborhood, my feeling of dread began to lift and I began to feel kind of tingly and excited – the way you get when you're anticipating going to a happy event. Armand's neighborhood was a bit on the cookie-cutter side, with a definite tendency toward taupe. But I found this soothing. Everything was neat and usual; no surprises. Although I put myself in check, realizing that perhaps I was suffering subconscious reactions from my crazily colored walls. However, I also realized that certainly, if Armand thought this little eatery expedition was worth the trip, we lay eaters were sure to be impressed.

But even with my barking feet, I was not about to miss a chance to enter Armand's foyer. Entering Armand's foyer is like entering onto a Fred Astaire and Ginger Rogers movie set. K. followed at my heels. He loves Armand's foyer, too.

We stopped and looked back at Ida Rose; she was still sitting in the backseat, waving a fan (how did she fit that in her sequined clutch?) and talking to an imaginary stranger. We shrugged and walked up the path toward Armand's house.

Armand's foyer has a lovely cathedral ceiling with a crystal chandelier, a marble floor and curved staircase that leads up to a sort of mezzanine. Also, Armand's home is spotless. But K. and I suspect that is largely due to his widowed mother and widowed sister moving in with him a few years ago.

Apparently Armand was looking forward to our epicurious adventure, too. He opened the door, dressed in Calvin Klein blacks, and gestured for us to enter. His mother and sister, both clad in black wool, hovered along the walls behind him.

“Good evening, please.” Armand gestured us into the foyer.

K. and I attempted to enter at the same time and wound up walking shoulder to shoulder together through the double front door.

We stood in the midst of our Forever Foyer and sighed. We drank in the lily-scented cool air, tinkling music and glimpses of exotic flowers placed carefully in a crystal vase standing in the middle of a round walnut table.

"Please, please, you come?" Armand's mother questioned us, motioning us past the foyer and toward the inner sanctum.

K. and I immediately brightened. Neither of us had been allowed beyond the foyer before. In fact, we made it a secret challenge between us to see who might be the first to gain access.

"Mama," Armand said quietly while kissing his mother on the cheek. She sighed and shrugged.

His sister cast furtive glances and landed on my sandals.

"Oh, beautiful!" she cried, pointing toward my feet. I shut up my throbbing toes and reminded them it wasn't how the felt, it was how they looked that mattered.

"Thank you," I said, blushing.

Armand's mother said something to Armand's sister that did not sound remotely encouraging. His sister sighed. "My mother reminds me that I am still in mourning," she answered simply.

"How much longer?" I asked sympathetically.

"Just six years!" she said brightly.

"We'll go shopping," I whispered toward her.

Armand's mother muttered something that sounded a lot like a curse. I mentally tossed salt over my shoulder, and was relieved that we had our resident pixie in the backseat of Vito's Towncar to remove spells.

As we walked toward the car, K. said, "I'm sorry about your brother-in-law passing, Armand."

Armand sighed. "He died in 1999. My mother made it a condition of immigration that my sister remain in mourning until her stateside matchmaker could find her a suitable husband, or the year 2016, whichever come first. I have a feeling my sister, she will hold out," he said.

K. patted him on his shoulder.

Ida Rose smiled as Armand opened the back door to sit beside her. "Oh my, this is almost like a gentleman caller!" she teased.

Armand stared at her. "Glass Menagerie or Hot Tin Roof?" he asked simply.

"Menagerie, of course," she replied normally.

Armand nodded and sat beside her. K. resumed navigator position and I resumed driving – very grateful to not be standing on my already very sore feet or sat in the backseat with Laura and her gentleman caller.

The atmosphere in the car grew festive as Ida and K. managed to elicit more than a grimace from Armand. Actually, by the looks of it, Armand was excited, too. Well, as excited as Armand could appear. He nodded a lot, while both Ida Rose and K. prattled on about gourmet menus they'd read about and how they'd manage the wine pairings. This was where Armand became animated and actually offered more than his usual mono-syllabic answers: “Syrah.” “Bordeaux.” “Pinot.”

I led us back downtown via Lititz Pike to Prince Street, and made a left on Lemon toward Walter's high rise apartment building. Geographically, it would have made sense to gather Armand last, as he lives so close to entrance to 222 and therefore Route 76/Pennsylvania Turnpike. However, as Walter is gravity challenged, and I didn't want to risk a visit to the ER and Trixie, I decided we'd pick up Walter last. All of us.

Walter lives in one of the few high rise apartment buildings in downtown Lancaster. K. went up for him. K. returned without him. I looked at K.

“The elevator's weight capacity does not include guests,” K. said simply.

I shook my head. We love Walter and he has a big heart. But he has an even bigger appetite and we all worry about when said big heart will need replacing with a new one.

Walter emerged from the lobby and into the summer swelter. He stood panting on the front walk. Armand and K. leapt out to help him. Hovering on either side of him, they walked with him toward the Towncar. Armand opened the door for Walter to climb in. Ida Rose leapt outside to offer Walter more room. Or maybe to not be sat upon.

“Wow. Sure is hot out here! Got a lot hotter since April...”

Unfortunately, or fortunately, Walter is a freelance writer and literally, not virtually, lives on the internet. His major claims to fame have been ghost writing and editing cookbooks, parapsychology magazines, self-help books (not dieting), commercial website content and some comic books. He doesn't leave his apartment unless he absolutely, positively must. He's managed to find local grocers and drycleaners and beer distributors that deliver. I am equally amazed and worried by his resourcefulness and his inertia.

Walter, too, had decided to dress for the evening. While most persons of Walter's girth might try to subdue their bulk with dark or neutral colors, Walter prefers a livelier palette. Tonight he sported miles and miles of fire engine red and white vertical stripes in a cotton short-sleeved shirt, which he tucked into a matching pair of fire engine red slacks, which were hemmed in with a wide white canvas belt. He accented these with white canvas sneakers. All in all, he looked like a pizza delivery man.

Walter eased into the backseat, and I felt Vito's Towncar sag. K. scoped out the remaining real estate in the backseat, and took Ida Rose and Armand to the exterior of the car for a quick huddle. I looked in the rearview and saw Ida Rose nodding understandably. Then she climbed in petitely next to Walter and exchanged pleasantries. Meanwhile, I watched as Armand and K. performed 'Once! Twice! Three! Shoot!' fingers. Apparently K. lost. He handed his maps to Armand and wedged himself in on the other side of Walter. Armand climbed into the front seat next to me with all the social graces of a hockey mom. I was glad he didn't have a whistle.

I maneuvered us out of downtown and back toward the Gass-up! on Oregon Pike, since I realized Vito's Towncar was running on something close to fumes. And I assumed the nearly zillion-dollars per gallon might be closer to double the closer we got to New York.

I pulled up to the gas tank, and Armand put a hand up. "Please," he said, and went to fill up the tank. He might prefer to use only one word at a time, but he was nice about it. Then again, he's been living in Lancaster for almost two decades.

At the same time, K. decided he needed a frozen latte, Ida Rose was desperate for her monthly horoscope and Walter had forgotten he hadn't eaten anything since a couple of hours ago and was concerned about his blood sugar.

We left Gass-up! a few months later.

CHAPTER 16

(Saturday afternoon)

As we finally pulled onto Route 222 North, we enjoyed a few sparkling moments of amicable solace. K. slurped at his frozen latte. Ida Rose read her In-Depth Personal Monthly Horoscope aloud while Armand grunted sagely in response and Walter chewed. Even the pungent smell of onions from Walter's sub wafted peacefully in the air conditioned breeze.

Once on Route 76, the landscape became far less scenic, so our imaginations got going. Armand began to speculate about the evening's fare. While he was still phobic about the lack of bonafide wait staff or tablecloths, he was beginning to ease himself into the role of patron.

"Hearts of palm," he sighed. "And pesto! Something must have the pesto!"

K. leant forward to speak into Armand's ear. "Maybe with sun-dried tomato!"

Armand attempted to turn around to concur but unfortunately got choked a bit by the seat belt anti-whirling around thingy.

"I certainly wouldn't mind something Champagne-ish," Ida Rose chimed in.

"Or maybe frozen-vodka like... with Beluga caviar," I sang.

Glancing at a portion of Walter through the rear-view mirror I saw him blush. His face began to match his outfit. "I know it's summer and all, and folks like to mostly eat on the light side," he began, "but if it's a nice air-conditioned room, I sure could get around a nice rack of lamb, with some organic rosemary, new potatoes and maybe a braised vegetable ragu." Clearly his recent cookbook editing was shining through.

Ida sighed. "It truly does not matter to me about our entrees or appetizers. Aunt Gladys' diabetes is the death of me and I would surely kill for a lovely decadent dessert – especially profiteroles with heaps of chocolate sauce and clotted cream... or chocolate cheesecake with a smashed chocolate crumb crust... with heaps of chocolate sauce and cream..."

We all sighed affirmations in unison.

As we passed Kutztown, Walter passed gas. Windows were opened and apologies were made, along with a good many "Excuse me," and "Beg pardons!" thrown in for good measure. Ida Rose re-consulted her horoscope by waving it frantically. K. stroked his forehead and complained to himself in the third person about the beginnings of a brain freeze. The delicate straps of my fancy dress sandals cut into my swollen flesh like dental floss. Armand smoked.

A couple of hours later, riding along with windows open and the AC blasting, Walter lay sprawled in the backseat asleep, pooting softly. Ida Rose lay slumped across his belly holding her nose in her sleep. K. lay full back, snoring, with his arm on Ida's shoulder, oblivious to everything. I glanced sideways at Armand. He smoked.

Finally I found our way down Canal Street and into the West Village. As this is generally the land of sell-your-first-child-for-a-parking-space, I was relieved and grateful that K. made sure our 'invitation' included a parking privilege.

K. had printed out directions from a mapping website, and read them at me as we wove our way around the same blocks repeatedly. Finally, K. screeched and I turned into what seemed a miniscule driveway. It was actually a long, narrow alley that led us downward into a steep pit.

I turned the Towncar's lights on, took Auntie's sunglasses off, and eased the car downward slowly. We reached the very bottom and a very locked gate. I thunked my head on the steering wheel repeatedly.

"How do we get in?" Walter asked from the back.

"Well there must be a person who's paid to attend, and who clearly is on a break," Ida Rose said matter-of-factly.I banged my head on the steering wheel some more.

"Well, it's not exactly like we can just back up!" K. cried.

We looked in plural out the back window at the cavernous path leading upward at what appeared to be a near 90-degree angle. Nope: no backing up here, even without Walter in the backseat.

K. smacked himself on his forehead with his clipboard repeatedly. Then he looked at a note that fell out.

"Oh, well, of course!" he sang out. We stared at him and his newly creased forehead. "Just press the BUTTON!" he instructed.

We looked at him. K. pointed past me, toward a somewhat hidden and very dirty round intercom-like button mounted in the brick wall just before the gate. It was black and unlit. It looked like a plain, old, black coat button, sitting next to a similarly large, black, oblong coat button. I squinted, wondering which button to push. The oblong button scuttled off. The round button didn't. I pressed it.

Miraculously, instead of scuttling off or biting me, it buzzed.

"Hell-ooooooooo!" a cheery man's voice answered.

K. yodeled back, "Hel-loooooooo!"

"So glad you have joined us! Password please!" the gatekeeper answered.

"Oh, piss," K. muttered, furiously flipping the pages of his disheveled clipboard. "Oh, alright! Here we go!" he exclaimed.

"Ready?" the disembodied voice requested.

"Quite!" K. chimed happily. He removed the password text page and began to sing.

"Sorry, but we really can't hear you, dearie," the disembodied voice transmitted.

Armand sighed, got out and exchanged seats with K., lit a cigarette and stood outside the car. He had to. If he had a lit cigarette in the backseat, with Walter's gas and Ida's antique fluttery garb, someone would have been set on fire.

K. hopped in next to me and leaned across me – literally – and began to sing the first phrase of 'New York, New York' across my boobs and into the not-roach coat button.

The gatekeeper responded with a final, "Neee-wwww Yo-ooork!" and buzzed the gate open to the garage.

Armand stomped out his smoke, and climbed in next to Walter. I sighed and gunned it, glad to be through, but wondered what four-part harmony they'd make us yodel to get ourselves out of here at the end of the night.

"Well, where to from here?" Ida Rose muffled from underneath Walter's armpit.

"Yeah, I mean, you got an address and all, right?" Walter asked.

K. spit forth placating statements like a deranged Pez dispenser. "Yes, yes, yes! No, no, no! Of course! Absolutely!"

Once K. was through, he registered my stare. And he noted that I noted his cold sweat.

"Wazzup?" I asked.

He leaned forward into my lap in order to whisper to me while pretending he was examining at my S&M shoes. "I forgot to write the stupid address down," he confided.

Shit.

"Okay, it's not so bad," I said. He looked at me. "You've got the phone number, right?"

K. shook his head. I sighed.

Armand cleared his throat. "Simple, stoopid sheet," he said.

"Huh?" K. asked brightly.

"Jez go and prezz de button," Armand instructed.

"Of course!!" And off he skipped.

Armand reclaimed his gun seat. I looked at him. "How'd you know?" I asked.

"I read laps," he said.

"I think you mean lips."

He shrugged. "Whatever."

K. came back happier and sweatier and invited us to join him outside of the car. Which we did. Which was why I understood why Armand was smoking incessantly when he stood outside of the car, even more than his usual addictive self. Summer in New York. The distinct smell of urine, combined with a hint of sweat and decaying attitudes, was steeped into every available concrete surface. While the Doo-doo had experienced some recent issues, these were nothing to the well-spring of historic stench coming from the parking garage. Ick. Ick. Ick. How do people live with this smell? In Lancaster, there are newly fertilized pastures I ride through in the springtime that are less offensive than this. But we ride along holding our noses, safe in the knowledge that fertilizer tilling lasts for only three weeks. This? I was pretty sure the urine I smelled dated all the way back to Fiorella LaGuardia.

"Hey, guys, are we here? Are we going?" Walter called.

"Yes, if this is the correct place of destination, I suggest we put forth," Ida Rose chimed.

Armand nodded. "Yes, ve are cooking," he assured through his cigarette plumes.

Armand opened the back door of Vito's Towncar on Ida's side, and we pulled Ida out from underneath Walter, her antique attire a bit the worse for the wear. She looked like a rumpled moth.

Then came time to extricate Walter, which was the hardest part of the whole process. Armand smoked. He stubbed his butt out beneath his left shoe. He surveyed me, K. and Ida. He sighed.

"Ve needs lev-er-aggghe," he instructed.

"Huh?" we all asked.

He sighed again and explained and re-explained a few hundred times. Finally we got it.

Armand would push Walter out of the back seat, while we pulled him out. A lot like Winnie the Pooh and the honey pot story. With Armand having cast himself as Rabbit. Poor Pooh. I mean, Walter.

We pushed and we pulled and finally all the King's men pulled Walter out of Vito's backseat. Where he'd been sitting remained a seriously sweaty puddle. Which, it being a Towncar, was leather. I fretted. Armand shrugged and wiped the backseat with an exceedingly crisp looking handkerchief which was clearly for showing, not for blowing. Armand rung out the handkerchief. It dripped red.

"OH MY GOD! Walter! You are bleeding!" K. screamed and flailed about with a series of motions that looked like he was on fire.

"LOOK! LOOK!" Ida joined in, now as Lady Macbeth, and pointed dramatically toward Armand's handkerchief.

"Walter, are you alright?" I asked.

Walter's ears began a crescendo that came close to matching his red pizza outfit.

"No, I'm not bleeding; just stupid," he began. "I wanted to look extra spiffy tonight. So I dyed my white pants to match the red of my new shirt my mom got me... but I forgot to wash them first before wearing them, like the dye directions said. Sorry about your seat..."

I felt awful. We all did. Especially Lady Macbeth. I mean Ophelia. That is, Ida. We were all obviously trying very hard to impress, especially poor Walter.

After several choruses of my mistake, sorry, nothing to worry about, just over-dramatic that's me, we continued our pilgrimage. I spluttered and limped as I went: the sandals were truly taking their toll.

"Okay, where to now, chief? Are we blindfolded and led to this place?"

"You know that really would be wonderfully dramatic but probably cause a lot of undue attention... and cost a lot more," K. replied thoughtfully. "Walking directions are right here," he added, waving his clipboard and some notes he must have jotted down while he confirmed our reservations in the parking garage. He might have confirmed reservations. I knew I had many.

I've heard about the death marches in Japan during WWII. Luckily their marches ended in death. We marched two-by-two up and around the various passageways of the parking garage's ramps, toward the street. With no respite in sight, we passed out of the stinky garage and onto city sidewalks hot enough to fry eggs. Literally. A pigeon's egg had plummeted onto the pavement moments earlier and lay sizzling. (Flung by a pro-choice apartment dwelling tenant? The choice being theirs?) A small, sad, scrambled (non-embryo thank-you-Lord) egg in a cracked half shell lay sizzling on the pavement. I stared and wondered how I could achieve that presentation – sans pavement, of course – with a normal egg for a normal person. Presentation-wise, it would be very dramatic, with the half shell and all. Like oysters.

Anyway, apparently the main entrance to the building was around the corner, the distance of about two city blocks. Given my screaming feet, this was equivalent to walking to Kuwait.

K. and Armand, being the professionals of the evening, led the charge while Ida fluttered along helping Walter, and I brought up the rear reviving my Quasimodo impersonation.

After the twelfth pause to allow Walter to intake his albuterol inhaler – for which my feet throbbed gratefully – K. perceived Mecca. "There it is! The Front Door!" he rejoiced.

We stared blankly at him. K. slapped himself repeatedly in the forehead with his clipboard. People walked by ignoring him. He acted like every other New Yorker. He then stepped furtively toward our pack, glancing about to ensure privacy amongst the several hundred passersby, and explained, "Our Supper Club is in this building!"

We collectively perked up. OMG – soon food, chairs, beverages and honest-to-gosh-air-conditioning would be ours, just a few paces away. And maybe it even had fancy restrooms where they give you mouthwash and perfume and Band-Aids. Especially the Band-Aids.

As we rounded the corner, we saw what seemed to be an exceedingly reputable apartment building, and well-paid professional residents entering and exiting. We smiled.

In the vestibule K. rang the buzzer for apartment #1A. The buzzer answered cheerfully and we were admitted into a spacious and newly updated lobby. There was a glorious blast of cool air, and the heavenly fumes of basil and garlic and a myriad of other spices teased us toward the elevators.

We advanced, but K. stopped us.

"Oh, no, we don't take the elevators up: we take just one shortsy-wortsy flight of stairs down," he said, and motioned to the other side of the lobby, toward what looked very much indeed like a service door.

We made Walter descend first lest he tumble and kill us all. Then the rest of us followed down some very ordinary cement steps and even more ordinary cinder block walls. At the bottom we amassed as a small congregation, and collectively stared at the single door ahead of us.

K. skipped forward, smiled happily at us and said, "Here goes!" and knocked on the door.

From the other side of the door came the clicking of high heels, then the unlocking of what appeared to be a great many dead-bolts and chain locks.

The door opened and we were greeted by a large round elf. Or at least she appeared to be a large, round elf – middle-age-ish, round, bleach blonde hair in a whispy pixie bob, wearing a lime green chiffon kaftan and matching day-glo green drop earrings. I looked down and saw she was wearing very sleek, stunning heeled sandals, which I admired. Then I realized the fat cow was wearing the same sandals as mine, but in lime green. And worse, apparently her brutes hadn't gnawed her feet as their shiny black cousins had mine. The blues of my toes whined in agreement, pulsing angrily at the elf's unscathed hooves.

A small, skinny male elf, wearing all black with a large gold peace-sign necklace leaped out sideways from behind the large, round green elf.

"Greetings, and welcome, one and all! Welcome to our little Supper Club!" the male elf sang. "I am called Groggin," he said, with a hand on his chest to indicate himself.

"And I am Perpetua," the green elf said, following suit identically.

"And we are delighted to have you here!" they said in unison, with arms outstretched.

I was unsure about whether or not they meant the Royal We or the Plural We but that would have to wait.

Perpetua said, "Besides having a wonderful supper planned for you, we'll all learn a little bit about each other. We might even enjoy a virtual '6 degrees of separation' experience! It's possible that by the end of this evening we'll discover we are all connected! Now then – do please come in."

Her unmauled feet clicked happily down the hallway as she led us inside.

"Now that you've arrived, our party can begin!" Perpetua waxed hostess-like.

"But first let's dispense with the formalities," Groggin added.

So we did the obligatory round-robin introductions and obligatory writing of checks to 'cash'. I noted Ida's confusion at not knowing who Mr. Cash was while she was writing and made a mental note to advise her much, much later.

The other parties in the room consisted of a middle-aged gay couple, an elderly woman and her retro-punk granddaughter, what appeared to be a streakily 'tanned' used car salesman type grinning wildly like the recipient of too many facelifts, and newlyweds from Nebraska.

As we shuffled into the main room, I tried to take heart that perhaps this might not be so grim after all. This studio/condo/thingy was like a loft, but underground and shorter. The cement floor was badish but an exposed brick wall gave it a nice feel. The remaining walls were a normal white wallboard, hung with absolutely gigantic paintings in bright oranges, fushcias and blues. Because there were some soft green streaks stemming from the bright blobs, Walter and I guessed they were flowers. Recessed lighting focused on the paintings to ensure good, even blob viewing.

Toward the back, against another exposed brick wall, were several long, worn, wooden picnic tables hemmed in by various types of chairs, loveseats and benches. Old-fashioned milk jugs and pump pitchers held sunflowers, gladiolas and snapdragons, dotting the caravan of tables. Every place had some version of a Mason-jar drinking glass and each setting was a hodgepodge of antique china. Nothing matched and it all looked lovely. Things might not be so bad after all.

We were invited to sit down, and we all did. There was a momentary heightening of alarm as Walter lowered himself down onto his own bench, which required the bringing of some additional chairs for the rest of us. Then all of us sat and grinned sappily at each other. Of course the facelift salesman had little choice. But a sense of calm and expectation settled as it slowly dawned on us that somehow we were all on the inside loop because of this very private, hush-hush party. I felt better for that. I actually started to feel a bit special. I even started not minding the $150 prefix. I started to befriend what remained of my toes and slid my sandals off underneath the table. My feet plumped up like ballpark franks.

We began our rounds of introductions. The grandmother and punk-daughter were enjoying a silent auction prize from an anti-puppy mill benefit. The gay couple had friends who had attended Perpetua and Groggin's 'Barbados Bash' last month and happened to have a pet-sitter in common with Perpetua. The used car/facelift salesman was actually an anesthesiologist whose nurse introduced him to Groggin (in the hopes of a raise no doubt). The newly-married couple from Nebraska were on their second marriage. Each had grown children from their first marriages, one of whom knew a friend of Perpetua's, and had purchased their dinner tickets as a wedding present. K. waxed lyrical about our little van load and Gillian, who is Groggin's hair stylist. I stared at Groggin. I hoped Groggin's hair styling was intentional because his head was shaved clean.

"Now that we're a weensy bit acquainted – let's begin!"

Perpetua's paws pounced upon a bell and rang in the feast. From someplace in the back we heard a heavy metal door open, the scuffling of feet and the squeaking wheel of a trolley. My Lancaster friends and I sat stupefied in horror as an Amish couple approached us. We stared blankly at each other wondering if they were lost, and where would they have found parking for their buggy anywhere near Bank Street?

"Here we are!" peeped Perpetua.

The woolen-clad bearded man in the straw hat sulked toward us and thunked a 15lb block of cheese onto the middle of the table. Next to him, his wife (or sister? they looked uncannily related) shuffled a plastic basket somewhat filled with Trisquits next to the cheese, along with a platter carrying an extremely large and phallic-looking summer sausage. She, too, was clad in black wool and looked very hot indeed. (What else could she be, wearing black wool in August in New York?)

Walter, Ida, Armand and I stared pointedly at K. Were we really in the right place? But K. was engaged in a serious interior design discussion with the anesthesiologist (Dr. Brad, apparently soon to be K.'s next client). I heard a snort and gazed at the punk grand-daughter, who was convulsing and nodding to her grandmother at the uncut summer sausage. Her grandmother sniggered. I looked down at my place setting and silently hoped that neither they – nor anyone else – would go all schoolgirl on us about the giant wiener.

Whistler's father and mother went back to their cart and returned carrying two very large, worn wooden handled knives. Brandishing these toward us, they simultaneously stabbed the cheese and whacked the sausage penis in half.

"Be careful, they are very shc-aaararrrp," the man glowered at us, sounding a bit like Colonel Klink from Hogan's Heroes. Ida held her napkin over her nose in reaction to Col. Klink's wool clad armpit reaching across her face.

Col. and Mrs. Klink went back to the cart, looked reproachfully at us, and squeaked back with their trolley. We heard the opening of what we assumed was the kitchen door and the very loud bang of its closing.

"There now! Isn't this wonderful!" Perpetua piped. I crossed my fingers and my bleeding toes and wished for a logical explanation and a decent meal. "Welcome," Perpetua beamed, "to the Amish Affair!"

Amish Affair? Talk about coals to Newcastle.

Silently, in one accord, my car load slowly and Children-of-the-Corn-like gazed at K. All the blood ran out of K.'s face, leaving it white as flour. Armand looked pointedly at the summer sausage, then at K. Ouch.

"Gee, to think we drove – all the way up – from Lancaster – for Amish food – in New York," Walter puffed, sucking on his inhaler.

"Oh, well that's marvelous!" Perpetua preened, "Amos and Angie are from Lancaster! They must be one of your six-degrees!"

Again we stared as a unit at K. The white in K.'s face was replaced by a slightly greenish tinge.

"My, my," twittered Ida, slipping back into a Tara Ophelia drawl, "sometimes what is common sincerely is just that." Her arrow flew straight and true and sank right into K.'s chest. He flinched.

"Zees are not vaiters," growled Armand, reaching for his cigarettes. "Zees are mammas and pappas."

"Oh, no, no, no – we are a no smoking facility!" Perpetua proclaimed.

"K., you vant come outside for smoke, yes?" Armand directed. We gazed from Armand to K., wondering if K. would return home with us.

K. burbled, "Actually, I'll just nibble on a little piece of this delightful cheese."

Armand gnawed on his unlit cigarette. Suddenly I realized that K. was clearly as embarrassed and disappointed as we all were. However, as no one knew the 'theme' for this evenings fare (or unfair) I realized we couldn't quite blame it all on K. – directly, at least. Indirectly would have to do.

But looking around I saw everyone else was chatting happily and truly enjoying the anticipation of Amish food. I sighed. Alright, so the menu wasn't exactly what we'd hoped. I shrugged.

"Hey, you buys your ticket, yous takes your chances," I said.

K. leaned forward to our little group and whispered, "I had no idea!!"

Walter said, "It's alright. Amish food, if it's not tourist food, is very good; simple home cooking." We looked at him. "It might lean toward the country side, but if it's good it's all made with very fresh, all natural ingredients," he explained. "Seriously, I just edited 'Cooking for 20 – Everyday Amish Dinners'."

We all nodded effusively, and pulled up our respective big girl and big boy panties and behaved as much like adults as we knew how.

As the cheese and sausage were far too heavy to pass amongst us, we passed our plates around for those closest to the Flintstone-like food to hack and serve. The cheese and sausage weren't bad, just usual – for us at least. We fell silent, chewing. I wanted mustard. And I definitely wanted a drink.

"Excuse me, Perpetua," I said, "but could we do with a bit of something wettish?"

"Cert'ly," our hostess gobbed through her cheese.

Groggin tinkled the bell. Again we heard the response of the banging door and squeaking cart. Angie appeared, looking as though she'd just taken a shower. But she hadn't.

"What would everyone like to drink?" Perpetua proffered.

"Vodka tonic," I began, chimed in by the others, "Merlot", "Cosmo!" and "Fuzzy navel!"

Perpetua pouted. "I'm afraid that because this is a supper club, we are not quite that well-stocked except with whatever complements the meal. Groggin and I highly recommend the sparkling water."

Everyone at the table, particularly the punk grand-daughter who had just turned 21, met Perpetua with steady, angry gazes. Even the punk's grandmother frowned.

"And of course we can't sell alcoholic beverages to anyone, so we offer what we have – complimentary – on the house!"

I thought maliciously of how much of my $150 to Mr. Cash would be consumed by complimentary beverages if I hadn't been the driver.

"Uh, what exactly do you offer, dear, beverage-wise, that complements the, um – Amish Affair?" K. ventured.

"Well, actually, to savor a truly Amish experience we wouldn't want to suggest anything alcoholic – so homemade root beer would really be the beverage of choice," Perpetua began, then realized the not-so-friendly-stares radiating toward her and wishing her demise. "However, as apparently we are not Amish, and in keeping with the flavor of the experience, we've struck a weensy loophole and are pleased to offer you – Amish Beer!"

Perpetua puffed proudly, plunking back into her seat. We sighed and placed our orders with Angie. No one – including Gramma – ordered root beer or water.

Amos appeared carrying large pitchers of what appeared to be a dark, thick beer and set these along the table. Most of the attendees leapt upon these enthusiastically. But our company held back; we were all too familiar with Bauser's Amish beer.

We peered in at the leaves and twigs floating toward the top. Just our luck. Krumpthf's. It had come to this. Krumpthf's.

However, Armand, with his waitering disorder, was determined to serve someone, even if it was only us. We sipped leerily, pulling out the occasional bit of debris. After awhile, the Flintstone cheese and phallic sausage wasn't so awfulish. We all ordered more pitchers of Krumpthf's, much to Perpetua's economic dismay.

"Tell you what," growled Karen, the punk granddaughter, "I'd rather the Amish dudes made money serving up food rather than puppies for profit," she said, hacking a piece of sausage and eating it from the knife. "We won't have a good night if I find out they're even related to a puppy mill farmer," she said pointedly at the kitchen door, embedding the knife firmly in the table for punctuation.

"Well I thought that they were all rclatcd, somchow," said newlywed Nancy from Nebraska.

The conversation flew around puppy mill breeders and how no form of punishment or torture would be too severe for them, they ought to be put in their own kennels, forced to breed, starve, freeze, be scalded, etc. All Amish Affair attendees were apparently responsible pet owners and happily in one accord against puppy mill owners, Amish or otherwise.

Amos was summoned again by Perpetua to replace the emptied vats of brew. We fell silent upon his entrance, each one of us glaring silent puppy mill accusations at him.

As soon as he'd departed, our chatter resumed.

"Being from the Amish area," began one half of the gay couple, Ken, "what do you know about them?" he queried Ida.

"The Amish?" Ida asked. "Well, they're like people... but they dress like Johnny Cash."

Next came hot bowls of steaming cream of cabbage soup. Now, unless your personal habits are in need of becoming regular quick, cream of cabbage soup is to be avoided. The five of us looked at each other, with the exception of Walter who happily had begun to lap his soup. We stared at Walter. He continued to eat. We sighed. This could only be the harbinger of a long and fragrant ride home.

Next came some huge portions of pot roast and gravy, spooned over extra wide noodles. These were buddied with a tray of what appeared to be fried potato patties. The evening was eerily rekindling visions of church suppers gone bad.

After a bit, we took apologetic and surreptitious trips to the restroom. This was, in fact, a former broom closet that had been made to resemble a single use powder room. I locked the door after I sat down so that my knees wouldn't knock it open, since they literally touched the door. I returned and watched Perpetua's panic peak, as she mentally tallied up the tankards and trips to the loo. Clearly her profits were going down the drain.

However, the featured course of the evening finally arrived: a ground beef casserole partnered with mixed frozen vegetables and covered in a cheese sauce. All arrived in more vat-like containers with a single serving utensil plunked inside each casserole. Amos and Angie moved into the shadows, and waited. We all looked at each other, not quite sure of our hostess' serving intentions.

Armand commanded Amos, "You vill serve, yes?"

Amos stepped out of the darkness and stared at Perpetua.

"Actually," Perpetua piped, "we serve ourselves family style – Amish style!"

She beamed. Amos moved away. Armand glowered.

The rest of us shrugged our cumulative shoulders, the Amish beer having washed away any pretense toward any gourmet dining we had entertained earlier. We all sat with our steaming plates full of ground beef and cheese sauce and mason jars full of Krumpthf's. We toasted Perpetua and Groggin, and even included Amos and Angie.

"You know, I sometimes edit cookbooks for a living," Walter glubbed amiably. "This casserole is certainly interesting. What do you all call this?"

Angie stepped up from the shadows and barked, "YUMMUCK!" Mrs. Klink style.

"My," Walter said nicely, "I sure would like the recipe."

Angie looked through her pockets. "Here it iz," she answered, Mrs. Klink style again.

YUMMUCK! for 24 persons:
6 lb. ground beef
Dash salt and pepper
2 cups brown sugar
1 medium onion
6 cans cream of tomato soup
6 cans cream of chicken soup
Gherkins
12 packages flat noodles
8 packages processed 'American' cheese
Stale pretzels - smashed

Brown the ground beef with the salt and pepper and onion. Add the brown sugar at the end. Mix in the cream of tomato soup (undiluted). In a separate pot, combine the cooked noodles with the cream of chicken soup (undiluted). Layer the hamburger mixture into a greased casserole dish. Place a layer of the slices of cheese, top with sliced gherkins. Then layer the noodle mixture. Place another layer of the slices of cheese, with another layer of sliced gherkins. Repeat. Sprinkle a layer of smashed stale pretzel crumbs on top. Bake until done.

I read the recipe from over Walter's shoulder. I tasted some. I ended the recipe in my mind with a last instruction: Throw the whole mess out the window and order a pizza.

I prodded the mess about my plate with my fork. I wasn't sure I couldn't eat it, much less finish it. I didn't even like touching it.

Nancy from Nebraska leaned toward me. "My! Is this what authentic Amish food is like?"

I puzzled for a moment, looking to Ida for support and a politically correct phrase.

"It looks like food," said Ida.

"Next ve have ze dess-ssserrrt!" commanded Amos.

"Oh yes, oh yes!" applauded Perpetua.

The remaining plates, platters and pitchers were removed noisily and hastily onto the metal cart. Then Walter sneezed several thousand times in a row.

"Gezundheit! Gezundheit" shouted Amos and Angie.

"Dankeshune," sneezed Walter.

"Bitte!" cried Amos and Angie.

"Vielen danke," retorted Walter amidst continued sneezes.

"I think it's just wonderful how you people can communicate with the Amish," the anesthesiologist said.

"Are you all able to speak Amish?" asked Nancy from Nebraska naively amidst Walter's sneezing.

Ida looked at K. sweetly and said, "Er hat bin be-phlegmled by schnooks."

"Ja, ja, mit de all-around-de-hausen ach-too-ee machen," K. added, using the faux Amish the three of us came up with eons ago while up way too late and way too snookered. Remarkably we'd remembered some of our made-up language.

"My, what kind of dialect is that?" Nancy asked.

We replied in unison, "Phlegmish."

We waited while Amos and Angie removed the dirty cart and returned with the dessert. I watched sadly as Ida Rose bounced up and down in her seat with anticipation. Clearly, anything calling itself a dessert was alright with her.

The cart squeaked its sad return, covered with what cheerfully looked like raspberry pies. I sighed in relief. The pies were thunked on the table along with very worn pie servers, tubs of Whip-Whip cream, carafes of coffee and coffee mugs.

The cart retreated hastily in the distance. Armand jumped up to serve the pies.

"Pleeze," he growled at Perpetua.

"Well of course," she replied, sitting back down.

Armand thrust a pie server into a pie, and bore down. Then he bore down again. Finally, we heard a crack and realized he had made it through the crust. This was repeated several times, until pie and coffee had been passed around all of us.

I bit into my piece of pie and crunched and almost lost a molar. The crust was exceedingly hard and very salty. And what I hoped was raspberry curd was in reality some kind of Jell-O. Even Walter raised his eyebrows.

"This is very interesting, Perpetua. I don't think I've come across anything quite like this. What do you call it?" he asked politely.

"Pretzel Pie! An Amish favorite!" Perpetua and Groggin cried together.

My," Walter replied. Though he didn't ask for the recipe this time.

Didn't matter. Angie appeared from the shadows. "I have zees, too," she said, and laid another recipe card in front of Walter.

PRETZEL PIE
(1) large box of stale pretzels
Your favorite Jell-O flavor
Lard
1 tub of Whip-Whip cream

Basically, you smash the stale pretzels and blend with enough lard to form a pretzel crust in a pie shell pan. Then you top with Jell-O. You serve this, chilled (which explained why the crust was difficult to break through) and if you're feeling rakish, top with Whip-Whip cream.

We all pushed our pretzel pies about our plates. Except for Ida Rose, who chiseled herself a second piece and took the recipe card from Walter.

After many polite goodbyes and a skirmish at the door with Perpetua and the punk grand-daughter about appropriating a mason jar, we bid adieu. We made our way out into the still warm humid streets. I looked at Walter, now re-wilting in the August haze.

"Tell you what," I offered, "how about K. and I get the car and return here for the rest of you?"

After many thank-yous K. and I walked on, leaving our little group in the air-conditioned safety of the apartment building's lobby. K. put an arm across my shoulders.

"Thank you," he said.

"For what?" I asked.

"For putting up with my delusions of grandeur. You know, we would have been better off having our own party and cooking for ourselves. At least we wouldn't have had to eat that awful food, or have a three hour drive back home," he added.

"Well, it won't kill us," I offered, "but my shoes will. I think I have only two good toes left, and those are broken," I said, limping along the pavement. My stockings were mangled; they'd come apart at the ankles earlier. Now I walked the streets of New York City barefoot.

"I'll drive home, if you want... it's the least I can do," said K. as we got to Vito's car.

"Okay," I agreed. I was tired.

We got into the Towncar, buckled up, miraculously got out of the parking garage without more obstacles or passwords, and made our way back toward our little tribe. We pulled up into the no-parking zone just in front of the sidewalk to the lobby doors. K. beeped three times. We looked; Ida and Armand sheparded both sides of Walter.

K. smiled wanly. "So what do you think you're going to do next weekend?"

"Guess I'm going to finally get serious about painting the walls," I replied, and sighed.

After we successfully ballasted Walter back into Vito's Towncar, K. wove our way away from Bank Street, back toward the Henry Hudson, G.W., and points Pee-Ay-ward as we hit the Jersey turnpike. The NJ Turnpike soon morphed into the PA Turnpike, and I woke up while K. was yawning.

"Next rest stop?" I asked. K. nodded.

Next exit, K. pulled off, following a rest stop sign. After several mis-negotiated turns, choices of fast food and one-way lanes, we descended on our usual fast food chain, Buddy Burgers. K. pulled the Towncar into a parking space, shut it off, and then we glanced at each other in mutual exhaustion.

I looked behind us, at Walter and Armand and Ida snuffled softly in the backseat, like two kittens with their over-sized mastiff. Then they all jolted awake with a start. "Where are we?", "Are we home?" and "We're not still there are we?"

We tumbled out of the Towncar. "Right then, potty break," I said. Except for K., who snored like he could use a lot of beauty sleep.

Walter and Armand strolled into the men's room. Ida and I stood behind the fifty or so women lined up outside the entrance to the women's restroom. As usual, we crossed our legs and commiserated with all the women in line about the usual diss'ing of the fool architect who didn't realize that women can't share urinals, and we wished him an excruciating period just once in his lifetime, etc.

After feeling like we'd grown visibly older, Ida and I finally got our potty break turns.

We finished and found Walter and Armand waiting for us. They had already consumed two burgers and shakes apiece, while K. had woken up, taken his turn in the men's room and was happily munching on the various salad stuffs he'd ordered in his Buddy Basket. Ida and I shook our heads and shrugged.

"You want a soda?" I asked Ida.

She nodded. "I'll come with you. I need another dessert."

The boys said they'd wait for us in the lobby. Then they walked off to take turns at losing change at one of those fake arcade games – the kind that cons you into thinking you can pick up a stuffed toy you don't need with a mechanical arm-hook thingy that doesn't work. But K. was intent on winning Flopsy Bunny.

Ida and I stood in line and wove our way through the cattle maze that snaked its way around and eventually made its way up toward the Buddy Burger counter. The couple behind us bickered about what they were going to order. Mrs. Couple made a crack about Buddy Burger's plastic combination-hybrid utensils.

"Yes, be careful, they are very shc-aaararrrp," Mr. Couple replied.

The couple laughed. Ida and I turned around and gaped open-mouthed at them.

"YOU!" Ida pointed, now fully returned to Lady Macbeth mode. "You are NOT AMISH after all!"

"Shhhh!!!!"

"Hsss!!!" Ida responded.

I rubbed my neck. My feet barked.

As fate would have it, Mr. and Mrs. Couple were indeed the Amish Col. and Mrs. Klink who had served (or not served, according to Armand) us our Amish Affair. Except that now, instead of being clad in black wool, they were wearing his 'n' her cargo shorts. And Mrs. Couple wore a purple tube top, and sported a very large tattoo of an eagle with a fish in its talons that covered her entire left shoulder. Mr. Couple wore a worn black t-shirt, '$E=MC^2$' printed across the front in white letters.

I stared at them. "What the?" I asked to no one in particular.

"NEXT!" the sweaty, middle-aged, overworked man behind the counter yelled nicely at us all.

Ida was immediately jolted back into the current plane of time. "I'd like a cappuccino with 2 shots of extra flavoring, a Chocolate Fudge and Marshmallow Pie Pocket, a Cherry Pie Pocket, a large Berry-Berry shake, and an 'I Win! I Win!' energy bar," she instructed quickly.

The stout man behind the counter wiped his brow and looked at her. He shook his head. "You want a Buddy tooth brush with all that?" he asked nicely. Ida shook her head. "You?" he asked me.

"Medium cola and a small order of fries, extra ketchup," I said automatically – my usual travel mode fare.

Then, as Ida and I were about to interrogate Col. and Mrs. Klink, they were ordered to place their orders too. We waited. They ordered a cheeseburger, large salad, onion rings, fries, a strawberry shake and a coffee. Then the four of us were dismissed to trudge down the line toward collecting our food.

"You are NOT AMISH!" Ida hissed.

Mrs. Klink shrugged. "It's a job," she said simply.

"Look, we'll pay for your orders, okay? Just please don't rat us out to Perpetua and Groggin, okay?" $E=MC^2$ boy begged.

Ida and I considered quickly. I wished that I had ordered dinners for the rest of the week. Too bad I wasn't more opportunistic.

"That might be sufficient," Ida answered for us both. I stared at her. "Considering an explanation. And an additional order of

Buddy Burgers for Mina. She is, after all, without Gainful Employment," she said pointedly.

I patted Ida on the back. I was glad at least one of us was opportunistic.

"Gee, really? Tough gig, man," $E=MC^2$ guy answered.

He reversed gears and made nice with the overworked burger guy, and added a Buddy Beasty Burger to my order. I groaned inwardly. A Buddy Beasty Burger is basically a humungous combination of meat-type patties featuring various farmyard animals, topped with a generation or two of their offspring. I shuddered. I wish I'd ordered a Furry Friendly pizza they could pay for instead. Oh well. I could always give the Beasty Burger to Bauser. Maybe he'd trade me for something a bit further down the food chain.

We carried our trays to the check out line, where $E=MC^2$ guy paid for us all. Ida was exceedingly more pleasant to him then.

The non-Amish couple looked around and put their trays on a table, and Ida joined them. I looked around for the boys. Walter and K. and Armand were still vying over the arcade game. I shrugged and joined Ida and our non-Amish couple.

Ida was already emptying additional packets of sugar into her extra-corn-syruped cappuccino. I cringed. It made my teeth ache. But Ida looked happy. Clearly she must have felt as though she would not be allowed out on another dessert outing until half-past Christmas.

Mr. and Mrs. Not-Klink sipped their beverages and eyed us nervously. I eyed them back nervously. Ida gulped down her diabetic nightmare. Then, fully pumped, she began.

"So, why the subterfuge? Are you wanted by the Feds? Did you actually kill someone? WHERE'S THE BODY?"

Mr. and Mrs. Non-Klink and I shoved backward against our seats aghast. Where the heck did Ida come up with this stuff?

"First, let's get this straight," Mr. Non-Klink said. "I have not, nor have I ever – or plan to – killed anyone or hidden their body," he said.

Mrs. Klink snorted. "Are you kidding me? It was murder to get him to stop here at a burger joint. My brother's completely vegan," Mrs. Klink said. "We're twins," she added.

Twins? Oh. Well. That would explain their appearing related. Especially since they were not Amish.

"I'm still not sure about consuming the shake," Mr. Klink said nervously.

"Oh, puh-leese, it's like completely soy," Mrs. Klink said, adding, "And where the hell can a girl find a place to smoke around here?"

Ida diplomatically introduced Mrs. Klink – Dody – to Armand, who was immediately sympathetic. As well as serviceable. He and Dody made their way to the parking lot to smoke. Mr. Klink, whose real name was Jody, filled me in.

"Look, I'm not proud of this, but at least it's a gig, man," he said, retro hippy-style.

I nodded. "That's cool," I said, retro hippy back. "But what the?"

Jody nodded understandably. "Look, I used to be the manager of the music department at a Buy-A-Lots," he said. "Anyway, after a bunch of the fires took place, and a few micro-managing binges from my boss, I got laid off."

"Sorry," I replied sympathetically.

"Anyway, since a lot of the Mom & Pop shops have shut down, it wasn't an exactly ideal job hunting environment, if you want to be in retail music," he said. "So I started trolling the internet. And then I came on a site that was asking for 'convincingly authentic' Amish servers." I raised my eyebrows. He nodded his head. "Hey, man, do the math. And it's not like they were asking for real Amish servers; just 'convincingly authentic' ones! I'm telling you, Dody and I showed up to our first New York City cattle call and aced it. And besides," he added, "we're pulling down a full week's pay for just three nights work."

Okay, it was all as clear as mud to me now. But I had to ask.

"So, as an ex-Buy-A-Lots employee, what's your take on the burning Buy-A-Lots?" I asked.

"Are you kidding me?" Jody said. "Who wouldn't want to burn a Buy-A-Lot?"

After some more pleasantries we strolled out, collecting the rest of our crew. K. and Walter were in the midst of arguing about who properly owned the newly possessed and coveted Flopsy Bunny, which ended with Walter sighing and relinquishing Flopsy

Bunny to K. in exchange for a package of ancient HoHos from the vending machine. Then we met Dody and Armand outside, who were comparing notes about clove-scented and party-colored cigarettes. Dody and Jody chatted with Ida about a downtown Lancaster coffee shop that would make surreptitious deliveries of Extra Mocha Syrupy Lattés for a small surcharge and a large tip, as well as where to get the really best Amish Food.

"Schwenks," they told us, nodding in unison.

"You're welcome," we replied.

We said goodbye, exchanged phone numbers with Dody and Jody (they were convinced they could help me find gainful employment) and re-loaded Walter and the rest of us back into the car. K. insisted on continuing the drive home. I ended up snoring and drooling in the takeout bags in the passenger's seat.

A couple of lifetimes later, we pulled off the exit ramp to Oregon Pike, and took it south, past Armand's McMansion complex and headed downtown toward Walter's high rise apartment complex. Armand pulled, we pushed, and after we hoisted Walter onto the freight elevator, we deposited him safely back home.

We doubled back and left Armand in front of his house; it was too late for any foyer visiting now. Then we headed back across town, and pulled up to Aunt Gladys' mansion. Ida Rose's eyes glowed wildly in the backseat, lit by high fructose corn syrup and manic levels of caffeine. She rolled up her pit-stop bounty back into its bag and thrust it at me in the front seat. I took it and nodded.

"And don't forget," she hissed. "I'm going to need this tomorrow! I might actually go into withdrawal!" she stage whispered.

I nodded and again agreed to make some kind of a plan to get her sweets back to her sometime, and we pulled out of the drive once more, under Aunt Gladys' radar. K. made a right and then a left onto State Street, and pulled up in front of his house. He yawned and undid his seatbelt. I copied him and slid out from my passenger's side seat, stretched, and hopped back into the driver's seat.

"Good night, sweetie. Call you tomorrow," K. whispered. I yawned and hugged him.

I headed back toward Columbia Avenue and my half of the townhouse on Clover Nook Lane.

I pulled up the driveway, turned off the Towncar's headlights and shut the motor off. I went inside and found the TV on and Vinnie stretched out on the sofa sleeping, sans Vito. Or Muriel. Or anyone else. I mentally genuflected.

I wandered into the kitchen and found a note from Vito telling me to listen to my answering machine, and to help myself to a plate of leftover pierogies and ham steak in the fridge. After tonight's culinary adventure, these leftovers seemed practically exotic.

I put the plate in the microwave, poured myself a Mug o'Merlot, deeply grateful it did not contain twigs, leaves or other organic matter, and sipped. I put the mug on the counter, then carefully walked upstairs on my shredded feet. I walked into the bathroom, tore off the remaining shreds of my pantyhose, and pulled on a clean pair of jammies. I hobbled over to the answering machine, saw the flashing light, and hit PLAY.

"Mina, dear, it's Auntie," Aunt Muriel's voice announced. My eye twitched. "I'm very sorry to bother you, dear, but it's kind of an emergency. Would you please call me as soon as you get in?"

The message ended. I looked at my alarm clock; it read 12:28. I sighed. I picked up the phone and dialed Auntie.

"Hrmph?" she answered.

"Sorry, Auntie. It's Mina. Just got in," I explained.

"Oh, thank you, dear!" she said.

"What's up?" I asked.

"Well, you're not going to believe this, but just about every member of the Coffee Committee called in ill for tomorrow!"

"OK."

"Well, it's Fourth Sunday!"

"Huh?"

"Fourth Sunday. St. Bart's always has an especially nice coffee hour after the service. And Squirrel Run Acres always gives us very nice complimentary brunch trays."

I figured Squirrel Run Acres – a local wedding factory – found a smart way to unload its end of the month leftovers for a tax break.

"Uh huh," I replied.

"Well, the problem is, so many people on the Coffee Committee called in ill at the last minute that no one is available to pick up the trays from Squirrel Run Acres," she said.

I yawned. "Okay, so you want me to pick up deli trays from Squirrel Run Acres in the morning for you?"

"Actually, brunch platters. If you don't mind, dear; it would be such a help. I just can't set up for the coffee hour and pick up the donated platters without missing the church service."

I agreed, got the particulars and arranged the pick-up and delivery of Squirrel Run Acre's leftover donations for early in the morning. So much for a leisurely Sunday. Oh well. From the looks of the unemployment ratings, I'd probably have my fill of leisurely Sunday mornings before the year was out.

Vinnie followed me upstairs, and was rolling around on his back on top of the bed, begging for belly rubs. "Jelly cat," I said, rubbing his belly.

Marie yodeled from her bedroom.

"I didn't forget you," I shouted.

I petted Vinnie's noggin adieu, and opened the door to Marie's room.

I jumped. There in Marie's room, quietly watching the end of 'Top Hat', was Annie McKay.

CHAPTER 17

(Saturday night into Sunday)

"Hi, I hope I didn't scare you," Annie started, getting out of her chair and accidentally kicking a Buddy Burger bag full of empty wrappers across the floor. Marie screamed. I looked over and saw a piece of Buddy Burger bun shoved next to her seed cup. Well, that was nice. At least Annie broke bread after breaking and entering.

"How'd you get in here?" I asked incredulously.

Annie shrugged. "Skills of the trade," she said ambiguously. "I mean ex-trade. I quit." She sniffed, and blew her nose into a Buddy Burger napkin.

"Oh jeez, in this economy? Are you nuts?"

Vinnie trilled next to me, and concurred by shaking his head up and down inside of the Buddy Burger bag. Marie shrieked and threw fluff up in the air. It looked like New Year's Eve in Times Square but with cockatiel dandruff instead of ticker tape confetti. Yick.

I picked Vinnie up and scooted him out of Marie's room, his head still inside the bag.

"Hey, c'mon downstairs. I really can't let Vinnie hang out in Marie's room," I said, blowing a path through the fluffed air in front of me.

"Agreed," Annie said, swatting the fluff in front of her face.

We left Marie's room, and trotted downstairs, Vinnie leading the way. We walked into the kitchen.

"You want something? Soft drink? Coffee? Wine? Juice? Seltzer? Water?" I asked. I wasn't sure of the appropriate protocol of offering hospitality to someone who had just entered your home without permission, except for maybe Vito.

Annie held out her half-full gallon cup of Buddy Burger Birch Beer. “Thanks; I'm just about floating away already,” she said.

I picked up my Mug o'Merlot from the counter, and gestured for Annie to sit down. She sat at the dining room table.

“I was thinking of quitting, anyway,” she began. “The field work just makes me feel dishonest and sneaky. And the desk work leaves me completely bored.”

I nodded with complete understanding. “Sometimes jobs can be just like jobs,” I said.

“I've actually been thinking about this for a long time, and I'm going back to school,” she said.

“Really? But I thought you had a college degree?” I asked. I didn't know a lot about U.S. Marshals, but it would seem kind of odd if having some kind of degree in criminology wouldn't be a prerequisite.

“I do,” Annie nodded. “I was also the top of my class when I was in Basic Training as a GS-0082 Deputy. That's seventeen and a half weeks of basic training – otherwise known as Dante's Other Ring.”

“Wow, that's impressive,” I said. “So are you going to go into some kind of social work?”

“In a way. I'm going to become a veterinarian. I got an offer to start as an assistant vet tech from a great shelter in Utah.” I looked at her. “You have no idea how distressed I was about letting your Vinnie out accidentally,” she said. “Which wouldn't have happened at all, if I hadn't been spying on Vito,” she added.

I shrugged. “Yeah, but if it hadn't been you, it would have been someone else. And the someone else probably wouldn't have gone to the extra lengths you did to make sure Vinnie got home safe,” I said.

Annie sighed. “That's what Mike said. He doesn't like my emotional involvement with my cases. Anyway, I sent a resignation email to him while he was doing field work today. It's timed to be delivered tomorrow morning – this morning – about 7 a.m..”

“Isn't that kind of sneaky?”

She shrugged. "Comes with the territory, I guess. I'm supposed to be on assignment until midnight tonight watching you and Vito, anyway. Besides, if I gave it to Mike in person, he would just talk me out of it again. It's a pretty big decision. Once you're out, you're out. And it's a big training loss for them."

"Again?"

Annie sighed. "I really haven't been very happy in my work," she replied.

"So, umm.... thanks for visiting. But don't you think you could have called?" I asked. Annie shook her head.

"Your phone's tapped," she answered simply.

"MY PHONE IS WHAAAT?"

Annie shrugged. "It's done all the time really; no biggie," she said.

I hung my head. I wondered how many CIA or FBI or whatever technicians were chuckling at the mini-melodramas of my life. Yikes.

"It's not like they listen to every word," Annie assured me. "There's software that monitors for buzz words, and if any of them are picked up, then a real human person listens to the entire conversation," she answered, as if reading my mind.

I sighed.

"So, how come the visit then? Just to let us know you've quit?" I asked. Annie nodded.

"I felt it was important to let you know I'm not 'official' anymore," she said. "At least, in the next month or so I won't be. I probably will have to go through some kind of debriefing period," she mused. "But before I'm officially re-sworn to secrecy, I wanted to advise you – and Vito – to quit the prescription sample gig. You really are nice people, even if you are a bunch of screwballs."

I smiled. "Thanks." Wow. I guess I was fitting into Lancaster, after all.

"Besides, I don't think I could handle putting a gang of senior citizens in the pokey," she said.

I nodded. "As far as I know, Vito's on it," I assured her.

"Good," she said, "because there will be some new attendees at St. Bart's services tomorrow, if you know what I mean."

I gulped. "Yikes! What do we do?"

"Nothing. Except make sure everyone's there and no one's out on deliveries. Especially at Madam Phang's," Annie said.

"Madam Phang's gonna get busted?" I yelped.

Annie shook her head. "Nope. Just sort of visited while nobody else is there," she said, sipping through her Buddy Burger Birch Beer straw. Annie looked at her watch. "Okay, this is way past my bedtime. And you have to pick up the brunch platters and be at St. Bart's by 9:00 a.m.."

She got up, walked toward the door, and opened it. Then she turned back.

"Remember, your phone conversations are, umm... not exactly your own. So I wouldn't make any phone calls tonight, if I were you," she said.

I smacked myself on my virtual forehead, erased all thoughts of calling Auntie and getting her moving on her church's phone chain, and waved goodbye to Annie from the front porch.

Annie drove off at about 1 a.m. I plodded over the driveway and rang Vito's doorbell. There came the sound of Stanley yapping, then Vito's footsteps shuffling down the stairs. The porch light came on.

Vito stood, rubbing his eyes, with Stanly snarling and hanging on his PJ cuffs. "Whatsa matter, Toots?" he yawned. "You need an emergency Swiffering?" he asked matter-of-factly.

"In a way," I said, swatting at the moths collecting around Vito's porch light. "Can I come in?"

"Sure, sure, sure, Toots," he said, dragging Stanley inside and opening the door for me.

I looked around. This was the first time I had been in Vito's house. It was pretty much nondescript, and pretty much what I expected. Contractor painted antique white walls and ceilings, with wall to wall beige carpeting. A decent quality but oversized brown leather lounger in the living room. There was also a glass coffee table that was supported by a statue of a large resin polar bear posed coyly on his back. And the kitchen floor really was an orange and olive green plaid. Yikes.

We chose not to talk in Vito's kitchen.

I sat down on the edge of the leather chair, careful not to stare directly into the baby polar bear's eyes.

"Cute, huh?" Vito grinned. "It was one of the few things the Feds let me bring with me from my old life," he said. "Marie loved that table," he added mistily.

I lied and made a happy face and nodded. Vito looked down at my feet.

"Hey, what did you do? Walk home from New York?"

I shook my head and handed Vito back his car keys, promising to give him the details during a normal wakey time. Then I filled Vito in about Annie and the upcoming Sunday surveillance scenario. That woke him up, and quickly.

He nodded. "This is serious."

Stanley snarled from Vito's tattered PJ cuff. "Dość!" Vito commanded. Stanley let go immediately, and hopped onto the arm of my chair, next to me, nose height. I got up.

"I'll take care of this, Toots; don't you worry," Vito assured me. "You just act like business as usual."

I agreed, left Vito's and walked back across to my side of our homes. I had my hand on the front door knob to my house when I heard Vito's garage door open, and saw his car backing out quickly and quietly before heading down the street. I locked my front door and thunked my head against it.

I was about to head upstairs when the phone rang. My eyes rolled ceilingward of their own volition while I answered.

"Sorry, dear," said Auntie. "I thought you might still be awake. I just wanted to make sure you wore something appropriate for coffee hour tomorrow."

"Appropriate for delivering leftovers?" I asked.

"And for serving, of course, dear," Auntie answered.

Oh. I hadn't figured Auntie had volunteered me as a coffee hour server too, but I should have.

"Okey dokey," I said. I did a mental shrug. I was going to be there anyway, right?

I hung up, refilled my mug and went upstairs. I made sure Marie got tucked in properly. Vinnie chattered away at me about how happy he was I was keeping his hours now that I was unemployed, and how much better the daytime really is for sleeping. I washed my face, and filled the tub with cool water. I sat on the edge of the tub, soaked my mutilated tootsies and sipped my wine, convincing myself that tomorrow was a new day. Then I fell into bed.

Sunday morning I woke up to the alarm radio blaring 'Manic Monday' and sat bolt upright, petrified I'd slept through the church brunch thingy. I bolted upright smack into Vito, a mug of coffee and Vinnie all at the same time. Luckily the floor caught the brunt of the coffee.

Vinnie and Vito shook themselves off. I stared at them.

"Jeez, Toots, it's like you have post dramatic tress disorder," Vito said, wiping at the graffiti-like splotches of coffee across his once white shirt.

I thought about my bad perms of days gone past. Vito could be right.

Vinnie trilled in agreement and wiped his paw on his forehead to clean off the splatters of coffee he received. His eyes brightened and got bigger. Mental note to self: cats get decaf.

I looked at the clock: it was six-thirty. I drummed my fists and feet on the bed. I glared at Vito.

"I had my alarm set for SEVEN-THIRTY!"

"That's what I figured," Vito said, holding up an apologetic hand, "that's why I'm here. I kinda overheard you." I looked at Vito. He handed me what was left of my coffee. "Here, drink this. Squirrel Run Acres is out in the country like." I gulped at the coffee, and frowned at Vito. "You don't think you can just goes in there and pick up brunch platters and all, without a little chit-chat, right?" he asked. I looked at him. "Look, if it was a normal pickup, that was paid for, you probably could. But this here's a donation," he explained. "You can't just kinda eat and run, if you know what I mean. You gotta be complimentary about it.

I hung my head. "Got it. Right. Sorry," I mumbled.

"Hey, why don't you get yourself moving, and I'll take care of Vinnie and Marie?" he asked. I looked at him. "Feed and clean them. Sheesh. You been watching too much TV." And he sauntered out.

Vinnie shook a back leg at me in agreement while hopping off the bed to follow Vito.

"Traitor," I muttered.

Vinnie called something back to me about slaggards and absentee breakfasts when he was absolutely famished. Well.

I got up and found my feet were not very happy about starting the day either. I looked at them and surveyed the damage. Ugh. I heard Vito rummaging around in the kitchen and promised myself again to change the locks on my doors.

I showered and dressed quickly, opting for my white shirt from last night, black pants and a pair of extremely worn but comfortable black Crocs. I had to; they were the only shoes that wouldn't re-gnaw my feet. Not exactly a fashion statement, but I was only serving at church, not going out on a date, right?

What my outfit lacked in fancy, it made up for in quick. I went downstairs and found Vinnie and Vito curled up on the sofa reading the newspaper. Vito sported a non-coffee streaked pink Oxford shirt.

"Well, what do you think about that?" Vito asked Vinnie. Vinnie nodded back and continued reading.

"What's up?" I asked.

Vito looked up. "You gotta read this article," he said. "You won't believe it. It turns out that it wasn't just your old boss behind the burning Bent-A-Lots."

"Really?" I asked.

"Yeah. Did you know some guy named Myron?" Vito asked.

"Yip."

"Turns out, he did some sneaky computer stuff to steal information about Buy-A-Lots, through some hack outfit in Bangladesh." Huh. So Norman was right. "Anyhows, he was selling the information, for a profit, to a big competitor of Buy-A-Lots; Världen Vänder."

"Världen Vänder?" I asked.

"They're in Sweden," he said.

"Why would a Swedish company want that kind of information?" I asked.

"Competition," Vito said. "I remember reading a couple months ago about how they beat Buy-A-Lots out of a bid for a store front in the Pretzel Nuggets Mall."

I remembered. Wow. Vito was right.

Världen Vänder was the oddish bulk grocery store that made you 'rent' your shopping cart for a quarter. You could only get a shopping cart if you put a quarter into the slot to release the lock to the next cart. You got your quarter back when you put your cart back. And they don't provide grocery bags – just packing boxes. Odd. But they do sell a very nice brand of lingonberries.

Vito stood looking out the living room window and waved.

"Hey, Toots, I gotta go."

I peered past him. At the bottom of Mt. Driveway was a yellow Cougar, Miriam seated behind the wheel. She wore a Doris Day kind of sheer headscarf with Elton John type sunglasses, and was waving paddy fingers at Vito.

"I got a bunch of, ummm... errands... I gotta run before me and Miriam meet you at church," he explained.

"Church?" I asked. "I thought you're Jewish?"

Vito shrugged. "Miriam and me talked it over. We figure it's okay, since we're not too kosher," he answered, and patted Vinnie on his noggin and hustled out the door.

I shrugged, gulped the last of my coffee, grabbed Vito's keys and my pocketbook, and headed out to Squirrel Run Acres.

I made the right onto Running Pump and drove through the residential section that leads to the mini-commercial warehouse buildings. I slowed down at the speed trap, and saw that a police car had pulled over another victim ahead of me. It had pulled over a black SUV and an irate driver who was wearing a white cotton jacket and banging his head on his steering wheel, while the officer smiled and wrote out a speeding ticket. Where the heck would anyone be speeding to at seven-thirty on a Sunday morning?

I shrugged and continued and eventually pulled into the parking lot for Squirrel Run Acres. The small employee parking lot was packed. Luckily, the space closest to the kitchen door was empty. I sighed with relief; I wouldn't have to double-park Vito's car to load the brunch trays.

I walked up the back steps and peered in through a screen door. A guy wearing black pants, a white shirt and an apron bounded out past me with a cigarette in his mouth. He lit it in the parking lot. He looked at me and nodded.

"Go ahead," he puffed, pointing his head toward the screen door.

"Uh, thanks," I said brightly.

I guessed I was supposed to go in and sort of help myself. I walked into a small back room, where a couple of stressed bleach-blondes were ripping lettuce with a vengeance onto individual salad plates. They looked at me.

"Finally," one of them said.

"About time," said the other, ripping another leaf.

I looked blankly at them.

"Well, go on," said the first one.

I shrugged and entered the kitchen.

I've never seen the inside of an ant colony, but I imagine a commercial kitchen provides a pretty accurate likeness of one. There were dozens of workers crisscrossing each other, carrying plates and bowls and supplies, pushing carts, carrying trays and dumping leftovers into large trash bins. Others were mixing, frying, washing and sautéing. No one stood still. Everyone sweated.

I looked around, and found some large take-out platters on a stainless steel trolley with 'St. Bart's' emblazoned in large black capital letters on them. There were eight of them. Yikes. Clearly, I'd be making several trips.

I heard the screen door slam, followed by shouting.

A nerdy kid with red hair and freckles and streaky eyeglasses thrust a large white plastic bottle labeled 'Ranch Dressing' at me. "Here, look busy!" he whispered.

"What?" I asked.

"You do not want to irritate Chef Jacques!" he instructed.

"Oh," I said smartly back and stood there, holding the half gallon of salad dressing.

"Fill the pitchers!" he hissed, and pointed me toward a rolling cart with about a couple dozen small empty creamers.

"These?"

He rolled his eyes and nodded and zipped past me on his mission. I shrugged and started dolloping dressing.

I heard more screaming and more banging as a tall, dark, handsome and irate chef strode into the kitchen. He had curly black hair, dark blue eyes and the vein on his neck throbbed handsomely beneath his scarlet skin. It was Sir Speedy – the driver I saw pulled over at the speed trap on Running Pump Road. He was waving his hands in the air and screaming, "Where's my filet? Where's the turkey?"

One of the two salad girls came running in after him. "We put them in the walk-in last night, like you asked us to," she said, rolling her eyes.

"The freezer?" he cried.

The manager rolled her eyes again. "The refrigerator," she answered.

"Oh, sorry," he said. She shrugged. He leaned on the stainless steel counter and muttered. "Great. I'm late. Get pulled over at the stupid speed trap on the stupid shortcut. And someone parked in my stupid parking spot," he mumbled.

The manager stared pointedly at me. Chef looked at me. "What are you doing?" he asked.

"Dressing?" I answered.

He shook his head. "We don't need that now."

He had incredibly deep blue eyes. In fact, he looked pretty handsome, when he wasn't acting all pre-seizure like.

"Can you prep celery?" he asked, folding his arms and looking down at me. I looked up. This was a nice change. Chef was easily well over six feet tall.

"Sure," I said.

He nodded. "Good. This way."

He directed and had me follow him to the back of the kitchen, over to a large stainless steel counter that fed into an industrial size steel kitchen sink.

"Here," he said, plopping a bunch of celery on the counter in front of me and walking away.

I shrugged, rolled up my sleeves, picked out a knife and set out to help. I guessed Vito was right. Instead of exchanging pleasantries, it seemed Squirrel Run Acres preferred to exchange services. It was a good thing I had some time to spare before getting to St. Bart's. Well, you know what they say. There's no such thing as a free brunch.

I just finished and dried the celery and set it to one side, and started to walk over to get the donated brunch trays. "Not so fast," the manager advised me. She looked over at my cleaned and cut celery. "Not bad. But you're going to have to work a lot faster or you'll be here until Thanksgiving."

"Huh?"

"Here," she huffed, pushing a large tub that held about fifty bunches of celery.

"Are you kidding?" I asked.

"No, I'm not!" she said and walked off, shaking her head and muttering.

The nerdy red-haired kid came up to me. "You don't want to irritate our manager, either," he whispered, and started throwing bunches of celery into the sink to get washed.

"I wasn't trying to," I answered.

He shrugged. "It's okay. My first day was pretty bad, too," he said.

"First day?" I asked.

"Sure," he said, throwing more celery in the sink for me and walking away with the tub full of celery leaf crumbs and dirt.

I shrugged and turned the faucet on. A few minutes later, the manager came up behind me and tapped me on the shoulder. I turned around. Her face was beet red.

"I just picked up a voicemail from SNAP Employment," she began. "They said the temp kitchen worker they assigned us for today called in sick. So who are you?" she asked.

"I'm Mina," I answered, washing.

"What are you doing here?" she asked, hands on hips.

"I came to pick up the brunch trays for St. Bart's."

The manager clapped her hand to her forehead. "Harry!" she shouted. The nerdy red-haired kid appeared. "Finish up here," she instructed, and led me away.

We walked over to the trolley with St. Bart's brunch. The manager started rolling the trolley toward the kitchen exit. "Ira! Rich!" she hollered. A very old man in kitchen scrubs and a thirty-something guy wearing a white t-shirt and a full-arm tattoo appeared. "Load these up in this young lady's car," she said.

They both nodded, and Rich pushed the trolley out as Ira followed behind. Chef looked up from a large cast iron skillet that held a couple of sticks of melting butter.

"What's going on?" he asked the manager.

"This is Mina. She came to pick up the donations for St. Bart's. She's not our SNAP temp," she answered.

Chef's eyebrows flew to the top of his head and his jaw dropped. I smiled stupidly back at him.

"Bye!!" I said, and wiggled my fingers at Chef and skipped out the door.

I drove to St. Bart's with Vito's car full of brunch trays and my head full of questions. My first foray into a commercial kitchen wasn't so bad. Especially considering my mistaken identity and all. And now that I knew how short-handed they were, maybe I could get a job? It wouldn't be exactly unpleasant working with Chef Jacques, either. That thought made me feel tingly where I hadn't felt tingly for a long time. I blushed.

I pulled off of Mulberry and into the parking lot of St. Bart's. I walked into Fellowship Hall and found Aunt Muriel fussing with setting up coffee and tea and juice dispensers. Plates and napkins and utensils lay all lined up on another big table, with a vast empty space where the brunch platters were supposed to be.

"Mina!" Aunt Muriel and Ma screamed happily. "Where are the trays?"

I told them, and in a few minutes a couple of teenagers were roped into unloading Vito's car.

"We'll have to hurry; the service will be out soon," Aunt Muriel said, checking her diamond-crusted wristwatch against the first chorus of the recessional hymn floating over from the sanctuary.

"What kept you?" Ma asked, unwrapping platters.

"Oh, they needed a little extra help," I said.

Auntie shook her head. "If I'd known that, I would have sent you there a lot earlier," she stated. I sighed.

Ma looked at me. "You look tense," she said.

"Do you want another massage?" Auntie asked.

"Maybe..." I answered, shifting gears between tall, dark and angry to blonde, muscular and chilled.

"Mina?" she asked, waking me back to reality.

"Did Massage Man ever tell you he used to be an investment broker?" I asked.

Auntie nodded. "And after all poor James went through to get the massage training to help his girlfriend," she added.

I sighed again. "She's pretty lucky," I said.

"Well, I don't know about that, but I guess she's happier," Auntie said.

"It sure can't hurt to have a boyfriend who's a masseuse."

"Oh for heaven's sake, she certainly does not have a boyfriend. She dumped poor James for another lingerie model."

"You mean a girl?"

"Do you know any men who model lace panties?"

I didn't and hoped I never would. Ticker tape thoughts ran across my mind. James not gay. James single. James attractive. Huh. I looked at Auntie.

"And, he's very, very nice," she added.

"And so is his portfolio?" I asked.

Auntie shrugged. "There's nothing wrong with a good investment," she answered.

A tag-line Amen at the end of the hymn, a benediction and the good-natured stampling of feet across the courtyard arrived, and Fellowship Hall was full of hungry Episcopalians. And Evelyn.

"Why, this is marvelous," Evelyn congratulated Auntie, waving both eyebrows.

Auntie gazed at her. "Thank you, Evelyn. So glad you recovered," she said evenly.

Evelyn held up a manicured right hand wrapped in mummy-like gauze bandages. "Yes, I'm so sorry I couldn't be of any help to you."

"You could pour the juice." Evelyn started to open her mouth to protest, but Auntie finished, "I know you're a south paw."

And that was how Evelyn was roped into pouring.

I was about to leave when I ran into Ed. Who'd shaved his head.

"So what do you think?" he asked, eyes akimbo.

I looked around and saw I was the only one within conversational range, so I figured he was talking to me.

"Very urban," I said, and hoped it sounded like something he wanted to hear.

Ed nodded enthusiastically. He chirped the mayor's downtown slogan at me: "Lovin' Lancaster! Lucky for me my hair burned off, or I wouldn't be the fashion statement you see before you!"

Burnt hair?

"Hey, quit stealing my girl," eyebrowless Ernie joked, joining us.

Henry came up from behind. "So who's going to seed the kitty?" he asked. I know it sounds dirty, but he meant who would throw some dollar bills into the donation basket to encourage real donations for the coffee.

After a mini-version of 'Once! Twice! Three! SHOOT! between Ernie and Ed, Ernie ponied up $1.58 and a cough drop. I shook my head, patted backs and went for a stiff cup of Joe.

I was behind Henry in line. He turned around. His nose was bandaged. He looked like Scarecrow from the Wizard of Oz. I stared at him. I didn't mean to, but I did. I mean, it was as plain as the nose on his face.

"Accident!" he said, nodding enthusiastically.

"Sorry," I replied.

Henry nodded up and down some more in agreement. He got his coffee, and I dawdled behind, trying to leave a good, large space between us. This was getting weird.

I got my coffee, turned around, and bumped right into Mrs. Miller's walker.

"Watch it!" she snapped kindly.

Her wrist was bandaged. Huh.

Then I backed up into a man with a sliding toupee and a Band-Aid on his forehead. I apologized, extricated myself and stood in line at the brunch buffet while contemplating running vs. walking away. I looked and saw a lone remaining profiterole. I sighed gratefully, took a napkin and reached for it when a wheelchair rolled over my foot.

"OUCH!"

"Sorry," the wheelchair driver said.

"Really is crowded here today, isn't it?" I tried politely, rubbing my dead foot.

The wheelchair maven peered around. "Yes. This church could use a few good funerals," she said, grabbing the profiterole with her gauze bandaged hand, and rolled away.

I looked at the buffet table, and quickly slid a donut and some grapes on my plate. I exited the line and took a seat at an empty round dining table. I sipped my coffee and looked around. The line of seniors waiting at the brunch buffet looked like the parade of the walking wounded. A bunch of kids ran around, their moms chasing after them. Some teenage boys conspired in a corner. Near them sat Mike Green and four other suits. Gack.

I turned around quick. I pretended to sip my coffee, thankful I was on church grounds so my prayer about not putting my family or friends in jail hopefully went on the express lane. I looked straight ahead, keeping my eyes averted from the U.S. Marshal table, and saw Ma and Mu and Tina Phang in a huddle in the kitchen. Oh boy.

Just then, Vito and Miriam ambled over and sat down next to me.

"Hiya, Toots," Vito said.

"Good morning!" Miriam added, bobbing her head up and down excitedly. Her plastic red and yellow polka dot drop earrings swung wildly with her head. Which was okay, because they matched her red and yellow polka dot sundress, red and yellow polka dot head band, and an equally matching polka dot neck scarf and sandals. It was impressive.

Miriam sipped her coffee, and tucked into her slice of seven-layer chocolate cake. Vito speared a piece of his cantaloupe.

"Good morning," I said, shifting my eyeballs repeatedly to the right, toward Mike Green's table.

"Whatsa matter, Toots, you gotta somethin' in your eye?" Vito asked.

I sighed. "Not exactly," I replied, leadingly.

"Huh?" Vito asked.

I rolled my eyes and threw my napkin on the ground. Vito shrugged and bent over to pick it up. I bent over quick and grabbed the napkin with him.

"Green's here," I hissed, doubled over, shifting my eyes to the right again.

Vito sat up and handed me my napkin. "Yeah, I know," he said and shrugged, and ate some more cantaloupe. I shook my head.

Just then, Trixie and K. joined us.

"Morning!" K. gushed, looking around at us all, then waved to Mike Green. I sighed and looked over. Mike Green nodded from behind his sunglasses. The others suits copied. Yeesh.

"Well, isn't this nice!" K. went on.

I looked at him. "Since when do you go to church?" I asked.

"Oh, I just thought it would be a nice change," K. lied, and bit into his apple turnover.

Trixie leaned in. “Since your Aunt Muriel gave us all marching orders last night,” she whispered. K. choked.

“How did Aunt Muriel get you to come to church?” I asked.

“She traded invitations to the Conestoga Cabana Cup,” Trixie said, smiling.

K. nodded. “I understand there's quite a diverse crowd,” he beamed.

“Yeah, with uniforms,” Trixie sighed.

Well, their social lives were looking up.

Just then, Mike Green sat down at the table with us, along with a Junior suit. He took off his sunglasses, and looked directly at Vito.

“Good morning, Vito,” Green said.

“Vlad,” Vito answered.

Green blanched. “I'm sorry, I think...” Green began.

“My name is Vladimir Pryzchntchynzski,” Vito said.

“Gezundheit,” a man at the table next to us answered. Vito nodded thanks.

“Otherwise known as, here in Lancaster, Vito Spaghetti,” Vito – Vlad – finished.

Mike Green hung his head. “You know what this means, right?” he asked.

Vito nodded. “It's time I come out, Mike,” Vito answered.

“Oh, you go, girlfriend!” K. cried. We all stared at K. “Well, coming out of the closet needs support!” K. said.

“Wrong closet,” Vito answered.

K. looked at Mike hopefully.

“Sorry, no closet,” Mike said.

“Oh well.” K. shrugged and finished his apple turnover.

“Really?” Trixie asked, looking all hopeful at Mike.

“Really,” Mike answered, looking back at her just as hopefully.

I rubbed my neck, because I couldn’t rub the pain in my butt.

“So, where do we go from here, Mike?” Vito asked.

“Dunno,” Mike answered truthfully.

Trixie pushed her untouched slice of lemon meringue pie at him. “Here, you'll feel better. Really; Mina always says so,” Trixie said. I kicked her under the table. She kicked me back.

“Thanks,” Mike Green answered simply, and had some pie.

After chewing for what seemed a millennium, Mike turned to Vito. Vlad. Whoever.

"This means you're not in the Witness Protection Program anymore," he said. "It's out of my hands."

Vito nodded. "No problemo."

Mike Green sighed. "It was nice knowing you, Vito. Vlad."

"Same here," Vito answered.

"Shame about your niece's boyfriend and all," Green added.

"Fiancé."

"Really?" Vito nodded. "Well, I wish them both luck once he's out," Green said.

"They've got good heads on their shoulders, mostly," Vito said.

Green nodded. "They're pretty much just kids. Hopefully this was just a good scare to set them straight."

"What's wrong with not being straight?" K. asked.

I looked up and perceived Jr. Suit standing up straighter with what appeared to be righteous indignation. This was going to be a bit of a change for Green. Then I looked down and saw Trixie's hand on Green's knee. Green was going to be in for a lot of changes, too. Costume changes, that is.

"Well, gotta be going," Green said, extracting his knee from Trixie's clutches.

"What about the Burning Buy-A-Lots?" Trixie pouted, upset at the abrupt departure.

Mike shrugged. "Who doesn't want to burn a Buy-A-Lot?" he asked. We all nodded. Mike looked at Vito. "By the way, I thought you were Jewish?"

"We're converting!" Miriam piped up, standing up at Green in full polka-dots and non-moonbeams.

Green rubbed his forehead. "Let me see here. I just want to make sure I've got this straight, okay?"

"I wish there was a lot less emphasis on straight," K. muttered. Jr. Suit sniffed.

"Okay, Vito – Vlad – is out of the closet; no more witness protection policies," Green said. Vito nodded. "Next, no one here in this room has anything to do with any of the burning Buy-A-Lots, right?"

"Agreed!" sang the chorus of burnt onlookers.

"Last," Green added speculatively, "does anyone here have any kind of prescription sample boxes they've actually bought in the last month or so? You know that buying and selling prescription samples is illegal, right?" Blank looks abounded. "I thought so," Green said. "Just to be clear, selling prescription samples – for whatever reason – is punishable by law."

We hung our heads.

Trixie bounded up and grabbed Green's elbow in hers. "So what are you up to while you're here in Lancaster? Care to see the sights?" she asked.

"Of course!" K. added. "We've got extra tickets to Polo!"

Trixie glowed at him.

"Actually, I don't know..." Green began.

"I do," Trixie answered, and led him out of the door under minimal false protest. The other Suits followed.

Jr. Suit handed K. his card. "Call me," he mouthed. K. nodded happily.

I stood up from the table and hoped to beat a hasty retreat. I figured I had done my Sunday morning's work for God and catering. Then Ma appeared.

"What's the matter?" she asked.

"Kind of a headache," I said.

Evelyn, Henry, Ed, Ernie and Mrs. Phang immediately offered up sample size boxes of pain relievers, anti-inflammatories and diuretics. I looked at their outstretched, gauze wrapped hands. Either they were all severely accident prone or they were pretending to be extras in a Curse of the Mummy remake.

"Or you could have some of these," Miriam said brightly, standing next to me, holding her beach bag pocketbook wide open. I looked inside. It was a pharmaceutical tricks or treats bag. I reached in and grabbed a packet.

"Oh, those are really good. They work just like a charm," Miriam said from one side of me.

"Yeah, they come in real handy," Vito said from the other side. I looked at him. He leaned in. "They can be a real blessing sometimes. Just like a banana in the desert," he said.

"Don't you mean manna in the desert?"

"Hey, that's pretty good, too," he said.

I pocketed the packet, and walked over to a trash bin to toss out my empty coffee cup and any leftover logical thought. I saw Aunt Muriel, Ma and Mrs. Phang in full post brunch deconstruction mode. I pitched in, and we planned how they would pick me for the special Conestoga Cabana Cup polo match later that afternoon. When all that was arranged, I wandered off, wondering what social outfit I had on hand that would work with my Herman Munster Crocs.

Vito came up next to me. "Can I hitch a ride?" he asked. I nodded and handed him his keys.

"What happened to Miriam?" I asked.

"She's got a community theater audition," he answered. "Besides, we've been seeing a lot of each other. I need some time off for good behavior," he said, rubbing his forehead. I handed him my sample packet of pain relievers.

We headed out and Vito drove us back up Orange Street. A few traffic lights later, we were back on Clover Nook Court and parked in Mt. Driveway just behind Bauser's car. We got out and found Bauser, Jim and Norman camped out on my front porch, reading the Sunday paper and drinking Krumpthf's. Bauser and Norman, not Jim.

Stanley yipped his greetings from inside Vito's half of the townhouses. Vito opened up his front door and Stanley bounced out at Jim. Without looking up from his paper, Bauser threw a tennis ball absentmindedly into the front yard. Jim and Stanley barked after it.

"What's up?" I asked, sitting down on the stoop.

"Did you read the paper? Do you know about Myron?" Bauser asked.

"Sort of," I said.

Norman looked up from his copy of the paper, shaking his head. "Talk about the three stooges," he said.

"Why?" I asked.

Norman held up the paper and read, "...a trail of evidence found included an engraved wristwatch, address book and a color copy of Myron Stumf's driver's license."

"So that's what alerted the police to investigate Myron? But how did they find out about the packet sniffers?"

"That was easy," Norman said. "I just programmed the sniffer to send a confirmation transmission to Myron's work email," he said.

"That was pretty sneaky," I said.

"And unnecessary," Bauser added. Norman nodded. "Myron was either dumb enough or full of himself enough that he thought it was safe to use his work email account to communicate with the hackers in Bangladesh."

I shook my head. It was hard to imagine Myron and Howard in jail.

"Wonder who's going to take over for them both at EEJIT?" I mused aloud.

Norman and Bauser looked at me. "Didn't you know?" Bauser asked.

"What?"

"EEJIT's parent company, Effhue, got bought out by Wurst Marketing," Norman said. "In fact, they wasted no time. Their ad's on the same page as the article. 'The Wurst Group. Because your business deserves The Wurst.'"

We stared at each other.

"I like it," Vito said.

We looked at him. He shrugged.

Bauser folded his paper. "All this makes me hungry. Want to go out for brunch?"

Jim sat up, wagging his tail, and tilted over onto Norman's lap.

"Actually we just got back," Vito said.

"You went out to brunch?" Norman asked, crestfallen.

"Not really; just brunch buffet at St. Bart's," I answered.

"Oh, well that doesn't count," Norman said. "Maybe you could whip us up a little something?"

I shrugged. "Okay, but it's gotta be quick. Got another polo thingy with Auntie and Ma," I said. "You guys wanna come?"

"Actually, yes," Bauser answered truthfully.

"You want to borrow my bike helmet?" Norman asked.

I cringed. "No, I think I can handle it this time."

Norman shrugged. "It's your noggin."

"You think I can bring Stanley, Toots?" Vito asked.

"Sure; it's a family thing," I answered.

After some more polo Q&A, we went inside and I got Bauser to watch over a skillet of sausages and scrambled eggs, while Vito and Norman rummaged through my refrigerator to improvise a polo picnic. Jim, Stanley and Vinnie sat hopefully on the sidelines. I rolled my eyes and went upstairs to change into something that didn't resemble restaurant service industry wear. I didn't want to risk another case of mistaken identity again while amongst food servers.

My answering machine light blinked hello at me.

"Hi, Mina, this is James," James' voice said. I smiled. Well, he was pretty good-looking. And had great hands. And was reasonably calm. And, I realized, available. And calling me! "I've been hired for a bridal massage party next Saturday," he said good-naturedly. "The bride was asking me about finding a low-key caterer, nothing too fancy, to cater for her and her girlfriends. So, umm... I thought of you. It's just a small party of 5 ladies. Give me a call if you think you'd like the job," he said, and left his phone number. "Oh, and maybe afterward we can go out and get a bite to eat, too," he added, and hung up.

It may have been several hundred years since my last boyfriend, but this sounded vaguely familiar. It sounded like an actual invitation to an actual date. Huh. And gainful employment. Double huh!

I hummed happily to myself, went into my closet and suddenly saw dozens of wardrobe possibilities. I opted for an upscale Bohemian look, to pull off the comfy Crocs. I even put on make-up and cologne, and trotted downstairs.

The boys were standing about happily munching sausages and eggs, including Vinnie and Stanley and Jim. I looked on the counter, where several hundred deli items had been lined up. Vito shrugged.

"We got confused," he said.

I went into the pantry, dug up a loaf of French bread, slit it in half and spread one half lightly with mayonnaise, and the other half with jarred pesto sauce. I piled on the assorted lunchmeats and cheeses. Then I grabbed my rolling pin and pressed the sandwich until it was flattened into a mouth size height. I wrapped the whole thing up in plastic wrap, and grabbed some pickles and pasta salad to round out the meal. I looked in the freezer and dug out a chocolate cream pie that only needed to be defrosted before being served. Then, lastly, I placed everything in both coolers, including Bauser's Krumpthf's, several bottles of wine, Pelligrino and some doggie biscuits.

The doorbell rang, and Vito let Ma and Aunt Muriel come in. They stared aghast at the stocked coolers, while Bauser and Norman explained. Ma and Aunt Muriel heaved collective sighs of relief. I patted Vinnie on the head and locked the door, as the boys carried the coolers out of the house. Then I climbed into Aunt Muriel's Lexus, while the boys loaded the cooler into the trunk of Vito's Towncar.

"Wow, that's a really big trunk," Bauser said.

Vito nodded. "Yeah. You know, even with all that stuff, it can actually fit an entire person, all rolled up like," he said. Bauser and Norman stared at him. "You wanna try it?"

"Maybe some other time," Norman said, closing the trunk.

Vito shrugged, whistled for Jim and Stanley, and threw a doggie Frisbee into the backseat. Jim and Stanley leapt in after it. Bauser and Stanley did a quick 'Once! Twice! Three! SHOOT!' behind the trunk of Vito's car. Bauser climbed into the front seat. Norman sat in back with the dogs. I wasn't sure who had won.

We wound our way back across town, and eventually onto the polo grounds. The pleasant lady we'd seen collecting entry fees last week was back at her post.

"Well, welcome back, so nice to see you again," she began, handing Aunt Muriel a large packet of information. Then she stared at me. She backed way and reached into a basket with more pre-printed information. She returned, and knocked on the window in the backseat. I rolled the window down, and she handed me a bumper-sticker size warning: POLO BALLS SOMETIMES EXTEND BEYOND THE PLAYING AREA. WE ARE NOT RESPONSIBLE FOR ANY BODILY INJURIES. ALSO, PATRONS ARE REQUESTED TO EXTINGUISH ALL CIGARETTES, CIGARS, PIPES AND OTHER LIT SMOKING TOBACCO PRIOR TO ENTERING THE CHUKKER TENT.

I cringed, waved bye-bye and we set off to find a spot to park. We found one near the end of the field, very near a goal post. Aunt Muriel and Ma looked at each other nervously.

"It's okay," I said. "We're going to be in the Chukker tent, right? That's in the middle. It's pretty far away from both goal posts."

After some discussion, Ma and Aunt Muriel agreed and said that I didn't have to wear the construction helmet or the fluorescent orange vest Aunt Muriel borrowed for me, after all.

We got the boys situated around Vito's Towncar with their man stuff tailgate picnic, complete with Krumpthf's. Norman and Bauser took Stanley and Jim onto the empty pre-game polo field to play doggie Frisbee. Vito lay stretched out comfily in one of his recliners, reading the polo propaganda from the hundred or so handouts we'd received at the entrance. Aunt Muriel and Ma and I strolled off toward the Chukker Tent.

It was a beautiful day. This time the tent was gleaming white, instead of the dingy color it had been last week. Then I realized: this tent was new. I hung my head.

Aunt Muriel looked at me. "They were due for a new tent, anyway," she said.

Ma rolled her eyes. "Let's get a beverage," she said brightly.

We walked into the tent and I entered the realm of extreme tailgating. Conestoga Cabana had not just provided a polo picnic, but a full scale outdoor catered reception. One side of the tent was filled by an enormously long buffet table. It was draped with linens and decorated with sculptures and flowers and huge vases filled with lemons and sunflowers. There were baskets of artisan rolls, huge bowls of pasta, seafood salads, green salads, Waldorf salad, trays of sandwich wraps, and dozens of other side dishes and appetizers. This line-up culminated in warming trays filled with Chicken Rossini, stuffed shells, a stroganoff, and pans of stuffed shrimp. At the very end, Armand stood at a carving station, waiting to serve an impossibly large roast beef and a gigantic turkey. He saw me and nodded and glowered at me from beneath furrowed eyebrows. I waved back. I hadn't seen him this happy in a long time. I figured he must be ecstatic to be working weekends again.

Auntie and Ma and I got something to nibble on. Another table housed various metal tubs filled with ice and bottles of wine and mini bottles of spring water. We each got a glass of white wine, with a spring water chaser. We looked around at the dozen or so bar height tables that were dotted around the tent area. We saw someone leaving what became a lone empty table, and claimed it quickly.

I felt a tap on my shoulder. It was Trixie. She was wearing an electric blue sundress, a large orange sun hat, electric blue retro bobble earrings, and a big smile.

"You look great!" I said, hugging her. "What happened to Green?"

"Left him at the train station," she answered.

"And?" I asked. Trixie smiled brightly at me, and pointed her chin toward a polo player, sitting on his horse and chatting to some patrons on the sidelines. "Married? Separated?" I asked dubiously.

"Nope. Completely single and complete with uniform," Trixie winked at me. I opened my mouth, and shut it. Some things are better left unknown.

Trixie needed a beverage, so I walked with her to get a glass of wine.

"White wine, red wine, or a soft drink?" the waitress manning the beverage table asked.

As I reached to receive my white wine, I gazed directly into Lee's face. She was clad in black and white service wear, complete with a bronze SNAP ID badge with her name engraved on it. It read 'Lee'. Yup, it was her alright.

"How's it going?" I faked, hoping an exit strategy would present itself immediately.

Lee reached for my wine hand, I jolted, and sent six ounces of Pinot Grigio straight up in the air. The pitter-pat of wine droplets pinged off of Trixie's sun bonnet.

"Sorry!" I cried, backing away and squeezing the wine out of my ponytail.

Lee wiped her head, and her sleeves. "It's okay; here," she said, pouring me another glass of wine. "I'm actually glad to see you," she added, looking somewhat chagrined.

Trixie leaned in at her. "Really?" she asked, a glint in her eye. Lee winced.

She looked around, then leaned in toward us. We huddled. "I'm really sorry about Bauser and the Plan and everything. And

I'm really glad to see you're alright," she said. I shrugged. "I got put on the Plan right after he did."

"Really? For what?"

Lee shook her head. "After they got rid of you, they made me responsible for office supplies." I nodded. Being the Gatekeeper of Office Supplies kind of goes with the territory. You have no idea how many office workers have sticky fingers. "I know. Except when it came to the checkpoint review, they faulted me for failing to order backup tapes for the server," she said.

I looked at her. "Corporate IT does that," I said.

"I know," she said.

"So they fired you for not ordering something that you weren't supposed to order?"

"Precisely." Yeesh. "Anyway, before all that I was kind of desperate. Howard kept threatening to fire me if I didn't help him. I've never been unemployed before, or fired," she admitted.

I nodded understandingly and drank some wine.

"Guess it's all part of the human experience," Trixie offered, and began wandering off toward her polo player, who was sitting on his horse toward the far goal near Vito, chatting up a petite blonde.

Lee looked around again. "Anyway, I'm sorry I hurt you," she said.

"Huh?" I replied brightly.

Lee rolled her eyes. "Look, please don't make this any harder than it is. We haven't exactly been buddies," she said. She had a point there.

"Being unemployed isn't so bad. Except for the not having any money thing," I said.

Lee shook her head. "I'm not talking about your getting fired. I'm trying to apologize for landing on you and knocking you out."

"What?"

"I was kind of hiding in the ladies' room. But then all the fire alarms went off and I kind of panicked and I crawled up through the ceiling tile and kind of got stuck." She grimaced.

"You crawled through the ceiling tile in the ladies' room?"

"I told you, I panicked!" she snipped.

"I'll say," I said. "So, did you take my purse, too?"

"Yeah." I glared at her. "But I wasn't trying to rip you off! I swear! I thought you had a key to the HR cabinet in Howard's office," she said.

I looked at her. "There's no key to that cabinet," I said.

"But there's a lock on it," she countered.

"Howard broke that the first year I worked there," I said. "All you needed to do was open the drawer." Lee hung her head. "So, how do you like your new job?" I asked, trying to switch gears.

"It's pretty good," she said. "But it's just temporary. In a couple weeks, I start my new job at Krapf Communications."

"Oh, great. What are you going to do there?"

"Nothing big; just entry level," she admitted. "But I think I have a real knack for slogans and such," she said.

"Oh?"

She nodded enthusiastically. "I nailed my interview with a tagline for them," she said. "Want to hear it?"

"Sure," I lied.

"Krapf Communications," she began: "When you hear us, you know it's Krapf."

I examined the ground for lost lottery tickets.

After exchanging a few more pleasantries, I relieved Lee of an open bottle of Pinot Grigio and some clean glasses. Then I made my way back to the table where Auntie and Ma were nodding and smiling with K. and his new date, Manny. We exchanged some introductions and wine.

Auntie consulted the diamonds on her wristwatch. "The game should be getting started very soon now," she said, nodding to herself.

"I better tell the fellas," I said. "I'll be right back."

I wandered past the various families and groupings of friends showing off their tailgate ware. As I approached the boys, I saw a couple of car loads of Auntie's church buddies parked on the other side of Vito's Towncar. I recognized Evelyn and Eddie and Ernie and Henry. They were talking with animated gauze bandaged hands, arms, noses and noggins and smiling with Vito, Trixie and her polo player. Beside them was another carload of people chatting, too.

Norman and Bauser walked over to me with Jim and Stanley. "So, what do you think about the burn victim ward?" Bauser asked.

"I don't want to know," I replied automatically.

"Nor do we," Norman added.

We walked over toward Vito's Towncar tailgate. Trixie was waving bye-bye to her polo date; he was trotting down the field to kick off the first chukker. Then, when he was gone, she turned and faced the gauzed grannies.

"Now I know most of you were admitted during my shift in the ER," she stage whispered. There was much shuffling around of feet and walkers in response.

"It was supposed to have been a coordinated effort," Henry said.

"LA LA LA LA LA LA LA! I don't want to know!" Trixie sang, waving and walking back toward the party tent.

I looked at Vito. He shrugged.

Helena popped out from his side.

"Hi!" she sang, holding a chubby and adorably beautiful baby girl against her hip. She smiled. "I talked it over with the family, and they've agreed it's time Uncle Vlad – Vito – met his grandniece," she said.

Vito nodded. "Seems like I'm out of the woods now, so to speak," he said.

Mrs. Phang walked over from the church mummy crowd, wearing an expensive ivory colored silk pant suit and some striking gold jewelry, set with jade. "Honesty is the best policy," she said, handing Vito a glass of wine, and the baby an animal cracker.

Norman held up his can of Krumpthf's and we all raised our drinks.

"To happy endings," he toasted.

We clinked.

"So you guys are definitely out of the prescription sample business, right?" Bauser asked.

Vito nodded. "Too much risk," he said.

"Besides, we're investigating homeopathic therapies now," Mrs. Phang offered.

"Huh?" I asked.

Helena nodded. "Mickey's been doing a lot of reading in prison. Herbal remedies are the way to go," she said. "They're completely unregulated, so there're no rules to break," she added helpfully.

Vito nodded sagely. I drank the rest of my wine quickly.

The players lined up on the field, and the first chukker started. We watched the horses race up and down, Vito and Bauser alternately shoving me behind anything possible each time the polo ball came remotely near our section of the field.

An air horn sounded a short time later, and the first three chukkers were over. Patrons were invited to the field for the traditional stamping of the divots. With the traditional warning to avoid the steaming divots.

"Game?" Norman asked me.

"Sure," I said.

We ambled out onto the field with St. Bart's crowd and their assorted walkers, canes and wheelchairs. I looked down the field, and saw Ma and Aunt Muriel laughing with K. and Manny, happily spilling wine and stomping divots. Trixie was petting her polo player's horse and his thigh. So to speak. I looked toward the party tent, and saw Lee actually smiling while she was working. Huh. Maybe she wasn't so bad after all. Maybe she just hated her job as much as I did mine. Armand frowned intensely and served briskly, happy in his work.

I smiled to myself, turned around, and stepped right into a pile of poo.

"Shit, shit, shit!" I said.

"Uh, yes, it is," he said.

I looked up and saw the non-irate chef from Squirrel Run Acres.

"May I?" he asked, kneeling down and picking my foot up out of the horse manure. He pulled out a few thousand paper towels from his pocket and took my shoe off to wipe it.

"It's really okay," I started.

"I'll be right back," he said.

I stood on the field, one foot in the air like a flamingo.

K. hurried over. "OMG, girlfriend! He's just like Prince Charming!" he whispered.

"He took my shoe," I said simply.

"I know! Isn't that fabulous?" K. said, then beat a hasty retreat.

Chef came back with my wet shoe. "It needed to be hosed off," he explained.

"Oh," I answered brightly.

"Here," he said, and offered my shoe for me to put back on. I squashed my foot into the soggy mess.

"Thanks. What's your name?"

"Jack," he replied.

"Really?"

He shrugged. "Chef Jacque in the kitchen. Jack everyplace else. My mom's French," he explained. "What's yours?"

"Mina," I said.

He smiled. "So, Mina, I hear you like to cook," he began.

ABOUT THE AUTHOR

Lizz Lund loves Lancaster. Since 1999, she's been having a terrific time here and thinks everyone else should, too. She is a newlywed and head-over-heels about her chef husband; she made him move from New Jersey, too. *Kitchen Addiction!* is her first novel of the Mina Kitchen series. Lizz grew up in Glen Rock, New Jersey and still hasn't recovered. She holds a BA in Musical Theatre from Syracuse University, but has never learned to waitress.

LOOK FOR THE SEQUEL TO *KITCHEN ADDICTION!*
COMING SOON: *Confection Connection.*

Stay tuned! Check out Lizz's site for updates!
www.LizzLund.com

For quick, fun reads: Lizz's blog - Simmerings
www.LizzLund.com

Connect with Lizz:
Twitter: @FunnyAuthor
Facebook: Lizz Lund - Author

9798648R0022

Made in the USA
Charleston, SC
14 October 2011